ALL THE CASTLES BURNED

ALL THE CASTLES BURNED

A Novel

MICHAEL NYE

Turner Publishing Company
Nashville, Tennessee
New York, New York

www.turnerpublishing.com

All the Castles Burned

Cover design: Maddie Cothren
Book design: Glen Edelstein

Library of Congress Cataloging-in-Publication Data

Names: Nye, Michael, 1978- author.
Title: All the castles burned : a novel / Michael Nye.
Description: Nashville, Tennessee : Turner Publishing Company, [2017]
Identifiers: LCCN 2017045217 (print) | LCCN 2017052693 (ebook) | ISBN 9781683367628 (e-book) | ISBN 9781683367604 (softcover : acid-free paper)
Subjects: LCSH: Preparatory schools--Fiction. | Teenage boys--Fiction. | Friendship--Fictoin. | Domestic fiction.
Classification: LCC PS3614.Y43 (ebook) | LCC PS3614.Y43 A79 2018 (print) | DDC 813/.6--dc23
LC record available at https://lccn.loc.gov/2017045217

Printed in the United States of America
18 19 20 21 22 10 9 8 7 6 5 4 3 2 1

For Kathy and Robyn

ALL THE CASTLES BURNED

PART I

I

In 1994, when I was fourteen years old, I was a new freshman, one of four hundred young men attending the Upper School at Rockcastle, a sprawling single-story building raised as a temporary structure in the 1930s that had, for some reason, remained permanent. Several short wings had been added over the years, including a science lab on the southern edge, its windows looking down into the small forest that secluded our campus from the outside world. The entire building was always drafty and cold, and seated in class on windy days, I could hear a low whistle trill through the hallways. Yet when I pictured Rockcastle, I imagined it the way you would see it from the street: a pristine, elegant private day school stretching in all directions, guarded by massive red oaks, the surrounding gardens immaculate, and the tall windows of the Upper School shining triumphantly in the morning light. This is where I met Carson Bly.

It's been years since I've seen Carson Bly, whom I once considered my best and only friend, and I believe my eyes are better trained to see it now, but even then I recognized that he was a pure basketball player. Athletic grace like he had is breathtaking. When he shot the ball, he leapt straight up, and his feet came down in the exact same spot. If we had been on a beach and he had been shooting for an hour, there would still be only one set of footprints. He raised the ball above his right shoulder, his elbow angled directly beneath his hand, and at the top of his jump he snapped his wrist, arm extended like a salute, and the ball spun perfectly through the air until—without touching the rim—it fell into the net with a whisper.

It was October and raining heavily, the steady waves of rain hammering loud on the roof of the small gym. The dilapidated gym that linked the Fieldhouse to the Upper School did not have a name—it was simply known as "the small gym." The scuffed wood floor was in regular need of cleaning, and the sidelines stopped right at the walls, whose wood ran in vertical strips and smelled like the pages of old and rarely opened books. Everything about the gym—from the floors to the walls to the rusty cables that suspended the old backboards off the walls—looked damp and exhausted. I stripped off my blazer, turned it inside out, and neatly folded it on the small bench on the sidelines, then took off my tie, rolling it into a coil so it wouldn't wrinkle. I folded my sleeves up, yanked my shirt out from my pants, and lofted short jumpers. My heels raised out of my brown loafers no matter how careful I was.

I don't know how long Carson was watching before I saw him. But when I did, he was standing with his arms crossed in the archway of the entrance to the Upper School.

"Owen Webb," he yelled. "You need to spread your fingers more."

I appreciated again, as if for the first time, that he was striking, perhaps handsome. He was six feet tall and had fair skin, eyes of such blue they were almost gray, and dark hair thick as a lion's mane. I was proud and surprised that he knew my name. He glided toward me, shucking his blazer as he moved, which he tossed in a pile over by my neatly folded clothes. There wasn't a single imperfection on his high cheekbones.

"You're snapping your wrist," he said, "but you aren't getting enough rotation. You need to spread your fingers."

"Thanks for the advice."

"Don't be a dick, I'm just trying to help. Go ahead, try it."

He walked under the basket and flipped his palm upward. Stretching out my fingers made the ball unsteady in my hands, but when I took the shot, the ball rotated rapidly, clanked off the backboard, and swished through the net. Carson snatched the ball and threw me a bounce pass.

"Don't watch the ball," he said. "I'll watch it for you. You just look at the rim."

I breathed deeply, trying to shake the fact that I was talking to Carson Bly. I had seen him in the halls, and had heard about the Bly family: one of the richest at Rockcastle, Carson a fifth-generation student. Yet I had always thought of him as aloof. During the last two months, when the weather was warm and autumnal, students sat outdoors between the Upper and Middle Schools. There was a large field of immaculate green, long enough for an impromptu game of touch football, Frisbee, or hacky sack, yet small and contained enough that every boy's face could be seen clearly through the windows, allowing teachers to, when necessary, stop any misbehavior. Carson always sat alone, frowning down into a book on existentialism or gun rights, the author's photo displayed on the back cover, always a white man's face, always a face turned into the same angry glare that Carson wore as he furiously scribbled notes into the margin. Yet in the halls, his face was relaxed and open and smiling, a transformation I thought couldn't possibly be real.

I frowned at the basketball in my hand. With both hands, I pounded the ball twice, knees bent and head down, pulling the ball over my shoulder as if I were slinging on a backpack. Who was he to tell me how to shoot? I suppressed the urge to tell him to fuck off, and continued taking shots. Some rattled in, some went through perfectly, some missed. Carson rebounded each one without comment; I tried passing the ball back to him so he could shoot, and he fired the ball back without speaking. After a few minutes, I worked up a decent sweat and hit several shots in a row, the ball snapping from my hand with accuracy and precision.

"Not bad, Webb," he said. "My turn." Carson dribbled out to the three-point line, then held the ball to his hip with his left hand and used his right to tuck his tie into his shirt. Tie out of the way, he dribbled once and released his first shot.

The ball swished through the net and bounced twice before I picked it up. When I raised my eyes, his knees were crouched, hands up by his chest, palms out, waiting for the pass.

He hit eleven shots in a row before he missed, yelling out "Short!" before the ball caught the inside of the front of the rim, skipped off the backboard, and ricocheted out. I rebounded and fired the ball back to Carson, who was shaking his head at the miscalculation; he proceeded to knock down ten straight. When the last one settled through the net, Carson nodded to himself and raised a hand to indicate he was done. He then walked to the bench and sat down next to his blazer.

"Sixth bell is almost over," he said.

Every Rockcastle student received "free bell." It was exactly what it sounded like: one class period designated to allow the student to do whatever he wished. Seniors based their schedule around free bell, which they always placed before or after lunch period so they could leave campus. There was no clock in the gym, and Carson didn't wear a watch—I wondered how he sensed the time. Dribbling the ball between my legs as I walked, I went over and sat down next to him. He didn't appear to be out of breath. He hadn't even taken off his tie.

"You're a good shooter," he said. "You playing this year?"

I nodded.

"We need you. Our starting point is this senior—Jamie Osher, do you know him?—and that guy can't do anything right. Total fucking asshole. If you chew him up this month, you can start on varsity."

"Really?"

"You shoot better than he does. I haven't seen you play, but you look like you get it. How's your left?"

"Nonexistent."

"Work on that. Jamie's a lefty. He absolutely cannot go right. Work on going both ways with your dribble. If you can finish at the rim with your left hand, you're set. Do you do anything else here? Debate team or something?"

"No."

"You should. Sports won't be enough." His eyes were focused across the room on the scratched wall, peering at it intently as if it were a threat to him. "You're a bit inscrutable, aren't you?"

I didn't know what that word, *inscrutable,* meant. All the boys at Rockcastle used words I had never heard before, and I had developed the habit of scrawling words into the margins of my textbooks—*s-o-teric? air-u-dite?*—in the hope that at home with a dictionary I could puzzle out the correct spelling and meaning.

Carson tilted his chin upward, his skull scraping against the wall, and looked at the ceiling.

"Do you see those missing panels?"

Above, between the rafters and the circular light fixtures, the ceiling had several black holes, like missing teeth.

"Every now and then," Carson said, "for no good reason, people throw stuff up there. Basketballs, soccer balls, softballs, erasers, soda cans, a mouthy first-year's shoes, whatever. All the students know about it, but I don't think anyone goes up there to clean it out. Sometimes you walk through here and there is a stray ball or scrap of something on the gym floor. A raccoon or something must push it out. Or the wind, I guess."

I pictured the inside of the roof, all the dust and dirt and filth up there; all the years of items, artifacts of all the boys who had been here before me; all the years that had passed.

"No one goes up there?" I asked.

"Not even the janitors. Strange, isn't it?"

"I like it."

Carson lowered his chin and looked at me. His eyes seemed delighted.

"So do I. Why is that?"

"I don't know." I held the basketball, my fingers tapping the leather. "Because it shouldn't be that way."

"They've been planning to tear this gym down. I mean, they've been talking about it for decades, so I don't know if it'll ever happen, but they talk about it."

"Tear it down for what?"

"I don't know. More classrooms. A teacher's lounge. Because some wealthy fuck gave us money and we have to build something new with his name on it. My father went to school here, and he said that until recently, it hadn't changed much. He said most of the buildings were old and drafty. But they just built the new junior high, the new primary school, redid the track, even the kindergarten playground. Everything but the Upper School."

Rockcastle did have a polish to it, a veneer hidden behind all the ivy covering the brick, a place that was reinventing itself—one building, one donor, at a time—until it was the kind of private day school it believed it should be. I couldn't articulate that feeling at age fourteen, but I certainly felt that my world was being reimagined, and that Carson was absolutely right.

"The Fieldhouse is pretty sweet."

A look of contempt crossed Carson's face, but just as quickly it passed, and he nodded to himself and said, "Yeah, they did give us that. You and me, Webb, you and me."

He took the ball from my hands and stood up.

"You and me, what?" I asked.

"Varsity basketball. Conference title." He dribbled twice, then palmed the ball, leaned back, and fired it up into the ceiling through one of the gaps. There was a distant thud, then a softer one, and I listened intently to hear the ball come to a stop. For a moment, I feared retribution for losing gym equipment, then realized that no one had seen me take the ball. Still, for reasons I didn't quite understand, I wanted it to bounce back, fall through the gap, drop to the floor, and roll to rest at my feet.

"Be here tomorrow, same time," Carson said over his shoulder. "We'll work on your game. And bring basketball shoes, something to sweat in." He strode back to the Upper School, clutching his blazer in his right hand. Even after he disappeared through the double doors, I stood watching them for what felt like a long time.

No one entered the small gym, and there were no sounds at all, as if the entire world was frozen over and the slightest noise would send fissures through the surface and plummet me down into icy waters. Then the bell rang, cracking the silence and signaling the end of sixth period, and the distant sounds of opened doors and heavy footsteps filled the air. Four upperclassmen entered the gym, laughing and shaking their heads, taking no notice of me. I followed them into the Upper School, dazed as if in a trance, and only when I collapsed into my assigned seat in English did I notice that my undershirt was soaked with sweat.

When the last bell of the day rang, I walked over to the cafeteria to buy a soda, then got my books from my locker and returned to the classroom. I pushed a desk in the back row up against the windows, which looked out onto the front drive. Every day after school, I sat here for two hours, started my homework, and waited for my mother to get off work and pull into the circular driveway. The school faced west, and the setting sun turned the sky dark; it was peaceful and beautiful to watch whenever I glanced up from working my way through biology, algebra, and Western civilization.

Last winter, fed up with my low grades and frequent cutting of school to wander from College Hill down to Clifton to read magazines in drugstores and play arcade games like Bad Dudes or Operation: Wolf in bowling alleys, my mother spent three hundred dollars for me to take Rockcastle's placement exam. She insisted, with a ferocity and seriousness that the public-school vice principals found amusing, that I was a bright, friendly kid who was bored by an unchallenging curriculum, and that despite my delinquent behavior, I was capable of academic excellence. No one was more surprised than me when I placed in the ninety-sixth percentile on Rockcastle's notoriously difficult entry exam. After a series of meetings in which my mother confidently pleaded for my acceptance, certain that the conformity and rigorousness of Rockcastle's curriculum was exactly what a troubled boy like me needed, I was accepted for admission.

Along the walls of Rockcastle's main entranceway were photographs of students in poses from around the world: arms raised in triumph atop a snowy mountain; camp counselors and their campers beaming despite their sunburns and unwashed hair; award ceremonies in New York and San Francisco with the winners holding their medals and trophies. There were also framed articles from the *Cincinnati Enquirer, U.S. News & World Report, Time, The Guardian,* and other periodicals about both Rockcastle on the whole and our individual teachers, scholars who shunned universities to work with a younger, less jaded generation. Gazing up at all the accomplishments of decades of Rockcastle men, their lives on display in oak frames and behind clean, unbroken glass, I remembered how uncomfortable I was just wearing my school clothes.

My first day at Rockcastle, walking the hallways and clutching a computer printout of my classes and their room numbers, I felt every smirk from the upperclassmen. How could I hide the fact that I was a freshman when I didn't know where I was going? But by the end of the second day, catching on quick to where my classes were and how to get there, I figured out that the smirks weren't about my course schedule or the fact that I said "freshman" rather than "first year." The derision was about my clothes. The only students who wore insignia blazers were kids on scholarship.

Scholarship kids like me were easy to identify. I only had two ties, and they were all wrong: my knot askew and the fabric thick as a tablecloth. My blazers were a little too bulky, the sleeves too long, and my shirts, whether they were blue or white, were overstarched, lacking in texture and breathability. Even in the nineties, when pleats were acceptable, the drape of my pants was wrong, the fabric too heavy. And my mouth revealed all: I had brilliantly white teeth from brushing, but the lack of braces meant my teeth were gapped and uneven. I only spoke in class when called on, keeping both my uncertain answers and less than perfect teeth hidden.

Even in their similarities, Rockcastle boys seemed otherworldly: their skin maintained a healthy glow, even in the winter. Shaggy hair was common in 1994—among soccer players, Latin scholars, hippies—an unkempt mess that hid eyes and ears as those who possessed them slouched smugly in their seats when called on to answer a question they hadn't even heard. Every Rockcastle boy wore a tie, but some had mastered their father's Windsor knot while others got away with an ironic bow tie or a food-stained Looney Tunes tie. Braided belts were common, the long end dangling off the hip like a holster. They wore scuffed oxfords or Birkenstocks, both acceptable under the school dress code as long as they were brown and sandaled toes were hidden by socks. Outside the walls of Rockcastle, we all dressed the same: flannel shirts, Starter jackets, collared shirts in loud colors, oversized T-shirts and basketball jerseys, everything loose and baggy.

The hallways were wide, not just to allow students to walk three deep in each direction, but also because all the doors to the classrooms opened outward, and we needed room to pass without taking a suddenly opened door in the shoulder. In all directions, boys exchanged ironic handshakes, playfully slammed each other into lockers, which reverberated the length of the hallway, bringing out our teachers, who scolded us to knock it off as we feigned innocence at any inquiries as to who started what.

Yet there was a small group of boys who were different from all of us. Boys like Carson Bly. Years later, in college, I stumbled across the term *blue blood* for the first time and instantly thought of my classmates at Rockcastle who fit this description. Much the way the eye gravitates unbidden toward symmetry and beauty, I wasn't consciously aware of the allure of these boys—the ones who everyone liked but nobody knew, the ones from mysteriously wealthy families, the ones who were brilliantly smart and amazingly athletic but refused to give maximum effort in either their studies or sports. They walked with their shoulders back. Their haircuts were perfect, teeth immaculate, ties dimpled, blazers bespoke to the exact measurements of their wide shoulders and lean arms, their strides confident and relaxed, as if the whole world already belonged to them. In some way, I suppose, it did.

• • •

I looked up from my homework. Outside, scattered leaves lay under the red-oak trees. There were very few of them, enough to suggest that autumn was here, and the remaining leaves, withered and golden, clutching to the branches above, would soon fall. Sitting by the windowsill all alone, I saw the trek of upperclassmen heading to their cars in the lot across the street: how beautiful it all seemed that afternoon—the sky spotless, the light shimmering through the oak leaves, and the sense of the future as belonging strictly to us. This was the beauty I expected at Rockcastle, what I had hoped for from a new school. What I remember of my first days.

I spread my hands out on my notebook, my blue-ink notes from world history disappearing beneath my palms.

The paper curled, sticking to my fingertips, and I imagined palming a basketball, picturing it until I felt not paper beneath my hands but the textured leather of the ball, the grooves of rubber spinning in my hands. Point guard. Starting varsity. The vision seized my mind, and I spent the next two hours dreaming of game-winning jump shots, behind-the-back passes, fast breaks, and a group of friends I did not have jumping up and down on the sidelines as I brought excitement and victory to Rockcastle.

And from where I am now, I remember that such beauty was wrapped in ribbons of loneliness, an angry solitude from which I have never completely escaped. Despite all that has happened, despite everything I have done, I remain the lonely boy by the window, a child with no purpose but to observe the happiness of others. There is something wrong with continuing to see myself locked away from the world, and yet I can imagine nothing else.

II

My father was a mystery to me. All I know of my parents comes from my mother. My father, I now know, is incapable of telling the truth.

The Friday before Thanksgiving, after school, my mother picked me up already dressed for the wedding she and my father were attending that evening. I threw my backpack into the back seat, then got in the front seat and closed the door before I noticed my mother's striking appearance. Her hair was down, eyes smoky with liner, tiny gold earrings in her lobes, nails shiny with polish, and she wore a dark purple cocktail dress that peaked out from the hem of her coat, which was, strangely, buttoned all the way up to her neck. On her feet were a pair of white Nikes.

"I'm already dressed," she said, killing my question before I asked. "But your father insisted I needed to do the grocery shopping today, not tomorrow. So we're gonna grab some things, and then you'll have to put everything away yourself." We hurried through Kroger, the grocery list all in her mind, and I watched the way her coat billowed around her knees, the flash of purple, her legs bare, the new white shoelaces in her two-year-old everyday shoes. We sped home, and she parked the car in front of our detached garage and popped the trunk. She raced inside and left me to carry the groceries up the concrete steps on the side of the house to the inside landing, where we discarded wet or muddy shoes, dropped an umbrella or snow shovel or any other mess my mother refused to let us carry through her house. Any groceries that my mother normally stored in the basement—frozen dinners, soda, beer—I left on the landing floor. Once the groceries were out of the car and the side door clicked shut, I took half the bags into the kitchen, then scooped up the bags on the landing and went down into the basement.

Our basement comprised two large rooms: the rec room, where I stood, and my father's workshop across the way, which was accessible through one door that always remained locked. Off to my left were the washer and dryer, my father's dress shirts and my mother's dresses hanging on flimsy portable racks, waiting to be ironed. The rest of the room was furnished around the big-screen TV that I remember the delivery men struggling to get down the steep basement steps. There was an old but comfortable wraparound couch, a La-Z-Boy recliner, shelves stocked with Betamax tapes of movies my father recorded whenever we got free HBO for a month, sports memorabilia from my father's high school and college days, an encyclopedia set no one used, *National Geographic* magazines in some semblance of order, and mass market paperbacks we never got around to discarding.

I went behind the bar, opened the fridge, and shoved the frozen dinners and pizzas into the freezer, the cans of Coke and my father's Miller Genuine Drafts into the fridge. I folded the paper grocery bags—as I had been shown to do—into a neatly ordered stack on the end of the bar. When I finished, I looked up to see that the door to my father's workshop was open.

I had been in there before, but always with my father supervising me as I made a pinewood derby car or regatta boat for Cub Scouts. When we were finished working, as we exited the room, he pulled the door closed and locked it. Usually, he was in there alone with the door cracked. I stepped around the bar, pushed open the door, and flipped on the workshop light.

My father had two long workbenches positioned at a ninety-degree angle in the corner; above one bench was a pegboard with an assortment of screwdrivers, wrenches, sockets, and power tools hung in an order I recognized but didn't understand. Above the other bench were two window wells sealed with glass blocks, below which hung vinyl bags with screws and bits, labeled by centimeter and the year and month they had been purchased. On the bench's shelf down by my feet sat several metal toolboxes. My father must have owned nearly a dozen of them, and they were all closed and, I knew, locked. Over in the far corner next to the boiler was a full-sized mattress. There was nothing on the walls or under the bed, and I recognized the sheets as older. I knew that my father sometimes—and of late, often—slept down here rather than in my parents' bedroom. I also knew that this fact was not to be asked about or discussed.

I stepped closer. On the workbench beneath the windows were several of his coin books, their dark blue covers with the year written on them in a font I always associated with government documents. Several sleeves of coins lay loose on the bench, and there was a spiral notebook, with yesterday's date—November 14, 1994—written on the open page's top right corner in my father's sloppy handwriting. My father never taught me about his coins; I only knew that the shapes, sizes, years, and countries were to be oohed and aahed over. I touched nothing. Over the years, I had been spanked, slapped, and grabbed by the collar and shaken like a misbehaving puppy for touching my father's things. My arms remained hugged across my chest, afraid of even leaving a finger trace in the dust in his workspace. And then I saw it.

In the far corner behind a gray desk lamp was a clay pencil holder that I had made for my father when I was in third grade. A small gasp of disbelief escaped me. I hadn't seen it since I'd given it to him, a Father's Day gift he had frowned at with aggravated confusion. The pencil holder looked more like a misshaped human heart, with the sides painted orange and the middle painted blue. Two mechanical pencils speared the top, and the oblong dish at its bottom held paper clips. I held it in my hand like it was a wounded bird, running my thumb over the smooth clay surface, and wondered why he'd never told me that he liked it.

I set the pencil holder back down and shuffled my feet, and that's when I toed something heavy that scraped on the concrete floor. I bent down. At my feet was a gray shoe box with a black top. I lifted the lid. Inside were a bunch of newspaper clippings, single-paragraph items about armed robberies in Ohio, Indiana, and Kentucky. There was also a yellow rectangular box of bullets for a .38. and a crumpled brown paper bag. I knew what was in it before I opened it. But I couldn't resist. I picked it up, its weight heavy in my hand, and cautiously pushing aside the worn folds of paper, peaked inside. Down at the bottom was the first gun I had ever seen in real life: a silver revolver with a brown handle.

I crushed the bag shut, pushed it back into the shoebox, closed the lid, and shoved the box farther beneath the work bench. My heartbeat echoed in my head, and my mind went blank. I sat there for what felt like a long time.

From above, my mother yelled, "Owen!"

I ducked, as if my mother could see me through the ceiling. I turned off the workshop light, quietly pulled the door closed, and yelled back, "Coming!" I hurried to the bottom of the stairs, and then stopped to compose my face. Somehow I knew that my mother didn't know about the gun. I looked up the length of the stairs and out into the night through the window of the side door.

My father always entered the house through this door, and I almost expected to see him standing there, arms folded, glaring down at me. I don't remember a specific time when it started, perhaps around junior high: my father, with increasing frequency, came home and went straight down to the basement. Sometimes he would be there for only a minute or two and then come upstairs. But more and more often, he would head down to the basement and turn on the television or drink a few beers or tool around in his workshop. With each step, I banged the stairs hard to let my mother know I was on the way. She was in the kitchen, changed into high heels. The groceries had been put away, the paper bags flattened and folded on the kitchen counter.

"Did you put everything away?" she asked.

"Sure."

"You all right?"

"Sure."

My mother set both hands on her hips. "Really?"

I looked at some point to the side of her face; over her shoulder was her *Ladies Home Journal* calendar pinned to her pushboard, surrounded by coupons, receipts, and house bills.

"C'mon," she said. "Sit outside with me. Your father is still getting ready."

We took our coats from the hall closet and the portable radio from its regular spot on the shelf and headed to the front porch, the hydraulic hiss of the storm door sealing us out. Even in autumn, all of us loved sitting on the porch, wrapped in our coats, looking out across our small front yard. My whole family loved listening to the radio outside, as if the sound were distilled pure by the outdoors. In the summer, we listened to news talk or music or baseball, the station choice made by whoever carried the radio out to the porch. My father loved baseball, and both my parents loved Led Zeppelin and the Stones, the music of their teenage years. I loved Snoop and Dre, Nirvana and Soundgarden, but back then it was easier to find my parents' music on the radio than mine. During these nights on the porch, my mother and I never talked much, and I think what we both craved was the shared silence of being with someone who loved you.

She lit her cigarette and inhaled sharply. In 1994 she was thirty-five years old, a number and age that meant nothing to me then. She was a slim woman who maintained her weight through smoking cigarettes and eating like a bird, and regardless of the weather, every weekday afternoon she walked over a mile to her part-time job at our local library. She was pretty in an unapproachable way, her expression often religiously placid as if a calm and regimented life would be penance for her past. Her legs were crossed at the ankles, and she had put on black panty hose.

"Where are you going again?" I asked.

"It's all on the fridge." She tapped her cigarette into an ashtray. "Number of the hotel's front desk is on the fridge. We'll probably be home pretty late. Are you going out tonight?"

"Where would I go?"

She shook her head. "You know in two years you'll never be home. You get that driver's license, and you'll be out the door."

"That's not true."

"I'll be sad if it isn't." She tilted her chin toward me. "You don't see any of your old friends."

Only with great effort could I pull up their names and faces—Bobby Bishop, who was getting into motorbikes; Lance Tucker, my partner in swiping cheap merchandise from Kmart; Tony Collins, whose comic books and sci-fi movies we used to read and watch together in almost total silence—and even then, they seemed so far away that they might as well be on the other side of the moon. They belonged to a version of myself I no longer wanted to be.

"What about new friends?" she asked. "You've been at school for almost three months, and I don't think you've mentioned a soul. I talked to Dr. White last week. He says you're doing well in school, but you're a bit of a loner."

I shifted in my seat and blew on my hands. "Basketball's been cool."

She was silent for a moment. Basketball practice was right after school, so she was still picking me up at five thirty, like nothing had changed. I actually wondered for an instant if she had forgotten I was on the team. She asked, "When's your first game?"

"December 6. I had a good week of practice. Coach Snyder said so."

"I didn't know you liked basketball that much. I thought you were into baseball, like your father. Something change?"

I pictured Carson tugging his tie loose and tucking it into his shirt.

"You can't practice baseball by yourself. I've been spending my free bell shooting jumpers in the gym. I got better."

"You could do homework."

"My grades are fine."

At the sound of gears shifting, she looked up the street, and we watched a Ford F-150 creep toward us and then turn left. "No, your grades are good. That's what Dr. White said. I was worried for a while. But I'm glad you've found something to do besides school."

"Why were you worried?"

"Mothers always worry." She hugged herself, her gaze still down the street. "So. Basketball?"

"Yeah. I've been doing really well in practice, Mom. Really well." The hours in the small gym with Carson had improved my game—off the bounce, catch and shoot, dribbling with my left hand. The first two weeks of practice were conditioning—wind sprints and defensive footwork drills—and walking through our basic offensive sets and defensive principles. I had made it through both our first and second round of cuts and, most likely, earned the starting point guard spot on junior varsity. I regaled her with stories of our scrimmages, where my quick hands and sharp shooting had earned me some respect from the seniors. Even knowing that the details didn't matter to her, I couldn't help myself, diving into all the minutiae of the drills and scrimmages, seeing the game with the same untrammeled vision Carson did. I didn't mention how I berated upperclassmen about turnovers, missed shots, and lack of effort, castigating them so much that after yesterday's practice, Cam Taylor, the varsity's power forward, came up behind me while I was standing in front of my locker wearing only a towel. He put his massive hand on the back of my neck and said softly, "You need to chill with all that yelling, Webb."

When I finished, she had a soft half-smile on her face. "Your father was a great athlete, you know."

A new silence fell. Despite his love of baseball, my father rarely spoke of his high school days. Almost all

I knew about their lives came from my mother and the strange, trancelike soliloquies she would fall into when we were alone.

"You should have seen him," she said. "He really was amazing."

I began to feel cold then. Mom, unmoving in her chair, gazed down the street. A car came into view, a new Grand Cherokee, clean and polished. It moved haltingly in our direction, then turned left. Something better than our house seemed to be down that side street.

"Cheri?"

"We're outside," my mother yelled. She stubbed out her cigarette and exhaled all her smoke and breath into the air.

"You two are nuts," my father said, stepping onto the porch. "It's goddamn November."

"You sit out here all summer long."

"Baseball on the radio is like church. Better than church. Someone actually wins."

"You look handsome."

My father, Joseph Webb, spread out his arms, palms up, sweeping wide and flashy like an arrogant politician greeting a rabid crowd of supporters. He wore black slacks and his best dress shoes buffed to a perfect shine, and his gold blazer had a hint of blue that caught my eye before my gaze drifted to his silver cuff links. His face was freshly shaven, his dark hair parted as if a bullet had been fired through it; he wore too much cologne, but his brilliant, wolfish smile was that of a boy who believed he could always get away with more than he should. But in that moment, he was my father, and my mother looked at him as if there were no other man in the world.

My father always believed that someone else was responsible for his unhappiness, and his inability to identify why or by whom he was so wronged led to a dormant anger that, by the time I reached high school, was beginning to erupt. At the University of Cincinnati, my father discovered a few of the things that would permanently shape him into the man I knew. He discovered that the charm that had worked on high school teachers did nothing for distinguished professors and their graduate assistants. He discovered that he had no idea how to study. He discovered that no amount of tutoring from my mother, who was his high school sweetheart, was going to be enough to get him through four years of college. For several years after dropping out, he drove an interstate truck route. Somehow he turned his incomplete college degree into a job as a chemical technician at Procter & Gamble. He worked at their offices out in Sharon Woods. One of the perks of his job was free household goods; once a month, he came home with large, clear plastic bags filled with things my mother never had to buy: Crest toothpaste, cans of Pringles, Betty Crocker cake mix, Tide laundry detergent, Brawny paper towels. But even as a boy, I sensed that he was somehow disappointed with his life; in moments of quiet at home, whether in his recliner reading a Tom Clancy novel or down in the basement watching television, he would get a faraway look of sad, simmering anger.

But on the porch that night, his charm was full wattage. He flipped his hand out to my mother, and she took it with just three fingers. He delicately pulled her to her feet. They seemed to be in their own private production. She kissed his cheek, then looked down at me. "See you later," she said. She leaned toward me, and I tilted my cheek up to receive her kiss. My father nodded at me, and they took the steps carefully. He held the passenger door open for her, something he never did, and I waved as they pulled out. I stood on the porch with my hands deep in my coat pockets, watching until they disappeared from view.

Inside, I shucked off my coat and threw it on the couch. I took a soda from the fridge and went to the living room. The cable box was on the floor by the TV, and I untangled it from its wires and carried it to the couch; after clicking a few buttons, I found the NBA doubleheader. My evenings had been spent like this the entire time I was at Rockcastle: homework in front of the television on the nights when my mother wasn't home, homework in my bedroom when she was. Often in such moments, alone in the only house I remembered, surrounded by the same furniture we'd had for years, friendless on a Friday night, I tried to convince myself it wouldn't always be this way.

• • •

The phone's ringing woke me. I hadn't realized that I had fallen asleep, and I stared at the game on TV to figure it out: it was the first quarter of a Lakers home game, so it was clearly after ten. I picked up the cordless and beeped it on.

"I'm in your neighborhood," he said, skipping a hello. "What's your address?"

"Carson?" I sat up on the couch. "How did you get this number?"

"There's this new invention. It's called a phone book. Anyway, that's not important. What is important is that I'm coming to get you. Asher Schmidt's parents are out of town and he's throwing a party. You know him?"

I didn't; Asher was a senior who didn't play basketball and therefore was of very little interest to me.

"I'm a freshman. No one wants me at a party."

"Everyone is gonna be too drunk to notice. Plus, you're on the basketball team. After this week, everyone knows who you are."

"Really?"

"Hey, I'm in a McDonald's parking lot. Do you want something? I'll bring you something. Hop in the shower. Your parents home?"

"No."

"Okay, leave the front door unlocked and we'll just come in. See you in a bit."

"What do you mean 'we'? Who's with you?"

But he had already hung up. I stared at the phone for a moment as if I didn't know how it had appeared in my hand, then dropped it. I rushed to the bathroom and turned on the shower. Knowing he was at a McDonald's didn't give me any sense of how close he was. I slid back the deadbolt on our front door, then undressed in the bathroom. Soap stung my eyes, and scrubbing quickly, I was convinced this was the fastest shower possible. When I shut the water off, I stood still for a moment, listening for any sound of people in the house; the game was still on and there was the distant hum of the crowd as the home team did something worthy of cheers.

In my bedroom I quickly tugged on underwear and jeans, then stood before my closet, entirely unsure what to do next. My T-shirts hung to one side, my button-downs and flannels to the other, and nothing appealed. All my shirts suddenly appeared ratty to me, a collection of sports team logos and absurd one-liners, baggy and inappropriate for a Rockcastle party. I didn't know how long I'd been standing there when the front door opened and I heard girls laughing.

"Webb!" Carson yelled. "You back here?"

He opened my bedroom door without knocking, and

I gave him a quick wave, then rubbed my arms like I was cold in order to cover up my chest. He set a McDonald's bag on my dresser.

"Ready yet?" he asked. He dropped on my bed and slurped from a soda.

"I'm still picking a shirt."

"You're so white. Look at you."

Still clutching my elbows, I smirked, trying to be cool, and looked at the floor.

"C'mon, dude, it's just me." He bounced up and made a small circle with his finger, pointing at me. "You have wide shoulders. You're gonna fill out. Step aside, Webb, lemme help you."

He placed his hand on my chest. His hand was warm and sticky, and he pressed with its entire length, from palm to finger, steering me from his path. He stood before the closet with his hands on his hips and nodded to himself as he pondered my clothes.

"Do you have a sweater?" he asked.

"Sure."

"A little preppy, but they'll think you're cute." He reached into the closet and removed a blue oxford. "This and a sweater. Brown not black. Okay? We'll cultivate this."

I buttoned up my shirt and tugged a sweater over my head. Carson suggested I leave the oxford untucked and frowned at my shoes. I said I didn't have anything else, and he said, "We'll take care of that another time." Voices rose in the living room, someone shrieked, and then there was loud, hyena-like laughter.

"Who's out there?" I asked.

"Couple of girls from Roger Bacon. You'll love 'em. But don't worry about that."

"I'm not worried."

"Eat." He pointed at the bag and sat down on my bed; with nowhere else to go, I sat at my desk chair, facing him, and started eating a quarter pounder. "They're nice. But here's the thing. Don't go thinking they *like you* like you—you know what I mean? Play it cool. You aren't getting laid tonight, all right? Here's the deal. We're going to a party. We're gonna get fucked up and have a great time. Meet some folks, puke in someone's potted plants, the whole thing. It'll be fantastic. Speaking of folks, where are yours?"

I had no experience with drugs; the effects of cocaine and alcohol didn't register with me then, as I was sitting across from him, mesmerized by his speech. I said they were at a wedding.

"Awesome. We'll leave a note saying you're staying at my house. Cool?"

"It will be until tomorrow."

"They can be pissed off tomorrow then. In the meantime, I want you to work on your persona. The image of Owen Webb."

"What are you talking about?"

"Look," he said, leaning forward, elbows pressed into his knees. "You and I want the same thing. We want to be masters of the universe, show these trust fund babies what's what. In order to do that, you need to continue working your magic on people, making that mysterious silent thing you've been doing at school hold up outside of school. You've got fight in you. People either have that or they don't, you know what I mean? That doesn't just come out of the blue, fall from the sky, a meteor or something—that's who you are. And yet you never show that, you never lose it in school, you never mouth off at anybody, nothing. Except on the court. The way you lay into dudes on the team! I love that! That fire is there, man, but you reel it in.

Same thing tonight. You have to get all fucked up, because that's what you got to do, but you still have to be that mysterious cool dude at the same time. You need to keep that in mind."

I finished my sandwich and wiped my hands on a napkin. Leaning forward, mimicking his pose, I stretched out my hands, then pointed my fingers downward, raising my knuckles.

"Do you see these?" I asked. "Do you see the scars?"

He scrunched his eyebrows and leaned closer. With my left hand, I traced the scars along my right hand, on the second and third knuckles.

"Last year at school," I said, "I was coming up the stairwell and this kid Mark Gordon tripped me. Knocked me on my ass. Except I was on the stairs, you know, so I hit the stairs and all that, got banged up pretty good. Everyone laughed. Everyone. I start crying, you know, cause it really hurt, and Mark is at the top of the stairs cracking up, and he goes down to the second floor and he thinks that's it.

"I jumped up. I haul after him, and I'm running down the hallway and I grab him by the back of his collar and swing him around and slam him against the lockers. He wasn't a big guy, but he was bigger than me, and he wasn't expecting that. And I just started whaling on him. I'm punching his head, his neck, everything, and no one pulls me off. I mean, everyone just stands there, watching. I'm beating the shit out of this guy, and I hear a teacher yell for me to stop and I know I've only got one punch left.

"And so I leaned back and aimed for the side of his mouth and hit him as hard as I could. Knocked out two teeth. One went flying, and the other one got stuck in my hand. That's how I got these scars."

"Jesus," Carson said. His hair smelled oaky and masculine.

"I got suspended for that. After? I fought before and after school. Sometimes people would pick on me; other times, I just wanted to fight somebody, anybody. I'd just pick someone, a ninth grader I didn't like, for whatever reason, always looking for someone bigger than me."

"Do you always win?"

"If you fight, you're gonna lose some."

He leaned away and tilted his chin toward the ceiling, his Adam's apple bobbing up and down, and when he leaned forward again he sprang to his feet and threw jabs into the air. I often remembered him this way: triumphant, young, handsome. Dancing around the room, firing out punches like a boxer, I believed that he and I were kindred spirits, and that we would always remember this moment when we looked back on our lives.

Carson stopped and stared at my desk. He raised a finger and pointed at my computer like an accusation.

"Holy shit," he said. "Is that an Apple IIc?"

"Yeah. Why?"

"You need to get a better computer. Fuck me, is this the one with the green-and-black screen?"

My cheeks burned red. When I was a kid, my mother had given me a gift of programming books that taught me ASCII by instructing me to write code for a series of easy-to-play video games. I wasn't sure how old the computer was, only that I needed it to type my papers.

"It works," I offered.

"Get a Gateway. Much better. The Internet is just phenomenal. My dad had to get a separate phone line for me to dial up. Wait—does this fucking thing even have a CD-ROM?"

"I don't know," I lied.

"Fuck, well, ask Santa or something. C'mon, let's go." He pushed me down the hallway and latched my bedroom door closed, and when we entered the living room, he threw his arm across my shoulders.

On the couch, each on a separate cushion, sat three girls: one blonde, one brunette, one redhead, as if Carson were offering variety.

"Ladies," he said, "this is my friend Owen Webb."

I dropped my eyes to the ground as they all said hello, so I never knew which one uttered, "He's cute!" When I looked up, they were smiling in our general direction without looking at us, and they had the air of privilege I recognized from Rockcastle: there was the perfect fit of their clothes shaped to their narrow shoulders and slim legs, makeup that made it seem like they weren't wearing makeup, and hair that was full and gorgeous. All three of them were generically pretty and none of them offered their names. In the hands of the blonde was one of my father's coin books.

"Would you put that down, please?" I said.

"What?" she said.

I pointed. "That's my father's. Would you put it back?"

"But it was just sitting on the table. Are these worth something?"

I crossed the room and snatched it out of her hand. On the coffee table were three of my father's coin collection books, which he kept fanned out on the edge of the table closest to the television. When I came home and saw him panning through the books, I always knew not to greet him and to silently leave the room.

"They're my dad's." I rearranged the books the way he'd had them. My hands trembled, and I quickly stuffed them in my pockets. "He doesn't like anyone messing with them. That's all."

"So why does he leave them out?"

I often wondered the same question. What I had

decided was that it was a sign of power—I didn't know the phrase *passive-aggressive* then—that he could leave something valuable but untouchable in front of me and my mother and silently demand that we respect his coins as a sign of respect for him. But before I could try to evasively answer, Carson clapped his hands and yelled, "Who cares? Let's roll out!"

His car was a gleaming silver Audi, a brand I had never heard of before. I sat behind Carson, pressing my body against the door; the speakers shook when he cranked up Alice in Chains on the CD player. He opened the sunroof, and the cool November air raced in; Carson blasted the heat, giving us a mixture of hot and cold air. In the middle seat was the redhead. Her hair was a rich, dark burgundy, magnificently curling down past her shoulders. She smelled like lavender, and when she leaned into me, she reached her right hand across her body and clutched my arm.

"I'm Vanessa," she said. "I should have introduced myself earlier."

"That's okay." I couldn't think of anything else to say, so I asked how she knew Carson.

"My dad's an attorney, and his firm represents Carson's father. They play in the same adult soccer league. Super competitive. Boys really don't stop being boys just because they get older."

Everything she said was names, dates, facts: her mother was a vice president at Great American insurance; her house was in Indian Hill; she went to Roger Bacon because her mother had; she wanted to go to Columbia for college; she played tennis; she was going to Vail for Thanksgiving. At some point, she reached into her purse and pulled out a bottle of pear-flavored vodka, and we passed the bottle back and forth, my first taste of alcohol a mixture of familiar fruit juice and an acidic burn down my throat.

The car stopped abruptly, and I realized we were there and that I had no idea where we were. We got out, and as my feet hit the curb I realized that the unsteadiness in my legs was the alcohol. In front of us was a long, immaculate lawn that rose through a cluster of thick oaks toward a Tudor-style mansion. The lights in every window blazed. Off to the right was a driveway that wound up to the front of the house, and on the other side the lawn fell away into a woods. We were on a cul-de-sac, and up the street were BMWs and Benzes and boxy SUVs. Vanessa held onto my arm, leaning against me, and even though her eyes were alert, her footsteps were drunkenly unsteady.

"Whose house is this?" I asked no one, forgetting that Carson had already told me.

"Oh my god, you don't know?" Vanessa said. She started laughing but didn't answer. One of the doors of the three-car garage was open; inside, hidden from street view, was a Ping-Pong table set up for beer pong. It seemed like every one of the two dozen boys and girls in the garage was smoking cigarettes. Carson ignored them, so consequentially we all ignored them, and beelined for the door into the house.

All around us, teenagers in designer jeans and expensive sneakers milled about, a red plastic cup in everyone's hand. Pink Floyd blasted from speakers I could feel but not see. The brightness of the room made my eyes ache, and then, as if on cue, someone started flipping the lights off until there was just the haze of cheap Christmas lights strung along the perimeter of each room. Someone handed me a red cup, and I gulped down the cold beer. I didn't see Carson, and I didn't notice when Vanessa let go of my arm. In the kitchen, around the island, a circle of guys argued about football. I went out through the sliding door, and in the backyard tiki torches lit the patio. I sat down on a lawn chair among a mixed group who seemed to be arguing about who'd had the best skiing accident. I finished my drink and started in on the torn-open case of Icehouse at our feet, passing beers whenever someone asked me for one. I'm not sure how many beers I drank. Soon, one guy dropped his pants to show off the scars on his knee from reconstructive surgery to repair a torn ACL; his boxers, which depicted little upside-down sailboats, made everyone howl with laughter, and he shook his hips in a weird luau dance before pulling up his khakis and collapsing back into a patio chair, immediately falling asleep.

My ability to focus on the conversation drifted, but I heard someone mention a fire pole.

"What fire pole?" I asked.

"You haven't seen it?" the girl next to me asked. "Really? C'mon, I'll show you."

She took my hand and pulled me into the house. She wore an oversized black sweatshirt and jean shorts; I couldn't fathom how her legs weren't freezing. Her calf muscles were shapely, her skin surprisingly tan, and I was pleased that a pretty girl was holding my hand, tugging me up dark stairs, spinning around couples making out on the steps. One kid was passed out on the landing, and we seemed to climb endlessly, as if racing up the turret to the hidden tower of a castle in the air. On the floor where we stopped, a stereo played the Doors, and the only light in the hallway came from a single lamp on a side table; above the lamp was an oil painting of a yacht. The girl dragged me down the hallway. A boy burst from a room on our right and raced ahead of us. He zigged into what I assumed was a bathroom; a sound like a toilet seat slapping porcelain was followed by loud, painful vomiting.

"Lightweight!" the girl yelled. She pulled me into the opposite room.

We were on the third floor and standing in an otherwise unoccupied living room. The only light came from the distant windows along the back wall, the outdoor lights from below throwing weak light into the dark room. Around us, large couches filled the massive space; a coffee table was covered in red cups and ashtrays, and along the walls, pristine white bookshelves held nothing but hardcovers. In the middle of it all, running from the ceiling down through a hole in the floor, was a fire pole.

"That's impossible," I said.

"I know, right?" she exclaimed. "Devon told me about this and I was like, no way! But it really works, and it is so much fun. C'mon, let's slide!"

The fire pole shined as if it had been regularly polished. It came to a halt at a steel base attached to the ceiling by bolts the size of saucers. Around the fire pole were two half-circles of railing. Down below, the pole disappeared into a thin circle of blackness, then reappeared in a lighted room just like the one we were standing in, another overfurnished living room. I stepped back and stood on the other side of the railing.

"Is it safe?"

"You're hilarious!"

She reached out and wrapped her hands around the pole. She sprang, coiling her legs around the brass, and screeched pleasantly, holding herself in place with her pretty legs. She turned her head toward me, mouth gaping open in delight. Even drunk, I recognized such happiness, however momentary, as elusive to me: I never possessed the ability to immerse myself in the reckless abandon of play.

She loosened her grip and began to descend, closed her eyes, and howled. Speeding up, she dropped through the hole, and when I looked down she slammed into the floor, never getting her legs underneath her. The jolt made her roll onto her back and laugh louder. I climbed over the rail, grabbed the pole, and slid, crashing next to her, banging our legs together.

"Let's do it again!" she said.

We raced up the stairs, stumbling over and sometimes stepping on couples, and slid down the pole three more times. On the fourth trip up the stairs, she gasped and wheezed, started coughing, and then sat down on a couch. I collapsed next to her, and she leaned her head against my shoulder.

"That was so amazing!" she said. I wondered how anyone could always speak only in exclamations. I nodded at her, my head lolling forward.

She smiled at me and placed her hand against my cheek; I didn't know what to do with my arms. I was leaning forward, my right arm taking my weight, my left hand lying placidly on her hip. Her tongue slid into my mouth, and I was surprised not only that it happened but that I liked it. Our mouths opening wider, our tongues flicked back and forth, teasing, exploring, and a sigh somehow escaped her. We kissed for a long time, until our lips were beginning to chap. When she slid her hand down on my chest, I somehow knew we were done making out. She leaned away, opened her eyes, and gazed at me, then pressed her face into my chest.

"You're so nice."

She was asleep, and before I too passed out, the thought occurred to me that I didn't know her name. I wrapped her arms around me and pressed my lips to the crown of her head. My head rocked backward into the couch cushions, and my eyelids were tremendously heavy.

• • •

I woke with an urgent need to vomit. The room was dark, and the shadows of unfamiliar couches and chairs and tables lurked like wild animals. I leaned forward and heard the gurgling in my stomach. My legs were rubbery, but with a rising in my chest I raced out of the room, crossed the hallway, and threw myself into the bathroom. I vomited in the direction of the sink, splattering the mirror and walls, a thick stream like oatmeal covering the porcelain. I turned on the cold water and retched until my empty stomach ached. Dropping to my knees, my hands gripped the sink, and I waited for the next wave of pain. When I was sure I was finished, I stood up and staggered back to the couch.

The girl was gone. I tried to think through what had happened, where I was, anything I could do to orient myself. Other than the bathroom light I had left on, the hallway was dark; So was the room. I turned away and leaned against the wall. Music still played downstairs, but there were no voices. Down the hallway, half-empty bottles and red cups and ashtrays were scattered on tables, around the banister, along the wall. I crossed the hall and looked into the backyard: an impromptu football game was being played, and there were people still sitting on the patio, still drinking. I just wanted to sleep. Seeking a bed to pass out in, I took the stairs to the top floor.

Everything was pitch black. There was a window at the end of the hallway, and it threw only a mute gray light that illuminated nothing. The ceiling seemed low, the hallway too small compared to the rest of the large, twisting house. There were four doors, one near each end of the hallway and two in front of me. All of them were closed, and for the first time all night I had the sense that I was an intruder in someone's home.

I turned left and opened the door. It was someone's bedroom. The ceiling sloped downward, ending at the floor across the room, making only about half the space useable. Waiting for my eyes to adjust to the darkness, I clutched the doorknob. Posters taped to the walls were of rock stars: Janis Joplin, Jimi Hendrix, Bob Dylan, Tom Waits. There was a large bed, a dresser, a small desk, and piles of clothes scattered throughout the room; on top of the dresser, the numbers on a five-disc CD player blinked, the sound apparently off. I lurched to the bed, ran my hands over the sheets to make sure there was no one there, and then collapsed.

• • •

I woke up in the darkness to find Carson taking off my shoes. He untied them carefully, removing one at a time, and set them gently on the floor next to the footboard.

"Carson?"

"Hey, pal, how you feeling?"

"Sick."

"That's cool. Listen, dude, I need to move you, all right?"

"Where?"

He answered by taking my arms and wrapping them around his neck. Then he slid one arm under my knees and the other beneath my back. I rolled my head into his chest and felt the bed fall away from me. I couldn't see his face. His body and breath reeked of tobacco. But in his arms, protected and warm, I felt my queasiness give way to a drunken happiness. He lifted me across the room, said, "Easy, Webb," dropped to one knee, then set me on the floor. I rolled onto my side.

"Go ahead and pass out now, all right?"

Someone laughed. I opened my eyes and saw Carson's silhouette move away from me. A girl closed the door, and everything was in shadows. She came to him and kissed him with a ferocity I had only seen in late-night movies on cable. She yanked on his belt and reached into his jeans; he leaned his head back and groaned, his lips curling into smile, his teeth white and wolfish. With one quick, expert motion, she pulled his jeans and boxers down. His erection arched away from his body in a thick, perfect line, and she took it in her mouth. She used her hands and mouth, bobbing up and down. My own erection was massive and painful.

Carson laced his fingers behind his head, mumbling softly, then dropped his hands and held the girl's hair back. He reached down and placed his hands on her shoulders, lifting slightly, and she released him. Her lips glistening with saliva, she stood up and kissed him hard. He yanked her sweater over her head, peeled off her undershirt, and unstrapped her bra with one finger. Before he lowered his head and kissed them, her nipples, hard and upright, stood tall, her breasts round and perfect, and she gasped when he kissed her. They stood kissing this way, Carson's pants around his ankles, his ass turned toward me now, stark and bare in the moonlight, and I could see the dark hairs climbing up his legs and disappearing into his cheeks. He pivoted her and then lifted her up, cupping her ass with his arms and tossing her on the bed. She laughed loud, then in low giggles, she said, "Carson, Carson, Carson."

He kicked off his shoes and pulled his remaining clothes over his head. He was now naked. With my eyes adjusted to the dark, the curvature of his body was laid bare: his sinewy arms, his wide shoulders, a surprisingly thin chest bereft of hair, and a slick, lean stomach. I had never seen him, or any of the other boys, in the locker room; I always turned away, dressed with my eyes down, facing my locker, and it was exciting to see him as a faceless body, hungry and yearning for sex, vivid before me in a way I could never imagine.

He kissed her stomach; she ran her fingers through his hair, now messy and disheveled. He unbuttoned her jeans and yanked them off, and I almost raised my head to see what she looked like between her legs. But they were too far away, the bed too high up from my spot on the floor, and all I got was her beautiful lean legs, smooth and perfect, arched outward, her toes painted a color I could not discern. Carson dropped his head between her legs and she gasped loud, threw her head back, mouth open.

Then he stopped. He stood up and turned away. A drawer opened; there was a tearing sound. Carson's chin was dipped, and only then did I realize he was rolling on a condom. Then he came back to bed, leaned all the way over and kissed the girl deeply. They lay this way, kissing but otherwise unmoving, for what seemed like a long time, and then he arched his hips and dropped a hand between his legs, and when she clawed his back, I knew he was inside her.

For a while they were lying this way, long, face to face, his hips moving slowly. Then they rolled away from me, and she was on top of him. Her grunting and moaning became more urgent, and she arched her body away from him. She gripped his ankles and kept saying, "Yeah, yeah, yeah." She leaned over him, kissing him again, hands on his face, her hips never stopping. She demanded that he get behind her. He slid out from beneath her and grabbed her ass; she was on all fours, her head turned toward me as she tried to see behind her, to see him. He reentered her, and there was a steady smack of their bodies colliding as he fucked her. They were both loud, the guttural noises they were making no longer controllable, and when he came he grabbed her hips hard, as if he could pull her body into his.

He slapped her hip, and she laughed. Their teeth were white, straight, perfect. He collapsed onto his back and she lay next to him.

"My legs are quivering," she said. Carson reached down, yanked off the condom, and tossed it on the floor.

"Gross," she said.

"Not our room," he answered.

Their breathing slowed. They turned themselves toward the pillows and climbed under the covers. After they fell asleep, I rolled onto my right side, away from them, and let the images of their sex lull me to sleep.

When I awoke, it was daylight. I raised my head to look out the window and guess at the time, and pain shot behind my eyes. I blinked, lowered my head back down, and cataloged the ache, the pulsating behind my skull, the dry taste in my mouth like I had swallowed cotton, the gurgling noises in my stomach. *This is a hangover,* I thought. I propped myself up on my forearms and glanced over at the bed. They were gone.

I ran my palm down my face and wondered if I had imagined the whole thing. I placed my hand on the bed; the tangled sheets remained warm, as if they had just left, and the smell of sweat and sex still lingered. Outside, the day seemed bright and cold; wind whistled over the roof, and what remaining leaves clung to the tree branches were brown and dead. I sat on the bed and tugged on my shoes and socks. On the floor was Carson's discarded condom.

In the hallway, all the doors were shut. On the third and second floors, the same: dark brown doors were closed, and the debris of the party lay in the hallway and around the banisters. Downstairs, a few kids were asleep on the floor, the lucky ones on couches or chairs. I didn't see Carson anywhere. My head throbbed, and in the kitchen, every inch of surface covered with sticky, clear alcohol, I opened the fridge and removed the orange juice. I found a clean glass in the cabinets and gulped down two glasses. I left the container and glass on the counter next to dozens of liquor bottles and beer cans and red plastic cups and walked out through the garage.

The reek of cigarettes clung to the air, and there was now a single car in the garage: a jet- black Audi, which seemed to be the automobile of choice at Rockcastle. A cheap card table sagged under the weight of beer bottles and empty beer cases, ashtrays filled with cigarettes, and what looked like several decks of ratty playing cards. One of the garage doors was open. Absently, I palmed a football from a shelf of sporting goods and stepped into the autumn air.

The chill was a palpable relief, the air down my throat as soothing as drinking cold mountain water from a stream. I opened my eyes wide and inhaled the world deeply. It was one of those perfect, beautiful autumn days when the sky is overcast yet bright, the leaves are dead but beautiful, and there is a damp chill on the entire world. Holding the football between my hands, I knew that this moment was one I would remember for a very long time.

I'm not sure how long I was standing there before I heard someone walking behind me. I turned. A shaggy-haired kid I had never seen before smacked his lips and whipped his arms in wide circles. He wore a plaid shirt and a blue vest and had an expression as if he was trying to hawk a loogie.

"My head hurts so fucking bad," he said. "Jesus."

I said nothing. In the last three months I had discovered what a powerful and interesting effect silence had on people and was beginning to enjoy the discomfort it created.

"I mean, wow," he continued. "Asher knows how to throw a party. Dude." He shook his head. "Do you know what time it is?"

I looked out into the street. Carson's car was gone.

"I need a ride," I said. "Can you drop me off?"

"Sure, dude. Which way you headed?"

"Clifton."

"Where is that from here?"

I frowned. "Actually, I don't know where we are."

The kid stared at me and smiled. Then he started laughing hard, hopping up and down, and bellowed.

"Fuck, yes! 'Where we are'! Fucking brilliant, man, fucking brilliant!"

He folded his arms across his chest and leaned back on his heels, shaking his head. He said his name was Sam. He said he had to grab his friend and disappeared around the corner of the house. I walked to the edge of the driveway and peered into the backyard. Around the patio, a wide swath of various shades and shapes of red brick were laid out with an elegance designed by a person who clearly cared about every detail. Three boys were passed out on lounge chairs, winter coats draped over their bodies, the ground beneath them littered with cigarette butts and beer bottles. The sheer number of alcohol bottles, both here and inside the house, was tremendous, and I wondered how teenagers could so easily acquire this much alcohol.

Sam reached down to a kid with a stocking cap pulled low to his nose; he opened his eyes just enough to recognize Sam. He raised an arm for help, and Sam yanked him up, still grinning the way he had in the driveway. His friend stumbled forward, almost being carried, and the three of us walked down the driveway and into the street, the electronic beep that unlocked Sam's car guiding us to the right SUV.

We shoved his buddy into the passenger seat and clicked the seatbelt tight. I climbed in the back, sitting behind Sam so he couldn't see me. The leather was cool to the touch, and the world seemed pleasantly isolated from the inside of a car. Sam lit a cigarette, turned the ignition, and slipped in a Weezer CD, set to a low volume.

"So," Sam said, "best guess what neighborhood this is?"

Around us were large homes that looked new, and yet the surrounding woods must have been hundreds of years old. Who would be so careful to cut such detailed, precise lots, surveyed and scaled and planned and engineered, without doing any damage to what surrounded it?

"We're east," I said. No one at Rockcastle, it seemed, was from western Cincinnati. "Hit a main road and head toward the city."

"Can do."

Sam wound us through a series of back roads with no sidewalks. The slow curves rose and dipped through clumps of leafless trees, the wet black branches reflected in the car's windows like ghost limbs. The heater was turned high, and the cigarette smoke clung around Sam's head; he cracked a window and the whistling wind ripped through, drowning out the music. We cruised at a low speed, and somehow Sam never seemed lost or frustrated. After driving down a handful of cul-de-sacs and side streets that dropped us right back where we had first entered, we found a long, straight shot where the speed limit was higher, and suddenly we were at an intersection of gas stations, phone wires paralleling the sky.

"I think I know where we are," Sam said. "This is 50. We're in Anderson."

I nodded. I knew only that Anderson High School had a good soccer team.

We turned right onto a road with a speed limit over fifty miles per hour. On both sides of the street were a series of low, flat shopping centers with small parking lots. The guy in the passenger seat gave one choking snore and rolled closer to the window.

"This guy," Sam said, "should never mix weed and beer. You know what I mean?"

We drove into the city, the landscape changing from single-story chains on their way out of business to three-story brownstones. The road climbed uphill, surrounded by heavy clumps of trees, and began to wind and curve in harmony with the Ohio River, its banks visible off to the left. We crested the hill and the city appeared below us, skyscrapers rising like a thousand triumphant arms at a concert. The road we were on led into the heart of Cincinnati. I pressed my palm against the window and watched the faint sun tumble behind me as the car veered north and we took the highway up and out of the city. We didn't go far; Sam exited at Martin Luther King and raced west, crossing the northern border of the city, passing the university hospital, the wide stretch of phone wires crossing the sky like a warning. Then we were back in Clifton, and everything seemed like home again.

Once we passed the University of Cincinnati campus with its rolling lawns and red brick buildings, we were in downtown Clifton.

"Where we going?" Sam asked.

"Turn right here." The street was a T-intersection, and Sam steered onto Clifton Avenue. Across the street were a series of buildings affiliated with the university—Hillel, a Newman center, fraternities pushed far from the campus, the Hebrew College—and when I saw Ludlow Avenue, I asked to be let out.

"Where?"

"The corner."

"You live here?"

I didn't answer but thought it best that Sam thought I did. He veered to the right and pulled up to the curb.

"Thanks for the ride," I said.

"No problemo, hombre. I'll see you next week." With that, I exited the car, closed the door, and watched Sam race through a yellow light as it turned red, the wheels leaning perilously as they accelerated across Ludlow, rising briefly as they headed north on Clifton, and then disappearing from site. I never saw Sam again.

It took me a moment to realize I was still carrying the football. It didn't click that I had stolen it. Tucking it under my arm, I watched the intersection and the flow of cars for a few minutes, holding the football dumbly, my mind empty and the cold creeping down my face and neck, chilling me to my feet. I guessed the walk home was about twenty minutes.

Behind me was Burnet Woods, a city park my mother took me to when I was a boy. I walked to the nearest fountain; the water was off, the moat drained, and inside it were scattered dead leaves, cigarette stubs, discarded soda cups. I wondered how often someone came by to clean it out. The faces from last night's party swam around in my mind, and I focused on the girl I'd kissed. My first kiss. And I had no idea who she was, not even something as basic as her first name. Sunlight filtered through the clouds, briefly, then faded away, leaving the world slated in muted colors, and the day's promise somehow seemed disingenuous. The trees were desolate and bereft of leaves. Spinning the football in my hands, I waited for a feeling to settle in my chest, but nothing happened. I was empty and blank, and I found I didn't mind this at all.

I walked home—thinking of excuses, imagining my reasons, preparing for yelling—and wondered how long I would be grounded. The sidewalk rose and fell due to the tree roots that pushed the concrete slabs up. I spun the football between my fingers, trying to make my face regretful. But when I got close to home, I saw there was no car in the driveway. I entered the house through the side door, which I knew didn't creak like the front door. Inside,

I stood on the landing and listened. Hearing nothing, smelling no coffee, I crept into the kitchen and surveyed the room. No jacket, no shoes. I crossed to the hallway and looked toward my room; my bedroom door was still closed. My parents' door was ajar, and when I peeked in I saw that the bed was made. Back in the kitchen, the red answering-machine light blinked "2."

"Hey, kid," my father said. "We're going to stay at the hotel tonight. Better safe than sorry. Drinking and all that. Yeah, yeah, yeah, I'm telling him. I'm telling him! Okay, so listen, we're at the same hotel as the number on the fridge. I don't know what room we're gonna stay in, but that's why they have clerks at the front desk working all night. You know your mother worked at a hotel once? Front desk. Graveyard shift, but don't ask her about it and don't call it the graveyard shift because then she'll tell you about the robbery and she hates telling that story and it gets me in the shitter for even bringing it up. Forget I said anything. Hope this didn't wake you—okay, hold on, hold on. Yeah, that's mine. I'm right here, Jesus, Mary, and Jos—"

The machine beeped. It had cut him off. I hit delete. The second message played. The time stamp was after two in the morning. Loud music, screaming, several voices talking all at once. The music, indistinguishable bass and guitar, could have been from Asher's house or from the wedding. I held my breath and waited for a voice, any voice, even a quick "sorry" so I could identify who it was on the other end. But no one spoke. Not one word. There was suddenly a muffled noise, the phone banging, and then a click, silence. The machine beeped, and after a moment of staring down at the football still in my left hand, I again hit delete.

III

Since the party three weeks earlier, Carson hadn't invited me anywhere. During that time, he and I continued to shoot baskets during our free bell, and I saw him daily at practice and in the hallways. In school, he always said, "Hey, Webb, what's up?" in that disarming and friendly way he had with the world, but it was always said in passing as he strolled away, just a quick greeting, an easy interruption from the conversation he was having with his older friends. I closed my locker and looked down the length of the hallway, and watched as Carson stood speaking with three other students and a math teacher, Mr. Rudolph. With their broad smiles and relaxed posture, they seemed to be sharing a great story.

"He's a little out there, isn't he?"

I turned. Standing next to me, gazing down the hallway, was Spencer Foote. He was the varsity's starting center, the focus of our high-post offense and our defensive anchor, an undersized junior with thick shoulders and a wide ass, our best player. His success was due to his nimble and big, soft hands that could scoop any erratic pass. Until that moment, he had never acknowledged me other than at practice, and even that was only with a nod or a finger point.

"He fits right in," I said. "Everyone loves him."

"Pay more attention, Webb. Everyone is afraid of him."

"No, they aren't."

"None of us hang out with him on the weekend. Or after school. Not just ballplayers, I mean, nobody. He plays basketball, and that's it."

"What's that, then?" I tilted my head in Carson's direction.

"Yeah, sure," Spencer said, "he's always talking to someone. He plays the part. Kind of an Eddie Haskell."

"Who's Eddie Haskell?"

Spencer laughed and shook his head. His eyes were merry, and he seemed to be enjoying my education. He cocked his head as a directive, and I followed him down the hall toward my next class.

"There was a kid," Spencer continued, "that he was close to freshman year. Augustus Wexner, a cousin of the more famous Wexners up in Columbus. Gus was a beanpole, real shy—not a bad kid, just didn't seem to know how to tie his shoes without help, you know? Those two were inseparable. Gus came to all the basketball games and everything."

"He wasn't on the team?"

"Gus? Shit, that kid was too scared to touch the balls between his legs, let alone big ones. He wasn't into sports. He was into hunting. Liked to be out in the woods really early. Deer, ducks, pheasant. I heard they used to go on hunting trips together; their fathers were business buddies, or something."

Spencer's family owned a regional bottling and

distribution company. Even now, I often can remember what a person's parents did for a living before I can recall their names.

"So what happened to Gus?" I asked.

"No one knows. I mean, he's not dead at the bottom of Red River Gorge or anything. He just never came back for his sophomore year. I heard he's up in Cleveland now. Anyway, your pal Carson? Sophomore year he came back doing this stuff, the glad-handing and captain-of-industry routine. But he eats lunch by himself. Always reading something by an existentialist, as if this is the 1950s or something. Like any of us came back from a war, you know?"

"I think he's cool. He's helping me with my game. He seems to have this place figured out."

"Nobody has this place figured out." Spencer placed his hand on my shoulder and steered me around a corner. "Look, I'm not saying he's a fag or anything. There are some gay guys at this school, and that's whatever. What I'm saying is that something is wrong with Bly. Bad wiring or something. Just pay attention, okay, Webb? There's a part of that guy that just isn't there."

"What do you mean 'isn't there'?"

"A detachment. And not in a Buddhist way, either. He always seems to be watching his life, watching us, and he gets this look on his face like he doesn't like what he sees."

"Why are you telling me all this?"

Spencer sighed. "I don't know. Never mind. Fucking forget it. You know, just, whatever, Webb, I'm just saying. Bly is different from the rest of us. Okay?" He clapped me hard on the shoulder, and my body bounced under its weight. "I'll see you at practice."

Spencer lumbered down the hall a few more steps and then steered into a classroom.

• • •

The first game of our basketball season was on a Friday night in early December. Cincinnati was covered in the first of what would be three days of sleeting rain. In the locker room, my shooting shirt draping halfway down my thighs, images of the game flashed through my mind: what our set plays were, how to space the floor, my feet sliding defensively side to side, keeping my hands down to avoid fouls, and to pass to the open man.

We weren't a very good team. We had only two guys with any size—Sonny Lewis and Derek Bremer—and they were only big compared to our team's collection of guys less than six feet tall who loved to shoot from the outside. When we missed, it only seemed to steel our belief that the next one would go in. And god forbid if we made a shot, because it only encouraged us to shoot more. All of us believed we were sharpshooters, including me, which led to our opponents getting a bevy of long rebounds, quick outlets, and easy layups.

Carson and the varsity team were required to sit in the stands during the junior varsity game. Those fifteen upperclassmen sprawled together over several bleacher rows, their blazers and ties on but loosened and wrinkled from a day of classes. It showed solidarity with junior varsity but also made the gym look like there was a real audience. Other than the players' parents, no one came to the junior varsity games. It was only during our fourth quarter that our classmates and their friends and dates, parents and alumni, would trickle in, seeking good seats for the varsity game. The gym was noticeably louder in fourth quarters, which always put an extra bounce in our step, made our passes crisper, our shots smoother.

During warmups, I hit a nifty left-handed layup, scooping from the other side of the rim, a move I had worked on with Carson. When I looked to the stands to see his nod of approval, he was turned away, his full attention given to a girl. They sat very close, but she gazed out at the court, her eyes wide and pooling, as if she were looking at something awesome and incomprehensible. There was a hardness to her smooth, pretty face, as if skeptical caution had been chiseled into her cheeks. She wore a black bowler hat pulled down low on her brow, long brown hair that hung over her shoulders, and overalls with only one strap fastened. She bit her lip and nodded once at something Carson said.

"Yo, Webb!" A pass bounced off my right shoulder. Pulled out of my reverie, I grabbed the loose ball and dribbled back into line. When I looked up to see if Carson had seen my gaffe, I found that the girl was staring at me. I quickly looked away.

I tried to casually spy my parents in the stands. My whole life, my father never missed my games. He signed me up for Knothole League T-ball, which was Cincinnati's equivalent of Little League, and filmed all my games with his gargantuan camcorder. He labeled the videos and shelved them in chronological order alongside the other movies in our basement rec room. The first few years I played, my parents came together to my games. But in junior high, when I was roaming center field and batting third for the baseball team, then riding the bench all winter for the basketball team, my mother appeared less and less often, and then not at all.

So I was a little surprised when I saw my mother come in alone. She took a seat about halfway up the bleachers at center court. No one sat near her, and she made no effort to speak to anyone in our sparse crowd. During my games, she always sat hunched forward, hands covering her mouth, elbows embedded in her knees, her frequent clapping and cheers hidden behind her fingers as though they were some secret bird call coming from high and deep in the branches of a tall tree. When I spotted her, I nodded discreetly, and her fingers fluttered in a wave that wouldn't draw attention.

The buzzer sounded, and we huddled around the junior varsity head coach, Kelly Peters. In school, we always spoke to our teachers with proper respect: Dr. Yee, Dr. Bober, and so forth. But for some reason, all the boys called the athletic coaches by their first names. Kelly had sandy brown hair and an earnest, boyish face; the varsity guys teased him about playing in a church league, which Kelly always took with good humor and not a hint of embarrassment. He never looked comfortable in his jacket and tie, squirming at the collar and cuffs the way a small child would. I kept calling him "Coach," and along with my work ethic, this made him take a shine to me, something the other kids noticed and resented, though I definitely earned my starting spot at point guard.

I didn't see my father come in, but I was on the bench to start the second quarter, catching a breather, when I spied him along the far baseline, where we were on offense. My father detested hats, never once had I seen him wear one, so his bushy hair stood in high strands from the wind outside, and his cheeks were inflamed red. Whether this was from the intensity of the game or from the cold outside, I could not tell. He remained in the corner when I got back in the game. My father was always an offense man. When I played baseball, he stood up and crept close to the backstop for my at bats—silent, studying, a coiled rage, never barking at me or the umpire. But when I took the field, he would climb back up the aluminum stands and sit, fingers laced, like a man watching the ocean. Basketball didn't allow him such passive observation.

I entered the game and nodded at him; he didn't acknowledge me. His stretch of territory was roughly six paces in each direction, his arms behind his back, right hand gripping left wrist, and I swore I could see his left hand turn white from the circulation being cut off. He leaned forward like he was charging into the wind, his eyes never leaving the court. I looked over at Carson; he looked right at me but didn't smile or nod back.

My first quarter had been good: in six minutes of play, I had hit two free throws and a corner three. I needed to do the same now. I brought the ball up the court and called the set—a simple two-man action on the strong side, and back cut on the weak side—bringing the ball toward my father's corner. The big David Teague posted up weakly on the block, his defender inching him slowly out of the paint.

"C'mon, Owen!" my father screamed. "Let's go!"

I blinked. Sweat pooled on my lip. My defender inched up on me. I pounded the ball hard right, then stepped back, picked up my dribble, and faked a pass to Teague. I had room to make the pass—I don't know why I faked—and my defender recovered. Teague waved for the ball. I faked a bounce pass, tried to lob the ball in, and it slipped off my sweaty fingers. My defender tipped the ball, and it soared high over Teague, ricocheting off the backboard. Turnover.

"Goddamn it, Owen!" my father yelled.

I hustled back. No fast break. We got a stop, ran the same set. This time, my defender pressed, tipped the ball from my left hand, and when I slapped at the ball, I committed a silly foul. With my back to the play, I heard my father curse, then the ref say something to him about profanity at the game and that he would kick him out if he had to.

At the dead ball, my coach subbed me out. In the stands, Carson was looking directly at me but betrayed nothing. With my hands on my hips, I looked up at the rafters as I came off the floor and walked by my coach without saying a word. I dropped onto the end of the bench, and the assistant coach came down next to me.

"Hey," he said. "Don't let that rattle you, all right?"

I nodded.

"Webb," he said, repeatedly, until I looked up at him. "It's all right, okay? It's all right. Shake it off. You're going back in the game, and we're gonna need you. Okay?"

"Got it, Coach."

He patted my knee. "Good man."

In fact, I was benched the rest of the second quarter. Our lead evaporated, and at the half we were down by six.

When the horn sounded, Kelly clapped for us to hustle to the locker room. I lingered behind everyone, my chin toward the stands. My father climbed the steps and sat next to my mother. She clapped, staring at my teammates, seeking me out, not finding me, ignoring my father as he stared out at the court like a man awaiting a death sentence.

In the locker room, our shoulders slumped and we stared at the floor. Coach strode before us, hands on his hips and his tie yanked loose from his collar. Two years later, when he left Rockcastle to follow his wife's biotech career to California, this was always how I remembered him: his sandy, thin hair flopped around his eyebrows, total frustration that everything he had told us over the last four weeks—fan your man to the sideline, close out on the shooter, rebound with two hands—had been ignored. Coach reiterated our plan of attack and reminded us of all the things we had worked on in practice, and then sent us back out to get loose for the second half.

Instead of shooting, I dropped to the floor on the baseline and stretched. Above, jumpers clanked off the rim as guys jacked up off-balance shots, grinning ear to ear. Sonny and Derek parked under the basket, bumping each other, screaming as they put back easy rebounds, enjoying their mock ferocity. I dragged my knuckles across the floor until the bones ached. The halftime buzzer blared overhead. Varsity coagulated back into one mass and stood up, slipping their gym bags onto their shoulders; they headed toward the locker room to change. When he passed by, Carson nodded at me and flattened his palm: *be cool.*

My father came back down to the court and staked out the corner directly across from our bench, where our team would be on offense in the second half. *Ignore him,* I told myself. *Don't even look in his direction.*

I started off the third by hitting a runner in the lane. Then I hit a corner three in front of our bench. When my shot rattled down, my father bellowed and pumped his fist. At the end of the third quarter, we were tied, and I took a seat again, getting a brief rest before coming in for the final minutes of the fourth quarter. My father's steps became more furious, pounding the wood, his boots squawking as he pivoted, his clapping furious. Every time the ball came to me, I attacked the rim. Sometimes I would pause, make the defender hold steady at my triple-threat position, then blasting by him. The first two times I went right, into the lane, and got easy layups. The third time I faked right, went left, and was fouled. I hit both my free throws. Soon, the defense started shading my way, and I had to pass the ball away, but I simply cut the baseline, curled to the other side, and drove to the basket from there. I was fouled repeatedly, and I calmly sank my free throws.

When I attacked the rim, the physical contact was a rush, a surge through my chest that I hadn't felt since before

Rockcastle, when I beat other kids up, manufacturing some provocation in my mind. Getting by my defender was pretty easy: I had a quick first step and protected the ball. Beyond him, I looked for the big guy, the one who would try to plant his feet or who came swooping in from the weak side to swat away my shot. When I jumped, I saw that they wanted to foul: rather than jumping up, they jumped at me, pummeling me with their size or swinging their arms to grab my shoulders, arms, hands, whatever they could. The fouls racked up, and they were subbed out, and the bench players would do the same thing. The savoring of the pain happened after the contact, when I was flat on my back sweating onto the floor, when a teammate grasped my hand and tugged me up. Striding to the free-throw line was when I could replay the assault in slow motion, making each moment larger than it truly was, savoring the delicious rush that I could only hold for a moment or two before I stepped to the line, right toes slightly ahead of my left, spin the ball twice off the floor, exhale, and let fly an easy free throw.

With under a minute left in the game, we were down one, and I brought the ball up. Our meager crowd was on its feet—even my mother—and Coach Kelly had shucked off his blazer, rolled up his sleeves, and waved his hands to instruct us into our positions. All I could hear was my father screaming. The red clock on the scoreboard ticked closer to zero. No shot clock. We wanted the last shot of the game. I crossed just over half court and crouched into a low defensive dribble. My defender stepped back, and the ref spread his hands wide: no five-second count. Coach Kelly called the ball: high screen for me, penetrate, ball to the post, weak-side screen for the cutting small forward. Whether from the post or the cutter, we should get a shot at or near the rim. All I had to do was make the right pass.

The screener came up on my right and set himself just behind my defender. I dribbled left. Ten seconds left in the game. I crossed over to the right, and the screener's defender back-pedaled. I dribbled at him, continued to push right. My defender tried to double-team me, and my screener was now at the top of the three-point line, waving his hand furiously for the ball. Teague posted up hard, his legs wide, his off hand sealing his defender. He had great position. I pounded the rock. Eight seconds. I drifted away from the double, hesitating. I wasn't sure what to do. All I heard was my father screaming, "Take the shot! Take the shot!"

Six seconds.

The weak-side defender stuck a foot in the paint. Somehow, he knew the play. What Coach Kelly called was not going to work.

Take the shot!

The screener's defender leapt forward, all over me. I jumped back, unbalanced off my right foot, and rifled a pass to my screener at the top of the key. I heard my father: "Goddamn it!"

Coach Kelly's hands stopped moving; he held them out from his body like he was a bad sleepwalker.

My screener, Robbie Stern, caught the ball. After being open all this time, he clearly didn't know what to do. He took one step in, like he was going to drive to the rim, and stopped. He was still wide open. Four seconds. No one was near him. Everyone watched him as he jumped off the wrong foot, cocked back, and fired what could only be called a knuckleball at the rim, the ball barely spinning. It hammered off the backboard, shuddering the glass, and then off the rim, high into the air. Two seconds. Everyone in the paint jumped. Someone tipped the ball, and it caromed harmlessly toward center court. The buzzer sounded.

I glared at Stern, determined not to see my father glaring at me. Each team lined up and slapped fives. We headed to the locker room, where Kelly rounded us together to give us a brief pep talk. Good game, good effort, we were right where we wanted to be at the end. Hit the showers, fellas. Practice Monday at three thirty, right after school. We all stood, and I turned toward my locker.

"Webb," Coach Kelly said. "Get over here."

I walked over, head hanging.

"You run the plays I call," he said softly.

"Coach, weak side sniffed out. I saw it."

"So you put Stern in a position to take that shot?"

"It was the right play."

"But the wrong man. Wasn't it?"

I glanced over at the guys. No one was paying any attention to us.

"Hey, Webb. Look at me. You're the point guard. Do you hear me?"

I nodded.

"It's not just the right play. It's the right guy in the right position. Remember that."

Take the shot take the shot take the shot take the shot take the shot.

"Got it, Coach."

"Good. Hit the showers."

Back on the court, hair still wet, I stood on the baseline and watched the varsity layup drill. Carson came out of line.

"Tough loss," he said.

"Fucking Stern."

"You should have taken the shot."

"I was doubled."

"Doesn't matter if you drill that game winner."

"I guess."

"Hey, man. You're the best player on the team. Take the fucking shot. You staying for the game?"

On the far end of the court, by the doors to the parking lot, my parents stood together, apart, a gap big enough between them for other departing parents to pass through without even turning their shoulders.

"Doesn't look that way."

He followed my gaze. "You'd think they were the ones that played."

"Hey," I said, looking at the scorer's table. "Who was that girl you were talking to?"

"Which one? The real pretty one with the hat?"

"Yeah. Who is that?"

He raised an eyebrow and smirked. "That's my sister, dude. Caitlin."

"You have a sister?"

"Better get going," He nodded in the direction of my parents. "Don't want to make them more pissed for waiting."

"Good luck, man."

He winked. "Don't need it," and he jogged back into the layup line. I walked to my parents with my head down, and when I got within ten feet, my father turned and headed for the double doors. My mother shot me a look, and I shrugged. Starting last year he had become more and more incensed at my team's losses, and my mother and I had learned the hard way that it was best to remain silent and listen to his harangues rather than attempt to reason with him.

I was surprised to discover that my parents had driven together, and disappointed I no longer had the option of riding with my mother rather than my father. Though it was her Camry station wagon, my father drove, guiding us in a sullen, angry silence. In the dark, I couldn't quite make out his eyes, and when his chin tilted toward the rearview mirror, I felt, but couldn't tell, that he was staring directly at me. He didn't drive fast or slow, and the radio was at a murmur, tuned to the classic-rock stations he preferred. My mother and I remained in a tense silence, watching the city zip by as we took the lateral from 71 to 75 and exited to our neighborhood. The three of us still hadn't spoken a single word when we pulled into the driveway. My father killed the engine, then sat with his hands on the wheel. No one dared to get out of the car.

"Do you want to be a loser?" he asked.

"No," I said. "What?"

"Because that's what you were today. You know that? You were a loser."

His eyes remained focused on some point directly ahead of him. My mother raised her hand and gently, as if assuaging a wounded animal, touched his left shoulder. She said his first name softly.

"You aren't in junior high anymore," he said. "You don't play for fun anymore. You play to win. Do you think that friend of yours would have passed up that shot?"

I didn't say Carson's name. "It was the right play."

He spun around. The quick whip surprised my mother, and her hand bent back, sharp and awkward.

"Jesus, Joe!"

"What does that mean?" he screamed at me. "The right play? Are you fucking with me?"

"Goddamn it, Joseph," she said. "That hurt!" He glared at her, and her expression went blank as she leaned away from him, her back against the door. A tremor ran through his cheek, and then he twisted further in his seat to face me. He grabbed my knee and squeezed hard.

"Do you hear me?"

"Yes, sir."

He seemed to be looking around me, or through me, as if I wasn't quite in focus. His chin dropped and he muttered something inaudible, then he spun back around and exited the car, slamming the door behind him. My mother waited until he was inside before saying, "C'mon, Owen." We followed him into the house, just in time to hear him slam the bedroom door, too.

We stood in the living room, my mother staring down at the rug, her right hand absently massaging her left wrist.

"Are you okay?" I asked.

"Fine," she said to the floor. She didn't stop touching her wrist.

"No, I meant your wr—"

"I know what you fucking meant. Jesus."

I picked up my bag and stomped off to my bedroom. I pitched my duffel into the closet, kicked off my shoes, and climbed into bed, facing the wall. Rubbing my nose into the sheets, I replayed the last possession in my head over and over again, slowing it down, trying to see the court from above as if it were drawn on a dry-erase board. My door opened.

"I didn't mean to curse you," my mother said.

"I know."

"Just, when he gets angry like that, I feel—"

"I said, I know."

I reached out and dug my fingernail into the wall. After a moment, the door latched shut, and I waited to make sure she wasn't in the room before turning over and staring at the doorknob.

When I was a boy, she would tuck me in at night and read to me from one of the library books she brought home: *The Phantom Tollbooth, The Cricket in Times Square, Abel's Island, The Dark Is Rising.* After she was finished reading, stroking my hair back off my forehead, she would tell me about what she and my father were like when they were younger. I don't think she was ever really talking to me. To give a soliloquy to no one was an acknowledgment of her loneliness, and if I was her audience, then someone, no matter how young, was listening. Someone cared. Over the years, these stories were told on boozy breath. I learned to identify the various alcohols on my mother's breath: the pungent sharpness of vodka, the fruity tang of wine, the yeasty rise of beer. The rich tobacco of her cigarettes. To me, it was the smell of safety.

Staring at the doorknob, I thought, *Please come back*.

But she didn't. And when I stood up, I didn't go out in the hallway to find her. Instead, I crossed the room, locked the door, and climbed back in bed to think about the last play, how I had screwed it up, and what I could do to make it right.

Then the yelling started. Even with two bedroom doors closed and a hallway apart, our house was small, and the brief silence soon became a series of accusations and fury. I couldn't hear the words, but I knew anger, and I knew rage, and I knew that this could keep going for a long time. I slipped headphones on and flipped through radio stations, the music as loud as I could stand, but their voices found a way to rise above the music. I turned toward the wall, the plastic pressing against my ear. I looked up at the window, and decided, *Why not?*

I slid the window open and pushed the screen aside. We were on the first floor, and it was a short drop to the garden. I put on my shoes and coat, squeezed out the window, slid it closed with just a crack so I could peel my way back in, and raced across the yard, slowing only when my house was out of sight.

I trudged west toward North College Hill with my hands jammed deep in my pockets, chin tucked and head lowered as if I were walking into a wind. Cars raced by, headlight beams flashing over my face for a moment, then gone. My mother made this walk every day, and I didn't understand why she didn't just keep walking, start over somewhere else, reinvent, shed my father and me like an old coat, something to leave in the back of a closet, never to be worn, looked at, or thought of again. The wind picked up, and I hurried toward the only thing I knew was open all night, a Frisch's Big Boy. I took a booth near the phone, ordered a Coke, and watched the ice melt, standing up every fifteen minutes to call Carson.

"Hey, man," he said. "What's up? I just got home."

"You guys win?"

"Yeah, pretty easy. I had twenty. You should have seen this sweet reverse layup I made. What's all that noise?"

"Oh, that." I rested my forearm on the top of the phone box and stared into the coin slot. "I'm at—" And then I choked, coughing on tears I didn't realize I was holding in. I turned away from the diner and covered my eyes with my free hand, determined not to speak until I could do so without crying.

"Webb? Webb, what happened?"

Twenty minutes later, Carson breezed through the door, his hair wet and slicked back, wearing a gabardine overcoat, a loud red scarf, and fingerless gloves. He slid into the booth across from me without making eye contact and plucked the menu from over the napkin dispenser.

"I love these places," he said. "Chains. Fucking diners. They are the best. Think about how fucking cool it is that you can have whatever you want at any time. Day, noon, night, after dark. America at its finest! You know, there's this highway, called Route 66, and it cuts through America, all the way west, and there are diners just like this the whole way. It's, like, the greatest road trip the world has ever seen."

He untangled his scarf, and when the waitress arrived without a word, Carson said, "Hi, love! Two black coffees and an open-faced turkey sandwich with fries. Webb, what are you having?"

For the next three hours, Carson talked. Like the winding, spinning, freewheeling Route 66 that I would look up in the school library on Monday the next morning, tracing my finger from Chicago down through St. Louis and Springfield and Oklahoma City and Amarillo and Kingman and Santa Monica, Carson spoke with the breezy confidence of a driver with a full tank of gas on the first day of vacation. He explained how restaurants worked and why they preferred cash and how everyone smoked weed and bumped lines to get through double shifts. He detailed the rise and fall of the gold standard and why the strength of the US dollar was a grand conspiracy concocted in the New Hampshire woods by a Soviet spy. He noted how the Second Amendment was an incomplete sentence intentionally written to let true patriots protect their families and homes from the tyranny of not just kings but industrialists and globalists and other shadowy organizations. With his hands fanning as though he was a magician displaying two decks of cards, he took me on his family vacations to New Orleans, Jamaica, Rio de Janeiro, the blue waters of the Mediterranean, and told me how his first kiss was when he was ten with this Italian girl who was three years older than him and how they still mailed letters now and again. It was nearly two thirty in the morning when he slapped the table and said, "Young Webb, I think it's time to get you home."

He pulled up to the curb. We both looked at my house: all the lights were off, nothing on the porch, my window still visibly cracked open.

"You feel better?" Carson asked. When I turned back to look at him, he was looking out over the steering wheel at the street, both hands around the wheel, as if he were about to hit the gas on a getaway.

"I didn't really think about it," I said.

"Exactly. Don't. We're better than them. We're always better than them."

In profile, his skin pale in the weak street light, there was an empty defiance to the hard set of his jaw and his blank gaze, and all that remained of Carson after hours of talk was a simmering anger with the whole world. An anger that defined him, gave him shape. I hadn't said anything about my family, and I didn't need to: he understood that whatever it was, it was unfair, and the only true response that a person could be honest about was to be and remain furious.

"I'll see you at school," I said. I climbed out of his car, and as soon as the door was closed, he pulled from the curb, raced through a stop sign, and disappeared up the street.

• • •

The last day of autumn-semester exams was a cold and windy Thursday in late December. At the end of the day, I trudged through Rockcastle's empty halls. All my classmates and teachers were already gone, but I still had to wait for my mother to get off work. Carson and his family had left Wednesday for a ski trip to Gstaad, a place I had to discreetly look up in an atlas in the school library. There was no practice that week. With my footsteps the only noise in the building, I crossed the quad to the back entrance of the locker room and changed into my basketball gear. On the gym floor, I set up folding chairs and worked on my pull-up jumper, dribbling hard right or left, and then rising up on the other side of the chair, as if coming off a screen, and snapping my wrist on the shot. I did this for ninety minutes, shooting free throws when I was tired, and then the alarm on my sports watch went off. With my arms slick from sweat, perspiration dripping into my eyes, and my stomach growling, I restacked the folding chairs and hurried to shower.

I gathered my things and sat on the concrete bench at the front of Rockcastle and waited for my mother, who was running late. It had begun to snow. Faintly falling, tiny flakes melted on impact with the concrete, an early indicator of what would be an unusually snowy winter for Cincinnati. Somewhere, the janitors and grounds maintenance crews were probably still around, sipping from their cigarettes, lounging around the cafeteria and in no rush to get their nightly work completed. A fine dusting of snow sprinkled the surrounding roofs and clung to the faded grass now bereft of autumn leaves. My backpack was light on my shoulders: all my textbooks were in my locker, where they would sit until next year.

I tugged my stocking cap down over my eyebrows and dipped my chin into my coat so only my nose and eyes were visible. Snow flurries pelted my face. I wondered what it felt like to be Carson when he skied, how racing downhill, barely in control, must be an exhilarating rush. Did he think about anything at all? Could he turn off all the noise in his mind, like the noise that seemed to constantly be cluttering mine? I wondered if anyone had ever felt as angry as I did at the idea of going home and being forced to keep all that anger inside, deep in my chest, careful not to disturb the fragile ecosystem my parents had created. I wondered what it would feel like to explode.

IV

In January of 1995, halfway through the basketball season, I had established myself as our junior varsity's best player, a guy who could hit open shots and get others involved. I strung together three straight twenty-point games, all wins, one of which was on the road. But it was the third and final game of this string that I always remembered, because it was the first time my father didn't watch me play.

When I didn't see my parents during warm-ups, I assumed that I had missed them. When we stood for the national anthem, I scanned the crowd, ignoring the cassette tape that made the bombs burst in the air, and still didn't see them. We tipped off, and on the first possession I whipped a one-handed pass through the middle of the lane that nearly decapitated the ref, who was the closest person to the pass. He nearly choked on the whistle when he signaled the turnover. As I was jogging back up the court, my mother hurried through the double doors and took her customary seat halfway up the stands, and relief settled in my chest.

After a few possessions, I realized my father wasn't there. He wasn't staked out in one of the corners, and he wasn't up in the stands. *Big deal. Be a man. So your parent misses a game. So what?* But I couldn't help it. I couldn't pull the trigger on any shots, just passed and passed and passed. I played well enough that it didn't hurt us.

After having all halftime to sit and think about how my father always promised me he would be at my games, how it was the one thing he and my mother could seem to do together, the only thing I really asked of him, I took out all my frustration on the court. He was going to be sorry for missing this.

No jumpers. I went at the rim like it could save my life. In the second half, I took fourteen foul shots. I had never dunked a basketball in a game, but whenever we struggled, I would try to get to the rim, rise up like I could dunk, and I would invariably get fouled. Once I was back on my feet, I would look out into the stands and see my mother clapping. She always clapped in front of her mouth, so I couldn't see if she was smiling or frowning. My father never showed up.

After the game, Coach Duke Snyder waited for me by the entrance to the locker room. He wore an ill-fitting sports coat, a clean white shirt, and a striped red tie that, as was customary, he would loosen and eventually strip off and slam on the ground during the varsity game. Barrel chested, tall, and boyish, he had served in a series of interim positions when called upon—dean of students, Latin teacher, director of alumni engagement—but he was always content to return to the Department of Athletics whenever he could. His teddy bear personality vanished during games, when he would snarl, berate, and curse like a dockworker.

"Webb," Duke said, pushing himself off the wall. "Hell of a game, son."

I tried not to smile. "Thanks, Duke."

"I'd like you to sit varsity tonight. Jersey and shorts by your locker. I won't bullshit you—you probably aren't going to play. But just in case, okay?" He put his arm around me and guided me toward the locker room. "Played tough out there, Webb. I'll always notice that."

The junior varsity was huddled on one side of the room, and I joined them and listened to Kelly tell us how proud he was of how we played and to enjoy the weekend, remember practice at three thirty Monday, and get some rest. Kelly looked up at me, smiled, and tilted his head toward the other side of the room, where the varsity team was. "Go join 'em," his nod said.

I came around the corner, and Carson strutted over and slapped me a high five. "Great game, dude," he whispered, his breath minty and hot against my ear. I was smiling and not thinking about how the varsity usually was ready to warm up as soon as the junior varsity game ended. The rest of the upperclassmen ignored me. I knew it was too quiet. At the end of the row, I stood and looked at my locker, and waiting for me on the bench in front of it was my varsity jersey. I tried to be nonchalant and cool as I walked toward it. Then I discovered that between the neatly folded jersey and shorts, the creases newly laundered and perfect, my jersey was covered in a thick spread of shaving cream. My throat went dry. I clenched my left hand into a fist, let it loose with one rhythmic slow breath, and, masking my hurt, screamed, "Fuck you, guys!"

Everyone roared with laughter—"No, fuck *you*, Webb!" and "Why'd you jizz on your uni?" and "How's the fit, Webb?"—and I pretended to laugh, too. Across the room, Carson gave me an exaggerated wink, and I wondered what he saw in my expression.

"All right," Duke yelled. "Get your asses out there and warm up. Webb! Catch up!"

Standing in my socks, my feet sweaty, I stood alone in the cavernous open area where the team and coaches huddled before games, a space with portable chalkboards and massive laundry baskets for uniforms and towels lined up against one wall, and sinks and mirrors along the other; behind the mirrors were the toilets and showers, and all the concrete walls were painted white. The smell of mint toothpaste and athletic tape hung in the air. Behind me, beyond the towel racks, stood five long rows of lockers, their steel doors painted in Rockcastle's primary color of royal blue. I returned to my uniform and picked it up, closing my eyes and savoring my achievement in the temporary quiet, and inhaled the smell of Barbasol that would cling to me the rest of the night.

Once I wiped the uniform down as best I could, I proudly slipped it on. It was crisp and white, with "Crusaders" in blue lettering across the chest and blue-and-gold piping around the shoulders. The blue lettering and numbers were surrounded by a thin yellow line, as if a halo surrounded each significant detail of Rockcastle. A two-tone stripe ran down the side of the shorts, which, unlike the too-short JV uniforms, had ten-inch inseams that struck the knee. The shooting shirt was a long-sleeve, half-zip pullover with "Rockcastle" written in crisp Helvetica script, the cuffs snug around my wrists.

I jogged out of the tunnel and raced over to the stands. I saw my mother frown but kept my head down as I ran up the steps to her.

"Coach asked me to sit varsity tonight," I said. "Is that cool? Can you stay?"

"Varsity," she smiled. "Of course, Owen."

"Thanks, Mom. I'll see you after, okay?"

"What smells like shaving cream?"

The entire game I sat at the far end of the bench,

upright and with my hands folded neatly in my lap, watching the game with the same tense interest with which I observed everything at Rockcastle. We played well. Our players seemed bigger, stronger, and faster than our opponents, the team from Deer Park. Their slate-gray uniforms reflected their washed-out complexions and dispassionate play. Carson hit all five of his shots in the first half, most of which he appeared to take only when he absolutely had to—when he was so wide open that not shooting the ball would appear to be fearful or incompetent. In the second half, he got his points early in the third quarter—two fast-break layups and one jumper—and was yanked in the fourth quarter when we were up by fifteen and it was time for the bench guys to play. After he was pulled, Carson exchanged fist bumps with the guys and made his way down to me. He motioned to the guy to my right to make room and dropped loudly onto the aluminum bench.

"Don't act like you're tired," I said.

"Did you play?"

"You know what I mean."

"I'm sweating, right?" He was: the ropy muscles in his biceps and forearms glistened, droplets running off his hands and plummeting to the floor. "I don't have to go all kamikaze into the lane like you did."

"We were losing."

"No, you did the right thing. I'm not saying that." We looked up as a long, high-arching three bounced off the back rim and ricocheted out for a long rebound that my teammate Scott Duffer grabbed.

"What I'm saying," he continued, "is that watching you play is intense. It was like you wanted to take a beating."

If Carson had brought it up during our next free bell, when we were shooting jumpers, I would have talked about it like it was no big deal. But something about the way he asked was making me nervous.

"You saw that?"

"I was watching from the tunnel."

Three straight possessions ended in turnovers. A trickle of sweat ran down my rib cage.

"We couldn't hit any shots," I finally said.

"Is that your problem?"

"Of course it's my problem. I'm the point guard."

"The leader."

"That's right."

Carson wiped sweat from his face and sniffed loudly. "What are you doing after this?"

"Nothing, I guess. Eating dinner."

"Is your mom here?"

"Yeah, she's watching."

"Where's your dad?"

I shrugged. *Here's what you missed, Dad. Here's what you missed when I was on the floor, looking up at the basket I just made, the ref signaling to count the basket, and a teammate's hand out to help me off the floor. Took a beating, Dad. And kept standing up, again and again and again.*

Carson said, "Introduce me to her afterward." I nodded, and we fell into silence.

After the game was over, I showered, then changed quickly back into my school clothes and dumped my essentially clean varsity uniform into the red laundry cart against the wall. With my backpack between my feet, I stared at the locker across from me, waiting for Carson. Elbows on my knees, I pretended not to listen as my teammates bragged about their weekend plans, which parties they were going to, which girls would be there, whose parents were out of town. One at a time, I grabbed and twisted my fingers. Dinner with my mom? On a Friday night? Why had I told Carson that?

As if on cue, he came around the corner, beaming, his dark hair still wet, wearing a tastefully faded green flannel, Abercrombie jeans, and Kenneth Cole boots. His eyes wrinkled with glee at the sight of me in my school clothes.

"You weren't kidding, were you?" he said. "You really don't have plans for tonight."

My face reddened. I kept my head down and picked up my backpack. Since the night three weeks ago at Frisch's, I had followed Carson around Rockcastle, standing outside his first bell classroom with arms folded like a hall monitor, eating lunch with him in the cafeteria, our heads conspiratorially low and close as we discussed the day's classes, and, of course, in the gym on our free bell, working on our game. We would often be joined by classmates, young men like Whitney Rockwell, a British kid with shoulder-length curly hair and a fondness for quoting poetry we had never heard of; or Charles Brice IV, our best golfer and heir to a chemical-waste company; or Nick Derby, whose tall, lanky body seemed to contrast with his soothing, soft voice, employed years later to consult with patients after he graduated from Stanford Medical School. But they were always Carson's friends, joining our unruly lunch talk or hallway banter for him. The only friend I had was Carson.

"Come out after dinner," he said. "I'll pick you up. I know a guy at Elder who's having a party. His parents are in Columbus or Cleveland or someplace with a C."

I lined up the textbooks in my backpack and zipped it closed. Carson sat down across from me, his knees spread apart and his hands folded in front of him. He observed me as though he were a professor, waiting for me to discover the answer to my own question.

"What's wrong?" he asked.

"Nothing." I fumbled my bag up onto my right shoulder and stared at a spot to his left. The weight of my backpack pulled on my neck, and suddenly I could feel the soreness in my body from all the fouls I had drawn tonight. "I just want to go home. Cool?"

He studied me as if I was out of focus. Then he gave me his big open smile and offered his hand.

It was one of those odd, archaic gestures that only Carson could pull off without being phony, as if he really believed in the old prep-school codes of honor and integrity. I glanced over my shoulder; there was no one left in our row, and what voices I could hear weren't paying attention to us. I turned back, gripped my backpack awkwardly with my left hand crossing my body, and shook his hand. He put his arm around my shoulders and steered me toward the exit. He said, "Let's go meet the parent."

My mother stood at the foot of the bleachers, her purse on her shoulder, and I recognized that she held her bag with the same posture I used to hold my gym bag, as if anticipating that some petty thief would race by and snatch away our things. Despite this, her face held a serene expression. She was staring off into the distance, taking in the Fieldhouse. She wore a new pair of jeans that fit her well and was wrapped up in a sweater and a winter coat that I vaguely recalled often made her uncomfortably hot.

"Mrs. Webb," Carson said. "I'm Owen's friend, Carson."

"Nice to meet you, Carson." She smiled tightly, her eyes narrowed with amusement when she shook his offered hand. "I saw you out there with Owen. You played well. And, Owen, you played great tonight."

"Yeah, Owen thinks so too."

She released his hand and focused on some point directly over my shoulder. "I don't believe I've met your parents, Carson. Did your mother come tonight?"

"My mother died several years ago."

I turned. His face was tranquil but serious and bore no indication at all that this was a joke. There was a short, brutal silence among the three of us, and then it sunk in that this was the truth, and I hadn't known. My mother set her hand gently against her throat.

"Oh, dear, I'm so sorry," my mother said.

"Thank you. That's very kind. It was a long time ago."

"What happened?"

"Cerebral aneurysm. The doctors told us it was instantaneous, no pain. I'm grateful for that."

He gave her the Rockcastle nod, a thin, tight smile on his face, and I knew he was waiting for a polite moment to slip away from us.

"Mom, we should go."

"Owen."

"No, it's okay," Carson said. "Owen's heard all this before. I'm not ashamed of it, Mrs. Webb, and I don't mind talking about it. Just kind of a weird thing to bring up the first time you meet someone. This was ten years ago. My dad moved us into a new house right away, and he's always been there for us. I mean, it was tough, but, you know."

"She died at home," my mother said.

He smiled blandly. "We'll have to talk about something sunnier next time we meet."

"Yes, of course. I don't mean to pry."

"I know. Well, I know you guys are heading to dinner, so I'll get going." He slapped my chest and then pointed. "Give me a call, all right? Nice to meet you, Mrs. Webb."

"You, too, Carson."

We stood and watched Carson weave his way through the crowd. Then my mother said, "That all sounds very strange."

"What?"

My mother tilted her head and pulled her lips in, as if she was tasting something unpleasant. Then she said, very softly, more to herself than to me, “There’s nothing behind his friendliness, is there?”

Every few steps, he stopped and shook hands with someone’s father, the same expression of polite aloofness on his face, a politician on his way out the door, his posture immaculate, his freshly shaven face still glowing from the game and the hot steam of the showers. I felt then that I, like everyone else, loved him, even though I didn’t know him at all, and that my mother was being unfair.

“What are you saying?” I hissed, aware of people around us. “You don’t know him.”

She shook her head as if breaking a trance. “You’re right. Forget it, Owen. I’m just exhausted. Let’s go.”

I looked back at the court and considered his face, its handsome blankness. He had never mentioned his mother to me. In all the months we spent together, Carson never said anything about himself that didn’t sound embellished bluster or completely fabricated. I knew nothing about him at all.

• • •

I waited until we were in the car before asking, “Where’s Dad?”

She frowned into the rearview mirror and backed out of the parking spot. “Your father has a migraine. He’s in the basement on the couch.”

“A migraine?”

“That’s what he said. Look, I’m sorry. I know he’s disappointed he couldn’t make it.”

I folded my arms across my chest. “I don’t care.”

She exited the parking lot and accelerated up the street.

“I really don’t know why your father didn’t come. He didn’t use to scream at you. Not like he has lately. He shouldn’t behave like that.”

"Did you tell him not to come?"

"No. I did not tell him not to come." She leveled her eyes at me. "I can't tell him not to come to your games. He's your father. He does what he wants. I can't tell him what to do. I think he knows his temper has become a problem. That's why he stayed home. He's afraid of what he might do."

"Like charge the court and punch the ref?"

I thought this would get a laugh. It didn't. I remembered how her wrist bent back, how, accidentally or not, he was strong enough and angry enough to push her around.

"So he doesn't really have a headache," I said.

She answered by turning up the radio and then driving with both hands locked at ten and two. At home, I didn't bother looking for my father, who I assumed was down in the basement as usual. I went straight to my room, shut the door, and flopped down atop my comforter, my shoes and coat still on. Light snuck through the crack beneath the door, and down the hallway Mom banged around the kitchen for a few minutes before turning on the television, which she played too loud, as if to let me know she was up and available to talk. I never heard my father's voice or his heavy footsteps move through the house. From the vents in my floor, I could hear that the basement television was on; he was down there, doing something, refusing to come up. My eyes adjusted to the dark, and through the window I watched a sky of crossed lines: electric wires bowing from the wind, and tree branches bouncing stiffly like broken, arthritic fingers.

I rolled onto my side and stared at the wall. Carson hadn't told me about his mother. What else hadn't he told me? What other secrets did he hold back? My chest rose and fell, and my knees reflexively curled toward my chest, the wool of my coat scratching my neck.

• • •

On Monday, sitting tall in the front seat of the car next to my mother, while Q102 blasted pop hits between their unfunny and ornery commentary on the Bengals losing to the Giants, I was thinking about Carson. I stepped out of the car, my breath visible, loose twigs from the oak trees crunching under my feet, a thin sheen of frost on the grass and bushes. I walked through the front door of Rockcastle, and the heater blasted me full in the face. I believed that Carson would be there waiting for me, like normal. But he was nowhere to be found.

My eyes roamed the hallways for him, hoping to see my triumph in his face. I cruised down the main hallway, my lips curling in a satisfied smile, my head held high and shoulders thrown back. Students milled around their lockers, bottles of orange juice or soda in their hands, breakfast consumed on the run. I backtracked. A group of students sat atop the radiant heaters that ran along the thin walls between the Upper School and the gym. I crossed the driveway to the cafeteria. He wasn't there either, and I took a long loop, passing the science labs and the foreign-language rooms with their cassette players and oversized headphones perched on every desk. He was nowhere. I stood at the T-intersection at the far southern end of Rockcastle and dumbly wondered if he was already in class.

I shuffled down the hall, passed my own classroom, and stood at the entrance of Carson's class, calculus with Mr. Obel. It was a room I had never set foot in. The entrance to the room was a small corridor, only a few feet long, so that from my vantage point I couldn't see Mr. Obel's desk or the blackboard, all of which were along the inside wall. A large chunk of the classroom's desks were also out of view. Along the back wall, a row of drafty windows had their blinds open, the radiator humming and spitting as if it had a nasty cold, and I could see the driveway between the buildings and the row of Dumpsters filled with garbage bags of cafeteria food and all the variations of papers and plastics we didn't recycle.

Carson was talking to someone. The left side of his face was in profile; he was unshaven, the dark stubble running from ears to chin, and his hair was combed back and still wet from his shower. He smiled readily, his teeth white and immaculate, wholly at ease with himself. I stood in the hallway, feeling Rockcastle grow quiet as people entered their classrooms, and the building took on the great stillness that occurs when a school's students are all seated at their desks. I'm not even sure who it was that closed Mr. Obel's door.

My day passed miserably. When called on, I had no answers. I wasn't paying attention and truthfully couldn't even say what I had been thinking about—it seemed I was thinking of nothing at all, that my mind couldn't comprehend even the most basic things. I would have stopped breathing had breathing required conscious thought. At lunch, I grabbed my coat from my locker, crossed the Upper School with my head down, ordered two cheeseburgers from the cafeteria, and walked out the north exit. I made my way down toward the track and the music building for the Lower School and took a spot on the bleachers, making myself even more miserable by sitting in the cold, wallowing in self-pity as I chewed lunch with a dull, bovine intensity.

At the end of fifth bell, I trudged to my locker and removed my basketball shoes and threw in my books. I walked to the small gym without any thought: this was simply what I did for every sixth bell. A loose basketball lay next to the wall, so I scooped it up, changed shoes quickly, and dribbled to the low block, shooting bank shots, alternating from one side of the rim to the other, concentrating on keeping my elbow in, my arm straight, and snapping my wrist.

Carson walked in a few minutes later, and as usual he tossed his blazer and jacket in a haphazard pile next to my neatly folded clothes. He stood at the top of the key, watching as I moved out to the baseline and shot from farther and farther out. He said nothing but began rebounding, alternating bounce passes and chest passes back to me. I couldn't miss. I hit ten in a row, then twelve, then two dozen. My eyes focused on the rim, the anger rising in my chest. When I finally missed, after hitting thirty-seven in a row, Carson plucked the rebound without jumping, the ball falling in a low arc directly to where he was standing, as if he knew all along it would land there. He held the ball at waist level with two hands. Sweat trickled down my neck and forearms.

"You should have told me about your mom," I said.

"Everyone knows." He dribbled the ball between his legs, once, twice, then with one hand shot a short jumper that rattled in. He cupped the ball and looked down the length of the gym. "Most of the guys here have been at Rockcastle forever. I'm a junior, Webb. I don't pay any attention to who the first years are or what they know."

"But I didn't know. And I'm your friend."

The words seemed to be a dagger in his side. He grimaced and for a moment actually appeared ashamed. Something tremored through his cheeks, and I thought he might cry. I hadn't expected this, and then I became the person who felt remorse, even pity. His shoulder slumped and he wrapped his arms around the ball and held it high against his chest.

"My dad's home this week," he said. "Why don't you have dinner with us?"

"You and your dad?"

"And my sister, Caitlin. She's your age. Goes to Ursuline. You want to see her again, right?"

I hated the hot blush I felt running up my face. No one had ever looked at me the way Caitlin had. Carson laughed and slapped me hard on my shoulder.

"I'll call my mom after school," I said.

"Awesome." He visibly perked up. "That's cool. My dad's actually a pretty good cook."

He dribbled out to the three-point line, a joyful cadence in the bend of his knees and the swinging of his hips, playing against an imaginary defender. Then he turned and, jumping straight up, his feet slightly pigeon-toed, he launched a rainbow that almost kissed the ceiling, hung in the air as if paused, and fell through the net with a soft hush. We shot baskets in silence, and when it was time I rolled the ball to the other end of the gym, and we changed our shoes. Carson stood and said, "See you at practice," and that was it.

I stalked out of the gym to the cafeteria, the short walk between the buildings chilling the sweat on my neck and face, and I was shivering as I slid quarters into the pay phone to call my mom. It went straight to voicemail, and I said I was going to Carson's house after practice and if that wasn't okay to call the school and leave a message with Mrs. Bunker and someone would deliver it to me in class. During English, my eyes continued to shift to the door at each sound of footsteps in the hallway, readying excuses that I would need to give my mom when I called her back and explained, for whatever reason, that it was important for me to have dinner at the Blys'. But no student worker ever came to the door, and when seventh bell rang, I went off to practice and thought nothing more about my mother's feelings.

It didn't occur to me until the next day that Carson never apologized to me for lying.

• • •

It was nice to walk out of practice among the pack of my teammates, all of us weighed down by at least two bags, a little uncomfortable from the heat of the showers and the bundle of our coats against the growing cold of a January night, and rather than veering away from them to climb into my mother's waiting car, I stayed with them. From my mother's car, I would see the upperclassmen climbing into cars three or four at a time to go somewhere else together, or lingering to talk before they went their separate ways, the fluorescent lights of the parking lot high above making them appear shadowy and unworldly, members of a club I would never belong to. Now, here I was, side by side with Carson, one of the boys.

Around the highway, the hills were covered by thick pine trees; behind them towered ugly walls that had been raised to limit the highway sound from the homes on the other side. Carson's Audi purred as we accelerated north, taking the curves with ease; on the horizon was the Kenwood Towne Centre, our nicest mall with upscale department stores, the surrounding area a series of good restaurants and shops that I had never eaten at or entered. Carson exited here, steered us north, and shot up Montgomery Road. With Warren G's new album filling the car with bass and synthesizers, there weren't any moments to talk. I enjoyed seeing the world whip by, the roads surrounded by dark trees and the faint outline of large homes far back behind their large lawns, their location chosen so the world would notice their largeness. The only thing Carson said the entire time was when we zipped by an auto dealership. Under the bright lights we could see Mercedes Benzes and BMWs, and he pointed and yelled, "Only place in the city you can get those."

When we were somewhere I didn't recognize, he turned right, and a long two-lane road took us east. Split-rail fences protected the long lawns from the road—this must have been farm country at one time—and lengthy driveways led to ranch homes far from the street. A series of turns into the subdivision took us onto a long street with no sidewalk and no cars; a sign at the entrance indicated that the neighborhood was monitored by private security. All the houses seemed, somehow, to be on their own small hill, each its own kingdom, their yards separated from each other by tree lines of either pines or poplars, the garages alone bigger than my home. Finally, we came to a house with saplings on the lawn and a low brick wall that separated the property from the street, a protective barrier even I recognized as hideously ugly. We pulled into the three-car garage, and though I would see many of them over the years, its size was still a marvel to me.

He shifted into park and killed the engine. "Wanna see something cool?"

"Sure."

He nodded at the glove box. "Open it up."

I reached over and squeezed the latch. The box dropped down with a heavy thump. Inside were a couple of CD cases, the car's registration and manual, and a Crown Royal bag with an odd shape. He pointed at the bag and said, "Go ahead."

The velvet bag was heavier than I thought it would be, and when I pulled it toward me, the shape was like an L, not a bottle. I pulled the gold threading open and reached my hand in. Somehow, upon touching it, I knew what it was and looked at Carson with fright.

His face lit up. He nodded again, and from the bag I pulled a jet-black semiautomatic gun.

"Where did you get this?" I asked.

"It's mine. My father and I have done some hunting, but we also keep guns in the house."

"Does he know you have it?"

"Of course he knows I have it. That right there is a nine millimeter."

"Why do you have it?"

"Why not? Tell me it isn't fucking cool."

The gun rested in my palm. My fingers were splayed, a little afraid to touch the trigger. It fit my hand perfectly. The word that kept running through my mind was *cool*. My breathing echoed in my ears.

"Go ahead and grip it," he said. "The safety is on. Rule one, don't point it at anyone. Keep that barrel pointed either down at the ground or at your target. It's not a toy. Christ, I sound like my old man."

I put two hands around the gun and aimed at the floor. "Wow," I whispered.

"Right? Pretty cool."

The thrill, a palpable charge through my arms and into my chest, couldn't have been stronger or more real. I raised the gun and aimed through the windshield at the edge trimmer hanging from the ceiling.

"You're Bruce Willis, man," Carson said. "All right, put it away. I'll teach you to shoot it sometime. There's a gun range my father and I go to. You'll fucking love it."

"Yeah, all right." I lowered the gun, gently pushed it back into the Crown Royal bag, shoved it into the glove box, and closed the latch with a firm click.

"What does your dad do?"

"Death."

"What?"

Carson laughed and popped the trunk, and we hopped out. Behind Carson was a pearl-white 7-series BMW and a massive black Range Rover, both of which looked spotlessly shined. Along the inner wall of the garage ran a neat and clean series of steel shelves and doors, all of which I was sure possessed immaculate and expensive tools that had never been used by a single member of Carson's family.

"I love saying that," he said, hefting his bags out of the trunk. "My father is a property developer. He specializes in mausoleums, retirement homes, and cemeteries. It sounds grim, doesn't it?"

"That's a business?"

"A successful one, too. I know, sounds crazy, doesn't it?"

We entered through a mudroom and dropped our bags on the floor. The hallway had recessed lighting, clean and expensive carpeting, cornices, and crown molding, and all the doors on both sides were firmly closed. It felt like the corporate office of an Italian aristocrat. From somewhere down the hall came the sizzle of meat on a grill.

"Dad?"

"Down here!"

The kitchen appeared to lie at the exact physical center of the house. The ceilings had thick exposed beams and seemed to be twenty feet high, and two large skylights, like eyes to God, showed the clear night sky. Every appliance was a pristine stainless steel, and there seemed to be more oak cabinets than would be needed for a restaurant. I had never seen granite countertops before, but in the last few months I had learned to recognize the cost of such comforts. Across the great room was a long dining table, also made of some dark wooden veneer, and on the walls hung oil paintings of French cities and restaurants. The island housed a large range that contained several grills and burners, all of which seemed to be turned on, and in the center of everything stood a man of unremarkable height, with a graying beard and a smile of satisfied amusement on his face.

"Dad, this is my friend Owen Webb."

"Owen!" He came around the island, the food sizzling on cue, with his right hand outstretched. His grip was large and powerful, and with his left hand, he held my elbow. I'd seen President Clinton do the exact same thing. "Pleasure to finally meet you."

"Thanks for having me for dinner."

"Of course! I'm not always home, so my children often fend for themselves. But when I am," he said, walking back behind the grill, "I figure I should make enough so that they can eat during the week."

Carson said, "He's probably got a thousand pounds of food on that grill."

"Sounds right. Why don't you call your sister in here?"

"Owen, would you mind getting her? I need to talk to my dad about something." When I hesitated, Carson smiled telegenically and said, "Don't worry, she won't bite."

"She's watching TV," Mr. Bly said. "Down the hall to the left. In the TV room."

The hallway Carson and I had entered through continued on the other side of the kitchen, like it was the house's sole artery. I had never seen a house so long. But on this side, all the recessed lights were off, leaving the hallway dark except for the hazy glow of a television screen coming from one open doorway on the right. As I crept closer, I realized I hadn't given any thought to what I would say to Carson's sister.

I turned into the room. On the back wall was a large television, probably six feet wide, and Jim Lehrer's serious face and coal-black eyes had never seemed more bizarre.

The next spring, when I read *1984,* I would remember this moment. On either side of the television were a series of custom bookcases filled with videotapes. Along both side walls were old film posters—*The Third Man, Casablanca, Double Indemnity*. The room, despite the obvious care put into its display of film-buff enthusiasm, seemed remarkably stale. In its center was a large coffee table surrounded by a recliner and two couches, all of which were angled to face the television. On the coffee table lay several remotes and two empty Diet Coke cans, both turned on their side. As I moved toward the sofa I circled wide, as if I were approaching a wild animal.

Caitlin Bly was stretched out. Her left hand, with ringless fingers and nails painted orange, hung off the couch as if she were deciding what to do with it, and a blanket was draped over her legs. Her feet peeked out from under the fleece, showing white socks and a thin gold bracelet around her slim right ankle. Her white blouse peeked out from the top of the blanket, and the top buttons of her shirt were undone. She had pretty brown eyes and chapped lips, and her brow was furrowed in complete concentration. On her head was a Santa hat.

"Caitlin?"

"Yeltsin sent troops into Chechnya. Have you ever heard of Chechnya? I'm still deciding if this, like, matters to me at all." She shook her head and didn't look up. "Who are you?"

"I'm Owen. I'm a friend of your brother's."

A thin smile was forming on her lips. She tilted her head, and the white pompom of her hat lolled to one side. Her hand slid inside her blouse and rested against her collarbone.

"Owen what?"

"Owen Webb."

"That's a name. That's the kind of name where you have to use the first and last name. Owen Webb. It's the syllables. I like it."

She finally looked up at me. The whole room became an optical illusion, shrinking away until there was nothing but Caitlin watching me, a wry expression on her face, as if she had figured out some great joke whose punch line I still hadn't grasped. She appraised me with eyes narrowed in playful recognition. She tapped her neck with a single finger.

"Chechnya, Owen Webb?"

I turned. The screen had cut to images of Russian soldiers fighting on a city terrain of rocks and rubble that were all the same shade of gray. They carried AK-47s, swinging them around like they were extensions of their bodies, and I remembered the secret rush of holding Carson's gun in my hands.

"I don't know anything about it," I admitted. "Why are they there?"

"Rebels who want to break free and have their own country. Russia didn't like that too much. For my world history class, we have to turn in a paper every day about current events. My friends, they're always like, but what if nothing happened today? That's crazy! Something happens every day."

"I don't really watch the news."

"You should. It's just incredible. Remember the Gulf War?"

I shrugged, still watching the images of Russian soldiers, of tanks rolling up and over hills, and I became aware of the sound system as the mechanical churn of the tanks' treads filled the room. On all sides of us were speakers built into the walls. Everything in this house seemed to be customized, everything considered with careful attention paid to all one's senses—as if this were more than just a home but an experience of enhanced reality.

"They had those little cameras on the bombs," Caitlin said. "Remember that? The green and black screen, all grainy, and the way a city and then its buildings appeared in front of you."

I looked back at her. Caitlin was no longer looking at me but staring at some point on the couch in front of me, as if she were speaking to a person who was no longer there.

"I remember," I said.

"Everyone thought that was so cool. You know, because you, like, see the war happening right in front of you. Real time. What a stupid phrase. 'Real time.' As if time is anything else, you know." She shook her head. "When the television went all black, except for that little CNN logo at the bottom of the screen, it meant someone died. A lot of someones. Can you imagine that? Dying like that? You're in a building just doing your job and then you're dead. Incinerated. You probably don't even know it—just all of a sudden, your whole body is on fire."

"I hadn't thought about it," I said.

"I couldn't stop thinking about it." She placed both hands around her neck, a mixture of a hug and strangulation. "I'd have nightmares. In my dreams I'd be at the mall, and all of a sudden this huge fire would come racing toward me, filling the whole mall, and everyone was turning into ashes and screaming and running, and I'd just stand there looking into the flames until they consumed me. And I'd be in pain. It would hurt so bad. In a dream!"

"That sounds awful."

She raised her eyes at me then, and they were liquid with tears.

"It was. It was so awful. The worst part? No one else

felt that way. Everyone thought it was cool, like it was a video game or something. But it wasn't. People were getting incinerated."

She shook her head and lowered her chin.

"Dinner's ready," I said. "That's why I came down here."

She sniffed. "Right. Dinner. Thank you, Owen Webb. I'll be there in one moment." When she discovered I was still standing there, she said, "Did you hear me? One moment. I'd like to be left alone, please."

"Oh, yeah, sorry." I almost ran out. My heart raced and I swallowed, my throat dry, feeling stupid for what had just happened.

Carson and Mr. Bly were standing in front of the island, their heads tilted low toward each other as if they were planning a conspiracy. When I entered the kitchen, they stopped speaking and stared at me. Then Mr. Bly boomed a fake laugh, clapped his hands, and announced that dinner was ready.

Caitlin entered the room, and both Bly men transformed into attentive and caring family members, asking her about her day, setting plates of hot food in the center of the table, filling water glasses while offering something else to drink. She ignored them. Without knowing why, I began to help, grabbing bowls and plates of food from the island and setting them down in no particular order in the center of the table. We all seemed to be performing for her. Caitlin sat on the long side of the table, diagonal from me and as far from her father as possible. She folded her hands in her lap, sitting erect and expectant, watching us bring food to the table.

When we were seated—Mr. Bly at the head of the table, Carson to his left, me to his right—he said, "Owen, I hear you're a pretty good basketball player."

"I'm okay."

"Better than okay. Carson says you're the best player on the team."

"Other than me," Carson winked. I smirked in agreement.

"How many of Carson's games have you been to, Dad?" Caitlin asked.

"Basketball is the American sport," Mr. Bly continued, ignoring her. "Baseball might have been at one time, but that's over now. Basketball has that quality of individual grace within the structure of the team."

This sounded regurgitated from someone smarter than him, a sound bite heard in a documentary. Rolling green beans into my mashed potatoes, I nodded without comment.

"What about football?" Caitlin said. "What about the military-industrial comparison between American hegemony and the NFL?"

"I played football as a boy," her father said. "I was a linebacker. Can you believe that? Someone my size playing linebacker?"

"Actually," I said, picturing my father, "I can believe that."

"He has all the photos in his office," Carson grinned. He cut his meat into several small pieces without eating a bite. There was a hodgepodge of foods on the table: swordfish, pork chops, chicken Monterey, three bowls of vegetables, garlic mashed potatoes, about two dozen rolls of various grains, and applesauce. It was more food than I saw at Thanksgiving.

"I liked to prove something," Mr. Bly continued. "I liked to show people how tough I was, and football certainly did that. There was something to be said about de-cleating a senior running back who just kept yapping his mouth in practice, and having him on his back, looking up at the sky, and seeing little old me standing over him. Best feeling in the world."

"I like to hit people, too," I said quietly. Carson's head was down, eating in a steady but unhurried manner; he seemed used to this kind of talk from his father. But to his left, Caitlin stared at me from across the table with clear, level eyes.

"Now," Mr. Bly continued, "I wasn't good enough to play in college. That just wasn't my destiny. I had to go out and work and make something of myself in the world. My father, their grandfather"—he waved at Carson and Caitlin with his steak knife—"had a funeral home, and I worked there for many years before getting into my business."

"Carson said you build mausoleums," I said. Turning my head back to Mr. Bly, I could feel Caitlin's eyes boring into the side of my face.

"That's correct. The dead and real estate. Two things that there are always going to be plenty of. Do you know what you're going to study in college?"

"I haven't thought about it much."

"Carson said you were a freshman. You'll grow tired of the question. I know Carson has. Caitlin was probably tired of the question before she was born. I'm hoping Carson will go into finance, but frankly, advanced mathematics may be the better way to go. All the best minds head to Wall Street now anyway, and if you can do anything with numbers, you'll find work there."

This was the first moment it occurred to me that Carson would soon be leaving. He was two years older than me and a junior. College advertisements filled his mailbox every day; small state universities and liberal arts colleges that no sixteen-year-old had ever heard of bombarded him with their thick, glossy folders stressing their faculty-to-student ratio and wonderful campus culture. Where would he go? How far away would he soon be?

"I've never been to New York," I said.

"You should go. I've been to every continent. I recommend Tokyo. Just an amazing city. And getting out into the surrounding countryside is easy. Japan is a remarkable place."

Somewhere in the house must be thousands of photos of the Bly family abroad: photos of smiling children in front of the Vatican or the Eiffel Tower, riding horses in Patagonia, skiing in the Alps, doing all sorts of wonderful things that they would never fully appreciate because they always could do it. They simply couldn't conceive of a world that wasn't given to them with palms open and extended, begging them to take its offerings.

"So, then, Owen, what are you interested in?" Mr. Bly asked. "Perhaps I can give some suggestions."

"You love giving advice, don't you?" Carson said.

"Of course I do. I'm excellent at it. Now, Owen—your interests."

I didn't have any interests. I was interested in Rockcastle and Carson and not much else. Basketball, I suppose, but mainly because of the time it allowed me with Carson. The future was so distant that it might well have been on the other side of the moon.

"Chemistry," I lied. "I like chemistry."

Mr. Bly frowned and repeated the word like it gave off an unpleasant taste.

"It's the future," I continued. "How things work together, what happens when they mix." I stared at my plate, trying to come up with some continuation of thought. "All this food and how tastes are just signals in the brain."

"Neuroscience."

"I don't know. Maybe. But you were saying how there

is always a need for places to bury people and to buy land. In some ways, those two things are the same."

"That's right."

"You aren't interested in how people live. You're interested in where they end up."

He gave one sharp, loud laugh at this.

"I'm not really interested in the why," I continued, "but the how. When people have something wrong with them, they want a simple solution. Like a pill. They want something to pop each morning with their orange juice. Chemistry provides that."

"A pharmacist!"

I nodded, the idea gestating. "Yes, a pharmacist."

"Those companies," he said, pounding the table with his hand, "make good money."

"I guess."

"That's good, Owen. Thinking one step ahead, what the demand is of us, what we need down the road rather than right now."

It was a good idea, I decided, though I did not know the first thing about medicine or drugs or any other health care. Mr. Bly continued speaking. The three of us silently ate while he delivered a long and rambling soliloquy—on the changing demographics of Cincinnati, how the suburbs continued to expand and Cincinnati and Columbus would soon be one great metropolis stretching over a hundred miles, how mausoleums were as gorgeous as Greek coliseums, the challenges of being a single parent, the costs of putting a roof on a house and of finishing a basement, the quality and maintenance of an automobile, and virtually any other topic that crossed his mind, interrupted only by the occasional swallowing of his food. When his father's plate was empty, the gravy scraped off with warm dinner rolls, Carson stood and announced that we had homework to do. Mr. Bly acknowledged his statement with a wave of his hand, and I somehow knew to continue sitting in place and listening to him speak as Carson and Caitlin cleared the table, washed the dishes, and stored the piles of leftover food in reheatable glass containers that they stacked in the fridge. Finally, Mr. Bly stood and wrung his hands. Carson came over and slid a Coke across the table to me. Somehow Caitlin had slipped out of the room without my noticing.

"We'll work here," Carson said.

"Fine. I'll be down the hall in my office. Owen, a real pleasure to meet you."

"You too, Mr. Bly." He offered his hand and we shook, again with his politician's grip of my elbow, and then he strode out of the kitchen like a war general, leaving us alone.

"Sorry about that, man," Carson said, hefting his backpack from the floor. "He likes to impress people the first time he meets them, you know?"

"It's cool."

"No, it isn't. But what can you do?" He opened his Coke and slurped loudly. "What time do you need to be home?"

"Ten?"

"All right, that gives us a little time to work."

We didn't speak again for the next two hours. Our textbooks before us, we had our heads down, and the only sounds were the stereo in the background tuned to a jazz station and the scratch of our pencils and squeak of our highlighters as we marked our books and wrote down in our notebooks what to remember for exams. I worked on geometry then biology. It was warm in the kitchen, the smell of pork still lingering; outside, the sky was dark, and all I could see of the backyard was a dark forest running along what I assumed was the perimeter of their property. But mostly what I saw was our reflection thrown back at us: an image of Carson and me working on our studies, two prep-school friends in a warm kitchen, pleased to be in each other's company.

• • •

The next morning, my father was sitting at the breakfast table, feet bare and hair disheveled, reading the newspaper, eating his eggs and burnt toast. Without lifting his eyes, he asked how it went at the Blys. "It was fine," I said. "Their house is huge. Like, biggest house I've ever been in."

"That's good," he said, and shoveled more eggs in his mouth. I sat down across from him.

With my eyes down, I asked loudly, "Have you ever owned a gun?"

"What?"

"A gun. Do you own a gun?"

He smiled into the front page. "Why? You want to shoot somebody?"

"No. I'm just asking."

"Why are you asking? Did your mother say something?"

I shifted in my seat. "About what?"

He looked up from the paper with his mouth open and ran his tongue around his gums. He seemed to be paying attention to me for the first time. He set his paper aside and took off his glasses, and for a brief moment he actually looked scared. My father ran a hand down his face, pawing at his skin as if he could remove it from his skull.

"I wish she wouldn't talk to you about these things." He pulled up his reserve of charm and smiled grandly.

"After college, I had a hard time finding a job. Back then, it wasn't uncommon to not finish, or to not even go to, college. I really wanted to hit the road. I really wanted to get out more. We'd never left Cincinnati, you know?"

I nodded, unsure where he was going with this.

"I started carrying the gun because of my route. I never had to use it. Right after I finished trucking school and got my C-class license, one of the old-timers took me aside and asked me if I had protection. I thought he was making a joke, and I said, 'I'm a married man and don't wear condoms no more.' But he didn't laugh. Not even a little. He said he knew a guy, reputable, and that he could get me a weapon cheap. It was a .38. A revolver. I never fired it. Not once. After I bought it, held it in my hand, I thought to myself, *okay*, and kept it in the glove box of my cab. I thought of you, you know. Making sure I'd come home, making sure you'd have a father. Now, your mother found out only because she was going through my things. I brought my duffel in, and I had put the gun in there because I was going to take it down to the basement and clean it—you gotta keep a firearm clean—and she was looking for, I dunno, dirty clothes or dirty magazines or something, and she found the piece."

"When was this?"

"When I still had the route. You were a baby. Sold it the day I quit the job."

My eyes narrowed. "So you don't have a gun now?"

He picked up a different section of the newspaper. "Of course not. If your mother is telling stories about me, maybe she should do so when she isn't drinking her wine. Sounds like she's getting her years mixed up." He refocused on the opinions section.

I got a bowl of cereal and took the front page, and we ate in silence until he gathered up the sports page and his plate, stood, and walked away, dumping his plate in the sink. When I was done eating, I cleaned my bowl and spoon, then his plate, utensils, and the frying pan on the stove, setting them all in the dish drainer. A new question occurred to me. I turned around, mouth already open to ask, only to discover that his chair was empty. Somehow, without my hearing him leave, my father was already gone.

V

For the next game, two nights later, we were visiting Batavia, a team with minimal talent that seemed to be populated mostly with football players. All crew cuts and acne, the boys had thick necks and the large, undefined bodies of teenagers who were first beginning to lift weights. Early in the second quarter of the varsity game, their point guard faked hard to the right, then crossed over into the lane. Our senior point guard, Jamie Osher, who was guarding the ball at the free throw, extended his arms wide from his pudgy body, elbows unbent, his knees too stiff to move. He bit on the fake, and when he tried to recover, his right foot stuck to the ground, his ankle rolled, and his foot folded ninety degrees the wrong way. Jamie collapsed, grabbed his leg, and screamed.

Two bench players gathered Jamie's arms around their necks and helped him hobble to the locker room. Coach Snyder stood with his hands on his hips, staring out into the middle of the floor, a mixture of concern for Jamie and for the fact that we were already down ten early in the second quarter. He turned. Jaw stalwart, nostrils flaring, Coach pointed at me and said, "Webb! Get in!"

As if spring-loaded, I hopped off the bench and tugged my warm-up off in one quick motion. Before I could reach the scorer's table, Coach put his arm around me, his right hand enveloping my shoulder. He lowered his head, and the strong, distinct scent of Old Spice overwhelmed me.

"Look to me for the offensive sets," he said. "If the offense stalls and the ball comes back to you, drive. Man-to-man on defense, fan your guy to the sidelines. You're the general now."

I wiped the bottoms of my shoes with my palms and caught Carson's eye as I took my position. He held his right hand out, flat and level with the floor: *be cool*.

On the next made basket by Batavia, Carson took the ball and stepped past the baseline to inbound to me. The Batavia coach screamed from the sidelines: "Press! Press! Press!"

Everyone on our team ran back except for Carson and me. His defender hugged the baseline; mine clung to my hip and clutched my shorts. With a light shove, I pushed off and raced to the corner where they wanted me and caught the inbound pass with two hands. Carson's defender tried to trap me, which we anticipated, and Carson streaked to the middle of the floor, with me passing back to him on the way before the defense could get possession.

The execution of our press-break was perfect. Carson and I put everything into another gear. Our speed was breathtaking, a head-shaking moment for spectators. On our toes, we made passes without a dribble; when Carson's pass to me was in flight, I knew before I caught the ball where my pass back to him would go, what part of the floor he would streak to, the ball zipping through the defense like a laser. After we scored thirteen straight points on five possessions—four layups, one three from the corner, and two free throws from fouls—the press came off, and I jogged the ball up the court with the knowledge that Batavia had thrown its worst at me and I had survived.

The problem was that I had already played all four quarters in the JV game that day; under state rules, I could only play two quarters with varsity. Coach knew this and started me in the third quarter. In the fourth quarter, sweat pouring off my forearms and dripping onto the floor, I watched our lead diminish, vanish, and then reemerge in the last two minutes of the game thanks to Carson. He did what he had been capable of all year but had willfully refused to do: he played with the intensity of a man whose life depended on winning. His legs were wide and his knees bent on defense; twice he created turnovers through good footwork, trapping his man in the corner and forcing a bad pass. On offense, he attacked the rim, handling the ball like I had never seen, bringing it low beneath his knees and then rising up, drawing contact on his way, and laying the ball off the glass like a whisper. He hit his free throws, sank two long jumpers, and we held on for a five-point win.

Behind me in the postgame high-five lane, his breath in my ear, Carson rasped, "Couldn't let you lose your debut."

We didn't know how bad Jamie's sprain was until the next morning, when he showed up at school on crutches, an oversized wool sock pulled over his right foot to keep his toes warm. He said the sprain was grade three, the tendon stretched out like an old rubber band, and that he was going to miss the rest of the season. He said this without anger, as casually as if he were talking about the weather, and he instantly started in on baseball and how he'd be ready to start pitching in March. I knew then I wouldn't ever play on junior varsity again.

• • •

The night before our first playoff game, we had a light practice, and I caught a ride home with Carson. We turned up Dre's *The Chronic* as loud as the stereo would go, and the doors rattled from the bass. I rode shotgun with two seniors in the back seat, and I couldn't have felt more alive. I glanced at the glove box and thought about what was inside.

Carson dropped me off, and all three of them told me to get lots of sleep, big game Wednesday night, and so forth. They waited until I reached the front door before they pulled away, the bass rattling Carson's car. The front curtains of my house were drawn closed, but the blue glow of the television flashed through the translucent threads, and I assumed it was my mother sitting in front of the television, letting something in the kitchen cook.

When I opened the door, I discovered my father on the couch, hunched forward with elbows on his knees and staring down at the coffee table. He was looking at his coins. Stored in expensive, shiny leather albums strategically arranged among expensive, shiny coffee table books about coins, they continued to hold my father's attention even when I entered the house, bringing with me a brief rush of cold wind. I wondered when he had last rotated them. He seemed to swap out his display albums—the ones sitting on the coffee table or on the shelf below it—with the coin albums stored in his basement workshop at least once a month. I counted three weeks, not four, since I had last seen him do this. Neither I nor my mother understood this obsession, but we did understand the angry, satisfied look chiseled on his face. This was the side of my father—distant, quiet—that I most feared. On nights when he was looking at his coins, my mother and I remained as far away physically from him as we possibly could.

"How was basketball?" My father remained hunched over his coins.

"Good." It didn't matter if I prattled on for ten minutes or gave a one-word answer: my father wasn't really listening. "Light work today. Shooting drills. Our first playoff game is tomorrow night. Home game."

My father hummed in agreement, turned a page.

"Mom home?"

The smile vanished. "Of course not. How does tuna casserole sound for dinner?"

"That's cool." My father's love of tuna was yet another mystery. "Mom coming home?"

"We might eat in front of the television tonight. Okay?"

I shrugged, even though he wasn't looking at me. My mother had started working later at the library, sometimes not coming home until after nine. My father gnashed his teeth, tipped up his jaw, and ran a palm down the length of his neck. His arms retained a ropy muscularity; his calf muscles bulged over his socks from his days as a long-distance runner. But shirts, no matter how small, draped off his torso, and when we used to take beach vacations, I always marveled at his pale, concave chest.

"Okay, well," I said, "I'm gonna start my homework."

He didn't answer, just turned a page, the smell of burning tuna hovering in the air.

I couldn't explain when exactly I noticed that my parents were living separate lives. Late in my freshman year, my history class watched a videotape of the fall of the Berlin Wall and the different coverage of the event provided on each network. I thought then about my parents. They seemed like that—separate worlds that were linked mostly by a name and divided by something solid, something like a mass of concrete, brick, and wire. Our teacher told us that five years after the Wall came down, Germany was growing into a solid, unified, and strong nation. I thought that nothing would bring my parents back together. I don't know why I thought of them this way, but I raised my hand and asked to use the bathroom, where I locked myself in a stall, pulling my feet up on the seat so no one would know I was in there. I rested my face against my knees until I could control my breathing and pretend again that I was all right.

• • •

Varsity finished the regular season as the fourth-place team in our conference, earning us a home playoff game. Rockcastle had missed the playoffs the last three years, so our playoff game against Summit Country Day brought a full crowd to the Fieldhouse: most of our students, all the team members' parents, teachers and administrators, and alumni. It was standing room only: the place was filled with young alumni in varsity jackets and ironic stocking caps with puffballs on top, the girls from Our Lady of Mercy, parents who never came to the games. We had never had a full crowd until this game, and the bleachers buzzed with enthusiastic chatter. The air was thick and overheated; all of us players were charged up with adrenaline. My mother had arrived early enough to get her customary seat in the middle of the bleachers, and my father stood shoulder-to-shoulder with other spectators in the corners, his arms folded across his chest. More than once, I saw him chatting amicably with the men around him. Best of all, Caitlin was there. She was seated with three other girls about halfway up the bleachers, once again wearing an odd hat (purple with a white pom-pom) pulled down to her brow. We locked eyes, and she waved in an exaggerated motion like she was cleaning a window. I suppressed a grin and nodded, then concentrated on warm-ups, watching my shot spin off the backboard and drop through the net.

After three quarters of rugged defense, tons of fouls, and a lot of trash talk, we were up three, 53–50, and on defense with under a minute to go. The game was close in large part because Carson was disengaged. All the ferocity he had brought to our last game was gone; he never looked to shoot, his shoulders slumped, his hands were on his hips, his expression one of vacant boredom. "C'mon, man, let's go," was all I could think to say to him, over and over again, and when he looked at me it was as if he hated me. His eyes narrowed and jaw tight, anger rippled through his face until his chin sunk and his neck coiled. As the game continued, all of us on the team stopped speaking to Carson or looking at him. From where I am now, I know that I had witnessed a side of him, however briefly, that was to be feared.

As we clung to our three-point lead, the ball swung to the corner, then into the post to their power forward, who had already scored eighteen points. He held the ball up next to his chin. He leaned his shoulders back into our power forward, Dan Hollis, who had his right forearm braced into his man's lower back and his left arm up in the air, elbow slightly bent, ready to leap and block a shot. But Hollis already had four fouls and was giving up five inches; he widened his stance, focused on his man's eyes, and seemed to be trying to stay upright. I was at the top of the key, my body turned sideways, my left hand pointed out toward my guy, making sure I didn't creep too far off him. But this discipline eluded our small forward, Asher Schmidt, who was on the wing closest to the block: he tried to double the ball. When he came flying in with his arms raised, the power forward whipped a crisp pass to his teammate at the three-point line, who in one fluid motion caught the pass, raised up, and shot an open jumper. I thought, *goddamn it,* but the ref closest kept his hand down; the shooter's foot was on the line, making it a two, not a three. The shot rattled down, and Duke called a time-out.

"Why did you double?" Hollis yelled at Schmidt.

"He's been killing you all game!"

"What did you say?"

"Guys!" Duke yelled. "Get over here! Huddle up."

"Motherfucker," Hollis muttered.

"Pipe down." Duke drew up an inbounds ball on the whiteboard. "Okay. They are going to try to trap us and draw a ten-second call, okay? Once we break their press, we're going to hit our two free throws, and then play D hands up, don't jump, don't foul. Simple. Here it is. Webb!"

I watched the pen squeak across the board. I was to use a double screen, curl back toward the ball, and catch the inbound pass from Carson in the middle of the court. "Do not go to the corner," Duke said. "Carson! You hear that? Do not pass to the corner."

Carson looked up and through me. He shrugged his eyebrows.

I nodded and yelled, "Let's go!" and we broke the huddle. There were twelve seconds left in the game. Everyone in the gym was on their feet, the pep band finished a quick song, and there was a nervous energy as people stomped their feet, clapped their hands, and cheered our names and the schools' names. I stood at the three-point line, hands on my hips, eyes down. My defender stood between me and the ball, his head turned to see Carson.

The ref whistled. He handed the ball to Carson. I deked right, then cut left, streaking toward the free-throw line and my two screeners. My right shoulder brushed both screeners, and I curled sharply toward Carson, hands up, ready for the ball.

But Carson's defender, who had started with his arms up and leaping straight into the air, abandoned Carson and ran toward me, arms up. So, too, did the second screener's defender. I was double-teamed. My defender slid to the first screener; the first screener's defender slid to the second screener. I broke hard, turned up-court, and threw my right hand over my head like a wide receiver signaling to the quarterback for the ball.

With no one guarding him and both defenders' backs facing him, Carson threw a two-hand chest pass off the nearest defender, stepped on the court, waited for the ball to ricochet back to him, grabbed it, and waited for the inevitable and confused foul.

The home crowd roared with delight at Carson's tricky play. It had taken three seconds off the clock. Carson smiled as he strutted down the court, and we pounded his back with slaps. "Smart play, smart play, good shit, smart play." When I tried to slap him five, he grabbed my hand, squeezed it, and winked. He was suddenly back in the world. We weren't yet in the bonus, so Carson would shoot a one-and-one. But he was an excellent free-throw shooter, and this was as close to a guaranteed make as we would ever get.

There were four of us at half court: me and Schmidt and our two defenders. Duke yelled out at us, "No timeouts!" I turned to Duke and nodded. After the makes, Summit would race down the court and fire a quick three. Since I had the point guard, he was probably going to bring the ball up. But he was a good shooter, too. He had hit two triples already in this game, so there was a good chance he wouldn't just bring the ball up, but would take the last shot.

I stood at center court looking at Carson. I was not directly behind him, but behind his right shoulder. I wanted to see the trajectory of the shot, the flex of his shoulder and triceps, the way the ball rested in his fingertips. When he raised the ball—using his left hand to balance it but letting that hand drop at the peak of the lift so the ball remained only in his right hand—I wanted to see the cock of his wrist, and how the tip of his middle finger would be the last bit of skin to touch the ball before it spun in a perfect fifteen-foot parabola to sink into the bottom of the net.

I knew the instant he released his shot that he had missed.

Carson's shot was off to the right. When he released the ball, he hadn't completely cleared his left hand. His thumb was still touching the ball, and it was just enough pressure to change the spin and direction of the shot. It bounced off the inside of the rim, skipped out to the left block, and the Summit forward grabbed the rebound. My guy raced toward the ball. I glanced at Carson. He turned from the rim once the shot missed, and a flash of dismay ran through his face. He looked right at me, his mouth fearful and pleading.

Their point guard had the ball, and he dribbled up the far sideline. His eyes looked up and far above my head to check the game clock. Ten seconds. They were out of timeouts. I slid to half court and waited, knees bent, bouncing slightly from foot to foot. He crossed left, then right, skipping, trying to find a rhythm. I backpedaled, giving him enough space to move but not enough to get a head start. He crossed half court and came out of his low dribble, sizing me up. He was going to try to beat me one on one.

Everyone was on their feet and screaming. To goad their point guard, I clapped my hands, but I couldn't hear the slapping of my palms. I shaded to his left, he crossed over, and the ball was back in his right hand. He was where I wanted him, isolated on the sideline with no passing options, and if he shot a jumper, he would have to swing his entire body to square up his shooting arm. People sitting in the front row, on their feet now, leaned toward the court, chins and chests jutting forward, a human fence making us feel contained and dangerous. He slowed his dribble, crouched low, and I scooted back just a step. I couldn't let him get by me. I wanted him to take the shot. I wanted him to think he could make it.

His eyes upped to see the game clock. I didn't need it. I knew.

He made his move. He brought the ball to his left hand, and I shaded right. He made a hard bounce, and I knew he was crossing back over. When he did, I thought about ripping the ball from his hands, but the last thing I wanted to do was foul. He bounced hard to his right hand and took one step toward the baseline. I slid with him, ready for the pull up I knew was coming, loading up on the balls of my feet to leap. Cut off, he raised up, and I went straight up, high and true as I could, my eye on the basketball, making sure to stay vertical, toward the rafters, *don't reach don't reach*. I got two fingers on the ball, just enough leather. I never turned around. I landed and the buzzer blared, a long deep howl. I looked straight at the shooter—his shoulders were down, his face crumpled in on itself—and then my teammates grabbed me from behind and screamed in my ears.

My teammates spun me around and punched my chest and arms, and all I could do was grin back. "Shut 'em down, Webb! Lock him *up*! Yeah, man, yeah!" All the Rockcastle fans were cheering and screaming and clapping and leaping up and down, and the pep band's horns couldn't even be heard. And then Carson emerged from around the forwards, pointed once at me with his right hand, the one that missed the free throw, the one that put us in jeopardy, his one finger straight and true like the barrel of a gun. He kept it raised and aimed at me until he was right in front of me, his hot breath on my face, and he wrapped his arms around me—right arm over my shoulder, left under my ribs—and squeezed all the air out of my lungs. His uniform was soaked with sweat, his body odor spicy, arms dripping wet, and he grabbed my head, my wet hair, and pressed my ear against his mouth and said, "Championship defense, Webb. You saved me. You saved me."

He dug his fingers into my scalp and screamed out at the crowd, "Rockcastle defense!" Everyone roared back, and I could not stop smiling. Carson spun me around, and I faced the crowd. The cheering somehow became louder, and he grabbed my shoulders and shook me, his hands hooked on my uniform, shaking me like a matador waving at the bull.

Up in the stands, my mother stood looking down at me. Between the rows of faces, hats, coats, gloves, the clapping hands and big smiles, my classmates and the pretty girls, everyone's faces red and exclaiming, she stood still, her palms pressed together as if in prayer, the tips of her fingers covering her wide, tight-lipped smile, her eyes shining and wet. Then Caitlin screamed, "Owen!" and I turned to see her waving her purple hat and jumping up and down with her friends. Carson's hands were on my shoulder blades, under my uniform, his strong hands on my sweaty back, and it felt like he was about to push me forward to leap across a great distance I finally knew I could make.

At that very moment, it didn't matter that my father had missed a game. It didn't matter that just two nights later, we would lose by fourteen points. Surrounded by witnesses, showered in cheers, what mattered was that this was the moment I had wanted and believed I deserved all school year, the validation I needed that I could be thought of and seen and loved as one of Rockcastle's own.

I raised my arms high above my head and roared back.

VI

Once basketball season was over at the end of February, my days at Rockcastle focused entirely on school. Carson and I still took our free bell to shoot baskets in the small gym, and we would sometimes set up plastic cones and work on ball-handling drills. He recommended that I join the debate team, which I did halfheartedly, content to treat it as useful for law school, if I ever wanted to be a lawyer, and willing to be the weak link of the team, a researcher who was rarely one of the five debaters in our matches. My classes became more rigorous as we pushed into the spring semester, and I developed the steady weekday work ethic of all Rockcastle boys.

Without basketball, I had nothing to distract me from my parents' unraveling marriage. Every word they spoke to each other was tinged with a hidden, hateful meaning. When all of us were home, my parents managed not only to never be in the same room together, but to never even be on the same floor. In the evenings, they increasingly discovered ways to avoid being home: my father started working out at the local gym, spent Friday nights playing poker with his coworkers, took up golf on the weekends even though I knew he hated the game, and went to bad action movies by himself. My mother picked up extra hours at the library and started going on long walks around the neighborhood for hours at a time. When she was home, she watched television with religious intensity, her hands unconsciously bringing her wine glass and cigarettes to her mouth.

One day, I sat on the living room floor, my legs out in front of me, and stretched my arms back over my head. I was watching my NBA tapes. At Carson's suggestion, I had started recording every game I could, which was a limited package back then, whatever our cable company provided. I sought out any NBA game with a good point guard, recorded it, and then replayed it over and over, studying how a guard created space, how he got in the lane, how he read the defense. "Focus on their footwork," Carson told me, "not the basketball. The last thing you should watch, Webb, is the ball." My stack of VHS tapes was organized by point guard rather than team. I had just finished watching my Mookie Blaylock tape—I had so many Atlanta Hawks games from TBS—and was about to look for a tape of Gary Payton games when I heard the front door open and my mother enter. From the way her bags hit the floor, I knew she was in a bad mood.

I said hello but didn't turn around. She responded by banging around the kitchen. A wine bottle corked open. My mother's food processor whirled to life, and pots clattered on the stove. On the screen, Gary Payton threw a lob to Shawn Kemp; I rewound the play and focused on Payton's feet, how he slipped around the screen and kept his balance.

My mother sat down on the couch and clutched her wine glass between her hands. "Is this a tape?"

"From last month."

She watched as I let the tape roll, paused, rewound, then replayed a single possession five or six times. It was a designed two-man set, and I wanted to see how the guard faked his defender, how he always kept his feet under his shoulders, never getting too wide and unbalanced. She finished her wine, got up, and returned with a refilled glass.

"Did I ever tell you," she said, "about the time a gun was pointed at me?"

"What?" I took my thumb off the pause button, and the game silently continued.

"When your father was failing out of college," she said. "I got a job at the front desk of a hotel. I worked nights. Your father did, too. Oh, he was still going to class, but he was mostly bartending by that point, and I didn't want to be the type of girl to get drunk at a bar while watching her boyfriend work, so I got a job as a hotel clerk. It was in Northside, which was already going downhill in the seventies. Not many people came by the desk at night. Drunks, mostly. Businessmen coming in late with a girl. Do you know what I mean by that? How older men buy the company of young girls? Well, it doesn't matter. Nothing was happening that night. I was sitting at the desk reading *The Hotel New Hampshire* when the bell over the entrance rang. All I saw was that his head was shaped weird. It never occurred to me that a man would wear panty hose on his head. Even with his gun pointed at me, it didn't really register with me that I was being robbed. I mean, he had panty hose over his head! It was so strange. He stuck that revolver right in my face. I remember thinking that, too: this is a revolver, not an automatic. It took a good ten seconds before I could even process what was going on. All I could tell the police later was that he had a mustache. He got away with a couple hundred dollars. He didn't hurt me. Just took the cash and left."

My heart echoed in my ears. All I wanted was my parents to stop talking to me like this: cryptic memories spoken as justification for who they were now.

"It was summer." She squinted at the window. "Not nasty weather like this. I looked right into the barrel of the revolver. The opening was so tiny, and I thought, *could something coming out of that really kill me?* I think I was too stunned to actually be scared."

She ran her fingers through her hair, a cloud of black and silence. For some reason she was still wearing her avocado rain boots.

"Your father made me keep working there. He said if I didn't, I'd never be able to walk back into a hotel again. For months after that I had nightmares of being shot, bullets ripping through my skull. In some of the dreams, I'd still be alive and see my own blood and bones splattered around me. Over and over again. And your father never even finished college. Isn't that remarkable?"

She watched the game: the Sonics gave up two transition threes, and Coach Karl called a time-out. She took her wine glass and returned to the kitchen to make spaghetti.

My mother became prone to staring off into space, unblinking and unhearing, letting the cigarette at the end of her fingers burn itself down to a sliver of ash. My father's choice of ambush, however, was wrapped up in some sort of education. After dinner, if he wasn't watching a ball game in the basement, he sat at the kitchen table, attempting to educate himself about stocks and bonds, as if he were preparing to switch careers from chemical technician to stockbroker. Library books written by Peter Lynch and Burton Malkiel were marked with color-coded tabs. He charted high-dividend-yielding companies and sometimes forced me to listen to him lecture on the risks associated with foreign municipal bonds.

"Do you study economics?" he asked me one night.

"Not formally," I said, turning from the fridge. I popped open the Coke I had fished out. "It comes up as part of Western civ, but it's not a class Rockcastle offers until junior year."

"Save all the money you can and put it in a private account. And don't tell anyone. The markets are irrational. People are, too. Particularly your spouse. You never know what they're going to do with what you tell them."

I pulled the tab off my soda can and put it with the recycling under the sink.

"In fact," he said. "It's better to just not get married."

Through the window over the kitchen sink, I watched the tree branches. I wondered if it was worth risking a fight to ask if he knew the difference between microeconomics and personal finance but couldn't see what good a fight with my father would do. There was no wind. Good day to be outside shooting baskets.

"Your mother should have married the black guy," he said, sipping his bourbon. I glanced at my father, whose eyes were still buried in the charts he kept in a three-ring binder. If his non sequitur about my mother's supposed boyfriend had a story behind it, he didn't bother telling me. Cigarette smoke plumed around my father's head, almost as if it were steam from his anger rather than haze from the tobacco. After five minutes of our not speaking, I grabbed a second Coke from the fridge so I wouldn't have to come back and hid away in my bedroom for the rest of the night.

• • •

On a rainy night in April, my mother was sick with the flu. What had started out the previous weekend as just a little sniffling morphed into full-blown achiness by Monday, a doctor's visit on Tuesday, and daylong sleep on Wednesday. That particular night, she woke up just long enough to ask that my father get her more medication from Walgreens.

"You're coming with me," my father said to me.

"Why?"

"So I don't have to get out of the car."

I glanced out my bedroom window. "Dad, it's pouring."

"Exactly."

I dog-eared the page of my geometry textbook and stood up from my desk with an exaggerated sigh that he didn't acknowledge. I didn't own a raincoat, so I pulled on a hoodie and a jacket and a crappy Houston Rockets ball cap, followed my father through the kitchen and out the side entrance, and jogged to the car. I was already drenched by the time I slammed the passenger door shut.

My father was jittery during the entire ride: drumming his fingers on the wheel, pivoting his jaw toward the rearview and side mirrors, checking the time on both his watch and the car radio. He stayed under the speed limit and kept his hands locked on the steering wheel. The rain had slowed to a drizzle by the time we made the drive to Walgreens. He pulled his fat, cracked wallet from his back pocket and handed me a twenty.

"You know what your mother needs?"

"Yeah, I got it. Can I buy a soda, too?"

"Don't we have soda in the basement?"

"Mom's been sick, so nobody went to the grocery store."

He shook his head, then gave me permission to buy a soda with a wave of his hand.

Inside I bought flu medicine, cough drops, vapor rub, and some honey for Mom to add to her tea. I grabbed a Cherry Coke and lingered for a moment at the magazine rack, looking at the baseball previews I knew I didn't have money or permission to buy. Back in the car, my father sat smoking a cigarette, his right arm thrown across the seat, the air in the car smoky. He opened his palm to receive his change from the twenty.

"Thanks, Dad," I said, raising my soda in the air like a salute.

"We should grab dinner, too."

"Can we go to McDonald's?"

"How about Rally's?"

Rally's was a fast food company new to Cincinnati. They had two drive-thru windows rather than one, and their vegetables and meat were supposedly fresher than McDonald's or Wendy's, though why that was the case, I had no idea. My father had recently handed me a stockholder's prospectus for Rally's and instructed me to read, evaluate, and come back to him with a report on whether or not he should invest money in their stock. I didn't have any idea what quarterly earnings and price-to-earnings ratios were, but I knew when my father was demanding rather than requesting, so after three days I reported back to him with a thumbs-up on buying Rally's stock. I don't know why I thought that, and I don't know if he ever bought Rally's stock, but ever since then it was the only fast food place he would go.

"Rally's is good, too," I said.

"Good. There's one ten minutes away in Finneytown."

He lit a fresh cigarette and cracked the window; wind from the blackened nighttime streets whistled through the gap. He turned the volume up on WEBN, his favorite classic-rock radio station, and eased out of the parking lot like he had made up his mind about something profound and satisfying. We drove north up Winton Road, and on the corner was the Rally's, its red-and-yellow plastic lights glowing pristine and shiny, undamaged from decades in the sun and snow, popping out against the dark. My father turned at the corner and drove past the restaurant.

"You missed the turn," I said.

"Making a stop first, then we'll go."

My father banked left at a fork in the road, and we were now in a neighborhood I didn't recognize. The houses in front of us were massive, with long lawns that dipped from the house to the street; porch lights illuminated wood railings spotless of beer cans and ashtrays. These were the type of houses owned by Rockcastle families, the kind of homes that had rooms small children weren't allowed to enter. My father reached behind me into the back seat and grabbed a small black duffel bag.

"Where are you going?"

"Stay here."

My father stepped out of the car, carrying the duffel bag, and nudged the door quietly closed, pushing his hip against it to latch. He blended into the night: his dark pants, his dark coat, his dark cap, none of which I'd noticed him wearing when we left the house. He strode down the street and disappeared from view.

I reached for the radio and discovered that my father had taken the keys. I slumped down in the seat and removed the receipt from the Walgreens bag, trying to read it in the weak light glowing from the distant houses. There wasn't anything interesting about the price of my mother's medicine, the Ohio sales tax rate, or the receipt's serif fonts. But what else was I supposed to do? My stomach growled with hunger, and I took a long swig from my soda, letting the acidic burn of the cherry-flavored chemical slosh in my mouth before swallowing. My stomach expanded, and I let out a quiet belch. I rolled the soda cap between my fingers. What the hell was my dad up to? My breath fogged the window, and with the bottle cap, I wrote my initials on the glass.

The trunk flew open. I dropped out of sight like a spooked rabbit, then peered back over the headrest. My father pushed the duffel bag, now larger and shapely, into the car. He shut the trunk and hurried around to the driver's door, got in, started the car, and drove away quickly.

"Where'd you go?" I asked.

"Did I tell you I decided to buy some stock in Rally's?" The hair around his ears was slick with sweat, and his cheeks were red, the way he looked when he mowed the lawn on a hot Saturday afternoon.

"No, you didn't."

"So we're going there as shareholders. In a very small way, we're going there as owners."

My eyes narrowed. In the dark, and with his eyes on the road, he couldn't see the look I threw him that I wouldn't have dared give him if I knew he could see me. I knew better than to ask a question twice or hope that my father would explain what he had been doing.

"What should we get Mom?"

"Plain cheeseburger. You know she doesn't like all kinds of shit on her food."

I slumped into my seat. My father had a crazy smile on his face, his eyes distant, as if he were wrapped up in a dream.

At home, my father set the Rally's bag on the kitchen table, and I took the medicine to my mother's room. The door was cracked, and I knocked gently, pushing the door open as I rapped. She was in bed, turned away from the door, and a humidifier was the only noise, roaring from the foot of her nightstand. I sat down and touched her shoulder, and when she rolled over, her face was as open and eager as if she were expecting a Christmas present. It caved ever so slightly when she saw it was me, not my father, and she pushed her head back into the pillow to take me in.

"We got you everything," I said. "How you feeling?"

"Less than great. Did you go with your dad?"

I nodded.

"That was sweet of you. He doesn't like to drive when it's raining. Did you know that?"

"It stopped raining."

"Oh." She rolled her head in the general direction of the window, but didn't get very far before rocking back and looking at me. She patted my knee and closed her eyes. "I'm very proud of you."

Distantly I heard the trunk of the car close, then the creak of the side door opening and my father pounding down the basement steps.

"No, I mean it," my mother said, calling my attention back to her. "I'm very proud of you, Owen. Very proud."

"Should I get you some water for this?"

"Yes, please."

When I returned from the bathroom with her water, she was asleep again. I looked down the hallway toward the kitchen. I removed all the items from the bag and set them up on her nightstand, removing the tamper-proof tops, and hoped that when she woke, she would take them. I turned off the lamp and closed the door behind me.

The Rally's bag on the kitchen counter now had grease stains from the burgers, and a roar rose up from the basement, the sounds of the big attack scene from a war movie. I wondered what my father was watching, but not enough to go down there and find out. From the cabinet I got a plate and set my burger and fries on it. I took the ketchup from the fridge and squirted a massive pile of the condiment into the upper quadrant of my plate. I tuned the radio that resided over the fridge to the Reds game, keeping it to a low murmur so I wouldn't wake my mom; they were opening a three-game series in Atlanta. I thought about how good the Braves pitching staff was, and how Smoltz always beat the Reds. As soon as I sat down, I immediately lost both my thoughts about baseball and my appetite. I picked up two fries like chopsticks and pictured them as the legs on some sort of monster and made them run around the edge of the plate. Then I felt stupid for acting like a little kid and flipped the fries into the ketchup, refocusing on the broadcast and Joe Nuxhall's voice. I sat at the kitchen table and listened to Joe and hoped my parents would stay out of the kitchen and away from me for the rest of the night.

VII

In early May, with just six weeks left in my freshman year, my mother left the house without me one morning. She was always my ride to Rockcastle. My father usually left before I was even awake. Despite my best efforts to be a driven and determined student, my morning alarm clock had continued to be my downfall; even with two alarms and a snooze button, I couldn't drag myself out of bed without my mother coming in and gently bouncing my head off the pillow until I growled "All right" and swung my feet to the floor. Once, however, after my mother left my bedroom, I fell back asleep while sitting upright. Since then, she pressed her hand on the back of my neck and steered me to the bathroom, then waited to hear the shower turn on before she headed back down the hallway to get herself ready for work.

So it was a surprise not only that my mother had left me behind, but also that my father was still home. I dropped my bag at the front door and looked out at the driveway where my mother's car should have been. Plates clattered in the kitchen. I turned. My father stood in front of the stove, shirtless, pushing eggs around a frying pan.

"Where's Mom?"

"She went to Half Day for breakfast with a couple of her friends from the library. I told her I would take you in today."

"I don't wanna be late for school."

"You won't. Sit down, have some breakfast."

"Dad."

He turned his chin and smiled at me. "Sit. Eat."

I rolled my eyes and sat down at the table. I pretended to be impatient and pissed, but by this point the smells from the stovetop had me salivating. To this day, I love breakfast food: heaps of pancakes, too many eggs sprinkled with bits of ham or pepper or cheese or tomatoes, crispy hash browns, bacon and sausage. I even love yogurt and fruit. Loading up on food after sleeping for eight hours always felt like the best part of any day.

My father set down a Western omelet, salsa drizzled over the top, and I wondered why he had never opened a restaurant. The hash browns were burnt pleasingly crisp, and half an orange was cut into slices. He set down a glass of milk, then folded his arms and leaned against the counter.

"What's all this for?" I asked.

"You don't want it?"

I answered by digging into my omelet.

"That's what I thought." He plucked the cordless phone from the wall, and I admired my father's arms, their sinewy ripples, his calloused hands dwarfing the phone. With his other hand on his hip, he punched a number and waited.

"Mrs. Bunker?" he asked. "This is Joseph Webb, Owen's father. How are you this morning?"

I put down my fork.

"Listen," my father said. "I'm afraid I have some bad news. Owen is sick today and won't be able to come to school. Yeah. That's right. I know. I know. I hope it isn't serious, too. If I call you back this afternoon, could I get a list of his assignments? Yeah? Okay. That's good, that's good. I'll let him know you said that. Thank you, Mrs. Bunker. Oh, excuse me—Lila! Thank you, Lila."

He beeped the phone off.

"Now you can eat slower."

"Why did you do that?"

"Why, indeed." He drew his wallet from his back pocket, opened it, pulled out two tickets to the Reds game, and slid them across the table. I looked at the tickets. Back then, they still called a day game a "businessman's special."

"But, Dad, I'm not a businessman."

"Owen, it's just a marketing term. You don't have to actually be a businessman. But, if you're truly concerned about it, I'll put you in a jacket and tie and I bet no one will stop you. Look how tall you've gotten. Shit, son, you're taller than me now."

"Yes, I am."

"Look closer." He fat-fingered the tickets.

My father and I went to games all the time, ever since I was old enough to fall asleep in my seat. The first game he took me to was in 1985; I had no memory of it, but I still have the ticket stub: Reds vs. Astros. Mike Scott beat the Reds, 5–2. I fell asleep in the seventh inning. Since then, my father would bring home Reds tickets once a month, tickets he said he got from guys at work, and we would skip dinner to drive down to Riverfront Stadium, sit in the upper deck between first and third base, and gorge on hot dogs and soda. My father never drank at those games, always happy to share a soda with me. Often, I fell asleep on the car ride home, the shadows of the city somnambulistic as they fluttered over the hood of the car, the post-game show a distant murmur on the radio. My eyes would droop heavy as the city faded away during our cruise up the highway, only to wake up right as my father pulled into the driveway and parked in the carport.

What my father was pointing out were the seats: blue seats. Lower bowl. We never, not once, sat that close to the field.

"Holy shit!" I said. "I mean, um, sorry. You know."

He laughed. "Holy shit! Say it loud!"

"Holy shit!"

"Grab your hat and sunglasses, Owen. We're sitting in the sun today."

We cruised down 75 with the windows down, my father blasting Zeppelin, the temperature touching eighty, a perfect May day without any rain in the forecast. The Reds were good that year, too, a team that would ultimately win the division, and good weather or bad, every sporting event is better when the team is in the hunt.

We parked in the garage we always parked in, a dark concrete structure up Race Street, and let the incline pull us down toward the Ohio and the ballpark. I could smell the river, cool and slightly oily, and when we passed out of the shadows of skyscrapers and hotels, we stepped into bright sunshine, the vendors hawking bratwursts and peanuts, T-shirts and pennants and hats and buttons for sale on every corner. A parade of men without their suit jackets hustled around us, ties askew, dipping into the bars closest to the park and overtaking the patios, where they clinked beer bottles and laughed too loud. We all seemed to be getting away with something, looking at each other with glee, our greetings more like secret handshakes that were all inflection and just the right amount of eye contact to acknowledge that, yes, we were here, yes, we should be elsewhere in an office, and no, there was nothing wrong, not one thing, with this kind of happiness.

Up on the pavilion outside the ballpark, my father led us not straight to the gates, but around the edges. He strolled, lingered, as if waiting for a late-arriving airplane.

"Dad, c'mon. I don't want to miss first pitch."

"I know. Just a second." He scanned the crowd, and I followed his gaze. Just off the pavilion, on the sidewalks, amongst the businessmen and the vendors, were scalpers, nodding and raising fingers, indicating whether they were buying or selling and how many they had or needed. We beelined for a scalper in a wide-brim golf hat with a Reds emblem on the band. He wore an Eric Davis jersey, baggy navy shorts, and spotless white shoes. He was black and had thick glasses and a thin goatee.

"What do you need?" he asked my dad.

"Selling two." My father opened his wallet and pulled out not two, but four tickets.

"Where?"

"Lower bowl, about fifteen rows up."

The scalper looked at the tickets, which remained tight in my father's hands, and quoted him a price twenty under face value. My father asked for ten more per, and the scalper nodded. From his left pocket, he pulled out a wad of cash and handed my father the money in exchange for the two tickets, and they smiled at each other and said thanks.

"Hot dog money," my father said.

"You had four?"

"Guy at work had four." He didn't look at me but focused his gaze on the entrance that he was guiding us toward. "Did you want to bring someone?"

"No," I said, though it wasn't as if he had asked me. The first person I thought of was Carson, who had never once mentioned baseball. I couldn't think of a fourth person. "You just usually have two."

"I usually bring home two. That's not the same thing."

Inside, rather than taking the escalator up three levels, we walked straight ahead, and the crowd seemed better, louder, brighter down here, close to the field. The Reds were heading onto the field, ready to start the first inning, the starter marching out to the mound with his head lowered in concentration. Adrenaline pumped through my arms, and I followed my father down the concrete steps, so close to the field I could see the circular swirls in the dirt around home plate, the black borders of the white plate, the chunks of chalk etching the imperfections in the batter's box that looked immaculate from high up in the grandstands. We sat four seats in from the aisle, the sun already warming my forearms. I stretched my growing legs until my shins knocked the seat in front of me.

"Great day for a ball game," he said.

All I could do was nod.

The first inning moved fast. The Mets got a base hit and a stolen base but no runs. The Reds went down in order. My father and I didn't speak. I didn't even take my eyes off the field, stunned by how much detail I could see in the players' uniforms, shiny helmets, the squint of their eyes, the arcs of tobacco spit they lobbed throughout the game. I never noticed the couple that sat down next to us. I didn't see that they were tan and beautiful. I didn't see them at all until the middle of the second inning, when a cop stood at the end of the aisle and said, in a voice firm and crisp, to my father and the other man, "Fellas, can I speak to you for a moment?"

The four of us looked at each other for the first time. All of us registered curious surprise, and then the men stood up and followed the cop up the aisle. The woman smiled tightly, and her beauty made me nervous and quiet; I lingered over her watch, her diamond ring, and her long legs, all the way down to her toes that were painted a dark shade of orange. Embarrassed for ogling her, I turned in my seat. The cop in his light-blue short-sleeve shirt took the steps slow, his forearms hairy, the gun and flashlight and other accessories on his belt shiny under the sun. His partner stood at the top of the stairs, his face unreadable behind his sunglasses. I turned back to the game and wondered what the cops wanted with my father.

Half an inning later, the men were back. My father's shoulders were coiled tight, and he made fists with his hands, his cheeks red with anger. His jaw was set, cheeks taut, and I knew he was clamping his teeth like a starving dog with a bone. The other man looked at his wife and said, "Let's go. I'll explain in a minute," and she picked up her purse without a word and they headed up the steps.

"Dad?"

"Get up. We're leaving."

Fear shut me up. Certain that everyone was looking at me and talking about us, I lowered my chin, though I didn't know what I was ashamed of. But I knew the feeling: embarrassment and shame. I stood and followed right behind him, watching his thick calf muscles as we went up the aisle, onto the concourse, out the gate we had just entered, and across the pavilion to stand in line at a ticket counter. We reentered through a different gate, went up the two sets of escalators we always took, ascended another set of stairs, made our way deep into a row, and sat down, high above the field, far from the players and their perfectly ironed jerseys.

We watched the game in total silence for two innings. We didn't stand or applaud when the Reds scored two runs in the bottom of the third. We didn't get hot dogs or sodas.

I barely watched the game, glancing from the field to some field of vision between the seats and my father, terrified of making eye contact or asking him what happened.

Finally, at the top of the fourth, leaning forward, his forearms pressed against his knees, he said, "I'm sorry about that, kid."

I ignored my rumbling stomach. He gazed out at the field.

"Those seats we had? Those tickets were stolen."

"Stolen?"

He nodded, though it seemed more to himself than to me.

"If anyone asks," he said, "we bought those tickets from the black guy. You remember the scalper?"

"Who would ask?"

"If anyone asks, we bought those tickets from the black guy. You got it?"

"Yeah."

"Describe him."

"I don't know. Black. Glasses. Eric Davis jersey."

"That's good. That's what I told the cops."

I didn't understand how my father got stolen tickets. The idea didn't make any sense to me, as if the words were spoken in a foreign language.

"Let's not trouble your mom with this, okay?"

"Yeah, okay."

"Good." He pressed his hands together like he was cracking a walnut. "Good."

We sat in silence for another half inning, and then he said, "I'm going for some food, you want some food?" I said, "Sure," and watched my dad take the aisle very slow, as if his body were arthritic and broken. But when he returned, his hands full with four hot dogs and beef nachos and two large sodas, his face was boyish and happy, as if this had been his plan all along.

We got home around four o'clock, and I said I was

going to my room to do homework. He didn't answer. I sat down at my desk and tapped my pencil against my geometry book, thinking through the day. I wasn't sure what I was and was not supposed to tell my mom. When she left this morning, she thought I was going to school. Should I pretend I had? With my father in the front room, I figured I would just hide in my bedroom, say nothing, let him come up with the story, and I would back him up.

I went into the kitchen and got two sodas from the fridge. My father sat on the couch, watching television, the cable box perched on his lap, the long cord snaking across the floor. I remember how he refused to let us get cable for years, and then one day I came home from school and we suddenly had cable, my father changing his mind as easily as he changed shoes. From the kitchen, I asked if he wanted anything, and he ignored me. Back in my room I set the two unopened Cokes on my desk and sat down on my bed. I don't remember feeling tired or falling back against my pillows, but when I opened my eyes again, my room was slated in gray shadows. I rolled away from the wall and found my mother sitting on the edge of my bed.

"Hey, sleepyhead."

"What time is it?"

"After seven." She ran her fingers through my hair, and, not yet awake, I didn't resist, her fingertips soothing. With her palm flat against my head, I remembered a story she once told me. When my mother told my father that she was pregnant with me, he shot out of his seat and scooped her up in one sudden move. She howled and laughed and smacked his shoulders, "Put me down! Put me down!" It was the first time she had seen him happy in weeks. He spun her in wide circles around the room—the white walls decorated with movie posters hung with tape, the used and lopsided furniture, the faded linoleum of the kitchen floor, the chipped paint around the drafty windows—all of it whirled away as if tumbling down a drain, never to be seen again, leaving only what was clean and wanted. There was a promise in this. A promise my father strengthened with each slow spin.

My mother lay her hands in her lap. "You've been out for a while."

"Should I get up?"

"Only if you want to."

I closed my eyes.

"Dad said you went to the baseball game today."

"Yeah. Business-day special."

"Reds win?"

"Yup. Larkin hit a home run."

"Sounds like you had a good time with your father. It's nice when you two spend time together."

Her breath was cool and minty. She spoke very softly, almost in a whisper, like she was trying to send me to sleep rather than wake me up. My eyes remained closed.

"I'm sure you two loaded up on junk food, so why don't you just rummage for something if you get hungry, okay?"

"Okay."

She leaned down and kissed my forehead. The mattress rose, and when I knew her back was to me, I opened my eyes and watched her leave the room. I had lied to my mom before: when I threw crabapples at a neighbor's car, when I had gotten in fights at my old school, when I broke her hair dryer, skipped chores, stuff like that. The sort of things kids lie about. This lie, however, was a lie of calculated omission I made on the spot, a lie covering my father's lie, complex in its simplicity. At that age, I didn't understand why this lie felt heavier, more insidious, because of how close to true it was, but I understood that this kind of lie—with just one small swerve from the truth—was somehow worse.

The next day, all through class, I tried to understand what had happened. By the time free bell with Carson rolled around, I nearly burst telling him the story. We circled around the perimeter, each of us shooting twenty jumpers—he hit sixteen, I hit fifteen—our regular opening routine, always done in reverential silence, before I told him about the baseball game.

He listened while doing the Mikan drill, flipping easy layups and practicing his finish with each hand, and when I was done, he cocked the basketball against his hip and stared at me. A film of sweat covered his lip.

"So you didn't tell your mom?"

I shook my head.

"That's fucked up. And the cops are going to blame the black guy."

"I guess."

"Where did he tell you he got them?"

"From work. That's what he says. I just figured, you know, guys in his department can't use them, or the company buys them and hands them out or something. I've never really thought about it."

"My father's company has season tickets. Four. A couple rows from the Reds dugout. He hands them out as perks and thank yous."

"Should I tell my mom?"

"Why would you?"

"Because I lied, and what if the cops show up? Then I'm fucked."

He laughed. "C'mon, Webb. Two white guys just told a couple of beat cops that a black man sold them those tickets. Didn't you pay attention in Taransky's class?"

Taransky taught a spring semester seminar in twentieth-century African American history. He was a tall bald man with a bird-like face who literally screamed half his lectures, his tie loose and hanging like a plumb line. It was impossible not to pay attention in his class.

"Look," Carson said. "Parents lie. They lie to each other all the time. And usually they are lying about something they aren't even talking about. Duck and cover, man. If something goes wrong, let your dad cover his own ass."

"But where did they come from?"

"Who cares?"

Carson dribbled out to the top of the key and shot a jumper off the wrong foot. It clattered off the rim, and I rebounded it with one hand. I dribbled out to the three-point line and caught Carson staring at the floor as if puzzling out a problem. The enigma of my father was intriguing, with answers and explanations that at the time I never could have guessed. I stepped back and launched a shot, the ball zipping off my middle finger and swishing through the net. We took turns shooting without any conversation, his gaze often drifting to a spot on the floor, eyes narrowing as he lost himself in thought. Finally, with a few minutes left in our free bell, he pointed to the bench, and I followed him over and sat down.

We were both barefoot when he said, "I'll be gone this summer."

"What do you mean gone?"

"I usually go for a few weeks every summer, right after exams. Did a summer in Barcelona once. A summer program at Stanford. This year, I'm heading west with my old man and doing some river rafting in Utah. Caitlin is off to France for the summer. This is pretty normal shit for us."

"You're gone the whole summer?"

"Six weeks, maybe seven."

"Oh." I spun the basketball in my hands and let it bounce once. "That's cool, I guess."

"You're gone too, right?"

I shrugged. "Two basketball camps. Each one week. I mean, I'm not going anywhere like you are."

"You should get a job. You know, lifeguard or something. Look at the pretty girls."

I acted tough and said, "Fuck do I want a job for?"

Carson laughed. "Goddamn, Webb. That's right. Fuck work! I hear you. Got a whole lot of life ahead of us for that shit."

I nodded and pictured my summer, away from Rockcastle, away from basketball, away from Carson, stuck inside my house with nowhere to go and nothing to do. Staying in my neighborhood now felt like a prison camp, with a huge open yard to wander aimlessly but always surrounded by barbed-wire fences and guard towers. I could see my summer already: out on the front porch, listening to the radio, my mother and father always in different rooms, different orbits, careful not to acknowledge the other's presence.

"Webb," Carson said, clapping the back of my neck. "You awake?"

"Yeah. Wide awake." We stood on the baseline of the small gym at the entrance to the Upper School. Doors banged open, and footsteps clomped into the hallways. It wasn't even June yet and the afternoons were already cottony with humidity. I slipped my backpack off my shoulders, bounced the basketball once, then fired it up into the ceiling gap, the orange vanishing into the black, ricocheting in the dark, until it rolled slowly, finally, to rest.

VIII

It was after dark, mid-July, and I dribbled home after playing basketball at a park in North College Hill, which is mostly how I had passed my weeks of summer vacation. It was Midwestern muggy even after sundown. My mother was rocking herself on the porch swing by pushing the ball of her foot against the floor. I took the steps one at a time; a wine bottle and a full ashtray sat on the side table. She smiled up at me and held her wine glass to her chest like it was a child's toy.

"How was basketball?"

"Good. Fun. You know."

"There's a plate for you in the fridge. Heat it two minutes and you should be fine."

I dropped my bag on the floor inside and walked to the kitchen. Standing over the sink I splashed my forearms, neck, and face with water and wiped myself with paper towels. I pulled dinner from the fridge and lifted the foil: chicken Marsala, mashed potatoes, and green beans. Even today, I prefer my leftovers cold, so I skipped the microwave, pulled a can of Mountain Dew from the fridge, and went to the living room. I set my plate and soda on the coffee table next to my father's coin books.

The cable box sat on the floor below the television, its cord wrapped in neat circles, the way my mother always set it down. I picked up the box and punched the buttons in hopes of finding the beginnings of an action movie. With my free hand I cracked open my soda, slurped, then set it back down, while with my right thumb I punched and double-punched my way through all the cable options.

"What are you watching?" my father said.

I didn't turn around. From the sound of his voice, I knew he was standing behind me, next to the stairs to the basement and probably on his way to bed. His voice was mild and sleepy. I was just beginning to recognize that this was the voice of someone who had been drinking.

"Haven't found anything yet."

"Should be a late baseball game on ESPN."

"Baseball's for old guys like you."

"Who's old?" he chuckled.

I turned. And for a moment I saw my father as a happy man. He remains, even today, so clear to me now as he was in that moment. He was my father: clad in tube socks with three horizontal stripes—the type popular in the seventies, his muscular calves stretching the old elastic loose—and the athletic shorts he wore to cut the lawn. He wore an old UC sweatshirt, and he needed a shave. His normally neatly combed hair was disheveled and tangled, and his glasses were hanging down toward the tip of his nose. Frozen like that, he was a middle-aged man with a content happiness who could look around him and think, *This is a good life*.

But when I turned, my left hand spun with me, and I hit my soda can, tipping Mountain Dew all over my father's coin books.

"God fucking damn it!" My father leaped across the room like a lion. He snatched up his books and furiously wiped soda off the covers and onto the floor. "Get me paper towels!"

I hurried into the kitchen and grabbed the entire roll. I tore off a sheet and handed it to him, and he palmed soda off the coin book in his hand. He grabbed the entire paper roll and blotted the pool of soda, then each sticky drop from his five coin books, dabbing each droplet with harsh delicacy.

"Dad, I'm really sorry."

"Just shut up. Go get me a glass of water. I need to get the sugar off these things."

I did as I was told. My father was on his knees, his coin books fanned out on the couch to dry, and he was wiping the coffee table clean when my mother came in from the porch and asked what the yelling was about.

When my father didn't answer, I said, "I spilled my drink."

"You were careless and stupid," my father said.

"I'm sorry."

"Jesus, Joseph. He spilled a soda."

"I don't care."

"You leave them out in the open. It was an accident."

My father stood. "It's a matter of respect."

"Respect?" my mother laughed. "Are we on camera or something? The coins are in silicone sheets. There's no harm done."

His shoulders rose and fell. I took a step back. There was a couch between them, but nothing between me and my father. He snapped his head around.

"Where are you going?" He reached out and snatched my collar and pulled me close, his boozy breath like a razor across my chin.

"Do I go in your bedroom and knock things around?"

"Joseph!" my mother yelled. "What are you doing?"

"Dad, I'm sorry."

"Goddamn right you are," he said. He let go of me with a push, a light shove at best, but he had pulled me into the space between the coffee table and the couch, so when he shoved me, my legs hit the table and I fell. My legs got caught, my knees bent awkwardly, and, unable to throw out my arms, I bashed my head against the television stand.

"Owen!" my mother raced over and crouched next to me. "Owen."

"I'm fine," I said, looking up at my father. "I'm fine."

"You don't like 'em?" he screamed. "You don't like these? Fine! Fine! I'll sell them!" He snatched up all his coin books and hugged them to his chest. "You two can spill all the shit you want in here!"

"What's gotten into you?" my mother yelled. But my father was already hurrying down the stairs and into the basement. I twisted on my side, more concerned about my legs than my head, and pushed myself up. My mother clutched my hands.

"I'm fine," I said again. "Really. I just tripped."

"I don't know what's getting into him," she said. "Just go finish eating. In the kitchen. I'll talk to him in the morning."

I nodded and did as I was told. In the morning, my father left for work before anyone else was awake. The coffee table was bare, and I never again saw his coins or his coin books, in the basement or in the living room or anywhere else in the house.

• • •

I first caught strep throat when I was seven years old. For a day or two I would have a hard time swallowing, my throat growing more restricted and blocked, and then a fever would kick in, and I became achy and lethargic. My mother would dote on me all day long. Sitting up on the couch, pillows propping me up and a blanket covering my body, I watched movies on our Beta machine, usually something my father taped from the dueling VCR system he set up when we rented movies so that we could always have a copy of whatever we rented. Beta tapes were best since they could last six hours, and I never had to get off the couch. Even better, they were smaller than VHS, so when I was a boy, they fit neatly into my grip. My mom would open a Coke and insist that I "let it go flat." She made chicken noodle soup, ladling it into a coffee cup so I could drink it once it cooled from hot to warm, and also giving her an excuse to bring refills. Even though I was sick, I think now of those times on the couch as the periods when I felt safest and most protected. My parents failed to instill that feeling as I grew older and their marriage continued to crumble.

It had been three years since my last bout with strep throat, when the pediatrician jokingly scolded me, insisting that he would remove my tonsils if I ever caught strep again. I assured him I wouldn't, even if the idea of having a body part cut out, like something from the horror movies I secretly loved to watch, was thrilling.

I came back from a week in Indianapolis at Reggie Miller's Five Star Basketball Camp feeling good: out of seventy-two high school freshmen from the Midwest, I had played well, finishing second in MVP honors and hitting 45 percent of my threes in the games. During the car ride home that Sunday, I told my mother about the drills, the games, the other kids, and the Indiana Pacers, who showed up to camp for photos and to show us a few pro tricks. I didn't notice until Monday afternoon that I wasn't feeling quite right, and by Tuesday morning I was dazed and feverish, my body chilled and my throat impossibly tight.

"C'mon," my mother said. "To the couch with you."

We got into the doctor's office on Wednesday morning, and he prescribed medication that I knew from years of experience wouldn't make me feel better until Thursday. At noon, the first dosage in my system, my mother went back to work. I woke up once to change the Beta tape to a Schwarzenegger triple feature—*Commando, Red Heat,* and *The Running Man*—and fell back asleep.

When I woke up, the television was blank but still on, the green digits "03" glowing in the top right corner. The Beta machine was open; when the tape reached the end, it was ejected rather than automatically rewinding like a VHS. I ran my tongue over my teeth and smacked my lips to get the dry taste of sleep out of my mouth. There was a knock at the door. It had the urgent rap of a second knock, and I wondered if the first was what woke me up.

"Mom?"

I got off the couch and walked to the front door. I peered out through the peephole at two rumpled men in short-sleeve dress shirts and ugly ties. I opened the door.

"Owen?" the man on the left said.

On the street were three nondescript American cars. I nodded.

"Son, I'm Detective Grogan, and this is Detective Williams. Is your mother home?"

"I think so." I turned around, holding my arm out and against the door as if I were barring their entry.

"Owen?" Across the room, at the edge of the hallway, stood my mother, hovering, like a ghost preparing to enter a room. She said my name as neither statement nor question, but as an expression of terror.

"Mrs. Webb?" Grogan said. "Is your husband home?"

"What's this about?"

Grogan took a step into the house, pushing me aside without laying a hand on me. In the air he lifted his left hand, holding a piece of blue paper folded into thirds. Williams entered right behind him and scanned our living room with his narrow eyes.

"Mrs. Webb," Grogan said. "Is your husband home?"

"What is that?" I asked, looking at the paper in his hand. Even when I asked, I knew it was a warrant.

"Owen," my mother said. "Go to your room. Right now."

I hurried past her and shut my bedroom door, the latch clicking loudly. I pressed my ear against the door, but I couldn't hear anything they said. Out the window, a third man in short sleeves and a tie walked around the yard, eyeing the house, his belt sagging from the weight of his holster and badge. This was, I was sure, about the stolen tickets. I had fucked up. I should have told my mom. But I didn't. I had lied, and now, because I hadn't told the truth, the cops were here, about to break down doors and arrest my father, all because I hadn't been man enough to tell my mom what happened.

I slinked to the floor, curled my knees to my chest, and pressed my hands against my head. All this was my fault.

With a knock, my door opened, and my mother strode into the room carrying her purse. Her eyes were red and raw, her cheeks bloodless.

"Get up," she said. "We're going out."

"What's going on?"

"I'll explain in the car."

But she didn't. In silence, she drove toward the city, hopped on the Lateral, and took us to the new Showcase Cinemas with the cushy green chairs that tilted backward. On the wide concrete pavilion outside the shiny new theater, my mother told me to stay put, and then she hurried over to a group of pay phones. She kept her back to me, gesturing frantically with her left hand. Once, for just a moment, she turned her face toward the theater, and in profile, I could see that her eyes were frantic and her cheeks streaked with tears. Her mouth moved rapidly and mechanically, like a puppet's.

Inside, she bought us a large popcorn and soda. We watched *Under Siege 2*—which I had already seen two times—without comment. Afterward, we walked outside and stood on the concrete pavilion. By then I was taller than my mother, and I dipped my chin a little downward to watch her scan the parking lot for our car, her eyes flipping from row to row, seeking something she clearly was in no rush to find. I knew we were in the fourth row to our left, but I didn't say anything. We stood there for a long time, and then she led us over to the curb and pulled on my hand to sit down with her. She stretched out her legs, and I pulled my knees up to my chin.

"Owen," she said. "I don't know where to start."

"It's my fault. Mom, I'm sorry, it's my fault."

"Baby, it's not your fault. No one made your father do what he did."

"But I didn't say anything."

She turned her head. "What are you talking about?"

"The tickets. The stolen tickets. Dad said that if anyone asked, I was supposed to say we bought them from the black guy, not that he got them from work. He said not to tell you."

"Your father told you to lie for him?"

"I didn't know what to do. He was so pissed. You know how he gets when he gets real quiet."

And then my mother got angry. Her eyes pooled, and all the muscles in her face tightened. "Goddamn it."

"I should have said something," I continued, tears running down my face. "I know I should have. I'm so sorry. I'm really, really sorry."

She closed her eyes and ran a palm up the side of her face. When she opened her eyes, she tried to smile. This only made me cry harder.

My mother reached up and pulled me against her shoulder. She stroked my hair, and I took in the strawberry scent of her shampoo. She cooed my name, and eventually my crying turned to sniveling and she let go; I sat up and wiped my face on her T-shirt, which I knew she hated. Mom looked out on the parking lot and sighed deeply.

"The police," she said, "didn't show up because of a couple of baseball tickets. There is a lot more to this. That's just one more shitty thing your father did. Apparently, your father has been lying about a whole lot of things."

And then she started explaining. How my father was a thief.

According to the police, despite my father having a career as a lab chemist, he had been breaking into homes for almost fifteen years. He broke door locks or cut windows and slipped in and took cash, jewelry, credit cards, electronics. Then he tore the homes apart, slicing open couches and chairs and mattresses, spray painting the walls, shattering all the glasses and dishes onto the kitchen floor. He didn't just steal: he terrorized. Not just homes of strangers who had more money than us, but those of neighbors, people who lived two or three blocks away. In the affectless voice of a victim still in shock, my mother explained to me how she had no idea, had never known, and she couldn't understand how she had lived the last fifteen years without really knowing the man she called her husband.

"So," she said, "your grandfather is coming up from Florida tomorrow."

"For what?"

"To help. To be here."

"He hates me."

"No, he doesn't," she lied. "He's just gruff. That's just his way."

When we arrived home, she parked the car in the driveway, and we got out and took in the emptiness: all the boxy police sedans were gone, and not a single light was on in the house. The lawn was littered with cigarette butts, which sat atop the grass like dead fish. Inside, things were gone: the living room television and the VCR, several lamps, even the refrigerator. I went down to the basement and found that our old fridge was now jammed with all the food from upstairs. In my bedroom, my computer and stereo were gone; so too were the autographed baseballs my father often gave me as birthday gifts.

My father didn't leave us a note. There was nothing from the police.

"Why is our refrigerator gone?" I asked.

"I have no idea."

"So we just call the nearest police station and say, 'Hey, is my dad in your jail?'"

"I don't know," she said softly. "Go to bed. I'll figure out what to do."

I folded my arms across my chest and watched my mother stare out the kitchen window.

"I checked," I said. "All our food is downstairs. We don't have to go to Kroger."

"Great," she whispered. After what felt like a long time, she said, "It's okay. I'll find out what's going on. Go to sleep. We've both had a long day."

My bedroom was different then. It wasn't just the missing stereo or the missing autographed baseballs. It was that everything seemed, somehow, artificial, as if all my clothes and books and posters knew something about the house that I had never seen. I didn't trust them. I didn't feel safe around them. I opened my closet and took down my largest duffel bag. I threw in my basketball shoes and shorts, a couple of T-shirts, socks, and underwear, not even thinking about how the clothes looked or what matched. I zipped the bag and stared at the clothes on my hangers. What was I doing? Where would I go?

I picked up the phone and called Carson. I hadn't heard from him since school ended, and I had no idea when he would return. Or if he had already. The phone rang and rang, and after what felt like a dozen rings his voicemail announced his mailbox was full and then disconnected my call. On the pushboard above my desk were three postcards from Caitlin. When I had received the first of her postcards, a picture of the Arc de Triomphe at night, I flipped it over, wondering who I knew in France. She said little in such a short space, but I was mostly delighted she had written me at all. She sent a postcard almost once a week, never with a return address; two had been written entirely in French, which I did not read or understand. The images included tacky tourist shots with heavy font screaming "PARIS," artworks like Klimt's *The Kiss,* and a black-and-white photo of Hemingway and Stein. I tapped the well-rounded corners of her most recent postcard, Toulouse-Lautrec's *In Bed,* and called Caitlin's line.

She, too, did not answer the phone. When my call went to her voicemail, I said, "Hey, Caitlin, it's me, Owen. Just, um, I don't know if you're back, but if you are, would you call me? I really need—" I stared at the beam of light coming from under the door, the only light in my dark bedroom, trying to think of what I needed, and my mind went blank for what felt like a long time. "I just need. I just need."

My voice cracked, and I wiped the tears welling up in my eyes. "I just need you to call back." I hung up the phone and held it in my two hands as if it could spring to life.

All my Rockcastle clothes, the button-downs and ties and blazers, remained untouched. School started in four weeks. Never looking away, I sat down on my bed and wondered what everyone would say about me.

"His name is Joseph Webb," I heard my mother say from the other room. "Yes, officer. He was arrested tonight."

• • •

When I woke up in the morning, I was still wearing the same clothes. I didn't remember falling asleep or getting into bed, but there I was, with the sheets pulled up high to my chin. I changed into clean basketball clothes and popped my strep medicine. My throat felt normal. In the kitchen, my mom was making a breakfast of eggs, sausage, and toast, while across the room, sitting by himself at the kitchen table with two newspapers, was my maternal grandfather. He wore a Polo shirt and khakis and boat shoes with no socks, his gray hair immaculately parted. Although he was not a large man, his presence seemed to fill the kitchen. I hadn't seen him in five years. When he looked up, he set aside the personal finance section of the *Wall Street Journal* and steepled his hands together on the table. His mouth smiled; his eyes didn't.

He was a Navy man, a fact he often liked to remind people of, and after the service he spent his entire life as an electrical engineer for General Electric. I didn't remember my grandmother—she died when I was four—but he never remarried, never seemed to think of women as anything other than a nuisance. He hated my father from the day my mother announced she was pregnant, and one of the few jokes my father and I shared was always at my grandfather's expense. When I was very young, we saw him at Christmas, and that was all; once a year, my mother drove down to visit him, and my father and I happily stayed home and ate pizza and burgers for a week. My grandfather had never shown any interest in me. He sent a birthday card and a Christmas card, usually with a check enclosed that bore the phrase "college education" scrawled in the memo space. In my baby pictures, he is smiling and proud while holding me in his lap, his grin wolfish and unnatural.

"Good morning," Mom said. "Why don't you sit down and eat something?"

I did as I was told. The *Enquirer* sat in the middle of the table. I pawed it open, looking for the sports page. The paper was still perfectly creased and apparently unopened.

"Where's the metro section?" I asked. I flipped the corners again and found sections A–E, but D wasn't there. I don't know why I asked. I never read the metro section. I looked up. Mom's eyes were lowered, but my grandfather was looking at me.

"We've had," he said, "an unfortunate situation here. Did you sleep okay?"

I shrugged.

"You're like me. No matter how bad my day was, I always slept at night. The Navy will do that to a man. It shows good character, I think." He flipped his palm upward and glanced at the ceiling. "Especially in a place like this."

"A place like what?"

"I believe in being direct with people, Owen. I don't like to dance around a subject. So. I've talked it over with your mother, and we agreed. How would you feel about coming to stay with me for a few weeks?"

"In Florida?"

"That's right."

I looked over his shoulders at my mother. Her eyes remained focused on smearing jelly onto toast.

"I'd rather stay here," I said.

"Just for the summer. Until school starts. Until things return to normal."

"I gotta stay here and play ball. Me and Carson are trying to start varsity."

"You mean 'Carson and I,' not 'me and Carson.' Speak properly." He sighed and spread his hands flat on the table. "Your mother has told me how important basketball is to you. And about your friend. I believe I can find a coach for you in the city, someone who can do some extra work on your basketball skills. Further, a friend of mine has a restaurant near the coast, and he could use your help. A summer job would be a really good experience for a young man. How does that sound?"

"Mom?"

"Owen." My grandfather did not blink. "You and I are talking."

My mother seemed so young then, unmoving and porcelain. She wasn't going to help me. I turned my chin back toward my grandfather.

"I'm not going to Florida."

"I understand why you would feel that way right now. But your father? He's in a lot of trouble. I'm going to post his bail today, and then he'll be at home until his trial starts. It might be better if you weren't around to witness these next few weeks."

"To 'witness' it? Is he being executed in the town square?"

Without taking his eyes off me, my grandfather said, "Does he talk this way all the time?"

"Dad, take it easy on him."

"I don't know what's going on," I said. I stared at the newspaper, knowing full well why the local section had been removed. "Where's the metro?"

"If basketball is all you care about, I'm sure we can find some sort of basketball camp you can spend all your time at. You'll come back here in great shape for the new school year."

"Is he serious?"

My grandfather's hand shot out, grabbed my wrist, and squeezed.

"You need to learn that when you're talking to an elder, you are talking to an elder, not to someone standing behind him."

The grip was painful and shockingly strong. I squirmed, mouth open in surprise. My mother raced over, but as if her father were a hot stove, she kept her hands to herself. Her eyes wet with tears, she pleaded, "Dad! You're hurting him."

I snatched the *Enquirer* and with it cracked my grandfather hard across the face. "Fucking Christ!" he screamed. My arm free, I bolted out of the room and into the garage, ignoring my mother's screams for me to come back, hopped on my bike, and raced down the driveway and into the street. Convinced they would follow me, I pedaled up a lawn and raced between two houses and through two backyards, zipped across the parallel street, up and through another two backyards, and then veered south, heading for Clifton. Colerain Road was downhill all the way, and I wanted to put miles between myself and home. After a few blocks I changed my mind, pedaled behind a church, and hopped off my bike. Bracing myself against a brick wall—legs shaking from exhaustion, adrenaline finally slowing—I started laughing.

I kept seeing my grandfather's face snap back. Over and over again. His eyes getting big, then—*boom!*—black-and-white print blocking out his angry face, his glasses leaping into the air like a cartoon. I laughed so hard my ribs hurt. I dropped down onto my butt and leaned against the wall, then breathed in deep and slow. Felt good to hit him. Felt really good to hit him.

"Fuck that guy," I whispered.

I picked up my bike and steered it to the pay phone at the Walgreens across the street. I called Carson and let his line ring twelve times before hanging up. I didn't know if he was back in town, but if he was then he'd certainly seen the news about my father. I hadn't really stopped to consider what I thought of it all. In many ways, my situation was the same as my mother's: I lived in a house with a complete stranger, yet some of the odd things—the baseball tickets, the mattress in the basement—started to make sense, the way a large puzzle looks more like the picture on the box after two or three major pieces click into place.

I stepped out of the phone booth and thought about what I should do next. I wasn't sure when I could go home, but I did know it couldn't be any time soon. I hopped on my bike and pedaled toward the courts down in Clifton. I'd find a game. I'd waste time there for a few hours and then call home, and maybe I'd only get chewed out a little bit rather than a lot.

Of the four courts, one had a game going, and two people were shooting solo on the second. Good enough. I leaned my bike against the bleachers and asked the two shooters if they had next. They said no, but we agreed to run together, and then the losing team shot competitive free throws for two spots. Everyone seemed a little bit older than me, but I couldn't tell if they were in high school or college.

I coasted through the first game, mostly passing, just getting a sweat up. Someone said, "Run it back," so we did, and this time I decided to start shooting. I realized pretty fast that the guy guarding me wasn't very good, and for some reason, I decided to let him know. At first, it was just a comment here or there—"Can't guard me," "Too late," "Not today, son"—but soon I was driving around him and flipping layups, and it became a running commentary.

He started talking back and grabbing my shorts, my wrist, my elbow, and I pushed him off, first lightly, then harder. One of the older guys told us to chill. "Just play ball," he said.

My team was winning, 11–6 in a game to 15, and I caught the ball at the three-point line. My defender clutched my right shoulder. With both hands on the ball, I swung my arms down and whipped the ball up to my left shoulder. I pivoted on my right foot, pulling my left behind me. He grabbed my right hip, digging his fingernails into my stomach, and stepped into my space. I swung the ball again, this time with my elbows high, and cracked the kid right in the temple.

He screamed and stepped back. All the other players straightened up out of their crouches, standing flat rather than on the balls of their feet.

"What's your fucking problem?" my defender screamed, clutching his head.

"You're my fucking problem! Keep your fucking hands off me!"

He stepped to me and shoved me with two hands.

"Fuck you!" he yelled.

I flew forward with a fist. His nose crunched. Someone yelled, "Damn!" I grabbed the kid with my left hand and punched him again with my right. He tumbled, and I crashed down on top of him and pummeled him with punches. Someone put me in a chokehold, and two other guys pulled at my arms. They dragged me off the court and shoved me aside.

"Goddamn, man," said one. "What's wrong with you?"

"Man, fuck that guy," I said. "He started it."

"Hey, look, whatever. You need to get out of here, okay?"

"Why do I have to go?"

"Do you see that fucking guy's nose?"

We all turned. On the pavement, sitting upright, was the kid I had just beaten up. His eyes were glassy and unfocused, and blood ran from his nose onto his shirt. There was already swelling around his eyes, and all the kids circled around him were staring back at me.

"So?" I said.

The guy turned back around. He was older than me, maybe a college freshman. He took one step toward me and lowered his chin.

"If anyone calls the cops," he whispered. His voice was very soft, soothing like a balm, and the sincerity of it made me look up. "Every motherfucker is going to point at you. Look, nobody wants trouble, okay? Just go. Get the fuck outta here."

Maybe it was his level voice or the idea of the police, but his words snapped through me, and suddenly I was scared and sorry and no longer recognized myself. I nodded once, then turned away. I tried not to run. Without looking back, I picked up my bike and pedaled away.

I spent the rest of the day wandering around the suburbs of Cincinnati. I zipped over to the pool and sat on the patio and watched teenagers jump off the diving board and kids splash in the shallow end. The bowling alley opened at noon, and I played video games there for a little while, then sat down and watched people bowl, wondering why they weren't at work. I wandered through a comic book store, reading *The Amazing Spider Man* and *Punisher.* I sat in a park and watched a bunch of college kids play a game of soccer. Soon it was dusk, then dark. All day long my stomach grumbled, but I had no money, and I got by drinking from water fountains until my stomach gave up on me and I no longer felt any hunger pains. Every time I saw a cop car, I braced myself for the lights to turn on, spinning punishing blues and reds, sirens howling, doors opening to throw me in the back seat and drag me away. But the patrol cars just passed me by. Three times that day I called Carson's line, and not once did the phone ring fewer than a dozen times, and not once did he pick up.

When I finally got home, it was well after dark, and my legs ached from pedaling all day. My hands were swollen from the fight, the knuckles scraped. Caked in sweat, I smelled horrible. I hopped off my bike a few driveways from my house and walked it the rest of the way. At our driveway, I froze. My mother sat on the porch smoking, a bottle of wine and the cordless phone at her feet. All sorts of excuses ran through my mind, none of them any good, and I finally crossed the grass and dumped my bike on the lawn. The stairs creaked under my weight, and I plopped into the chair next to her. She eyed me as if I weren't quite in focus.

"It's after eleven," she said.

"Sorry," I said.

She watched the street and let her cigarette burn down to the filter.

"Your grandfather left," she finally said. "Took a flight back to Florida this afternoon. I'm sure you already know that the offer to stay with him has been rescinded."

"Rescinded?"

"Don't know that word, prep-school boy?"

"To take away."

"Yup. Taken away. Lot of taking away going on around here."

I looked down at my hands. "Sorry."

"Whatever. It wasn't a good idea. Sending you down to Florida. I don't know what I was thinking. I mean, I was thinking that getting away from this shit would be good for you. But it must have felt like I was trying to get rid of you. I wasn't. I was.... Shit, Owen, I don't know what I'm doing. I don't know what to do."

"Neither do I."

"You aren't supposed to. You're fourteen, for Christ's sake."

Carson told me that when you don't know what to say in a conversation, count down from ten. Slowly. "People love to talk," he said. "Just wait them out." I only got to seven before my mother spoke again.

"Your grandfather," she said, "is a son of a bitch."

"I know."

"Did you see his glasses fly off?"

"No."

She tried to suppress a smile. "Really?"

I looked up and saw her grin. I shrugged. She laughed.

"How many times in my life," she wondered, "have I wanted to hit him in the face. A hundred? Two hundred? And then you bolt out of the house like the Br'er Rabbit. Jesus."

Ash tumbled off her cigarette.

"Mom? What's gonna happen to us?"

"I don't know, Owen. I really don't know."

She poured more wine into her glass and sniffed. I went inside and made a sandwich and grabbed a bag of potato chips and came back to the porch. I wolfed down my food, and she ate some of the chips. But for the rest of the night, we didn't talk anymore.

PART II

IX

I walked to the library and found the *Cincinnati Enquirer* from the day after my father's arrest. He was the front-page story in the metro section, with the headline "Average Citizen Held in Burglary Investigation." The Hamilton County investigators had been after him for years and were stunned to arrest a Procter & Gamble chemist, a college-educated man, rather than their original profile of a high school dropout. According to the paper, though my father was suspected of crimes in Kentucky, Indiana, and Ohio, he was officially charged with eight counts of burglary and robbery, ending what one cop called "a fifteen-year spree of terror" in the community.

The break in the case had been a sale just three weeks earlier of suspiciously rare coins to a shop in Northgate Mall. When I read that I knew: they were the coins from the coffee table, and my father sold them after I spilled soda all over them. The police spokesman stated that after all those years of careful work, it was almost like Joseph Webb was trying to get caught.

• • •

After my mother bought a new fridge for the upstairs, then carefully sorted through every food item to decide what to keep, after she went back to work and found her coworkers to be sympathetic, after she spent nights wandering the house and staring silently into open closets while cataloging all the things that had been in her home and wondering which had been stolen and which purchased with stolen money, she swallowed her pride and cashed the check my grandfather had mailed from Florida. She used the money to replace the living room TV and to purchase a used computer so I could type my papers. She decided she had been humbled enough and would drive to the Hamilton County jail in downtown Cincinnati to pay my father's bail and bring him home.

I was lying on the couch watching a Stallone movie when my mother told me she was going to get him. Carson and Caitlin were the only two people I wanted to talk to about what had happened, and when I hadn't been able to reach them right after my father's arrest, I decided I didn't want to talk to anyone. Not that anyone had called our house other than reporters.

"Is that okay with you?" my mother asked, cradling her purse.

"What's he gonna be like?"

"I don't know."

"I mean, I can't really say no, can I?"

"You could."

I shrugged, and with that, she left. I didn't see what say I had in the matter one way or the other. If I was honest with myself, I didn't know how I felt about my father coming home. I still couldn't picture what I had read in the newspapers, seen on the television news, and heard from my mother: my father, the thief, slipping into homes by picking locks, cutting glass, and disabling alarm systems, and taking whatever he could stuff into a small blue or black duffel bag. My time at Rockcastle made me conscious of how little I actually possessed—that my family was, if not poor, what a sociologist would call "lower middle class." Until I went to a private school, I never felt like I was really missing anything. I wore basketball shorts and hooded sweatshirts most of the year; when it got cold I wore jeans. We had cable in the house. It didn't seem like any of the three of us particularly bought much, we had two old but functional cars, and we never went on vacation. My father didn't steal to provide for us. He stole because he enjoyed stealing. He stole because it terrified and humiliated and haunted people, and inflicting this kind of horror is what he wanted more than anything.

Who was my father?

After she left, I decided I couldn't sit there and wait. I put on my shoes and headed out to the nearest court. It was still early in the morning, dew shimmering on the grass, no one in the park but morning joggers doing a few loops before heading to work. I shot jumpers, alternating sides of the court, twenty from each spot, until I felt enough time had passed. I dribbled the ball all the way home and entered through the always unlocked side door. The television, which I had turned off, was on, and when I came in through the kitchen, my father was on the couch in roughly the same position I had been: head propped up with his bent right arm, cable box on his stomach, shoes off, and feet up. I wondered if there were other traits in me besides seating posture that I had unwillingly inherited from him. It could have been any other day in his life.

"You're home," I said.

"That's right." He turned off the television, set the cable box down with great care, and stood. With his hands on his hips, he faced me, a grimace on his face. He seemed diminished somehow, not nearly as tall, not nearly as confident, his shoulder curling inward slightly, as if he was afraid of getting punched. "Shooting some hoop?"

I looked at the basketball in my hand as if I were unsure how it got there.

"Where's Mom?"

"She went to the grocery store. She thought it would be a good idea if you and I talked a little bit, just you and me."

"Oh. Right. Sure."

"You doing okay?" he asked.

"I guess so. I mean, it's pretty weird."

"Yeah. I'm really sorry, Owen."

"About what?"

"For all of it."

"That's okay." I really had no idea what to say to him, and I also had no idea what he meant, what he was referring to. Grammar from my English class floated through my head, and I wasn't sure what "it" stood for, and even if that was clarified, whether it had meaning to either one of us.

"No, it isn't," he said. "I screwed up. Really screwed up. C'mere, sit down."

I came around and dropped into the recliner across from him. He fell back onto the couch, his elbows on his knees, focusing his gaze on some spot between us.

"I'm probably going away for a while," he said. "It's still in discussion, but I might be looking at a long time."

"How long?"

"Fifteen years."

I snorted. This could not be real.

"What did you do?"

"I stole. I broke into people's homes and stole things. I'm sorry, Owen."

"But why?"

"I don't know. I'm still sorting that out. I've had a lot of time to think while I've been locked up. The important thing right now is that I'm not going to be here, and you're going to be the man of the house. You know? So, you need to step up."

"I'm fourteen. What exactly am I supposed to do?"

"Oh, you know. Help around the house. Not give your mother so much grief. Stuff like that."

"Stuff like that. Sure."

He leveled his gaze at me, and then shook his head as if discarding the idea of what he was going to say next.

"I know you're pissed at me," he said. "I'm really sorry."

"Stop saying that! Sorry for what?"

"All of it."

"Fuck you." I stood up, the ball bouncing to the floor.

"Owen. Son."

I walked out, went to my room, and locked the door. I slipped on my headphones and turned on my Walkman, and when my father knocked, I turned the music up louder. He continued knocking, then tried the doorknob. There was a souvenir from one of our Reds games, a black mini-bat with the fake signature of Dave Parker, on the floor of my closet, and I picked it up, tightening my grip around the small handle, and waited for my father to come through so I could finally have a reason to hit him.

But he didn't. The knocking stopped. I sat down on my bed, holding the bat, and waited. The song ended, then the next one, and then the next one. Then I was afraid. I didn't want to go out there. I'd seen how furious my father could get when he was angry, and I thought he might be waiting for me, fists up, chin defiantly thrown forward, on the other side of the door, looking for the honesty that you only find in a fistfight. I got off the bed and slid down to the floor, under the window, my knees pulled up toward my chin. I watched the door, waiting for it to split open and for my father to charge in.

I stayed in my room, despite my gnawing hunger. No way was I going out in the kitchen. When the phone rang, I picked up on the first ring.

"Hey, man," Carson said.

"About time."

"I got back from Spain yesterday. I just heard about your dad."

"He came home today."

"What's it like?"

"Fucked up." I heard my mother's car pull up and the engine cut out and the front door open. I cracked my bedroom door open. I looked down the hall; their bedroom door was closed, and when I looked right, my mother was setting down groceries on the kitchen table.

"I gotta call you back," I said, then beeped the cordless off.

"Where's your father?" she asked.

"I dunno," I said, looking at the empty living room couch, the black television screen. "In bed, I guess."

"Come help me finish unloading."

I went out to the car and carried two paper bags of groceries inside. Our kitchen fridge was a new, cheap model, recently purchased on credit because our old fridge had been purchased with a stolen credit card. Its doors remained bare: magnets sat in a pile on the kitchen table, and whatever scraps we had put on the doors over the years—my school photos, takeout menus, a whiteboard for notes to each other, coupons, numbers for plumbers and electricians—were gone. Thrown away, perhaps; I didn't know. I started unloading the food. My mother had bought enough to feed an army, and I wasn't sure why. We never ate this much, and we certainly weren't about to have any visitors. We unloaded steaks, chicken, and pork chops. Two dozen frozen dinners. Fresh vegetables and fruits: bananas, apples, oranges, tomatoes. There were two loaves of bread, cans of soup, three types of soda. It seemed like she had gone through the store and grabbed one of any and every thing that entered her mind. When we were finished, and the paper sacks were folded and stored under the kitchen sink next to the cleaning products and trash bags, she sat down at the kitchen table and lit a cigarette. "Get me a beer, would you?" she asked.

I popped one open, slid it across to her, and sat down. "You want one?" she asked.

"No."

"Have you tried drinking yet?"

I thought about saying no. But my father's worst sin was lying, and so I nodded.

"What did you think?"

"Tastes funny."

"It's an acquired taste." She sucked on her cigarette. "My father used to say that about his drinking. That it was for adults and everything. I hated that. It was so—" She flopped her hand in the air.

"Condescending," I said.

"Right. Definitely. Condescending." She studied her untouched beer and I wondered if she suddenly remember it was barely ten in the morning. "That party you went to with Carson?"

"Yeah. They had a keg. And bottles. And cans."

"Sounds like a good one."

"I drank it because everyone else did."

"That's how everyone starts drinking. No one really wants to. When I was a girl, I started with wine coolers. They're really sweet, like pop, and you don't realize how drunk you're getting. It takes a while to get used to the harder stuff."

We sat in silence. I stood up and grabbed a Coke from the fridge, its humming the only noise in the house. I thought about turning on the radio, but my mother continued to be on the verge of saying something. Something rose up in her chest, her eyes raised expectantly, and then it would sink again, back down into her stomach, and she ashed her cigarette instead.

Finally, she said, "Don't ever lie to me, Owen. Understand? Ever."

"Okay."

"I mean it."

I nodded. "Hey, could you give me a ride to Carson's house?"

"You're leaving already?"

"I don't have anything to say to Dad. And I don't want Carson coming here."

Her gaze, blank and unreadable, scanned my entire face. Then she looked at my shoulder and seemed to be once again weighing something she couldn't entirely find words for.

"I'll take you over there. Sure. Why don't you pack a bag for a few nights? You don't mind staying there for a few days, do you?"

"You sure?"

"You don't want to?"

"No, I want to, just, you know."

"Your father and I could use a little time. Just the two of us."

I picked up my Coke. "Now?"

"No time like the present."

Off the floor of my bedroom I picked up my duffel bag and shoveled in a random assortment of underwear, basketball shorts, and T-shirts. I threw in my sandals and enough socks, which I always seemed to forget. It only took me a few minutes to pack. I picked up the cordless and called Carson. He didn't answer.

But this time, I got his voicemail; if nothing else, he was checking—or maybe just deleting—his messages. I said, "Hey, it's Owen. I'm coming over. Things are fucked up over here so, you know, maybe we can hang out and stuff. Um. I'm on the way, actually, so I'll see you when I get there."

When I emerged into the hallway, my mother was waiting, purse and keys in hand.

In the car, she let me pick the radio station, and we didn't speak. Silent car rides were becoming normal, and in later years I preferred to drive in complete silence, no talk, no radio, just the whirling noise of the city outside, with me sealed off from the world. When we pulled up to Carson's house, the garage doors were open, and three cars were visible.

"Call me when you want me to come get you," my mother said.

It didn't occur to me for months that I was being abandoned. What my mother suggested—get away from here, Owen, run if you have to—was selfish of her, leaving me to fend for myself, sending me off to a family I knew she didn't like or trust. But my father, for all his flaws and lies and deceit and anger and abuse, was the center of my mother's world, and she couldn't look at me again until she had tried to make that world right.

I got out of the car, grabbed my bag from the back seat, slammed the door closed, and waved. She smiled and waved back as if she were merely dropping me off for another day at Rockcastle, and as soon as I turned away she put the car in gear and backed down the driveway, into the street, and was gone.

In the garage, without the direct sunlight firing down on me, I wiped my forehead, uncertain if I should just walk in or knock or if anyone would even hear me if I did. Carson's Audi was parked closest to the doors, the rims and bumpers shiny, the paint gleaming, as if the whole thing had just been freshly waxed. I peeked into the front seat hoping to see the glove box open and the gun sitting there, ready to be plucked like fruit from a tree. Of course, the glove box wasn't open and the passenger door was locked. An image ran through my mind of pointing the gun at my dad and making him drop to his knees in apology, tears streaming down his red face, begging. Then both the image and the anger were gone, and I entered the house through the garage. I walked down the long hallway, and outside the kitchen I dropped my bag on the floor. There were two empty cereal bowls on the kitchen table, the spoons speckled with bits of cereal and dried milk. An opened Diet Coke sat next to an empty glass whose insides were streaked with orange-juice pulp. I walked past the table and looked out onto the brick patio at the lawn furniture with its clean cushions and placemats. No one was there.

"Owen?"

I turned. At the threshold stood Caitlin, in shorts and a T-shirt, her hair pulled back into a loose ponytail.

"Your garage door was open," I said.

She rushed across the room and threw her arms around my neck. She smelled like spice and oranges, and when I finally hugged her back, I closed my eyes, pressed my cheek against her hair, and breathed in deeply. She stepped back, clutching my elbows, and appraised me.

"We saw the news," she said. "What the fuck is going on?"

"I don't know. He came home today."

"What did he say?"

"Nothing, really. I mean, he said he was sorry, but in that way like you don't really have anything else to say."

"C'mere," she said, pulling me toward the kitchen table. "Sit down and tell me. Do you want coffee?"

"I don't really drink coffee."

"Soda? Or I can put lots of sugar in your coffee. That's what I do. And cream!" She sat me down and bounded over to the counter. She brought back a full carafe and two mugs, then raced back to the fridge and grabbed three different types of creamer. From the island, she snatched a sugar bowl and set it directly in front of me. She shook her head while she poured a cup of coffee for me and then for herself. Even with the sugar and the French vanilla creamer I added to my mug, I could taste that the coffee at the Blys' was much better than my father's Maxwell House.

"So, oh my god, how are you?" Caitlin leaned toward me, her eyes wide.

"I'm okay, I guess. It's weird. We aren't really talking about it. Maybe we're all in shock." She nodded, and so I told her the whole story: about being sick and the cops showing up and how we came home to find things missing and no note from my father. About my grandfather showing up the next morning and how I'd hit him. About the fight on the playground. And how these last few days, my mother only talked when she was on the phone with the lawyer or with her friends, trying to gather information about what my father did and how much time he might serve. Otherwise, the phone had been off the hook to keep the reporters away, and my mother and I both remained silent—she watching television and me playing video games—as if we were waiting for a letter that we knew would never be delivered.

"We called, you know," Caitlin said. "Your line was always busy. But we've called."

I nodded.

"No, really," she insisted. "No one forgot about you."

I smiled tightly and stared at my hands. I wasn't sure I believed her.

"So, like, all the stuff in your house was stolen?"

"No. Nothing actually belonged to anyone else. He would steal stuff, then sell it or pawn it, take cash, credit cards. So the cops took what they could tie directly to the crimes. One of our televisions, but not both of them. One of our fridges. Some autographed baseballs. The washer and dryer. Rare coins. We still have furniture and stuff."

"So it wasn't to buy stuff. It was just to do it?"

"Yeah. Stealing just to steal."

She shook her head.

"We didn't need any of it," I said. "He wouldn't let my mom work. Or she didn't want to. I don't know. I mean, she had a part-time job at the library, you know, just afternoons, and that seemed okay. We don't have all this nice shit like you guys have, but we didn't want for anything, I don't think. I don't know. It just doesn't make sense. He had a job. He's a chemist."

"The paper said the cops were kinda stunned that it was him. They were looking for a high school dropout, not a middle-class dad."

"I didn't really ask if I could crash here, but—"

"Owen, c'mon. Of course. Stay with us. In fact, you aren't allowed to leave."

"Where's Carson? I just talked to him."

"Probably went back to bed. We usually stay up late in the summer."

I looked at the cereal bowls.

"That's from last night," she said. "Or earlier this morning. Fruity Pebbles are so good they might as well be dessert. Let's get you some sun. C'mon, we'll jump in the pool."

I changed in the hall bathroom, then went out on the patio and crossed the courtyard. Caitlin was yanking her T-shirt over her head, revealing that she was already wearing a green bikini, held her arms out, then arched her back in the sunlight and dropped her shirt melodramatically. She unbuttoned her tattered jean shorts, shook her hips, and pushed the shorts down the length of her tan legs. I stopped short, taking in her beauty. She turned her head and beamed, posing with her hands on her hips and her left heel raised off the concrete. Then she laughed uproariously and, with her sunglasses still on, she took two long strides and leaped into the pool, screaming at the top of her jump before cannonballing into the water.

"Owen! Hurry up!"

I did as I was told.

We didn't plan well, so we constantly were hopping out of the pool: to turn on the cabana stereo, grab cold sodas, grab snacks, find towels, sunscreen, and hats, and sunglasses for me. We played a couple of games of Nerf basketball in the water, and she started a monologue about Ursuline and the girls in her grade and her soccer and lacrosse teams. Her face was a master class in the variety of expressions one can make, shifting from horror to delight to terror to frustration to rage to shyness, opening up to me in a kaleidoscope of personality.

We were sitting on the steps in the pool, and she told a story about falling into mud at summer camp, a story that had her laughing so hard she clutched her knees. When she sat up, her hair was falling around her face, and I reached over and tucked it behind her ear, and then kept my hand lightly against her skin. She turned. Her face was filled with delight and surprise, the sun making her squint. I leaned in and kissed her. For a moment, we just held our lips together, and then she put her arms around me, the splash of water the only sound I heard. I don't know how long we were making out, but after what felt like several minutes, she pulled away and held my shoulders at arm's length.

"Wow," she said. Then she laughed, stood, and fell backward into the pool. She swam its length, her body stretching in slow, insouciant strokes, and when she reached the other end, she turned underwater and butterflied back to me.

We were still in the pool when Carson finally came outside. I didn't know what time it was. Our heads were bobbing in the water, and our conversation and laughter ended when he approached the edge of the pool. He loomed over us, unsmiling and appraising. He wore a wrinkled button-down and yellow basketball shorts. Either he slept in those clothes or had grabbed the nearest thing off the floor.

"You okay?" he said.

"We're fine," Caitlin said.

He sneered, "Not you."

"Yeah, I'm all right," I said.

"Really? Good. Let me know when you're ready to work."

"Work?"

"We haven't played all summer. I need to see how your game is." Then, finally, he smiled, turned on his heel, and walked away.

Caitlin's expression was now wiped blank, an adult look of controlled indifference. Drops of water ran down from her scalp and dripped off her chin. I had no idea what she was feeling, but after Carson vanished back into the house, her eyes dropped, and she tipped her chin toward the sky and backstroked away from me to the far end of the pool.

Back in the bathroom, the stench of chlorine clinging to my skin, I changed again and laced my shoes tight. In the driveway, where the black asphalt steamed hot, Carson skipped around the three-point line, a dotted perimeter painted in bright yellow paint. The basketball hoop was a Goalrilla with a high-end glass backboard, a breakaway rim, and a heavy-duty base. It was like having a Rockcastle setup on a playground.

"Let's warm up with Around the World," he said.

I missed my first two, and Carson made it to the top of the key before missing twice. We both were rusty: he was probably still half asleep, and I had spent the last hour in the pool. But on my third attempt I hit my first shot, then my second and third, and I went all the way around the arc without missing. When a shot went down, Carson plucked the rebound and held it. I remained crouched, waiting for the pass. He smirked. I nodded. He threw a deliberately bad bounce pass to my right; I slid over to grab it and hopped, setting my feet in what would have been out of bounds on a normal court. I released a high, arching shot from behind the backboard that rattled down through the net. I hurried to the next spot and waited for Carson's pass.

I won that game and the next one, and then Carson said, "All right, we're warm. Let's go one on one."

"Rules?"

"Ones and twos, make it take it, to eleven. All possessions back behind the three-point line."

"Cool. Let's go."

He flipped me the ball. I wrapped two hands around it, the synthetic texture hot and a little slick from the macadam residue picked up in the day's heat. The afternoon sun pounded down on us, and I stripped off my shirt and threw it into the garage. My shoulders had widened over the last year, but I was still thin and probably gave up at least twenty-five pounds to Carson.

I checked the ball. When he checked it back, I snatched it and zipped hard right; he was caught by surprise, so

I went by him easily, even though he shoved my left hip when I blew past. One to nothing. Back at the top of the key, I went left and fired a stepback, calling glass before it banked in. Then I missed a jumper, and Carson had the ball. He drove left, then crossed over and flipped in a layup over my outstretched arm. He buried a long jumper, then another, before I finally got a stop.

I won the game, 11–9, which didn't matter. What mattered is that at some point during the game, Carson started hand checking harder, squeezing my hip, then using his hands and forearms and elbows to bump and push and grind me. I didn't hit back, figuring it was some sort of test, but by the fourth or fifth extra hit, I had had enough.

In the second game, Carson, too, stripped off his shirt. He had chest hair, dark streaks around his nipples and sternum that striped his chest all the way to his waistband. His arms were rounder and more muscular than mine, all things I knew, but under the sun, sweating, adrenaline firing, my skin unbronzed from the summer, I was both in awe of and intimidated by the sight of his bare chest. On my first possession, I again tried to drive hard right, but he was ready, slid his feet, and slapped the ball loose. He grabbed it, and even though he was three feet behind the line, launched a shot that spun perfectly through the net. Two to zero.

I cursed under my breath and checked the ball. He drove left, slamming his right elbow into my chest, and shot a fadeaway jumper. It rattled out. I corralled the rebound and dribbled out to the three-point line. I bent at the knees and raised my head as if to shoot, and when Carson rushed out, I zipped by him and flipped in an easy layup. Two to one.

Short of a punch to the head or groin, all contact became legal. A person watching basketball for the first time would have thought that Carson and I were required to hit each other at least twice before even attempting a shot. Knees to the thigh, tripping, hacks on the wrist and forearm and triceps, knuckles ground into the spine. We rarely made eye contact; all cursing was directed at the air. I didn't know what we were fighting about, only that we were fighting, and the winner was the guy who would hit the eleventh bucket.

What ended the last game—our fifth—was when I broke the unspoken rule. I was winning, 10–7. Between possessions, our hands rested on our hips, feet dragging, the sweat running down us in a steady stream, sunburns blossoming on our lower backs and necks, muscles tight and aching. I dribbled left, right, lazy, hoping to catch Carson on his heels. We were both too tired to really fight anymore. I deked left, and he cut me off, ramming his forearm into my side, so I spun right. He grabbed my shorts. He held me in place, and I swung with my left arm to break his arm free, then raced toward the baseline. Carson cut me off. I pulled up, a tough shot, a ten-footer, all about touch and feel. When he jumped to block the shot, he swung his right arm up and into my ribs. Hard. The shot was up and over his outstretched hand, his fingers just under the ball. And when I came down, I curled my shooting hand into a fist and cracked Carson in the eye.

We landed, feet tangled, and fell. Carson crashed face first into the driveway. I landed on my left shoulder, my head banging back into the pavement, my face up. He clutched his face and screamed profanities while the ball bounced off the rim, the backboard, then swirled the rim, and fell through the net.

"What the fuck, Owen?" he said, face buried in his hands.

I rolled on to my side. "What?"

"Fuck you, you know what."

"Shot went in."

He leaned back on his heels, his right eye shut tight. "Really?"

I nodded, pushing my palms down into the driveway, to stand. I didn't know then that all my anger was directed at my father, not Carson. We weren't fighting about basketball but about something else. Only now do I know that we were also fighting about Caitlin.

Carson looked down the length of the driveway, blinked open his eyes, and spit. Every muscle in my back and legs squeezed when I tried to stand, and when I was finally upright, I stood over Carson and offered my hand to help him to his feet. He took it. It was unnecessary—he knew it, and I knew it—but it was an old-world gesture that we both believed in, or, at least, a gesture we imagined a certain type of man made toward another man when there was a winner and a loser.

"C'mon," he said. "Let's sit inside and do nothing for a while."

Inside, we raided the freezer and grabbed pints of ice cream, then went to watch television. Caitlin was sprawled on the couch where I first met her, a Diet Coke resting on her stomach between her two hands. She was watching Court TV, and Marcia Clark was pointing up, to a witness we couldn't see. Behind Clark was Christopher Darden. We couldn't see O.J.

"What's happening?" Carson asked.

"Crime scene stuff. She's cross-examining one of the crime scene cops. Mazzola, I think."

"I can't believe how long this is taking."

"I liked her old haircut," I said.

"The curls?" Caitlin sat up. "Those were hideous."

"She kinda looks like Sigourney Weaver now. She was more no-nonsense before."

"I think he's going to win," Caitlin said.

"O.J.?" Carson asked. "Are you serious? He fucking killed them both."

"I know. We all know, right?" she said, looking at me. I nodded. I didn't know a soul who believed that O.J. hadn't killed his wife and her friend "But, that glove thing? That is terrible. And these cops are definitely some racist assholes."

"Doesn't mean he didn't kill them."

"I know, Carson. Jesus. I'm talking about him being acquitted. I think he gets *acquitted*. No doubt about it."

The three of us watched for about an hour. It was a rather monotonous cross-examination of a defense witness, with excruciatingly dull questions about LAPD protocol when examining a crime scene, blood splatter, footprints, broken glass, and the handling of items in the house. And yet, it was absolutely riveting. I sat up a little bit every time the camera showed O.J., who tilted slightly in his chair, his dark gray suit snug and sharp, his expression that of a man attempting to be interested. I wondered if my father's trial would be like this: drawn out and dull. I wondered if I would be allowed in the courtroom, or if it would be on television somewhere, and everyone would look at my father the way I was looking at O.J. right then: as a guilty man, a terrible man, who should be punished in the worst way possible.

"You wanna play NHL?" Carson asked.

We left Caitlin unmoving on the couch and crossed the hall to yet another room with a television. We flipped on the Sega and played NHL '94 for a few hours, until Caitlin stuck her head in and said she was ordering pizza, and we realized we were hungry.

Outside, tiki torches burned along the perimeter of the patio, casting the three of us in a warm glow against the muggy, dark night. Carson opened a case of Bud Light and handed me a beer. He offered one to Caitlin, but she shook her head, raised a Zima, and drank half the bottle in one gulp.

"I don't know how you drink that shit," Carson said. "Especially with pizza."

"I'm a chick, you're not."

"That's not an answer."

"Sure it is. Just not one you like."

I asked, "So how do you hide all the cans and bottles from your dad?"

They laughed. Carson said, "Do you think he takes the trash out on Wednesday nights? Or even looks in the cans?"

"As long as we don't touch his scotch," Caitlin said, "he doesn't care."

"Really?" I said.

"Our dad likes scotch," Carson said, "because it sounds fancy. Aged sixteen years, twenty-four years, whatever. Ask him sometime about mash and peat and the Scottish climate and what it does in the right oak barrels, and he'll never shut up."

"Scotch is nasty," Caitlin said.

"So he really doesn't care?" I asked.

"Care, know, whatever," Carson said. "He lets us do what we want. He's been leaving us at home since I started ninth grade. Dad must be gone nearly two hundred days of the year. When he's home, it's great. All Ward Cleaver and everything."

"And when he's not?"

Carson flipped up his hands. "Look around. Are you complaining?"

My parents always seemed to be around. Even if it was just one of them—my father down in the basement with his tools and woodwork, or my mother on the front porch with her cigarettes and the radio's small speakers squeaking out the Doors or the Who—their presence meant, if nothing else, that I was always safe. But now I realize that as a kid, there was something else: I was also always angry and afraid.

"I don't know," I said. "Do you miss him?"

Caitlin stopped chewing. Carson belched and tossed his empty can on the table and grabbed another.

"For what?" he finally said. "My father loves me, but he has to work. All this—this house and this food and all this other shit—comes from him. Not from me or Caitlin. He has to work, and he has to be on the road. There's no big tragedy or meaning in it."

Caitlin wiped her hands on a paper towel and stared out into the backyard.

"Look," Carson said. "You're going to be fine." He pressed his beer to his eye, now swollen and showing the first hints of a bruise, then to his neck, and then took a deep drink. When I turned away from him, I discovered that Caitlin was watching me with a feral intensity. I looked down at the two pieces of four-meat pizza on my plate, picked one up, used three fingers to fold it in half, and burned the top of my mouth when I took a bite.

I swallowed my bite and turned and looked at the house. It seemed even more impressive at night, with all the stone and brick and cornices thrown in pleasant shadow from the outdoor lights. I couldn't even begin to count how many windows there were.

"Which is your room?" I asked.

Carson looked up. "I don't know."

"What about Caitlin's?"

On hearing her name, Caitlin turned back to the table. Her Zima was empty, and she twisted the cap off a fresh one. Her brother pointed at a window far down in the darkness. "She's in the other wing."

"She has her own wing?"

He crossed his arms and leaned back into his chair. The beer can was still in his hands, and with his disheveled hair and a wry smile spreading across his face, he was handsome, a college scion whose tantrums and failings somehow remained charming.

"We're like English gentry," he said. "Man, you have no idea. My bedroom is literally twice as big as yours, isn't it?"

"It's probably as big as my entire house."

"I never gave you the proper tour. Let's go inside. I'll show you."

I followed him into the kitchen, down the hallway, and into the grand foyer at the front of the house. He spread his arms wide, pulled his chest up toward the ceiling, and grandstanded like a master of ceremonies.

"This home is not just a home," Carson said in a deep, mock-heroic English accent. "But a cultural landmark of American heritage. An institution almost an entire decade old! Think of it! Think of all the months of history you are about to journey through!"

"Delightful, Mr. Bly, just delightful," I said, also with an English accent. "Tell me, good sir, what did you say the name of this place was?"

"The name? Ah, yes, the name." He squinted and nodded, as though conjuring the image before our eyes. "This place is called Tyndrum."

"Tyndrum? Glorious!"

"Ha! 'Glorious'? Yes, sir, it is. It means the castle on the ridge. An apt name, yes?"

No one will remember this now, but when he was like this—playful and smart, joy in his voice and smile—Carson Bly was luminous.

"Tyndrum," he boomed, "is the glorious creation of one Vilnius Bly, an important philanthropist and builder of final resting places for the recently deceased. He has used his Irish-German heritage to create a building of stunning stature filled with unhappiness! Tyndrum has twenty-three rooms of various usages. As currently constituted, Tyndrum has seven bedrooms, three entertainment centers, three libraries, two dining areas, and several rooms that have no purpose or name whatsoever. Let's begin! Onward!"

He sprinted up the stairs, and I raced after him. At the top of the stairs, he grabbed the banister and spun left like a cartoon character, then turned and backpedaled, waiting for me to catch up. We looked down the length of his wing at all its closed doors. Along the walls, a single painting hung in the space between each doorway. Down Caitlin's wing, all the doors were also closed, almost like the rooms were private tombs. He led me to the window at the very end of the hall.

"This window," he said, "provides a stunning view of the roof of the garage, the blacktop driveway, a majestic basketball hoop for sport and leisure, a low brick wall built in an insane Robert Frost homage, and a line of trees that makes the other, lesser monstrosities of bucolic Indian Hill difficult to see. That was the idea, anyway. And, what a stunning view!"

"Splendid!" I shouted.

"So, that happened!" Carson said. "Let's go to the entertainment room!"

We strode to the nearest door and flung it open.

Three massive windows, surrounded by thick red curtains that hung from floor to ceiling, looked out onto the front lawn. There were two rows of leather club chairs in a rich chocolate color, spaced by small cocktail tables covered with drink coasters and framed black-and-white photographs. Against the nearest wall was a massive television.

The sheer size of its speakers—the screen was easily sixty inches—made me think of how heavy such a thing must be, and I couldn't imagine how they got it in the room. On the walls, brass torch lamps that were surely refurbished originals lit the room. On either side of the television were game consoles: Nintendo, Super Nintendo, and Sega, and it hit me that he had all the same game systems downstairs. He had two of everything. There were doors on either side, and Carson opened one and beckoned me into the long, narrow storage room behind the television. It was lined with VHS tapes. There must have been well over a thousand of them.

"This is Tyndrum's video library," he said. "Mostly this is VHS, but we have some Laserdisc, too. We're just beginning to convert."

"How many movies do you have?"

He shrugged. "Lots."

Back in the main room, we looked out beyond the club chairs. There was a pool table, an old movie projector, a popcorn machine, a Coke machine that hummed pleasantly, and classic Hollywood posters: *The Third Man, Grand Prix, The African Queen, Vertigo.*

"The lord of the manor," Carson said, "instilled a love of cinema in his children. Even if they always watch the telly downstairs."

"What do you call this room, sir?"

"This room? Uh, Hollywood."

"That's lame."

"Give me a better one, guv'ner."

For a moment, I contemplated the room and all its beautiful attention to a Hollywood era long gone. "Belladonna." I pointed at the projector. "Does it work?"

"Just for show."

"You know, movies aren't on reels anymore," I said. "They're on platters."

"What?"

"There are three great big platters that movies rotate on. So, it spools out the reel, and then it sorta wraps around again so the projectionist doesn't have to rewind anything. The platters are huge, like wagon wheels."

"How do you know that?"

"I don't know. Read it somewhere."

He folded his arms across his chest. He didn't seem to like the fact that I had knowledge he didn't, and for maybe the hundredth time, I wondered why Carson liked me at all.

"C'mon," he said, without his mock British accent. "Let me show you the rest."

The next room also ran along the front of the house. It was a library. Along three walls were bookcases that reached the ceiling; there was even a rolling ladder to help fetch books from the top shelf. No dust or neglect was visible anywhere. Several leather chairs were situated around the room, and a couch sat beneath the windows. In the room's center was a table as long as a truck, the kind of table I had only seen in libraries. Its thick legs had been carved with intricacy and loving precision, patterns of nooks and crannies all along its edges, the rococo carvings and ornamentation mirrored in its eight surrounding chairs, all of which were pushed in except for one.

"I'm across the hall," Carson said in his normal Midwestern accent.

His bedroom was bigger than my living room. The blinds were black and drawn shut, the only light falling from a single desk lamp with a long metallic arm onto a notebook open to two blank pages. A stack of similar composition books lay to the right. Against the distant wall was a king-sized bed, the sheets and comforter rumpled, a massive stack of clothing surrounding it. To my left was a large television, the screen showing some kind of war game that was on pause, the controllers sitting on the floor in front of two beanbag chairs. Everything smelled moldy and wet. His desk and its lamplight were flanked on both sides by massive bookcases stacked with a mixture of hard- and soft-cover books, from many of which protruded tiny torn pieces of colored paper. I took one off the shelf and flipped it open; years later, when I was in college, I would recognize the same book, Hegel's *Phenomenology of Spirit*, and recall that moment, holding it in my hands, seeing the underlined passage on page 134, and finding the words incomprehensible. I put it back on the shelf next to similar books on philosophy and existentialism. Along with these, Carson seemed to have a wide range of books on anarchy, liberty, and political thought by men like Robert Welch and Friedrich Hayek. On every wall were hung posters—the corners unbent, the edges straight and neat—of beautiful and interesting buildings famous for their architecture: the Sydney Opera House, the Eiffel Tower, the Coliseum, the London Arcade, the Churchgate Station in Mumbai, and dozens of others whose names were written in languages I couldn't read. Directly above his desk, notecards were pinned into the wall. I leaned closer. They all had quotes written on them. Some were from famous men, such as Emerson and Churchill; others were things he heard in the halls of Rockcastle ("I, like, truly can't imagine who gives a shit about this at all." –GB). There was also one quote from Caitlin: "I was happy I found her like that."

On the other side of the television were a closet and a bathroom that rivaled any master bath. I peered into a U-shaped room with recessed lighting that housed racks of shirts, jackets, blazers, T-shirts, jeans, pants, and coats, all of it hanging neatly; below were endless shoes, all sorts of boots and dress shoes and slippers, anything a person could want. I looked left around the corner, and there was his bathroom. Strangely, it had two sinks. When I sensed he wasn't behind me, I walked back into his bedroom, then into the hallway, where he stood with his hands in his pockets as casually as if he were waiting for the bus.

"This house is awesome," I said.

"This wing. You haven't even seen half of it. We'll do that later. Let's go back outside. I could stand to eat and drink more."

• • •

In the morning, I woke up to find Carson sitting at the foot of the bed, staring out the window. I had taken the adjacent bedroom, which was very clean and obviously never used. It was more like a hotel suite: furnished with a king-sized bed, two side tables, an armoire, a television in front of a couch, and a desk that bore a thin layer of dust. Every drawer in the desk was locked. His face was in profile; he hadn't shaved that morning. His back was ramrod straight, a tension in his cheeks and neck pulling like a rubber band. His hands, tucked between his knees, were out of sight.

"You awake?" he asked, still staring outside.

"Sure," I said, propping myself upright. "What's up?"

"Get dressed. We're going out."

"Where?"

He answered by continuing to stare out through the open blinds into the backyard. There was a tree line there, but from my vantage point, still slumped low and sleepy, I couldn't tell what he was looking at. Even then, however, it struck me as a disingenuous pose. But something about the set of his mouth, that ugly tension in his neck, kept me from smiling and making a joke.

"Get dressed," he repeated. He stood up and refused to look at me. He wore camouflage cargo shorts and a black

T-shirt and a backward Detroit Tigers hat, all the clothes ill-fitting and wrong. On his way out, he said, "We'll eat on the way."

I dressed quickly, and out in the hallway, I glanced down toward Caitlin's room but heard nothing. Downstairs, finding the kitchen empty, I walked out to the garage, opening the door as Carson was closing the trunk of his Audi. He climbed behind the wheel, opened the garage door, and turned on the engine. I took this as my signal to get in.

In the car, Carson remained silent, but he turned *The Chronic* up loud, the doors and windows of his Audi shaking from the bass. The windows and sunroof were open to let in the roaring wind. We drove through a McDonald's, and Carson placed our order—"Do you mind if we get Cokes instead of coffee?"—with the charm he used among the spectators at our basketball games, his lips slightly upturned into a smile, the tension in his shoulders gone, looking the cashier full in the face when he said, "Thank you." But as soon as we pulled away, the mask fell, and he was again sullen and unspeaking.

We headed east; I pulled the sun visor loose and around to the side to keep the sun off my face. The city fell away quickly, and four lanes became two, the houses set farther and farther back from the road, the cornfields giving way to woods. I saw a sign for Hillsboro. Carson turned the car south, and we were on a road heading toward a forest. He steered onto a gravel road, plumes of dust surrounding us as we rumbled slowly down the tree-canopied path. He pulled into what looked like a small, unmarked parking lot with room for perhaps four or five cars. He powered the windows closed and killed the engine, then got out of the car. I hopped out too and watched as he stood with his hands on his hips, starting into the woods.

We were on a small bluff overlooking a creek that I could smell and hear but not see, and the chirping of birds whose names I didn't know called out from the surrounding forest. Everything was a dark shade of green, the branches lush and languorously stretching out and around us. Off to the right was a small pathway sloping down toward the creek, just narrow enough for one person. It was the middle of the week; I figured no one else was out here.

"Are we camping?" I asked.

He grinned. "We are furthering your education."

Carson opened the trunk; inside were three duffel bags with airport tags still wrapped around the handles. He pointed to a green canvas bag that had "1986 Aeronautics Show: Houston, Texas" printed on the side and said, "Grab that one and follow me."

He hoisted the other two and headed down the path. I picked up the bag. It was full but not too heavy; it clinked, loud and metallic, like it was filled with empty soup cans and bottles. The path, bone dry but slick, weaved through an overgrown, weedy underbrush and then broke through the trees and left us standing at the rocky edge of the creek. It was probably twelve feet across and fairly shallow. Carson scanned the area, then dropped one of his bags and headed upstream. A tree had fallen across the creek; its trunk was thick and round, so perfect for crossing that I wondered if it had been intentionally felled. Carson climbed on top of the log and unzipped the bag. From it he pulled out ten beer cans from the night before, lining them up equidistant in a neat row across the tree. When he was done, he dropped the bag on the edge of the creek, one corner landing slightly in the water, and walked back to me.

"Drop your bag, dude," he said. "Gotta teach you some safety first."

I put down my bag. Carson crouched over the second bag, unzipped it, and withdrew a revolver. It was different from the one he had in his car: smaller, shinier, and somehow less threatening.

"Target practice," I said.

"You should have seen the look on your face," he said. "All morning, getting more and more nervous and shit, but not saying anything. Man, you're gonna love this, Webb. You're gonna love it."

He removed the revolver from his pocket, keeping it pointed downward. "First things first. Never point the gun at yourself. Okay? That's like rule number fucking one. You point the gun down. Like the way your mom told you to hold scissors. Got it?"

He handed me the gun. It was heavier than I thought it would be, and oddly smaller in my hands.

"There you go," Carson said. "Down. Good. Now, flip that little lever. See? That's how you open a revolver. Now, look. All six chambers are loaded. You're looking at the back of the bullet. Go ahead, pull one out. See how light it is? Kinda cool, right? Okay, slide it back in. Yeah, it just falls in. Close it. Good. Easy, right? Okay, now by your thumb, on the inside, that's the safety. Flip that off. Good. Now you're ready to shoot. Look upriver and pick a can. Go for the one in the middle. You want to look down the barrel of the gun, down the sight, and see the can. It's just like shooting a basketball: look at what you're aiming at. Hold on, hold on, Owen. Owen? Relax. Okay, relax. Feel how tense you are in your shoulders, here, feel that? You aren't gonna hit shit that way. Relax. There you go. Cool. Now, look at your target. If you want to close an eye, fine, but you can always do it with two eyes open. Try it. See? The optics of it, how it seems like the can moved? But it didn't, that's just your brain working. With a handgun, I keep both eyes open. If you had a rifle and a scope, that's different, but with this, both eyes. All right, Webb, when you're ready."

The roar stunned me. I didn't immediately see the way the can spun in the air and dropped down into the creek bed. Instead, all I sensed was the incredible bang, the shocking reverberation from firing the gun.

"Beginner's luck," Carson laughed, slapping me on the back. "Great fucking shot, dude!"

I lowered the gun and stared at the pebbled handle. "What is this?"

"It's a .32," Carson said. "Larger the caliber, the larger the kick. You'll see as we work our way up."

The duffel bag, unzipped, seemed empty, nothing but a black hole.

"How many guns do you have?"

"My father's guns. I brought six."

"Those were in the trunk? There's no lock on them?"

"Do you see a lock? Look, man, that's why each gun has a safety. We're fine."

I held the gun away from my body. I didn't want to rest it against my leg, but I also didn't want to let it go.

"Did you come out here with Gus Wexner?"

His face darkened. "What do you know about Gus Wexner?"

"Nothing. Just that you two used to be friends."

"Who told you about Gus?"

"Nobody."

Carson shoved the gun into the pocket of his shorts as casually as if he were putting away his wallet. He put his hands on his hips and shook his head slowly, staring off into the trees.

"Some people," he said. "Some fucking people. What did they say? Huh? Did they say it was my fault?"

"No, nothing like that." I took one step away from him. "Just that you two used to be friends."

"Good friends. Great friends. We used to be. Yeah. Gus was—" He shook his head again. It strikes me now how theatrical and silly his physicality was when he felt cornered. He was performing, something I think I sensed even then, but it was almost like he was performing for himself, not for me. Pretending to act indignant only showcased how much he didn't truly care.

"Sure," he said. "Gus and I came up here. A lot. I showed him how to shoot a gun. Not at this exact spot, but out here, you know, in nature. He was a good guy. I didn't know he had problems. I didn't know he was suicidal."

"He's dead?"

He waved a hand as if to shoo away a silly question. "Failed attempt. Parents shipped him away to a different school. They didn't understand him. They didn't understand what he was about. I didn't understand that he wasn't, you know, he wasn't tough. I thought he was tougher. You know? But you are, right?"

"To do what?"

"To do whatever we want. To tell these fucking bozos that we aren't going to take their shit. We're in charge. We're the ones who know. We know how to play ball. We know how to ace tests. We know how to hold a gun, how to drink whiskey, how to just be, you know? Outside of all the rules and the bullshit."

"You're ranting."

"I'm ranting!" he yelled. "Ranting!"

"Raving."

"Raving!"

"Bellowing!" I screamed.

"Barbaric yawp!"

We both roared again for absolutely no reason, then we

grinned like idiots. “See, man,” he said, pointing a finger at me. “You get it. I knew you fucking got it. I could tell when I first met you. Okay. Enough of this sentimental shit.”

What was shocking and stirring about all this was not the ease it took to squeeze the trigger, the report of the gun, or the fact that we had been driving around with guns in the trunk of the car. What was shocking was how much I loved it. The roar and the kickback were so powerful, so loud, and they came from me. I looked down the creek bed at the nine remaining cans. I had hit one. First try. *Cool,* I thought. *So cool.* I snorted and looked back down at the .32. I lifted my arms, my left hand cupped under the grip, my right wrapped around it, one finger over the trigger, and aimed for the second can, pushing a calming breath up through my skull and down into my stomach, pressing my lungs out against my ribs. The world stilled. Then I fired—feeling that percussive roar—and hit the second can.

“My man,” Carson said.

• • •

After an hour of shooting, with my aim getting progressively worse as we moved up in caliber, we gathered what stray shells and cans we could, stuffed them in the duffels, and walked up the trampled path to the car. We threw everything in the trunk, backed out of the parking lot, and returned to Carson’s house, the whole time talking about anything but guns—basketball, girls, music videos, cars, clothes—as if we had both agreed that what had happened was our secret.

I lived with Carson and Caitlin for the next nineteen days. My parents never called, not once. For a few days I borrowed clothes from Carson, and then we drove to the Towne Centre and went on a shopping spree, all of which he paid for with his American Express card. For nearly three weeks our days were the same—playing basketball, swimming, getting drunk, watching O.J.'s trial, playing video games, a kitchen covered for days in food wrappers and condiments and empty cans and then cleaned up in one frenetic blur as long as the stereo was turned up ear-splittingly loud so we could sing along as we scrubbed the grime from the countertops—all occurring in the protective cocoon of this parentless estate. Every time I thought of my father's trial, I shoved the thoughts aside by jumping in the pool, shooting jumpers, or popping a beer. I didn't want to see or think about him for a second. They lived in the real world, while here, with Carson and Caitlin, I was happy and loved and unburdened.

Carson and I went shooting two more times. My aim got a little better but was poor compared to Carson's. We didn't talk much while we were shooting, just fired at our ten targets, set up fresh targets, and did it all over again. We rummaged through the garbage at home for targets: orange juice containers, beer bottles, soda cans, water bottles, half-used cans of pesticide spray bottles from the garage still covered in spider webs, anything we could stand upright and fire upon. When we were in the woods, an eerie calm came over us both, and we didn't discuss why we were there or acknowledge that we were getting away with something for which we should have been caught and severely punished. No one was ever out in the woods. And knowing what I know now about how the towns and woods around Ohio operate, I'm not sure it would have mattered if anyone did see us. People fired guns in the woods. That's just how life was lived there.

I never had any illusions that the three of us were a family. We were more like exiles, a trio of forgotten children left to our own devices in a place where we could do no harm, where no one came in or out. The whole month was hot and steamy, and I thought of us as baking in an enclosed space for a finite amount of time until we were ready to be taken out of the oven. We were on a clock. It would have to end.

When it did, when Carson told me my mom had left a message on their answering machine, he agreed to drive me home. Caitlin sat in the back seat. When we pulled into the driveway, with wonder she said, "This is your house?"

I turned, left shoulder into the leather seat, to look back at her.

"Hope you aren't disappointed," I said.

"In you, Owen Webb?" She winked at me. "Never."

"All right, Webb," Carson said, sticking out his hand. "I'll see you in school next week."

"I can't believe we have to go back."

"Castles in the sky, Webb. Eventually, it's always going to rain."

We shook hands. It's silly, I know, but I loved that gesture so much. I got out of the car and retrieved my duffel bag from the trunk. Caitlin stood waiting for me by the open passenger door. She hugged me, her right hand behind my head, and kissed my cheek. "Call me, okay?" she whispered. Then she let go without looking at me and hopped into the passenger seat and closed the door. The Audi idled in the driveway as I took the sidewalk to the porch, knocked once on the door, then cracked it open. When I turned to wave, they were already driving down the street, the car vibrating with bass. He honked twice, then sped away.

Inside, my mother stood in front of the stove, and my father sat at the kitchen table with a library book, a Tom Clancy novel. It looked like a staged scene, as if they were trying to convince me everything was just fine.

"Welcome home," my mother said.

"Hey." I dropped my bag and stood on the threshold of the room with my hands in my pockets.

"Enjoy your mini vacation?" my father asked.

I pictured the revolver in my hands. I pictured pointing it at him and making him afraid.

"Yeah, I did," I said. "Thanks for letting me go."

"We just thought a little time away would be good for you," Mom said. "Why don't you go wash up for dinner?"

I picked up my duffel bag and took it to my bedroom and dropped it on the floor. Afternoon light cast a dusty glow on all my things. My bedroom felt small and contained, like a prison cell. Comparing my life to prison, knowing what my father was facing, shamed me, and I forced myself to think of my summer reading list, a program Rockcastle took rather seriously. Then I remembered that when I walked the halls next week, everyone there would know about my father. I sat down in my desk chair and stared at the carpet, the vacuum streaks still fresh in the floor. What would I say to all my classmates?

Nothing, it turned out. The next week, when I returned to school in my crisp dress shirt and dry-cleaned blazer and the appropriately distressed boat shoes Carson had bought for me, not a single classmate or teacher mentioned my father. There was no way that they didn't know about it, but if a glance even hovered on me for an extra beat or condolences were on the tip of anyone's tongue, I could never tell.

I used to think that this was out of consideration for my privacy, respect for my family and our suffering. But that wasn't the truth. The truth was that like all Rockcastle scandals, my family's crisis was hushed rumor that we never spoke of in public. In locker rooms, hallways, classrooms, and house parties, I heard about the salacious missteps of Rockcastle families. Affairs discovered when a child hides in a closet, only to hear and see his father fuck his mistress in his parents' bed. A fourth-generation family business bankrupted from addictions to cocaine and alcohol and gambling. Pancreatic cancer that rots away a mother's body just four months after diagnosis. Carson's mother dead from an aneurysm. Everyone carried secrets. But as a blue blood, even a fake one, I pretended that nothing had changed. All was right with the world. Even if all the pretending meant that the anger, sadness, and fear turned inside, like a parasite, gnawing at me until there was no choice but to let out the unspoken.

X

On a Tuesday in mid-September, I woke up and dressed for Rockcastle like it was any other morning. In a few hours, at a Hamilton County courthouse, my father would be sentenced to prison. Monday afternoon, a jury had found him guilty of all charges: eight counts of breaking and entering, one count of possession of stolen property, one count of selling stolen property. We did not at the time know how many years the judge would sentence him to. From what I had seen in the O.J. trial, I thought the sentencing would take months.

But it didn't. My father would be sentenced the next day.

My parents came home on Monday night and sat down in the living room together, something they never did. We ordered Chinese food and ate silently, my father drinking a six pack of beer, my mother vodka and Sprite, me water. Over the course of the evening, steady and slow, they got drunk. When I stood and said I had to do homework, they said nothing, continuing to stare at the blue haze of the television as if I hadn't spoken at all.

In the morning, my mother was hungover and doing her best to pretend she wasn't. But I had learned to recognize the bleariness under the eyes, the smacking of lips and gums, the blinking and unfocused vision, the way she tilted her head away from the lights. She offered breakfast, but I said I wasn't hungry.

"Your father wants to drive you to school today," she said. "Is that okay?"

Not really, I thought. "Fine," I said.

He came out of the bedroom wearing his best black suit, a white dress shirt, and no tie, his dark chest hair showing near his neck. His hair was immaculately gelled, and he reeked of Old Spice. He almost looked ready to take my mother out for a night on the town.

"I thought we could talk in the car," he said.

"Sure," I muttered.

When we got in the car, however, my father drove in silence. Even with a forced look of serenity on his face, he drove abnormally, cautious and tentative, two hands on the wheel, slowing for yellow lights, tapping his fingers on the wheel, frequently cracking his knuckles.

We exited the Norwood Lateral, gliding at fifty around the expressway exit. Rockcastle was on our right, the campus rising up from the woods below, and the dew on the rolling hillside glittered in the morning sunlight.

"You know," he finally said, "your mother is going to really depend on you with me gone. I'm depending on you, too."

"I know," I said, not knowing what he meant.

"My lawyer thinks I'll get a long sentence."

"How long?"

"Close to the max. Twelve to fifteen years."

My fifteenth birthday was in October. I hadn't even been alive for fifteen years.

"So, you'll be in the city?"

"Nope. I'll be in Chillicothe. Do you know where that is?"

I shook my head.

"It's south central Ohio. Out in Ross County. In a few months, you'll be able to drive out there yourself. I'm sorry I'm not going to be around to teach you how to drive. Your mother isn't much of a driver."

I leaned away and pressed my forehead against the car window.

Catching the green lights, we made two quick turns and were pulling up to Rockcastle. My father steered into the line of cars, from which my classmates were hopping out of passenger seats, dragging their book bags behind them like chained balls, struggling to hustle up the front steps to class. On the concrete bench by the front door, Carson sat with his feet up, leaning back against the building, his hair dangling around his eyes. My breathing echoed in my ears.

"You can let me out here," I said. "You don't have to go to the front door."

"It's no problem."

"Just let me out here."

He pulled to the curb, and I opened the door, yanking my bag from the floor. I bent at the waist, keeping my head down and out of sight.

"Hey, Owen."

"Yeah?"

"I just want you to know." He blinked. I couldn't remember ever seeing my father cry. But if at that moment I could have drawn a horizontal line through his face, right across the top of his lip, it would be like two different people: the lower half, his mouth smiling, teeth showing, as though he were a game show host; above, the wide, sad eyes of a man about to go to prison. There was something terrifying about seeing my father like this, so I looked down at his right hand resting on the gear shift.

"I just want you to know," he said again, "that I'm sorry. Okay? I'm sorry."

"Sure, Dad. I got it."

"Good. All right, then." He turned and faced ahead, putting his right hand back on the steering wheel. I closed the door and stood, watching him, as he steered the car into the drop-off line, curved around the bend, and disappeared from sight. When I turned toward the entrance to Rockcastle, Carson was watching me. I waved. He didn't acknowledge my greeting but kept his eyes trained on me as I walked up the front steps to stand in front of him.

"What did he say?" Carson asked.

"Nothing. Nothing much."

"You all right?"

I shrugged.

"Okay, then," he said. "Let's go to class."

All day, I watched the clock, keeping my hand and head down in every class. Not one teacher called on me, which was rare. I assumed they took pity on me. After school, I did my homework until I saw my mother's car pull up. I went outside, and when I got in the car she looked over at me and smiled. She looked as if she had been crying all afternoon.

"You okay?" I asked.

"No," she said. "Are you?"

I shrugged, which of late seemed to be my answer to everything.

"I don't want to cook. Where do you want to go eat?"

"I don't care."

"I'm incapable of making any more decisions today. But I really don't want to go home."

"Some place by Tri-County?"

Mom put the car in gear and turned the radio up, and we drove north to the mall. I didn't ask about the sentencing. She drove into the mall's parking garage even though I hadn't said I wanted to eat at the mall. She parked and we wandered inside. I felt like an idiot wearing my school blazer, but I didn't say anything. When we went through the second set of glass doors, filtered air blasted down on our faces, and I was instantly cold. Off to our left was a nail shop and a Glamour Shots, and on the right an arcade, the new Mortal Kombat game positioned next to the entrance and surrounded by seven or eight kids. Dead ahead was the food court, the thick odor of fried food hovering over the tile floors.

"Can I get coneys?" I asked.

"Sure." My mom reached in her purse and pulled out a twenty. "I'll come find you."

I walked to the Gold Star and ordered four cheese coneys with mustard and onions and a large Mountain Dew and carried my dinner on a red tray to a spot in the center of all the tables so my mom could find me. I picked a table that had been freshly wiped down, the whorls of diluted bleach still visible on the surface. Carrying an identical red tray on which sat a salad in a transparent plastic bowl, Mom sat down across from me and started to pick at her food.

"He received the full fifteen years," my mother said.

"What does that mean for us?"

"Nothing, I guess. If he's gone seven or ten years, what difference does it make?" When she saw my frown, she said, "Parole."

"Did it take long?"

"No. Walk in, judge comes in, your father rose and made a statement, judge sentenced him, and then he was led out a side door."

"Sounds weird."

She speared a tomato but didn't eat it.

"Courts are open," she said. "The public can come in. Our neighbors were there. There were three rows of people who applauded. People we knew, Owen. Mr. Brady, who your father used to ride to work with. The Stewarts from down the street. He stole from people we knew, Owen. Christ, I was so humiliated. I couldn't look any of them in the face."

"Did they say anything to you?"

She shook her head. "After your father was led away, I sat down and waited through a couple of hearings before I stood up and left. I didn't want to see any of them. I couldn't...I mean, what would I say to them? I didn't know. I had no idea. I feel so stupid. So stupid."

"Mom, we didn't know."

Her mouth tightened into a small line, and she shook her head rigidly.

"I should have. I should have known. How could I be such a fool?"

"He fooled everybody."

"But I'm his wife!"

I set down my coney. This felt like a conversation she should be having with an adult, not her son. She placed her hands flat on the table as if she were going to push herself to her feet, but she never rose. Instead, her face seemed to cave in on itself in some mixture of determination and fear.

"I'm divorcing him." When I said nothing, she said, "Did you hear me?"

"Sure. You're divorcing Dad."

"Right."

I shrugged. "Doesn't matter to me. He's gone either way, right?"

She laughed sickly. "I suppose that's true."

"Can we talk about something else?"

"Sure." She picked up her Diet Coke and took a sip. "O.J. Simpson or the Unabomber?"

"I was thinking about people who aren't sociopaths."

Mom snorted into her drink, sending soda up and on to the table.

"Jesus Christ," she said. "I'm sorry."

"That's okay." I mopped up the soda with napkins, pleased I had made her smile. "Hey, do you know why Dad stopped coming to my games?"

"I really don't know. When you were a boy, your father went to everything you did. Baseball, soccer, all of it."

"Was he out robbing people instead of going to my games?"

She stared at me until I met her eyes. Moments like this always made the fact that I was six inches taller than her seem absurd. How could I physically tower over her and yet she was the one who could level me with a single sweep of her eyes? I caved and looked over her shoulder at some boys in line at Chick-Fil-A.

She said, "Maybe. Honest? I really don't know."

"So I was just cover."

"I don't know, Owen." She pushed her salad aside. She'd had maybe three bites.

"What did you do this afternoon?" I asked. "You know. After."

She said she had decided to go to the downtown public library rather than our local one, and even though it was cool out for late September, she walked the waterfront, which was empty of people, animals, even garbage, and watched the barges float west down the Ohio. As she spoke she waved her hands and bugged out her eyes, her voice rising and falling like waves; usually, she had a cigarette in these moments, jabbing and flicking and twirling, the smoke circling her head like a ghostly halo. She paused midsentence and stirred the ice in her soda with her straw.

"I sometimes wonder where they're going," she said. "The boats, I mean. What city they are stopping at next, or if they go all the way into the Gulf. Do people still transport things by boat? I mean, they must. I just watch the boats because I think they're beautiful, but I don't know what's on them. I can't imagine what would possibly ship that way when there are trains and airplanes, and they get there so much faster."

She continued for a while longer, and then I looked up and saw that she was staring at me.

"Did you hear me?"

"What?"

"Do you want to look around? For clothes or something?"

"No," I said, before thinking about going back to our house. "Well, yeah, I could look around. You know."

"Let's go."

We started at McAlpin's. I looked at Starter jackets I didn't want and at black and gray jeans, my mother hovering patiently. We wandered back into the mall, and I tried on basketball shoes at Finish Line and Foot Locker, even though as a Rockcastle player I had shoes in our royal-blue and gold team colors. We wandered into Cross Colours and Benetton and Abercrombie, but all I did was pull shirts off the rack, pretend to study the fabric and stitching, then hang them back up. My mother remained silent the whole time, never asking what I was looking for or wanted. In Sam Goody, I pushed around the awkward cardboard longboxes that housed the CDs, the images on the covers distorted to fit the boxes' elongated shape. After an hour, during which time I hadn't thought of actually making a purchase, the speaker system squawked that the mall would be closing in fifteen minutes.

Outside, our steps echoing in the parking garage, I was suddenly very tired. I climbed into the passenger seat. Once the car was started, my mother turned and looked at me, and I stared out the windshield, determined not to meet her gaze. With one hand, she reached out and touched the side of my face, a gesture I was too old for but nonetheless loved. She ran her fingers through my hair and stopped at the base of my neck. I waited for whatever was coming next. But instead of speaking, she let go, turned the radio on to a low murmur, and I fell back against the seat and closed my eyes.

When I woke up, we were pulling into our driveway. I glanced at the clock—I had slept for about twenty minutes. My mouth was cottony, and my legs had tightened. The cabin was warm and pleasant, and when I turned my head, a gentle ache ran across my shoulders.

"Awake, sleepyhead?"

"We're home?"

"We're home. Just you and me now."

She parked in the driveway, and we approached the side door. I pulled the screen door back, the rust on the screen noticeable under the bright porch light, and it wheezed and creaked open, banging against my calves. My mother keyed the lock, and we awkwardly steered our way up the narrow staircase into the kitchen, the wood steps creaking under our feet, the screen door slamming shut, me spinning on the steps to push the door closed and latch the deadbolt. My hand hovered there. The door had a large window, and it would be easy to break the window, slip a hand in, unlatch the deadbolt, and enter. I wondered if my father found break-ins this easy, this obvious.

My mother stood at the top of the steps looking out into our home. The lights were all off. In every way, nothing was different. Everything was still there. The couch, the tables, the lamps, the generic landscape paintings of places my parents had never seen. I crossed the room and turned on a lamp. When I faced my mother again, she had already turned away and gone to the fridge. She opened a bottle of wine, poured a large glass, and took a long drink. She set it down and refilled her glass.

"Now what?" I asked.

"You have school tomorrow. You go to school. I find a full-time job. That's it."

"I mean, do we have to move?"

"Your grandfather sent us money." Her face remained turned away from me, as if her shame was a pungent smell I might whiff. "Just enough until I get better work than the library."

"Work," I said. It was a word I knew she always liked.

"We could rent a movie. Drive up to Blockbuster."

"That's okay," I said, eyes on her second empty glass of wine. "I should do some homework. Study and stuff."

"That's probably a good idea."

I went to my room, shut the door, and flopped down atop my comforter, my shoes and coat still on. Light snuck through the crack beneath the door, and down the hallway Mom banged around the kitchen for a few minutes before turning on the television, which she played too loud, as if to let me know she was up and available to talk. I pulled out all my textbooks, stacked them on top of each other, and lined up the spines neat and orderly along the edge of my desk. Algebra two, modern U.S. history, chemistry, *Jane Eyre*. I ran my fingers over the rounded corners of the books then lay my head down on them. When I opened my eyes again, the house was silent.

I crept into the living room. On the coffee table stood an empty bottle of chardonnay and a second bottle that was half-empty. The ashtray was filled. I picked up the cork off the floor, wiped it on my sleeve, then placed it back in the bottle. I turned on the television. It was a little after eleven.

In 1993, Fox had become the fourth network-affiliated channel in the tristate area. Compared to how it was done on the other news broadcasts, the camera framing of the Fox anchors was bizarre. Viewers could see the entire desk, including the anchors' legs and shoes. Behind them was revealed a glimpse into the newsroom, where shadowy figures silhouetted in darkness shuttled behind the set, flickers of light emerging from computer screens, sheets of paper clutched between hands like religious symbols. The camera panned from main desk to weather to sports to local reporters standing off to the side—no cuts from camera number one to camera number two, just a panning action—demonstrating how the members of the Channel 19 News team were as close and comfortable as a family.

My favorite anchor, Jack Atherton, was on. With thick, jet-black hair and coffee-dark eyes, he had a classic Hollywood handsomeness that was mildly generic and wholly soothing. On camera, Atherton didn't stay in the frame. He read the news like a prize fighter, bobbing his head and shoulders, swiveling his entire body in his chair as if the teleprompter's words were punches he had to duck and counter, taunting the viewers as if they were a sparring partner. Tonight, however, Atherton sat upright and still.

"Today, a reign of terror," Atherton intoned, looking right at me, "has finally come to an end. Joseph Webb, a chemist from North College Hill, was sentenced in Hamilton County Court to a fifteen-year sentence for robbery and burglary."

Atherton vanished. The camera cut to a courtroom. The shot was from behind, showing my father standing tall. It was as if I sat in the rows behind him. I could just see his profile, his glasses protruding from his face but his eyes hidden, his fingers resting lightly on the table in front of him, his lawyer standing next to him. In the front row, her shoulders curled and head bowed, sat my mother, her body shuddering with what I knew were tears.

"I am so sorry," my father said, his words distant and echoing, "for what I did to my family and my friends."

The shot cut to the judge, a walrus with a pristine mustache. He stared down at his desk, as if my father's words were inaudible. On the voice-over, Atherton said there were ten counts, there was an armed robbery, coins, Proctor & Gamble, a jumble of words and phrases I couldn't make sense of that just became a noisy din.

My father was led away in handcuffs. Next, a shot of three rows in the back of the courtroom, all the spectators on their feet, applauding. There was John Herzog, our neighbor from three streets over. There was Mr. Wagstaff, who used to carpool with my father in his massive tan Econoline filled with six other P&G employees. There was my baseball coach, Mr. Davis. There were Mr. and Mrs. Acta, whose son Peter was on my Knothole League baseball team. There were more faces, none of which I could place but all of them familiar, and I suddenly understood my mother's shame as if it were a thick oil that had been poured over my head.

Back in the studio. The two news anchors, chitchatting, shaking their heads, admonishing, their body language the same as I had seen from scolding teachers and assistant principals for years.

Atherton looked right in the camera. "Webb got what he deserved."

Then it was over. They were on to the next story. My father's story was already yesterday's news. I turned off the television and sat in the dark and thought about how my father had never tried to explain himself, justify his behavior, make any sense of it at all. He could express the remorse, say the platitudes, but even in the moment his words felt hollow. It's like a part of being a fully formed human being didn't exist in him. I ran my finger over the cable box and thought about being hollow and whether a person like my father had always been this way. Or if it was like carving a Halloween pumpkin, cutting and scooping and scraping out the inside, only to take a knife and cut a smiling face into the surface and place a lone candle inside to shine that deceptive, grinning light.

XI

In February of 1996, we finished our regular season .500 and in fifth place in our division. We were a solid team, but undersized, and often lost our games due to getting out-rebounded. Because of our low seeding, our first playoff game took place on the road. We traveled to midtown to play at St. Bernard, a small Catholic school just north of Cincinnati proper that had one of the best home-court advantages due to its gymnasium, a relic from the 1940s. Their fans were rabid and loyal, and the bleachers rose taller than usual for a high school gym: the spectators seemed more like judges from a dystopian nightmare looking down upon us in stern judgment. The floorboards were warped and had a series of dead spots upon which a dribbled ball would simply stop, stick to the floor like glue, and then roll away. There was barely a step between the baselines and the gym walls, and opposing teams were always wary of barreling down the lane and letting their momentum carry them into the concrete wall. The rims were old and unforgiving, and the backboards were made of some ancient synthetic material rather than fiberglass. Even the trajectory of layups was an adventure.

Duke strode through the locker room and yelled, "Five minutes!" At this announcement, the room quieted, though the laughter and teasing and crude jokes never ceased, and everyone finished dressing. Exactly five minutes later, he clicked his stopwatch, shoved it back in the pocket of his blazer, and wheeled a chalkboard in front of us. He held a stub of chalk that seemed minuscule in his massive hands. His baritone and the scrape of chalk the only sounds in the room, Duke outlined our plan to stay in man-to-man defense and diagramed the basics of our offense that he insisted we already knew. When he was finished, he looked down at his palms as if he was surprised the chalk was still there. He said, "Gather around, men," and we came together and raised our hands up and stared at each other, a mask of anger on our faces, and loudly screamed, "Defense!" Then we raced out onto the basketball court to the small applause and cheers of our parents and friends.

I spotted my mother in the stands. She waggled her fingers in a wave, and I nodded, a tight smile, trying to be too cool to acknowledge her presence. I stole glances at the stands during warm-ups, and even though she sat on the right side of the gym with the small group of Rockcastle parents and students, she seemed to somehow be sitting alone, her hand covering her mouth, as anxious as ever. A couple of minutes before the game started, in walked Caitlin with two of her friends. She locked eyes with me but otherwise gave no indication she knew me and climbed halfway up the bleachers with her friends. I glanced at Carson, who was across the court stretching his back, and it didn't seem he noticed at all.

The horn sounded, and we came to center court. We all knew that St. Bernard's philosophy was taken straight from the New York Knicks: if you clutch and grab an offensive player early in the game, the whistles will eventually cease and the refs will "let them play," allowing a physical and bruising style of basketball akin to rugby that naturally favors the home team.

The opposing point guard had black hair cut close to his scalp and a thin, wispy beard. He was the only player on the team with facial hair, and he had the sinewy build of a wrestler. Every time I had the ball, his hands were on me: he grabbed my hip, forearm, shorts, hand-checked my lower back if I got around him, and slammed his elbow in my chest as soon as I passed the ball. Despite the number of fouls called, St. Bernard continued their physical game, and soon we started turning over the ball.

At the end of the first quarter, a back screen got Carson free to cut baseline to the rim. I rocketed a bounce pass through the lane; he dribbled once and rose up. The help defender slid over, and rather than jump and challenge the shot, he ducked at the waist and bumped Carson's legs in midair. Defenseless, Carson lost his balance and fell hard on his back. He sprang up before the whistle even blew.

"Motherfucker!" he screamed. "You piece of shit!"

Three players raced between them, and the fouler, a towheaded kid who wore the number 27, turned away and smirked at his bench. Both refs separated the teams, and we had to hold Carson back. When he screamed, saliva flew from his mouth, spraying all of us with his fury.

"Take out my legs! What the fuck is wrong with you?!"

Someone pushed, and then everyone on the court shoved toward each other, ready to fight. The coaches jogged onto the court and pulled us apart, and Duke shepherded our team toward the bench, telling us to calm the hell down. The crowd stood, and the shuddering bleachers sounded like a thunderstorm. My mother raised her head from behind her hands but didn't stand; Caitlin's expression was gleeful, and her friends pointed and yelled and jeered like everyone else.

"Duke, did you see what he did?" Carson said. "He took out my fucking legs!"

"I saw it. It's over, all right? We need you to keep your head."

"Piece of shit!"

"Carson! Calm down!"

"Goddamn, Duke, did you see what he did?"

I said, "Carson. Easy."

"You saw it, Webb!" He jabbed his finger at me. "You saw it!"

"Yeah, I saw it." I narrowed my eyes to tell him, *We'll get him.*

He understood and put his hands on his hips and blew out a deep breath. The anger seemed to vanish just as fast as it came. He even laughed.

"You and me, Webb." He shook his head. "You and me."

The refs called it a flagrant foul. Carson hit both his free throws, and we got the ball. Number 27 was subbed out and received high fives and fist bumps on the bench, his expression the contemptible smirk of a boy who knew no boundaries, who embraced fights, encouraged them. I saw myself in him. This was the person I could have been if I had never entered Rockcastle: thuggish, smug, contemptible. I couldn't keep my eyes off him. On every dead ball, I looked over at 27, and his face morphed into the image I saw in the mirror every morning: the same eyes, the same cheeks, the same spots of acne around the jaw and neck. Each glance made me hate him more.

Late in the second quarter, 27 reentered the game. He didn't guard me or Carson. On the surface, neither of us reacted to his reentry; Carson and I didn't even exchange a glance. But at the end of the second half, we held for the last shot, and the ball was sent to the corner, where our power forward, Scott Sugarman, forced up a jumper from just inside the three-point line. The buzzer sounded before the shot was released, and when it caromed off the rim and went long, there was no point to securing the rebound. But Carson did, grabbing it with one hand and coming down just outside the paint. And there was 27, his hands half-heartedly up. Carson turned and slammed his elbow into the kid's throat.

The kid flew backward, keeping his balance, then he staggered and dropped to a knee, clutching his neck, wheezing for air. Both refs missed it, and Carson released the ball and moved away quickly, knowing full well the effect and not needing to see its aftermath. However, the left side of the gym saw it and howled curses down on us. Our path to the locker room went right along the bleachers, and as soon as we entered the corridor, a hail of paper cups and ice and coins soared down on us. With a string of expletives, we raced into the locker room. Even from down in the bowels of the gym, we heard the PA announcer gurgle instructions on good sportsmanship, the refusal to allow any more food or drink in the gym, and something about the good standing of the St. Bernard community.

Inside the locker room, the dusty heating pipes that ran across the ceiling hissed like snakes. The room was so hot we all felt like closing our eyes and dozing off. Duke huddled us up and on the chalkboard diagramed the simple changes we needed to execute in order to win. When he was finished, he calmly placed the chalk back in the tray beneath the board and wiped the dust off his hands. Sweat poured from his hairline.

"As for that nonsense after the whistle," Duke said, "that needs to stop. These kids are punks looking to start a fight, and when this crowd gets going, they don't need any extra motivation. I yell at the refs, not you. Understand? You let me worry about the refs. Play the game, do your job, and we'll be fine."

His gaze settled on the players opposite Carson.

"The last thing I want to see," Coach continued, "is an errant elbow thrown at someone's windpipe. We're Rockcastle. We are the class of this conference, and we're better men than that. Do not embarrass me, yourself, your family, or Rockcastle with that horseshit. Are we clear?"

There was a gurgle of "Yes, sir" from us, and then Coach repeated the question while looking directly at Carson. Louder, we screamed, "Yes, sir!"

"Let's get back out there," he said. "If you just want to stretch out, do it near our bench and away from the bleachers. All right, men, let's go to work."

We lost the game. We moved the ball, making crisp passes and good decisions, but St. Bernard packed in their defense and dared us to shoot. Countless balls hit the back of the rim and shuddered out. Others rattled halfway down, bouncing between the front and back of the rim like pinballs, and then popped out. They weren't forced shots either: we executed the offense, sending the ball on a string, and our shots spun through the air in a perfect arc, wrists snapped, follow-through with the arm out, but nothing fell. Too late, we tried getting the ball inside, but St. Bernard smothered us. We had to start fouling. At the end of close games, fouling is pretty common. The only chance we had to catch up was to stop the clock and hope St. Bernard missed their free throws.

Number 27 was their best free shooter and was shifted to point guard. Naturally he had the ball, and naturally I had to foul him. I didn't hit him particularly hard—I wrapped my arms around him in a loose hug—but each time, he acted as if this were the most egregious act, flopping around, grunting loudly, performing to draw a whistle that was a foregone conclusion.

"What's your problem, man?" he said to me after I fouled him for the third time.

I looked down at the warped wooden slats of the gym floor and remembered Coach's words about Rockcastle.

"Mugging me and shit," he said. "What's that about?"

"Enough, guys," the ref said, stepping between us and leading 27 to the free-throw line. He dribbled three times, head down, and then he looked up and stared at me for a moment before shooting. He had hit his first four free throws.

"That ain't ball, man," he said to me again and again. "That ain't ball."

The more he talked, the more I hated him. The more he talked, the more I pictured myself at another school, a school like St. Bernard, talking like this kid, looking like this kid.

"Y'all don't know ball," he said, dribbling, ready to take his second shot.

Bent over, hands tugging the hem of my shorts against my knees, I said in his general direction, "Go fuck yourself."

"What?" He picked up the ball and stepped toward me. His left hand squeezed into a fist. "What did you say?"

I didn't move and spoke again in the same level voice: "You heard me."

He was right in front of me, his waist by my head, and I could smell his scent, a mixture of cigarettes and stale milk and sweat.

"What did you say? What did you say?"

The refs blew their whistles and raced in, and all of us were again clustered on the free-throw line. The crowd jeered. A St. Bernard player grabbed my shoulder and pulled; blindly I shoved him off. Players pushed and cursed, but nothing much happened. Then, Carson came through the crowd and headed straight for 27. He came from the kid's right side, spun him with his left hand, which put them just a little outside the scrum. Carson's right arm was back, fist cocked, elbow bent. The whole thing moved in slow motion, and I distinctly remember a smile coming across my face and thinking, *Yes, this is what I want*. Once 27 was completely turned in Carson's direction, I flew forward and smashed the kid full in the face.

My fist buried into the kid's nose, and like a water balloon, his face seemed to cave inward. There was a crunch of bone; the impact rippled through me. My punch came from the hips, twisting through them, driven with my legs, my fist merely the contact point for an effort that took every one of my muscles—a knockout punch so perfect that I realized I had been imagining it for the entire second half. There was blood, a small geyser that shot from the kid's nostrils on impact, splattering the air around them, like a brushstroke of genius.

I still see that confetti of blood in my dreams.

What caused all the trouble in the following weeks was not the punch, but the concussion. The punch broke the kid's nose, and the way it looked was probably bad enough: his head snapped back, his legs buckling, the crunch of bone. He never got his arms outstretched to take the impact, and when he fell backward, out of control, his head slammed into the floor. The impact, and not the punch, is probably what caused his grade-two concussion.

Not that it mattered in the moment. Someone from the crowd came running at me and threw a wild punch that missed badly. Another kid flew in and tackled me, and I was buried in the scrum, a whooshing sound escaping my mouth as all the air left my body and I slammed into the ground. Only later did I learn that Carson punched two other players and threw another to the ground before he too was swarmed. There just seemed to be a large pile of bodies. Whistles blew, and then there was nothing but the din of footsteps and profanity as kids stormed the court and parents came out to pull us all apart. The two cops standing near the entrance who were just there for easy overtime suddenly had work to do.

This was one of the greatest moments of my life with Carson. After the fight, for about five minutes, our team was in the locker room, all of us with scrapes on our knuckles, bruises forming on our hands and faces and ribs, the adrenaline still racing, and we stuck out our chests, screaming barbaric yawps at each other. In the locker room, when it was just us players, and the coaches were still outside the doors huddled with the cops and parents, trying to make sense of what happened, those were some of the happiest minutes of my life at Rockcastle.

The St. Bernard student taping the game, a senior with a tripod and a VHS tape perched high above the fray on the last row of the bleachers, didn't get my punch; he was busy recording the fray as it pushed from free-throw line off to the sidelines, and when the camera finally panned back to me, I had already been tackled, and all that could be captured was a steady stream of bodies racing to center court to enter the fight. There were people who claimed they saw the whole thing, and no doubt they did, but on a night like this—with so many versions of the fight, so many memories twisted and made unreliable by hearing other people's stories, the confusion from the person sitting right next to you seeing and remembering something completely different from what you remembered—all that was true and honest about your account suddenly became hazy and uncertain. No one was quite sure what they saw.

Instead, the only certainty was what the videotape caught: Carson, his body facing the camera, separate from his team, grabbing a St. Bernard player by the jersey, pulling him into a punch, and then stomping on the kid's head when he fell to the floor.

When the bus pulled up to Rockcastle, I got off last, uncertain of how my mother would react. She stood next to our car, arms folded, unlit cigarette between her fingers. She remained silent as I got in. I hadn't bothered to shower after the game—I don't know why—and just wanted to go home. She started the car, and I scanned the parking lot for Carson but didn't see him. I wondered how much my mother had seen: the fouls, the undercut, the elbow, the punch. I wondered if she knew how much I'd loved it. I turned on the radio; she instantly switched it off but still said nothing. After ten minutes of silence, I asked, "Am I in trouble?"

"I honestly don't know."

"I didn't start it."

"Yes, you did. I saw you. You threw that punch."

"If you were there then you saw what they were doing to me the whole game. That kid deserved it, Mom. Look, it was just a fight. I'm over it. No big deal."

She laughed sadly. "Goddamn it, Owen. You really don't see how dangerous that boy is, do you?"

"Who? Carson?"

"You didn't see what he did," she said softly. "What's the point? I know what it's like, what you're like. I'd be the same way. If I tell you to stay away from him, you'll just become closer. So I just ignore it, I guess, and pray that he graduates and goes away, and then everything is fine. What would you do?"

I answered by staring at my shoes. I couldn't think of anything to say, and her mood was something I hadn't seen from her before. I was proud of myself and of Carson, and yet, in front of my mother—a person who I knew had loved and protected me my entire life—I recognized with a sorrow that made my chest ache that there was a side of myself that I couldn't reveal to her. We pulled into the driveway, the headlights shining dully on our small house. I went straight to my room, stripped down to my underwear, and went to bed without bothering to shower.

XII

Early the next morning, my mother and I arrived at Rockcastle. She parked in a visitor's spot, and we walked in silence to Duke's office off the Fieldhouse. Along with being the basketball coach, he was also the athletic director. When we entered, he was seated at his desk wearing a tracksuit, reading glasses perched at the tip of his nose. His legs were crossed at the knees, and in his massive hands was a week-old copy of *The Sporting News*.

"Owen!" he boomed. "Mrs. Webb! Thanks for coming in early. I really appreciate it."

He tossed the magazine on his desk and removed his glasses. He shook hands with my mother and waved her to a pair of chairs facing the couch against the wall.

"How are you, Duke?" my mother asked.

"I'm all right. Considering."

"Yes. Considering."

They both looked at me. I slid my book bag off my shoulders and sat on the couch against the wall, facing their disapproval.

"I'm really proud," Duke started, smiling broadly, "of what Owen has done this year. He's really grown into a helluva basketball player and leader. His teachers tell me he's a terrific student, too. But, you know, this fight—this fight looks really bad. Now, I just want to say, I'm not out to get you, Owen. And I want to be clear, right now you aren't in any more trouble than any other player on the team. Okay?"

"Thanks, Duke."

"Good." He stood up, still holding his reading glasses in one hand, and took a VHS tape off his desk. He crossed the room and wheeled an old media cart from the wall, the television tube strapped down so it wouldn't tilt over. On the lower shelf was a battered VCR, and Duke pushed in the videotape.

"I got this last night," he said, "from the St. Bernard athletic director."

We watched the six minute and thirty-seven second footage that a St. Bernard student had filmed. The distorted audio captured mostly the noise right around the camera, which was stationed at the top of the bleachers and at mid-court. It panned back and forth from one side of the gym to the other. The cameraman hadn't been paying much attention when the fight began—no players were in the shot—but then there was a commotion, and the camera swiftly swung to the other side of the court and zoomed in on the brawl. My punch couldn't be seen. Individuals couldn't be seen. It was just a jumble of players pushing and shoving and coaches racing in to break it up.

What could be seen, though, was off to the left. Near the baseline, two players grappled, one from St. Bernard and one from Rockcastle. It was Carson, his face clear and naked in the shot. He punched the St. Bernard player in the face and then tripped him. When the boy was on the ground, Carson rammed his foot into the kid's neck, his head ricocheting off the floor like a ball.

Duke turned off the videotape and sat down.

For years I have thought about that moment and what the purpose of our meeting could have been. Duke never asked me to rat out Carson; obviously, with the videotape, he didn't need my testimony. Instead, he seemed to be cultivating the relationships he would need in the future—from me, from my mother, and probably from a few other basketball players and their parents—to further his claim that the Bly family, and Carson in particular, was detrimental to the integrity of Rockcastle. I understand now how Duke held so many roles for the school, how effortlessly he was able to shed one title and wear another, and I've long been impressed by what my head coach aimed to achieve. He tapped his reading glasses against his knee, letting the footage sink in, while my mother squirmed quietly in the seat next to him.

"Now, Owen," Duke said, "let's talk about your future."

• • •

Throughout the day, our teachers lectured us on the brutish and juvenile behavior of the Rockcastle basketball team. In Western civilization, Dr. Gregor gave an impromptu survey of history's most arrogant leaders, demonstrating how the overreach of rulers from Caesar to Napoleon to Mussolini reached across mountains and oceans only because of their military might, and how this pugilism doomed their leadership and their people. Dr. Headley's biology class turned into a lecture on ethics, during which he glared at me, his eyes bulging behind his glasses. Sweat trickled down my rib cage as I looked back at him with practiced blankness. This continued in geometry, when Dr. Yee explained how often immigrant kids, like himself, were picked on for being different, and that he only learned to win by not fighting back. In Latin class, we were treated to Dr. Bober ignoring all pretense of an antifighting message in the dead language. Instead, he fell right into an explanation of Rockcastle as an institution, a place that gave the state of Ohio its mayors, congressmen, and governors, men who left to make their fortune abroad and returned to give back to the city, shaping the halls of Rockcastle not only with their financial support, but as an example of moral certainty and responsibility—something, Dr. Bober declared, our current basketball team clearly lacked. By this point in the school day, the other boys slouched in their chairs and glared at me, not because of the fighting itself, but because the fight forced them to listen to these interminable harangues.

Duke hadn't told me what would happen to Carson. He only assured me that I would owe him a lot of suicide sprints during the off-season. I didn't offer up that I had thrown a punch, and Duke, it seemed to me, had been careful not to ask. So on my sixth bell, I went to the small gym like normal to shoot baskets. After fifteen minutes and no Carson, I underhanded a shot across the room—missing badly, the ball smacking loud and dull off the backboard—and walked to the main office.

The headmaster's secretary, Mrs. Bunker, with her gaze swinging from paper to computer monitor, kept her fingers hovered over the keyboard, a pen somehow intertwined in her hands while she typed. She set down her pen and looked up at me, hers the expression of an adult who could dole out punishments in such a way that students liked being caught.

"Owen, dear," Mrs. Bunker said. "What can I do for you?"

"Mrs. Bunker, I usually spend sixth bell with Carson

Bly, and I haven't seen him today. I know you don't really keep tabs on all of us, but have you seen him?"

At Carson's name, she visibly flinched, curling her shoulders and tapping her knuckles together beneath her chin.

"You haven't heard, have you? Carson isn't here today."

I frowned. "He's home?"

"Yes, he is," Dr. Charles White said from the doorway of his inner office. He was the school's headmaster, and he entered the room with a faraway look, batting his hands against his thighs, as if he was absorbed in a vivid, pleasant memory from his childhood. He wore a neat mustache, his thick gray hair pushed back off his forehead, and a herringbone jacket and dark tie. His build was that of an ex-football player who'd been told his entire life that he was too small for the sport.

"I was meaning to talk to you today anyway, Mr. Webb. Why don't you come on in?"

I looked at Mrs. Bunker, asking with my eyes if I was in trouble. She gave away nothing, and I briefly admired her professionalism cloaked in genuine kindness. I deadened my eyes and entered Dr. White's office with my shoulders back. Imagine, my mother always said, a wire holding your chest toward the sky. She had been a dancer as a girl, and this was the kind of advice she would give me in the mornings. Once inside the office, I remained standing by the door, as if I should be ready to run.

His office was that of an executive who knew the figures in the quarterly reports the same way he knew the face in the mirror each morning. His desk faced the door, and on its glass top sat a neat stack of folders and a single pen on the ledger. Two brown leather chairs in front of his desk were placed at forty-five-degree angles, and a circular glass coffee table sat between them. In the corner, on a small table, sat a glass sculpture of a sailboat; above it were framed diplomas from Kenyon, Harvard, and Yale and photographs of racing yachts on the open sea. Behind his desk were a map of the world and four small silver clocks set for times in New York, London, Moscow, and Tokyo. I couldn't fathom why the headmaster of a prep school in Cincinnati would need such precision about cities so far away.

"Please," Dr. White said. "Have a seat."

I took the chair facing the window. Rather than sitting behind his desk, he took the adjacent chair like we were pals, crossed his right knee over his left, and steepled his fingers against his chest. My gaze focused on the knot of his tie, and I estimated how much the tie cost.

"You aren't in your uniform," Dr. White said.

For a moment I was puzzled; I looked down the length of my body, taking in my sweatshirt and shorts and basketball shoes.

"Yes, sir," I said. "I have free bell before English. I shoot baskets in the small gym and change before class."

"I see. You shoot baskets by yourself?"

"Usually with Carson."

"You two are friends."

"Good friends."

"So I've heard." He gave me an unctuous smile. "And you two good friends were at the center of the fight at St. Bernard, weren't you?"

I looked again at the glass sailboat in the corner.

"Have you ever been sailing?" he asked, following my gaze.

I shook my head. I'd never left Cincinnati, let alone been on the sea. I felt him changing subjects, aware then that he was using tactics, and my faint desire to open up to someone was immediately slammed shut.

"It's really wonderful," he continued in his rich, stentorian voice. "An old classmate of mine has a summer home on Cape Cod, and my family goes out there for about a month every year. The ocean is this big, beautiful thing. Very peaceful. We have a crew team, you know. That might be a way for you to get comfortable with being on the water."

He turned his head back to me, and I parroted a smile. I didn't know what "crew" was.

"I recognize something of myself in you," he continued. "I didn't come from the best home either. I got in a few scrapes when I was young. That's just part of being a boy, isn't it? When I was your age, it was just me and my father. My mother died when I was very young—I actually don't remember her at all—and he always had to work, so I had very little supervision. When I first read 'Self-Reliance,' I already knew what Emerson meant. Well, that is neither here nor there. Have you thought about where you're going to go for college?"

"Not really, sir. My parents went to UC. Maybe there, you know?"

Dr. White smiled down at the floor. I appeared to have told some great joke.

"The University of Cincinnati," he said, "is a fine school. But a graduate of Rockcastle has the opportunity to go to elite institutions. Ivy League schools. Stanford, if you wanted to follow Greeley's advice and go west.

"I'm sorry—you look confused. My point is that here, at Rockcastle, you have something really extraordinary available to you. Our school has a national reputation. A student who excels in academics, athletics, public service—a well-rounded young man—has a world of opportunities available to him. You need to think bigger than just this city."

"You're here," I said.

"That's true," he beamed. "Very perceptive, Mr. Webb. I am here. And I'm proud to be here. To be honest, I've had opportunities to leave Rockcastle. But this city, and this school, are very important to me. We can never forget who we are or where we're from. You'll find that when you leave home, you quickly long to come back. But your appreciation of, and loyalty to, home, however you define it, will only be strengthened by seeking broader horizons and experiencing everything the world has to offer."

"Loyalty is important," I said. "I already met with Coach Snyder this morning. With my mom there. We watched the tape that the St. Bernard student made and everything."

With my hands folded in my lap, I remained silent and watched Dr. White's mustache curl around his lips.

"Why don't you tell me, in your own words, what happened."

"I'd rather not."

"I beg your pardon?"

"I said, I'd rather not."

Dr. White fanned his hands from his face, keeping his elbows on the arms of the chair.

"I think it would be better," he said, "if you just tell me what happened."

"Yes, sir, I understand."

We sat quietly for a moment, Dr. White observing me with narrowing eyes. I turned my gaze out the windows. The afternoon was darkening, overcast like a bruise, and the bare branches of the oaks outside quivered in the wind.

"I'm not out to get you, Mr. Webb. I just think it's important to hear your version."

"But you've already heard, sir. That's why Carson isn't here today, right? I already gave my statement to Coach

Snyder. All the more reason why I don't want to talk about it any further. Not without, at the very least, my mother here."

He leaned back in his chair, which issued a soft but audible squeak, and looked at me as if he had never truly noticed me before. Other than turning my head in his direction, my posture had remained unchanged.

"Mr. Webb," he said softly, "do you understand how dangerous that boy is? Do you think this is the first time I've had to deal with his anger issues?"

Had my mother said the exact same thing? I couldn't remember. All I was certain of was one word: *dangerous*. I pictured Carson's gun in my hand, pointing it out the windshield. I didn't know then how to speak about fear, how to speak about my father's arrest and my mother's misery, and how all the anger I had been feeling could come from a place of such sorrow. So instead, I said nothing. Dr. White let out a puff of air as if giving up on me. He seemed to consider his next words carefully, and then decided against saying anything more. He leaned forward, bringing the chair to a halt, and waved two fingers in the air.

"Mrs. Bunker will write you a hall pass." He stood and offered his hand. "Thank you, Mr. Webb."

I hesitated, hands on the arms of the chair, ready for a final accusation. None came. I stood up and shook his hand firmly and walked away with my shoulders pulled back. Mrs. Bunker, with her standard kindness, told me that she thought I had a very good basketball season, and she looked forward to next year. I did, too, I said, and admitted that I hadn't known she had been at the games. "Oh, some of them," she said. "Not all. I go when I can. You take care now, Owen," and with that, I had been politely dismissed. In the hallway, I clutched my pass in my left hand, an ache rippling through my bones, and studied the Rockcastle insignia affixed to the top of the yellow cardboard stock, my name, student ID number, time stamp, reason for my absence ("Meeting at the request of Dr. White"), and Mrs. Bunker's signature, all neat and orderly and proper. Hall passes at my old public school were scrawled on thin sheets of translucent paper, and I wondered how often Rockcastle had to order new passes. Then, remembering the time, I raced down to the gym and changed without showering and made it to class slightly out of breath.

During our discussion of *Othello,* my mind wandered to Carson. I didn't know yet that he was suspended for two weeks, didn't know how his father was protecting him. Somehow, all I could see is that I hadn't fought for myself, but Carson had. And what had I done, other than hide? I tugged on my tie, the knot around my neck like a noose, ashamed at my own selfishness. Dr. MacIntosh strode back and forth in front of the chalkboard, scrawling notes on action and thought and evil in his unreadable cursive, and he swung a yardstick like a watch chain, the pinwheel of this motion captivating when I couldn't follow what he was saying. I spent class figuring out how I was going to get to Carson's house and managed to somehow avoid getting called on even once. After the bell, I went to the senior lounge at the far end of the eastern wing. I knocked, a clear signal that I was an underclassman. Even though the door was never locked, only seniors entered the lounge. Even our teachers simply stuck their heads in and asked to speak to the student they were seeking.

"Enter, heathen!"

I swung the door open. Translucent tie-dyed drapes covered the two windows opposite from me. The light in the room came from strategically placed lava lamps set on upside-down milk crates and two strobe lights spinning from the ceiling. The walls were covered with concert posters of the Beatles, the Stones, Janis Joplin, the Doors—the sole exception to this décor being a Michael Jordan "Wings" poster. Norton copies of classics were scattered across the room, and the carpet was worn thin where students had walked over the years from dilapidated couch to dilapidated chairs. Spencer Foote looked up from his calculus text, his hand hovering over the equations he had been writing in his notebook.

"Hey, Webb," he said. "Sorry I can't let you in. Senior rules and all that. Feels like the whole team could use a place to hide out today."

"No, that's cool. I was wondering if I could ask you a favor?"

"Speak, heathen."

"Can you give me a ride to Carson's?"

For a moment, he gazed at me as if I were a Polaroid that had improperly developed, the colors bleeding into a yellow haze. Then he shrugged and said, "Sure," with the same pleasant, nonchalant attitude he used to approach all things off the basketball court. We lumbered out to the parking lot. A late February storm was coming in, and we all hoped that school would be cancelled tomorrow; already, wet flurries were falling sideways, the wind creeping between our collars and our necks. The weather didn't seem to bother Spencer at all. Though he wore a coat and stocking cap, he walked without hunching his shoulders, squinting into the wind with his head up, chatting amicably about the end of his basketball career and how he could now spend all his time eating and no longer caring about his weight. I couldn't remember if Spencer had been a brawler or peacemaker during last night's fight. Even then I knew he was a person who would be welcomed in any home and every business for the rest of his life, and the sense of disappointment and loss and regret that filled most adult hearts at least once would somehow elude him.

Spencer drove a Ford Explorer, the most common type of car in the parking lot that year, a steel box on an unstable chassis that shuddered on the roads. Under his massive hands, the steering shook and rocked in a remarkably chaotic and visible way, and I wondered what it would feel like to be in a rollover accident, if the sensation would feel—before the blood and broken bones and excruciating pain—like great fun, a roller coaster of dips and spins. Spencer chattered the whole way, a monologue punctuated only by my occasional "Uh huhs." I have no memory of what he actually said.

He dropped me at the curb of Carson's house and pulled away as soon as I waved. I stood at the foot of the driveway for what felt like a long time. The white snow fell in faster, fatter flakes and somehow made the house seem darker. All the lights were off and the front windows dark, except for the porch light over the door, and it seemed to be a false invitation. When I finally headed up the driveway, my footsteps crunched on the salt already spread in an even dusting across the wet macadam.

Before I reached the door, I was certain I saw something stir by the window. I rang the bell, and it reverberated loud and clear. It sounded like the bells of a Catholic church. I'm not sure how long I stood there, waiting, before I rang the bell again. I slipped my bag off my shoulders and set it at my feet. With the heel of my fist, I slammed my hand against the door.

Finally, Caitlin cracked the door and stared out at me.

"He doesn't want to see you."

"Let me in."

"He doesn't want to see anyone."

"I said, let me in."

"Are you deaf? What I said—"

I slammed my right arm against the door and pushed hard, sending Caitlin sliding backward on the marble floor. I threw the front door closed. A look of shock spread across her face, then she was on her feet and slapped me hard. I grabbed her right arm, my face stinging from the blow, and with her free hand she jabbed a finger in my face, screaming at me to get out of her house. I twisted her arm behind her hip, bear-hugged her, and pressed her hard against the wall.

"Get off me!" she yelled.

"Where is he?"

"Fuck you!"

"Where is he?" I yelled. She squirmed, trying to break my grip, but I simply squeezed tighter. "Caitlin. Stop it! Stop! Caitlin. Caitlin."

I closed my eyes and whispered her name, once, twice. "Please," I said. I lowered my chin. Her face was nearly touching mine, our lips close enough to brush, her breath minty, her eyes dilated. My knees pressed against her legs, and with shocking awareness, I realized I had an erection. Her chest heaved visibly, and I had no idea where all this anger in me had come from. I released her arms and set my palms flat against the wall. She softly placed her left hand against my chest as if she were soothing a wounded and scared pet, and her fingers clutched my shirt. We both seemed to recognize a part of our sexuality, something equally terrifying and delightful. She licked her chapped lips.

"He's in his bedroom," she said, her voice low and soft. "He hasn't left his room all day."

For a moment, I didn't know who she was talking about. There was just Caitlin, and her entire face filled my vision: her eyes deep and muddy, suggesting something I couldn't escape from; her porcelain skin sprinkled with freckles across the bridge of her nose. She was now running both her hands across my chest, and I didn't know when I had released my grip on her.

She said, "Go see him."

When I stepped back, we were still staring at each other, and she leaned against the wall as if she were exhausted from a long run. My breathing echoed in my ears. Without another word, I took the stairs to his bedroom and banged on the door.

"Carson? It's me, Owen."

There was some sort of shuffling on the other side, and distantly, the low murmur of a classic-rock song's long bridge and lonely chords. I knocked harder, my fist against the wood for a brief moment, the reverb running up my arm, before hammering the door again.

"C'mon, man, it's me. Open up."

I knocked again and placed my hands on my hips, looking like someone's father. After a moment I opened the door.

Eyes open and staring blankly, Carson was lying on his bed facing the window, smothering a stack of clothes that could have been either clean and folded or dirty and wrinkled. His arm dangled off the bed. Out of his reach and beneath his bed were several empty cans of soda and what appeared to be a bottle of vodka.

"You weren't in school," I said dumbly.

Carson rolled onto his back, knocking several T-shirts from his bed to the floor. He stared up at the ceiling.

"I met with Duke this morning."

"You cool?"

"Yeah, I think so. You?"

"I'm finished, Webb." According to Carson, Dr. White was roused from his late-night reading of the new David McCullough book with a phone call from the St. Bernard principal. The facts were laid out for him: a brawl, a St. Bernard student in the hospital, and a videotape of the assault. This morning, Dr. Gray called Vilnius Bly, who was reached via speakerphone in New York, to deliver the news and explain that in no more than ten days, the Board of Regents would meet for a formal hearing of Carson's expulsion. Carson's father, who—like his father before him—was a Rockcastle graduate and a generous donor, started making phone calls, first to his lawyer and then to his friends on the Rockcastle board, reminding them that he was the construction mogul who had helped to control renovation costs of the Lower School by making sure that the sealed bids were appropriately low and the dollar figures perhaps known before the envelopes were even opened.

"So you have a chance?" I asked.

"No, I'm fucked. I'm gone. My dad can't fix that. It's just a question of whether I'm 'expelled' or 'withdrawn' and that's up to Dr. White."

"What difference does that make?"

"If I'm withdrawn," Carson said with the flat affectation of concussed man, "I still have a shot at getting into an Ivy League college. If I'm expelled, I don't. And White has friends at all the good schools, not just Ivys. He's, like, really connected. All he has to do is make a few phone calls and fuck with the teachers writing my recommendations. Expelled or withdrawn probably doesn't even matter."

"Is that kid pressing charges?"

"According to my dad's lawyer, they haven't decided yet. We're worth quite a bit of money. I'm sure they will. My dad is going to kill me." His expression, ashen and vacant and defeated, was a look I wouldn't see on him again until one late, muggy night almost thirteen years later.

Then, like a surge of electricity fired through him, Carson yelled, "That guy fucking hates me! White's this idealist and shit about Rockcastle, and he doesn't get it. He doesn't get it at all. He thinks it's all about merit, and it's not. Fucking fascist! I should stab them all in the fucking throat." His chest rose and fell, the muscles in his face taut. When he was stretched out like that, I had the sudden image of him and that strange girl and felt again the thrilling intensity of watching them fuck.

I said, "You'll still go to college."

"Fuck, Owen, who cares about that shit? Of course I'll go to college. Even with my straight C's I'll go to college. But I won't go to the right college. I'm supposed to go to Princeton like my dad. And if fucking White starts shit, I won't get in. Can you imagine someone like me having to go to, like, Villanova?"

"You're a C student?"

"They take and take and take. You know? Some people."

He sprang up, swinging his legs to the other side of the bed. He bent down and grabbed a bottle of whiskey from the floor, opened it, and took a swig of the brown liquid. Then he looked at me as if he had noticed for the first time that I was even in the room. "Whose side are you on?"

I raised my palms. "Yours. Always."

He seemed to wake up then, and he studied the bottle in his hands, running his thumb across the lip, picking at the label until a corner popped loose. His anger gave way to resignation, and when he looked up and out the window, his face in profile, he appeared older and worn out, like a newspaper left out to dry.

"You can't afford straight C's," he said. "Can you?"

"I dunno," I said, looking at my feet. "I mean, what's wrong with Villanova?"

Carson laughed and ran his fingers through his hair. "I envy you, Webb. I really do. All right, then. C'mon."

We stood and crossed the hall to the library. Out the windows, the snowstorm was fully upon us; wind whistled, massive flakes descended, and all the lawns and driveways were already covered in snow, which was coming down hard. An assortment of thick books was scattered on the massive table, all lying open to what seemed to be random pages.

"When I bother to do homework," Carson said, "I usually do it there."

"Feels like there should be a fireplace or two in here."

"Maybe in the next house my father builds."

Across the room on a long table beneath the window was a phone. I thought about calling my mother and asking if I could stay at Carson's for the night. Then I thought, *Why bother?* Why should I ask her permission for anything? She was just going to go home and drink until she passed out. I'd been home alone, even when she was in the room, since my father got locked up.

"Where's your dad?" I asked.

Carson gave me a puzzled look. "What? Oh. New York this week. Why?"

"No reason. You hungry?"

He clapped his hands. "You're right. We should eat. I'll make us some Dagwoods."

"What's that?"

"Don't you read the comics? Jesus, Webb."

We went down to the kitchen. The appliances hummed their soothing and barely perceptible drone. Carson opened drawers and yanked open the fridge, and I was amazed again at the size of the fridge and how much food there was for just three people. He removed packages of meat, condiments, lettuce, tomatoes, and bread, dumping them on the counter behind him.

"The key," he said, "is to get as much on the sandwich as you possibly can but still have it taste awesome."

"Is there a secret?"

"No. I just wanted to sound mystical and shit."

We each slapped together a double-decker sandwich composed of rye bread and Swiss cheese. Beyond that, we used a mixture of things—of ham or turkey or chicken or roast beef or pastrami or bologna or salami, of mayonnaise and mustard and relish, of tomatoes and peppers and crisp lettuce and baby greens—the most haphazard sandwiches we could make. I grabbed both plates and an entire bag of unopened potato chips, he snagged a couple of Cokes, and we made our way back upstairs.

"So what are we doing?" I asked.

"Homework, Webb. Hit the books and all that." He hopped two steps to the top of the landing, and then turned. "I can't let you go to Villanova, Webb. And if you work, then I work. Knowledge is power and shit. Let's go."

In the library, we set our food down in the middle of the table, and without speaking about it further, fetched our backpacks, returned to the table, and got to work. I opened my history book, laying it flat on the table, took my sandwich in two hands, and began to eat. The wind blew hard against the windows, but there wasn't any of the familiar rattling I was used to at home; instead, I was fully ensconced and safe in Carson's world. Reading carefully, we ate our sandwiches, then slurped down sodas and chips, getting through our assignments slowly. I wasn't sure, really, what Carson was working on. Was he catching up, staying with the class, or working on his next assignment? But it didn't matter. We were together, and that made everything all right.

I didn't even notice when it was fully dark. Periodically, one of us got up to use the bathroom, but it was as if we were in a trance, performing a mechanical and bodily task, leaving the room in a fugue state and returning as if under the heavy influence of a sublime force. I read my history book with complete concentration, taking notes, becoming aware of historical links that were left unspoken in the text, writing out my answers in clear sentences and with careful penmanship. When I was finished I closed the book and pushed it aside and picked up my geometry book, because that's what I had second bell. I didn't just do the assigned problems—the odd numbers, which had answers in the back of the book—but all of them, and when I made a mistake, I tore the paper from my notebook and rewrote all of it, even my previous correct answers, not just erasing but removing my mistakes until all that would be seen was the precision of my work.

I don't know how late it was when he stood and walked to the window, his hands in his pockets. There was a great sadness about him, a slight smile on his lips, and I could see then what he would look like when he was an old man. He should have remained young and handsome forever: tall and brooding, staring out into a world that he had a part in shaping. What should have happened is that decades into our future, I would look at my friend in a similar pose by a similar window, maybe even in this house, when his hair was gray and his face chiseled by time, and remind my friend of seeing him in just this position during that awful snowstorm when we were boys. "Remember that, Carson?" I would ask. "Remember that storm and how you stood right there, just like that, with your chin dipped and brow furrowed, so youthful and handsome?" And he would laugh and say, "That was before I had three children and businesses on four continents!" Often I framed moments with Carson this way—*Remember this, Carson, remember that?*—like pictures, so that I could turn to them, as though they were pages in a photo album, and I would place my finger next to every moment. *Do you remember this? Do you see?*

He set his jaw and tugged his lips slightly inward, as if he had bitten something sour, and his eyes grew hard and distant. He wasn't watching the snow but instead seemed focused on an object that only he could see. He yanked his hands out of his pockets and wrung them together over his belt; they tremored, and he clenched them as if they were arthritic and painful and he could somehow force whatever was aching out of his body. He ran his hands over his face.

"I'm exhausted. I'm going to bed." He continued to face the window. "Take the guest room next to mine. There are towels in the armoire, and the bed should have sheets on it. Knock if you need anything."

He left the room unceremoniously, and once he was gone, all my energy seemed to go with him. I placed my books in a neat pile, closed the notebooks, left the pens on the table, and crossed the hall to my bedroom. I stripped to my boxers, climbed into bed, and fell soundly asleep.

When I woke in the middle of the night, the snow was still falling. From my bed, the heavy flakes against the night sky seemed unreal, and I stared at them, disbelieving, not remembering yesterday's storm, until I was wide awake. I went to the window and placed my hand against the cold pane. I looked around the bedroom. It was three in the morning, and once I discovered the time and blinked away the sleep, I realized I could hear music.

I tugged on my jeans and walked barefoot into the hallway. From Carson's room, music rattled, a thick and heavy bass line and angry guitars. The hallway was dark except for the window at the end, which emitted a funereal and cautionary glow. I turned away and looked down Caitlin's wing, and after a moment of hesitation, crossed the landing and entered her hallway.

Over the window at the end of her hallway, a heavy curtain blocked out all the light. There was a crack of gray light beneath only one door, the first one on the left. Like a ghostly mist, it spread out at my toes, and I assumed it was the glow from a television. I stepped closer, my footfall squeaking audibly beneath me, and I winced at the noise. Standing in front of the door, I raised my hand to knock, then lowered it when a shadow moved in front of the door's light and stood just on the other side.

Caitlin didn't open the door; I didn't reach for the handle. Instead, I set my hand against the wood, the brass latch clacking against the jamb, rattling softly. The door moved back in place ever so slightly, pressure from her hand on the other side holding it in place. I didn't understand what was happening, but I had no urge to open the door; somehow, opening it would be horrific, revealing that this moment—this strange urge to be near her without seeing her—would be proven false. We stood like that, palms flat and somehow touching despite the door between us, for what felt like a long time. Then the pressure on the door was relieved, the weight of my hand pushing it forward against the latch, and the shadows of her feet disappeared. The gray light on the floor vanished, and the moment was over. I crept back to my bedroom, climbed into bed, and buried my head beneath the pillow.

When I woke, I struggled to free my legs. I had fallen asleep in my jeans, which had twisted uncomfortably around my legs, which were themselves tangled within the sheets. All the adjustments I had to make to free myself forced me to fall hands first to the floor. I blinked. Outside the snowfall continued, slower but still steady, and there was no sunlight, just a drab grayness that bounced off the snow. There was no music coming from Carson's room; I glanced at the clock and discovered it was almost noon. The house was engulfed in a cacophony of silence, and I feared disturbing it. I entered the bathroom and turned the shower on at least in part just to hear the noise. I shut the door, stripped, and took a very long, hot shower. The vanity was stocked, so I shaved my face carefully until my cheeks were smooth and perfect, combed my hair, and brushed my teeth, a tinge of blood from my scrubbed gums coming out when I spit. I made the bed and sat on its edge, my hands folded neatly in front of me, uncertain if I should leave the room. When I finally did, I looked down the hall toward Carson's room as if there were something wild around the corner that would attack me. I heard nothing and crossed to the library. There was no one there.

"Come watch TV with me."

I turned. Caitlin wore jeans and a hooded sweatshirt and looked wide awake.

"I'll just wait until Carson gets up."

"Wait with me. Let's go."

I followed her down the hall to her room. Like Carson's room, it was massive. She had space for a loveseat and a coffee table and beanbag chairs and a television, in addition to all the normal stuff a rich girl's bedroom has: a massive four-post bed with a string of lights artfully dangled around its top and across the ceiling; a walk-in closet the size of a garage; clothes on the floor and lying on top of every piece of furniture. It seemed unfair that both of them had such large rooms in such large wings all on one floor. She picked up a remote and started flipping.

"Something you want to see?" she asked.

"How about a movie?"

"That's easy. New or old?"

"Old."

"Good answer. Do you like Barbara Stanwyck?"

"Who's that?"

"Well. That answers that question." She stood up and went to her wall of movies and pulled down an armful, then dumped them on the coffee table. "We'll start with *Stella Dallas* and go from there."

She went to her closet and returned with two cups, a bottle of orange juice, and a pint of vodka. She twisted the vodka open and poured a small amount into each cup, then filled the cups with orange juice, licking her fingers before recapping the bottles. There was a slight ripping sound when she lifted the cups off the coffee table, two sticky circular rings among the boxes of videos. She stood and popped in the movie, flopped back on the couch, clinked her cup with mine, and took a long drink.

We spent the day this way. There was a fridge in her walk-in closet and a shelf with snacks, and we stood unspeaking between movies to use the bathroom, get food, and drink more. I don't remember which movie we were watching when she lifted my arm and pressed her head into my chest. We watched *Double Indemnity*; *Sorry, Wrong Number*; *Ball of Fire*; *Meet John Doe*; and then we got off our Stanwyck kick and watched others. A second wave of snow was coming later that night, and temperatures would freeze, coating the city in a glaze of ice. Cincinnati would never again have such a blizzard, and over the next few decades when the first snow of the season fell, I would always think of this day on the couch with Caitlin.

She smelled faintly of strawberries, something I didn't realize until I was very drunk. It was late afternoon; the only light in her room came from a lamp in the far corner, leaving us in the shadowy light of the television. She ran her hand up and down my chest, and when I tilted my chin toward her, we kissed hungrily. We spilled our cups on the floor, and she put her hand between my legs.

"Want to?" she asked.

I nodded mutely, and she stood, tugging her shirt off at the same time, revealing her white bra and its thin shoulder straps. She walked to her bed and hopped up.

By now I was fully hard, and I'm sure it showed through my jeans.

"Come over here," she said. "Bring our drinks."

We didn't know yet what really turned us on—that aggression and anger would be, for both of us, what made sex so good. We were both still afraid of our desires. A spasm of tenderness rose in my throat. I fought it back and took a deep swig from my cup. I stepped forward, my legs touching her knees. This close, I could smell her sweat mingled with the sweetness of her perfume.

"You want to take my clothes off?" she asked.

"No. Stand up."

When she did, I curved my hands around her jaw. Her eyes were down; her lips trembled. I had no idea what I was supposed to do. Carson had lifted that mysterious girl into his arms, carried her to the bed, and threw her onto the mattress. I fingered her earlobes, and the image collapsed: it didn't seem like her, like us. However brief it might have been between Carson and the girl, there seemed to be intimacy there, love. Caitlin and I were something different.

"I'm a virgin," she said.

"Me too."

"And I want to lose it to you."

I nodded and ran my hands down her neck. I kissed her softly; she kissed back hard, biting my lip, and I kissed back fiercely. She grabbed my ass and yanked me close. I tasted blood and realized she had bit me. She began to unbutton her jeans, and I helped, hurrying her along, and she was gasping then. I yanked her belt off, and she shoved down her jeans and panties. With a shock I realized she was completely naked. Her pubic hair was lighter than the rest of her, a soft patch that was downy and golden and fair along her skin. She kicked out of her pants, smiling. We both looked down the length of her body, and she took my hand and ran it softly over her mound, her hand guiding mine slowly, gently, inside her. I had no idea how wet a girl would get; the feeling was complete shock, and when she tilted her chin back and moaned, I was momentarily stunned.

Then an urge hit me. I pulled her hair back and spun her around and ran my mouth over the base of her neck, her shoulders. I remember seeing this in a movie, how excited the girl had become, all Hollywood lighting and music, and for the life of me, I had no idea why this would be good for her. But I loved it. I realized much later that this—from behind, seeing Caitlin's ass, the bare, soft, spotless skin—would become my favorite way to fuck her. With a grunt, I pushed her down on the bed.

I licked the back of her knee, like I'd seen the guy do in the movie, and worked up her thigh. Caitlin was whispering something, but I didn't hear what. Her hips rolled back against me. At the top of her thigh, where her leg joined her ass, up over the mound of her right cheek, I bit the flesh a little harder than I'd meant to, only to hear her say, "Fuck, yes."

"You like this," I said. "Right?"

"Jesus, yes."

"I thought you did. Turn over."

She obeyed, then arched across the mattress and gripped the bedspread tight. I knelt over her and stared at her breasts. I had never seen a girl's breasts before. I bent down and kissed them all over. I tongued her pale nipples, bit them gently, then moved slowly down her stomach. There was the smell of Caitlin's perfume and of Caitlin herself, a faint but harsh smell from her vagina. I loved it. I was surprised I loved it. I circled around her lips with my mouth; I kissed her thigh, licked again, pulling lightly at her pubic hair with my lips. She groaned then, continuing to talk to herself. Her hips started to move, pressing against my face, and then I was lapping at her like a thirsty dog. I had no idea what I was doing, but her entire body seemed to be shaking as if possessed by a spirit.

"Take your clothes off," she said.

I raised my head. I had forgotten I was dressed. I stripped everything off, and then, naked, I stood in front of her. Now I felt shy; the sight of my erection embarrassed me, and my feelings seemed to create her own. Color rose in her cheeks, and she propped up on her elbows. My body was pale and wispy; whatever muscles I had at fifteen couldn't have been much, couldn't have been attractive to anyone. I dropped to my knees so that she couldn't see below my torso. One of my hands still rested on her knee.

"Don't be shy," she said. "You just saw me naked."

"I know."

She smiled, and I smiled back and we were kids again.

"Come up here," she said.

I obeyed and stretched out next to her.

"Just look at me, okay?"

I nodded. She rolled onto her side, and with a smile on her face, lowered her eyes down the length of my body. I stared into her hair, afraid to follow her gaze. She scooted downward, and I lowered my chin far enough to watch the top of her head. Her hands ran down my stomach, tracing the ridges of abdomen and hips, and my skin flushed hot beneath her touch, tiny beads of sweat pearling along my hair. I closed my eyes and pressed my cheek against the bedspread. She wrapped her hands around my cock. I inhaled harshly.

"It's cute," she said.

If it was possible, I grew even harder in her hands. She cupped my scrotum with one hand and with the other moved gently up and down my shaft. She moved very slowly. Strangely, I fought a sudden urge to yawn.

"Condoms," she said. Her hands were off me, and she opened up her nightstand drawer. She removed the box of condoms from a bag, a small orange box with a silhouette of a couple kissing. She ripped the box open and pulled out all the condoms; several tumbled to the ground, but in her hand dangled four of them, held together by perforated plastic, and she tore one loose, tossing the rest to the ground. With an outstretched hand, palm up and forearm shining with slick sweat in the sickly glow of the television light, she gave the responsibility to me.

I leaned on one elbow, turning away from her, and opened the wrapper. The smell of latex hit me, the slightly oily quality of it. I wasn't sure if there was a right or wrong way to put it on. I flicked the condom, and the receptor tip came loose from the wrapping. *Oh,* I thought, *I see it now.* I rolled onto my back, spread the condom over the tip of my cock, and rolled it all the way down, surprised at how tight it felt. When I looked up, Caitlin was smiling down at me.

She climbed into the bed, resting her head against the pillow, her arms at her sides and her legs stretched out in front of me. I rose, and the alcohol sloshed against my skull. I climbed over to her, both very horny and very drunk, my body heavy as I moved my palms and knees unsteadily across the mattress. As I crept closer, she spread her legs until I was where I thought I was supposed to be.

"Where?" I asked.

"I'll do it." Her gaze traveled below my chin, down my chest, and she grasped me by the base of my cock and gently pulled me toward her. I was too high. I shifted my hips down, then I was too low, and she pulled, and then I pushed, and she closed her eyes and gasped at the same time my eyes opened at the warmest, strangest, most wonderful feeling I had ever known.

"Am I in?"

She opened her eyes, focused at some point on the ceiling. She seemed both in terrific pain and wondrously happy. She nodded and placed her hands behind my shoulders. It was over fast, but when we were done and I had thrown the withered condom into the trash can and stood naked in front of the mirror, I knew something was entirely different without quite knowing what had changed. I did recognize, however, that I could see myself without shame. Shoulders thrown back, firm on my feet, I looked at myself naked: the faint hair on my chest and around my nipples and the large tuft of dark pubic hair; the barely visible outlines of my muscles in my chest and shoulders; the V-like cut of my hip bones jutting below my stomach; my thighs and the growing down of hair running all the way to my feet. Above, my eyes were dilated and wild, my hair tangled atop my head like a bird's nest. I could really see myself. When I returned to the bed, I saw that Caitlin had passed out, and that seemed like a good idea. I fell next to her and gazed at her in profile—lips slightly ajar, a soft breathing escaping from her mouth, her eyes closed—and thought, *This is how I will stay close to Carson forever*.

I didn't know what time it was when I woke. The television was still on, and the jump between show and commercial threw various gray rainbows of light around the room. My mouth was cottony, and I blinked dumbly down at the floor. When I raised my head, an ache ran through my shoulders, and there he was, standing at the foot of the bed.

"Carson?" I asked.

He didn't move. In the dark haze of the bedroom, I couldn't see his eyes or his expression, just an empty oval. His hands remained by his side, but his fingers twitched and curled, as if he held a deadly weapon. I glanced at Caitlin; the back of her bare shoulders peeked out from the sheets. When I turned back, Carson was already headed for the door. I didn't call out to him, unsure of what to say, and I didn't want to wake her. I thought about getting up and throwing on clothes and racing down the hallway—but to say what? My head ached something awful, so I pressed my face back against the pillow and tried to sleep.

In the morning, I dressed quietly and went down the hallway. Carson's door was open, and when there was no answer to my knock, I walked in. The bed was unmade, but he was gone. I checked the other rooms in his wing, then downstairs. Nothing. I went back to Caitlin's room and sat on the couch and started flipping channels until she woke up. She curled next to me on the couch, and she smelled so good and her body was so warm that, for just a moment, I forgot about Carson.

We ate cereal and drank orange juice and for nearly an hour, we didn't speak. Then, Caitlin said softly, "He's gone, you know."

"Who?"

"My brother. He left this morning."

Her head was under my chin; I couldn't turn and look down at her.

"He left? Where did he go?"

"I don't know. He's gone."

She laughed softly and rubbed her hand over my stomach.

"Don't let him seduce you. You're, like, way into him. I love him, he's my brother and all, but he's always been a little off. We used to have pets when I was a kid, and he'd torture them. Killed my cat."

"What?"

"It happened when no one was home. All I remember was my mother was really upset about it. After she died, all the animal stuff just stopped."

"Animal stuff?"

"I'm just saying, he's just a guy. He's a little off, but there's really nothing special about him. He's probably down in Clifton or at one of his sketchy friends' places or something. He does that. He disappears for a few days and then, magically, he returns. I'm just saying you shouldn't wait around. Don't wait on him. He's only going to disappoint you. He disappoints everyone."

Onscreen, there was some kind of dinner party, a widescreen shot, and a man was standing tall, enraged and controlled.

"You should call your mom," she said.

"Now?"

"Later," she said, pressing against me.

Caitlin and I stayed up there the rest of the day, and around four, I called my mom at work. She answered after one ring and said, with no emotion about me skipping school, that she'd be there soon. After I hung up, I went into the guest bedroom, packed my schoolbag, made the bed, wiped down the bathroom, and closed the doors behind me. Downstairs, in the foyer, by myself in a high-back chair, wrapped in my coat with my backpack between my feet as though I were some dazed and stranded traveler, the last days ran through my mind. It was a dizzying series of images. I couldn't quite understand how I had been at school just two days ago, that I had been in Dr. White's office, that there was an accusation and a fistfight—a punch thrown in defense of me—at the core of everything that had happened. It all seemed like moments from someone else's life.

My mother's car rolled into the driveway and idled. The wipers worked against the fresh sleet beginning to fall, and her face was obscured by the reflections of dead trees in the windshield. Still, for one moment, I wished that it was my father picking me up rather than my mother, as if he would somehow understand all this. The sudden ache of missing him surprised me, and I ran my hands over my face as if I could simply wipe him away. I stood and slipped my backpack on and opened the front door. I was half outside before I glanced up. Caitlin stood looking down at me from the landing. I raised my hand in a meek wave, and she waved back, smiling tightly, her gaze bouncing from me to my mother and back again, anticipating a confrontation that never happened. I closed the door behind me, the lock clicking softly into place. Exhaust smoke plumed from my mother's car, and all I concentrated on was the crunch of snow under my feet.

XIII

My mother decided that the fight during my basketball game indicated I was lacking the steady hand and influence of a male role model, and consequently, we should drive out to Chillicothe Correctional Institution to see my father. I now regard her decision as questionable logic and terrible parenting. This was in late February. My parents were not yet officially divorced; my father had filed appeals, which would ultimately continue all the way to the Ohio Supreme Court, during which time he refused to pay his taxes, so when the divorce was settled years later, there was no child support left for my mother. For the rest of my life, I never forgot that he was a petty, vindictive man.

After the first month of his incarceration, during which time my father had called home once per week, he stopped calling altogether, and I no longer picked up the receiver and said aloud, "Yes, I accept the charges," to the operator. I received a Christmas card three weeks late, and that was all. So when we drove to south-central Ohio to see him, it had been months since I had heard my father's voice, which was beginning to recede in my memory like the last, fading chord of a funeral dirge. My mother steered us up 71, and at some state route turned east and followed a two-lane road with a speed limit of fifty through a series of farmland counties and endless flatland. The view became speckled with rural settings: roadside clusters of small houses, single-lane bridges, backwater gas stations with only two pumps, dilapidated barns with painted advertisements for home-cooked meals. A faint whistling came from my window, and I thought about the route Carson and I had taken last summer into the woods to shoot guns and the thrilling mystery of that first drive. My mother and I didn't speak; the Discman adapter was plugged into the tape deck, and we listened to Fleetwood Mac on repeat until we arrived.

• • •

The protocol for entering the prison was always the same: cross the flat parking lot, present your name and the inmate's name to the guard, then sit and wait with a dozen other people who would rather be anywhere else. The brochures from universities and colleges I had never heard of had started showing up in our mailbox, places like Kennesaw State and Roanoke College, institutions with majestic buildings and endless stretches of lush green lawns. Chillicothe with its stench of poverty and failure was a reverse of Rockcastle, where the certainty of the future was the norm, and I wondered toward which of these divergent paths I was careening.

We only waited an hour before we were ushered through another set of guarded doors, thick slabs of steel that groaned when opened, and then out into a walkway surrounded by barbed-wire fence. A straight, narrow gravel path directed us toward the prison, which was a series of massive concrete blocks that rose four stories high yet had no windows. Inside, we walked through a bright hallway, the floors freshly cleaned, the harsh stench of bleach lingering, and then we were in a large, open meeting area. Along the nearest wall stood a row of snack machines and signs indicating no smoking; the distant, opposite wall bore a series of interior windows through which visitors could see the guards and prisoners shuffle from main lockup into the meeting area. In three even rows were heavy, nondescript tables, each with four chairs but room for six. The tables were bolted to the floor. Above, on the catwalk, guards patrolled, their uniforms dark blue, and they looked bored and restless. My mother and I took the closest table.

"You okay?" she asked.

"Fine, I guess. Are you?"

"I should have had a cigarette before I came in."

"This will help you quit."

"I'd rather have the cigarette."

I smiled and squeezed her hand. Like characters in a bad movie, we looked up at the same time, and there, walking toward us from the opposite corner, was my father.

He was a stranger to me. I knew that when I was an adult, I would somehow be like him. He was grinning, and he was much slimmer and smaller than I remembered, his bushy hair now shorn short and streaked with slivers of gray. As he strode toward us, I knew before I stood that I was taller than him. When I rose to my full height, over six feet, he did a comic shuffle backward in mock horror, his palms up, eyebrows arched, before stepping toward me for a hug.

"Look at you!" he said. "You're so big! You're practically looking down at me!"

"I am looking down at you."

"I can't believe how big you are. Wow." He held me at arm's length, kneading my shoulders. He wore a beige prison suit, the top button undone, revealing a blindingly white undershirt; his glasses were thick but the frames clear, like something a grandmother would wear, and along with my height, this diminished him in a way that pleased me.

He let me go and pivoted toward my mother, arms out. "Cheri," he said. She considered it for a moment, then let him hug her, and after a moment, even hugged him back. The three of us sat down, my father across from us, and he was still grinning. He smelled like shoe polish and Old Spice. I looked around, worried that someone had seen us, even though I didn't know anyone else there—and, of course, no one else cared.

After a few minutes of small talk about our drive up and the prison food, my father turned to me and said, "You must be dominating on the court now."

"I'm okay.

"He's being modest," my mother said. "He made varsity and was their leading scorer in the games he played."

"No shit?" my father said. "Can you dunk?"

"I can, but just barely. And only in practice, not a game."

"Cool, very cool. So? Tell me about it."

I frowned. My mother too was staring at me, her chin in her hand, waiting for me to talk to my father about... well, what exactly?

"There's something else," I said. "In our last playoff game, I got into a fight."

My father frowned.

"See," I said. "There was this other player who had been talking trash and pushing and elbowing and all that other stuff, and you know, it just got a little heated."

"It was a brawl, Owen," my mother said.

"Yeah, I threw a punch. A few. You know. The whole team got involved."

"And?" my father asked.

"And nothing. The whole team was involved."

"They threw his friend Carson off the team," my mother said. "That boy stomped on someone's head. It was ugly, Joe."

"You got in a fight. Okay." He studied my face. His hands were folded together, and he was leaning forward, forearms and elbows on the table, a look of amused confusion on his face.

"His scholarship?" my mother tried. "His college future?"

My father nodded and put a hand to his forehead and kneaded his brow. Then he looked at some point over my head on the back wall. I had seen this gesture before, when he placated my mother, attempting to play the family enforcer when I always saw that he found my misbehavior amusing.

"You didn't play football," my father said. "I did. Played middle linebacker even though I was a pipsqueak. This was before video cameras or whatever, so the point was, you did what you had to in order to win the game. In football, every play ends with a pile, right? I mean, sure, sometimes a one-on-one tackle, but for the most part, it's a bunch of guys in a pile. So you gouge an eye, punch a groin, twist a thumb, whatever. That's just the game. That's football."

"Joe!"

"You brought him here for a lecture from me? About what? Being tough?" He looked straight at me. "Don't punch people in the face. Okay? Are we all happy now?"

My mother's face reddened. She lowered her chin, bit

her lip, and closed her eyes. I didn't know what she had actually expected him to say. I sensed that changing the subject altogether, like Carson did, might save us all from additional embarrassment. This was her plan, her insistence, and it seemed that I would be the reason and the show, a chance for my father to do some good.

"Wanna know what else is going on, Dad?"

"Of course," he beamed. "That's why we're here, right?"

I told a long story about my sophomore year at Rockcastle. I talked in great detail about basketball, and how I had become the focus of the offense and how I had to earn trust and be tough and be a leader and all those other sports clichés. I talked about how Duke had found me an AAU team to play on in the spring and summer, and how he and I created a plan to work on my shooting mechanics and the different drills I devised for myself to improve my dribbling and footwork. I didn't mention Carson. My mother stood up and bought us sodas and chips while I discussed my course work, how I was doing with algebra 2 and physics, and what I was learning about centuries of Russian obsession with gaining open access to the sea. For a moment, I considered telling them about Caitlin, but that seemed to still be a secret I wanted for myself. Instead, I morphed into a detailed telling of Rockcastle anecdotes, making my parents smile and laugh and squint in disbelief, revealing a whole life lived without them. I was a puppet determined to show that I had no strings, and I kept this up for nearly an hour.

The truth remained an omission. I spoke about my life at Rockcastle because life at home was so unreal. Basketball had made me disciplined in the mornings, and I staggered up and out of bed, showered, dressed, and ate breakfast without prodding; my mother did the same on the opposite end of our small house. Then at seven thirty, we wordlessly went out the side door to the car. Our drives to and from Rockcastle were without conversation, accompanied only by the blare of the radio. At night, I did my homework at the kitchen table, and she sat in the living room watching syndicated sitcoms while eating Ritz crackers and drinking white wine until she was drunk. Then she watched the news, the primetime shows, and Letterman. She left the wine bottles and cracker box on the coffee table and staggered down the hallway to sleep, and I cleaned up after her before I went to bed, making sure the kitchen and living room were spotless.

I couldn't talk about any of that.

When I was done, we pushed our soda cans and empty bags of chips around the table. My father glanced at us, smiled, looked down, shifting his weight from hip to hip, nervous in a way I had never seen before. His discomfort embarrassed me, and I remembered another story that I hadn't told yet.

"I even tried out for the school play," I said.

"You did?" my father asked.

"Yeah, the whole basketball team tried out. We were just hanging out and talking during the JV game, and one of the theater kids was there, and he said something about how the spring play is going to be really cool, a fresh take on a classic, stuff like that. So the school is doing an updated version of *A Midsummer Night's Dream,* with the whole cast being sixties gangsters and hippies. And the best part is that Rockcastle is doing the play in cooperation with Ursuline, because the play needs girls and guys. So rehearsal is at their school for one week, and at our school for one week."

"Owen wanted to meet girls," my mother said.

Caitlin's naked body entered my mind, and I raced forward with my story.

"The whole team wanted to meet girls," I said. "We all told this theater kid, right then and there, that we all wanted to be in the play, and he said the tryouts were in two weeks, and we said, okay, cool. One of the guys got a copy of the play, and over the next couple of days, we all read parts aloud in the locker room. If you were reading, you had to stand up on a bench—you know, get used to being on stage and everything—and read your lines real loud, and then we'd drill the guy with basketballs and shit. We were so obnoxious one day, Duke got pissed at us and made us run suicides."

"Dish," my father said.

He had been saying this off and on the whole visit—*dish*—and, at first, I was confused and just kept talking. It seemed to be a conversation filler just like "uh huh" or "sure" or "right" or any other noise a person might make to prove he's truly listening. At some point, however, I figured out my father meant "dis"—he had picked up and mangled the shorthand for *disrespect*.

"I tried out," I continued, "for one of the smaller parts. I thought my chances of actually getting a spot would be better if I went for a smaller role. Like, five guys on the team tried out for Theseus. So I tried out for the part of one of the Mechanicals, Tom Snout. I didn't get it. I mean, I wasn't good or anything, but I think once Mrs. Jackson, the theater teacher, figured out what all the ballplayers were doing, there was no way she was taking any of us."

"Dish," my father laughed.

My eyes narrowed, and a ripple of anger traveled up my neck.

"What is that?" I asked.

"Dish?" My father shook his head. "It's something the brothers say."

"Dish."

"Yeah. It means disrespect."

"I know what it means. But it's dis. Not dish. Dis."

If my father was at all embarrassed, he didn't show it. He nodded like an eager student. "Dis. Huh. I guess the brothers just say it funny."

"Maybe you aren't listening."

"Dis. Yeah, that sounds better." He bobbed his head, wholly unashamed. I wondered how long he had been saying it wrong, or if he even dared to say it in front of the *brothers*.

"How are you, Cheri?" my father asked. "How's work?"

"Fine. Work is fine," she said. I looked over my father's shoulders. It was her turn to be a trained monkey. She had started a new job with Fifth Third Bank and headed to their downtown offices every morning after she dropped me off at Rockcastle. I didn't really care much about what she did, and I got the impression she didn't either. I cracked the pull tab off my soda can and tapped it between my fingers. I hadn't spoken to Carson or Caitlin since my time at their house the week before.

I mumbled about buying another soda and stood up and went to the row of food dispensers. The Coke slid down the chute and hit the bottom with a mechanical thunk. I kept thinking about Caitlin and having my hands all over her. Was Caitlin my girlfriend now? Had she called me while I was gone?

Smiling dumbly, I looked up from my reverie, and all thoughts of her vanished. The visiting room was half-filled, with inmates and their families spread as far apart as they could be. All the prisoners wore the same khaki pants and short-sleeve shirts, the thick black letters "D.O.C." across their upper backs. But other than that, they couldn't be more different. The men with families were relaxed, spreading their legs wide, their children sitting next to them, a toddler balanced on a knee or a teenager slouched down as if playing a video game. Others sat across from a wife or girlfriend, holding hands with them the entire time; after the allowed greeting hug, close contact wasn't permitted. When it was two men, they sat hunched and huddled close, as if they were playing cards, their expressions grim and serious. Up above, the guards chatted with each other, glancing down only on occasion. Nothing about the room felt threatening or dangerous. No one seemed to be smuggling drugs or discussing outside crimes or huddling with an attorney, none of the stuff I had seen on television, the scenes that in the last few months made me sit upright on the couch and pay attention to the smallest details of the actors' facial tics, gestures, words, and the grim overhead lighting in each scene. I studied those television scenes as if they could somehow explain my father to me. They never did. And all I saw around me were ordinary people, broken and desperate and sad, trying to act as if there weren't a time limit, pretending that family members wouldn't go their separate ways when the visit was over—one to a cell, the other to a car and a lonely drive home—to be alone with our fear, frustration, and anger.

My mother waved me back to the table. She was tired, her shoulders sagging. Whatever they'd talked about had pissed her off—the color in her cheeks was high—and she had the expression of a person trying to swallow spoiled food. We sat silently for what felt like a long time, my mother and me across the table from him, his hands folded together like a choir boy's.

"Did I ever tell you," my father asked me, "about my grandfather dying?"

"No, I don't think so." I glanced at my mother. She didn't seem to know this story.

"My mother's father. He lived over in Mount Airy."

"North or south?"

"South. Anyway, we went over there to visit one day. I was four. My grandfather and I were out in the backyard, playing cops and robbers. We both had toy guns, and we would hide behind trees, shooting at each other. We did this a couple of times. Sometimes we were on the same team. Somewhere in the yard, my grandfather would hide these big silver dollars in a leather pouch, and we would have to find them, shooting at the bad guys to get to the loot."

"Sounds Rockwellian," I said.

"This one day, we were on opposite teams. I was a cop, he was a robber. He crept across the yard in such a way that, you know, I was going to get him. You know how grandparents let kids win games, right? So he's coming across the yard, and he sees me and freezes, and I point my six-shooter at him and—bang! I get him.

"He drops his gun, clutches his chest, and staggers from side to side. At thc time, I thought how great it was, the way he sold it, the way he died so dramatically." I tapped the half-empty can in front of me. "I think about it now, and it's all different. How red his face was, the way his eyes rolled skyward. His dance was just a person staggering around trying not to lose his balance."

Next year, I would take a class in psychology. This was what we called *trauma*.

"Right there in front of me," my father continued, "he hit the ground, and, I don't know, there must have been something there that I recognized, something that even as a kid I knew wasn't right. He hit the ground in such a strange way. Normally, he just knelt down, then put his hand down, easing his way to the ground, making those dying noises you see in westerns. This was different. He fell hard. I still remember the way his whole body collapsed, as if he didn't have any bones. I remember standing there, looking at him, and I kept saying his name. 'Grandpa? Grandpa?' I started crying. And then I ran into the house for my mom. He was dead before the ambulance got there."

"Jesus, Joe," my mother said softly. "You never told me this."

"For a long time," he continued, "I thought that if I hadn't stood there for a minute calling his name that someone could have saved him. That those sixty seconds would have made all the difference. I know that isn't true. But I kept thinking about it."

The entire time he told this story, he held a small smile on his face.

"I've been messed up," he said. "For a long time. I'm sorry, guys, for everything I put you through."

I couldn't decide if I believed this story. In class, we had discussed sociopathy, and there was something about my father's tale, the way he told it and the way he smiled, that made me wary. *This is what penitence looks like,* I imagined him thinking.

"We have to go," my mother said. "Say good-bye to your father."

"Do you really?" he asked. "It's only been a few hours."

"Three. And it takes two hours to drive back."

He raised his palms. "Okay, I understand."

"No, you really don't."

She stood, and my father and I did the same. He came around the table, and when he believed she wasn't looking at him, he rolled his eyes, as if this could somehow be a joke.

"What did you say to her?" I asked.

"Great to see you, Owen." He bear-hugged me. "You'll have to come back when the weather is nicer and we can sit out in the yard.

"Sure. Of course."

When he hugged my mother, she didn't hug back. We turned away and waited while a security guard came down the hallway to guide us out. I looked back. My father had just gone through security in the opposite corner. Two guards stood in front of him, and one flipped up his hand, to which my father raised his arms parallel with the floor. The other guard took an electronic wand and ran it from my father's neck all the way down to his feet, then stood in front of him. He said something, and my father opened his mouth wide and stuck out his tongue. He turned, and his face was in profile, and I saw how old he looked. My father seemed to have aged thirty years, his expression blank and his face skeletal. He wouldn't be eligible for parole for another eight years, when he would be forty-nine years old. What does an ex-con pushing fifty do in the world?

• • •

Overhead, the late-February weather—a dome of gray clouds covering the sky, damp and bleak and portending snow—pressed down as if to smother us. My mother dug in her purse for her cigarettes. She yanked them out, jammed the first smoke in her mouth, and with a flicker of her lighter, inhaled deeply. I never understood the appeal of cigarettes; after being inside for several hours, the cold, fresh air was a soothing balm. She stared out at the empty fields surrounding the prison, shaking her head now and again, as if she were replaying every terrible thing my father had said, none of which I had heard.

"How is this my life?" I asked. "This is so fucked."

"Watch your language, please."

"Why? What difference does it make?"

She shook her head. "Fine, don't. I'm tired. I'm really,

really tired, and if you want to curse, go ahead. You're right. What difference does it make?"

"So that's it? You just flip around, first I can't do something, then I can? Why do I listen to anything you say? You're as bad as him. Great speech, by the way. Yeah, my fuck-up convict father is going to really get me with his Gipper speech about how I shouldn't start fights and should behave like a normal, upright young man. Great plan, Mom, great plan."

She exhaled and studied the crooked and cracked bumper of an ancient Chevy in front of us.

"Don't you get angry?" I said. "Doesn't it piss you off that we have to see Dad in a goddamn prison?"

"What good would that do?"

I folded my arms on the top of our car and stared at her. Since I had discovered that I was tall enough to do this comfortably, I often leaned on the roofs of cars like this. Even then I knew it was a pose, and knowing that I was posing, along with everything else that day, pissed me off.

"I don't know," I said. "Maybe feel alive? Show some pride? Not put up with his shit?" How could I have really known or understood what she was going through? Each jab at her was a puncture into her resolve to survive my father's deceit, to ignore the fact that she had never really known him at all in order to keep moving forward, not for herself, but for me. She had found a job. I kept my scholarship at Rockcastle. She had survived. But I didn't see then the toil involved in just surviving, which I pictured as something heroic and masculine and stoic. I didn't see how much energy and effort it took just to rise in the morning, to swing her feet out of bed and stand up, when it would be so much easier to roll over, curl up in the fetal position, shut her eyes tight, and wish the world away until someone else dealt with the problem. I saw her as weak, and this, like everything else, only made me angrier.

She crossed her arms across her chest and stared off into those flat Ohio fields. I waited for a response, not really sure what I wanted from her: did I truly want her to scream back at me and treat me like a small child who had spoken out of turn? I know I wanted a fight. But I also know I wanted the fight to end, too, and be resolved, knowing that she was on my side.

Instead, she flicked her cigarette into the air, and it bounced off a Taurus. She unlocked the car, and when I didn't move, she said, "If you don't get in, I'm leaving you here."

We backed out slowly, and my mother stayed below the speed limit, checking the mirrors too often, hands at ten and two. The CD player whirled to life, and Fleetwood Mac crooned from our speakers. My mother cracked the window and lit another cigarette, the cold, whistling wind accompanying us. After three or four songs, she rested her hand on my forearm.

"You're right. What difference does it make," she said.

I didn't answer. She took her hand off my arm and again gripped the wheel. Small droplets of rain pattered against the windshield. I saw the sign for 71 and the ramp to turn left and head south toward Cincinnati, but like anyone else in the world, I don't remember falling asleep, only waking up in the driveway of our house, opening my eyes to discover that she hadn't shaken me awake when she parked the car. Rain pelted the windshield, and I studied it as it fell, trying to observe each drop hitting the glass. I rubbed my cold hands together and tried to remember what it was we had been arguing about. I couldn't seem to remember any of my words.

My immediate memory of that day is factual: it was the last time I ever saw my father. We never visited again.

When I got my driver's license, I never once visited on my own. I never received another collect phone call or found a birthday or Christmas card in the mailbox. Years later, he must have been released from prison, spent time in a halfway house, found work in a factory or an oil change shop, and moved on with his life. But in doing so, he never reached out to me or to my mother. Not once. And this disconsolate fact doesn't fill me with sadness or anger. Instead there is a great absence, an invisible, airless mass, where normal feelings I should possess simply do not exist.

XIV

Once again, they both shut me out. For two weeks, I called Carson, then Caitlin, daily, and after leaving a message on their answering machines the first four times, I simply hung up and hoped that one of them would call me back. More and more, I wanted it to be Caitlin. She was all that was on my mind—the way her legs languorously stretched down the length of the bed, how tight she squeezed her eyes shut when we had sex, the way she fit in the space between my shoulder and head. The strawberry scent of her shampoo, the small size of her hands. Like her brother, however, she ignored me for long stretches of time for reasons I didn't understand.

Spring break promised to be boring. Because we lived in North College Hill, I was far from the homes of any other Rockcastle student, even the ones I wasn't good friends with. Not that it mattered. Most of my classmates went on real vacations: Vail, Hilton Head, St. Thomas. Me? On Monday, Mom asked me not to watch too much television and to stay out of trouble, and she went to work, leaving the clock radio in the kitchen turned on, as if the sounds of daytime soft rock would soothe me like I was a nervous toy dog. I watched the morning SportsCenter twice, then went to shoot jumpers in an empty park a few blocks from my house. I dribbled the ball back up my street, careful to avoid the cracks in the sidewalk that would send the ball spinning into the grass. It was March, still chilly, and Rockcastle had a spring break that lined up with colleges rather than high schools, so there weren't any neighborhood kids around.

I stopped and picked up my dribble. From down the street, standing under a canopy of trees just beginning to bloom, I saw a car I didn't recognize in my driveway. The unmarked cop cars that had parked in our driveway and idled at our curb had been four-door American sedans with unadorned hubcaps. This was a faded red Malibu, a teenager's first car. A boy in the passenger seat inhaled from his cigarette and ashed into my lawn. With the basketball on my hip, I crept up the sidewalk, thinking my footsteps were too loud. There was a second boy in the car, sunglasses on, head lolled back, right arm swept across the back seat of the Malibu. They watched my front door, and there, ringing the doorbell, then cupping a hand over his eyes and peering through the living room window, was Carson. He knocked on the door, then took a step back, like an experienced salesman, and slid his hands into the back pockets of his Abercrombie jeans. My chest tightened. I had longed to see him for days, yet now that he was standing on my porch, something about this moment filled me with dread.

I crossed my lawn. "What are you doing here?" I asked Carson.

He turned and leaned against the post. "I'm here to get you, Webb."

"For what?"

"For spring break."

I glanced at the car. The kid in the passenger seat wore sunglasses and pulled on his cigarette like he was auditioning for a mob movie. Probably menthols, I thought.

"Come on up here, man," Carson said.

I climbed the stairs and dropped onto the porch swing facing the street. Carson leaned back against the railing, facing me with his back to his friends, his arms crossed, and a strange smile on his face.

"Been practicing?" he asked, nodding at the ball.

"Yeah," I said. "Free throws, then catch-and-shoot, then one-dribble-and-shoot."

"You'll be all-conference in no time."

I ran my fingers over the tacky surface of the basketball.

"Where the fuck have you been?" I asked. "You just vanished. You don't return my calls, you're kicked out of school—you're, like, not around at all."

"I'm a free man now. I've been, you know, around. Hanging out. Doesn't matter. Fuck those guys. Anyway, that's not important. What is important is that you pack your bags. We're going on a little road trip."

"Road trip?"

"It's spring break, Webb. Time for us to get going. See the country. Hit the beach." He pushed his sunglasses up onto his forehead. "A run for freedom. I'm talking about the great American road trip! C'mon, Webb!"

"I can't just leave."

"Why not? You got something else to do?"

"No, man. Just—I can't leave town. My mom would kill me."

"Ask for forgiveness, not permission. Remember how we first became friends? Remember that awesome party we went to? You didn't get in any trouble for that. In fact, your parents were proud that you took initiative. I mean, they didn't even come home that night. They were out getting drunk, too, right?"

Did Carson know I was awake when he fucked that girl in front of me?

"One night and one week are two different things, man."

Carson sighed. "Same principle, dude."

"That doesn't make any sense. Who are those guys?"

"Friends of mine. Good guys, you know?" I would later learn that the kid in the front seat was Brian Reinhart, and the one in the back seat was Kevin Lordo. But in the moment, all I knew was that they didn't go to Rockcastle. They looked more like my old friends, the type of guys I ran around with at my old school, when I was always getting in fights, or shoplifting comic books, or throwing rocks at passing cars only to run away laughing when the driver screeched to a halt.

"Come on. I'll introduce you."

"I don't know, Carson."

"Picture it, Webb. Picture those rolling Kentucky hills. Picture the open road, the total freedom of being in a car. Kerouac and all that. Then, we're on a beach. Panama City. You don't have to worry about getting ID'd down there, man. It'll be no problem. Everybody drinks and parties down there. We'll take over, like, two hotel rooms, you know—those ones with the shared door between them—and it'll be one big celebration. Six days on the beach. It'll be fantastic. Get the fuck out of Dodge for a little while, you know? It's just like when you stayed at my place the other day. You didn't ask, right? You just did it. Because you wanted to."

"Sounds kind of nice," I said. Over the boys, over the roof of the car, across the street, and down a couple of driveways, a neighbor I had never spoken to was mowing his lawn. My parents would wave to him whenever we drove by, but I'm not sure they knew him either. An expression of dazed exertion settled over his face as he trudged up and down his grass, leaning forward, his mower sucking up dead leaves, clearing his front lawn long before it needed to be cut. No one else on the street had mowed yet. There wasn't a need.

"Haven't you learned yet?" he asked. "We make our own rules. Especially me."

"You got kicked out of school."

"And, baby, if I want to, I'll still go to Princeton."

With two hands on it, I kept the basketball in front of me, spinning it between my knees. Carson, still leaning against the railing, flipped his sunglasses from where they rested on top of his head down over his eyes.

"You know," he said. "Ursuline is on break next week. I bet we can get Caitlin to fly down this weekend. Meet us there."

Caitlin hadn't left my thoughts for over two weeks, and I lay awake every night wondering when I would see her again. My mouth dried, and I shuffled my feet.

"Really? She could do that?"

Carson laughed. "You're so naïve, man. Dude, it's kinda charming. Yeah, man, why couldn't she?"

The muscles in his forearms rippled. The kid in the front seat of the car fiddled with the radio, and I thought about the gun in the glove box of Carson's car. After all this time, Carson remained a mystery to me, in much the same way that my father was hazy and unclear. The surface of them: that's all I saw, and perhaps that's all there was to them. Sitting on my porch that day, I believed Carson. I believed he had it all figured out and that an insouciant attitude was enough. Even better: I was smarter than him. I had earned my way into Rockcastle. I had earned varsity. I had earned the right to go on a road trip with Carson and make new friends and have a real vacation and even have Caitlin swoop in just to see me, had earned the right to follow only the rules I made. I stood up and faced Carson. "Fuck it. Let me pack a bag."

He smiled triumphantly.

In a heartbeat, I was back outside with a duffel bag over my shoulder. I had thrown T-shirts, shorts, and underwear in a bag without really looking, took my toothbrush from the bathroom, and that was about it. I followed Carson to the car, and he popped the trunk. Inside were five bags haphazardly tossed in, and I dropped mine on top.

"Hey, Reinhart," Carson said. "Let Webb sit up front."

Without any complaint, Brian Reinhart opened the door and got in the back seat. Carson turned the ignition, revved the engine, and backed us out of the driveway, the doors shaking from the stereo's bass and my hands shaking with adrenaline. We raced up the street, zipped through a yellow light, and accelerated up the ramp onto the highway. Then Carson eased into traffic and cruised at a leisurely pace in the right lane as if he were in no rush to get anywhere at all. We turned onto 71 and headed south toward the river.

"I love that smell," Reinhart said.

The other boy in the backseat asked, "What is it?"

"Smells like vanilla."

"Jack Daniel's."

"Man," Reinhart said, "whiskey doesn't smell like that."

I pointed at the factory to our right. "It's a distillery. They're processing the grains that make whiskey. The smell comes from the process. After the grains and mash and water are aged, they need to be processed. Adding sugar gets the flavor you want, and then it has to be cooked. What you're smelling is that process."

"How do you know all that?" Carson asked.

"My father told me." The factory racing by suddenly seemed slower in my vision, and the tall gray structures and the smoky windows looked old and tired under the sun, as if they had been worn away by the heat. For years, we had driven by this factory, its strange smells of vanilla or strawberry, sweet and slightly buttery, and I pictured candy. When I was ten years old, I finally asked my father about the scent and was disappointed, and a little scared, that it came from whiskey. I had long associated alcohol with my father—the yeast scent of beer and the sharp pungency of whiskey a telltale sign he was having a bad day, the kind that made my mother and me slink away. I rapped my knuckles softly on the window, thinking about him, hating him, wondering why he had to ruin everything he touched.

"Ever hear of Panama City, Webb?" Carson asked. "I've heard about it at school. Nice average families go to Hilton Head. I've been there. It's a little boring. Families like mine go to Vail or Corsica or someplace tony like that. Now, Panama City? That's where it's at. That's where the grim is—these disgusting clubs where we can get in even though we're underage, and drink all the shitty liquor you can imagine. Down there, Webb, down in Florida, it's another world. The whole place is like one big Ponzi scheme. Man, you have no idea. You're gonna love it. You ever been down there?"

I shook my head. "My grandfather lives in Orlando, but we don't visit."

"We aren't going to Orlando, dude. Fuck that Disney shit. Look at this sunshine. If I was religious, I'd say we were blessed. Hey, Reinhart? Hand me one of your mixtapes."

Over the next few hours, I learned very little about Brian Reinhart. He was a skinny kid in baggy jeans and an oversized Hornets T-shirt, and when he handed me a mixtape, he did so with gentle, childlike reverence for the cassette. I opened up the cassette holder, popped in the ninety-minute tape, and as the bass of an E-40 track rattled the car, I removed and read the playlist, written in orderly printed handwriting. Reinhart did this with all his mixtapes, writing out in longhand a one-sentence criteria for each selection. He spelled poorly—"Ceaser complex" and "Jamahcian influence" were just two examples—but the printed words were unsmudged and in straight, parallel lines. He signed these playlists "Reinhart." Apparently, not even his parents called him Brian.

Kevin sat directly behind Carson and remained mostly silent the entire car ride. He had dark buzzed hair, an inconsistent goatee, and muscular shoulders; his eyes were dead so that even when he smiled, he looked like he was simply showing his teeth to a dentist. There was a cigarette tucked behind his ear, but I never saw him smoke or even hold a lighter. He frequently cracked his knuckles but otherwise remained volcanically still.

Sunlight flooded the car, and we rolled over the Ohio River, the metallic bridge rumbling underneath us as we cruised above the water, the massive barges below heading downriver toward places I couldn't even imagine. In a breath, we were across the river and into Kentucky, its rolling hills rising around us on all sides. At some point, one of us started rapping along to the music, and soon all four of us were singing along, pointing our fingers or hands or fists for emphasis, rolling our shoulders in a seated dance, just being kids.

All through Kentucky, I didn't think about my life. The anger that had been building when I saw Carson, when he challenged me on the front porch, when I inhaled the false-confectionary scents of the distillery, all seemed to vaporize under the loud music and rushing wind from our open windows. The early spring weather was just the right mixture of spring chill and hints of summer warmth. It was the kind of fun I hadn't felt in weeks.

A few miles from the Tennessee state line, Carson flipped on his turn signal, then veered madly across three lanes and cruised down an exit ramp for Williamsburg; the signs pointed toward Daniel Boone National Forest. At the bottom of the incline was a massive Marathon gas station, the kind with an entirely separate entrance for RVs and long-haul trucks. It was late in the afternoon and all the parking spaces directly in front of the multipurpose store were filled. Carson steered us over to the faded parking spaces along the far edge of the lot and parked. In front of me was a single pay phone, then an uncut field of tall yellow grass and wildflowers, and, out in the distance, the blossoming trees of the forest. I lifted my arms over my head, and a stretch rippled down my lats and into my spine.

Carson yawned. "Unless you're literally a brain surgeon, driving is the hardest thing you will do in your entire life, which is both amazing and sad, if you think about it."

"Want me to drive?" Reinhart asked.

"Fuck no. I just want you to appreciate my contribution, that's all."

"Whatever, man. Are we eating here?"

The four of us turned. The Marathon station had not only gas and convenience store merchandise, but showers for truckers and, sharing a space, a Burger King.

"Yeah. I want to get on the move," Carson said. He eyed a Malibu convertible that pulled into the nearest pump. "We should have a different car."

"What's wrong with my car?" Reinhart asked.

Carson didn't answer. It was too cold for the top to be down, but the middle-aged man who climbed out of the Malibu clearly didn't care. He wore boat shoes and no socks, a loose-fitting oxford, sunglasses, and a faded ball cap—dressed like a man about to put his boat into the water. He placed both hands on his lower back and arched toward the sky, his mouth sliding into a grimace.

"Little cold for a convertible," I said.

Carson nodded, and his eyes darted toward the pavement, as if making a mental calculation the answer to which was too good to be true. I clapped him on the back and jokingly asked if he was stoned.

"Just thinking," he said. "Let's get some lunch."

The four of us entered the gas station, the rusted bell above us trilling our entrance. Inside, the rows of Hostess snacks, candy bars, oil cans, work gloves, cheap T-shirts, and single-serving toiletries fanned out in long, straight aisles. The clerk had a line four deep, and the bathrooms were straight ahead. Hot dogs rolled under heat lamps by the soda machines, and off to the left and around the corner was Burger King.

"I'm gonna piss," Kevin said, heading toward the restroom.

"Me too," Reinhart said.

"Is this 'real America'?" I said.

Carson ignored my joke, watching the gas station clerk, his neck and shoulders tense. He crossed his arms. A trucker reached into his wallet and pawed at a wad of bills before handing the clerk a twenty.

"Wait," I said. "I forgot my wallet. It's in my bag."

Carson handed me the keys without taking his eyes off the clerk.

Back outside, I strolled across the parking lot, taking in the variety of cars, the license plates—West Virginia, Wyoming, Minnesota—the spray of dead bugs on the windshields, and the loads of baggage in back seats. Everyone seemed to be from somewhere else, and everyone had someplace else to be. It felt like we were all on a caravan to a better place, and the idea of heroic voyages and slaying dragons popped into my mind. I didn't even like that sort of thing, which is why I remember childishly thinking about knights and castles as I opened the trunk of Reinhart's car and stared down at our bags.

My duffel bag was on the right, and I unzipped it and fished around for my wallet. It was a brown trifold, cracked and bulky, a hand-me-down from my father that held only cash and my Rockcastle ID—no cards, no identification, not even photos. I stuffed the wallet in the right pocket of my basketball shorts, the trifold sliding down my thigh and batting against the top of my knee, and then considered all the bags in the car. There were four of us but six bags, and it had only taken me a few minutes to grab a toothbrush and T-shirts. Directly beneath my bag was a blue duffel with thick white handles and a faded logo for SeaWorld printed on its side. I shoved my bag aside and unzipped the blue duffel.

Crumbled pieces of the *Cincinnati Enquirer* stuffed the bag like it was packed to be mailed. Right on top was yesterday's edition, and I removed a single wrinkled piece and unfolded the local want ads, scanning with bored interest the calls for executive assistants, third-shift truck loaders, entry-level engineers, paralegals, and junior-level copywriters. I crumbled the newspaper into my fist and reached back into the bag.

I felt it first. A ripple of recognition, fear, and delight tingled through my fingers, up my forearm, and into my chest. My hand hovered for a moment, and then, like a caress, I ran my palm over a pebbled rubber, and then I wrapped my hand around what I knew was a gun. I gripped it, careful to keep my fingers away from the trigger, my gaze resting at some indistinct point slightly above the bags, at the back of the trunk. With a gentle pull, keeping my hands low and out of sight, I lifted the gun out of the bag and looked down. In my left hand was the grip of a .32 revolver.

My breathing echoed in my ears. I didn't recognize the gun. It wasn't one that Carson and I had shot in the woods. My thumb rose off the grip and edged toward the hammer as if magnetized. Then I froze. Using the muzzle, I pushed aside the balled pages of newspaper, and at the bottom of the duffel bag were three other pistols. My mouth went dry, and I watched my left arm shaking as if it weren't a part of my body.

I released the gun as if it were a scalding pot and looked over my shoulder. No one was paying any attention. Drivers stood outside their cars, one hand on the pump handle and the other on a hip or scratching their heads or covering a yawn, staring off into space. On the street, cars slowed down to ease onto the ramp to the highway, the steady hum of traffic the only noise I could hear. My tongue, fat and heavy in my mouth, felt swollen, and it was hard to breathe or swallow. I turned back around, used my T-shirt to wipe the handle of the .32 free of my fingerprints, and zipped close the gun bag. I stood up and put both my hands on the lid of the open trunk and held them there, at shoulder level, and looked out at the forest. I pictured my hands held even higher, as if I were under arrest. Or higher, pressed against a brick wall as a cop frisked me for weapons. Cops with guns drawn, screaming orders at me, willing to shoot me. Willing to kill me. Cops like the ones who had arrested my father, cops who worked in prisons, patrolling an area with dominant indifference. My heartbeat thumped in my ears, and I clenched my hands into fists, brought them up to my closed eyes, and tried to press them through my skull. After what felt like a long time, I ran my fingers down my cheeks as if I weren't sure they would still be there, and when I looked up again at the still, unmoving tree line in the distance, my vision was blurry and wet with tears.

I reached into the trunk, picked up my duffel bag, and dropped it on the pavement. I shut the trunk, went to the driver's door and locked the car, slung my bag over my shoulder, and walked back to the gas station. Carson, Reinhart, and Kevin were seated at a booth, trays of hot cheeseburgers and fries in front of them.

"Going somewhere, Webb?" Carson asked.

I tossed the keys on the table.

"I'm going home," I said. "Don't feel well."

"Buy some Pepto. Gas stations have everything."

"I'm going home." I turned and walked away and kept moving, even as I heard Carson say, "Hold up." I was already back on the sidewalk outside before he caught up to me and grabbed my shoulder.

"What's the matter?" he asked.

"What the fuck are you up to?" I whispered.

"Up to?"

"In the car. In Florida. Whatever it is, man, I don't want to know."

We were standing several feet from the entrance, next to a garbage can with a plastic ashtray top that hadn't been emptied all day. Carson stood in front of me and started nodding, slow and methodical. He crossed his arms over his chest and stared at me until I tucked my chin and looked at the ground.

"You opened a bag that didn't belong to you," he said.

"I just want to go home."

"You sure? You really want to go home? To do what?"

I had no idea. All I knew then, with startling clarity, was that I needed to be at home, on the couch, and away from all this. Away from everything that Carson was about. He was studying me the way he had a year and a half before, watching me shoot and miss jumpers in the gym, just a freshman with no friends and nothing else to do, sizing me up and deciding what I was good for, what to shape me into, recognizing in me just enough of himself and just enough of someone else that he decided he could mold me into his new best friend. It is clear to me now how long he had been plotting this, shaping me, leading me, guiding me to that moment in Williamsburg—a moment that would lead me to a point of no return. But right then, under his steady gaze, I didn't think anything other than this: *I am absolutely terrified of what he's going to do to me.*

"All right," he said. "Be a pussy. Go back to Cincinnati. Be a Rockcastle man. Keep pretending you can be one of them. You think everyone else doesn't know what you are? Just some white-trash faggot pretending to be something he's not. That's cool. I'm going back in there, and I'm eating my fucking Whopper, and I'm going down to Florida, and if you don't wanna come, fine, fuck you. Stay here. Good luck finding a way home."

He walked past me, slamming his shoulder into mine, knocking my bag off my shoulder. Tears ran down my face, and I furiously wiped them away, humiliated by what he'd said and even more humiliated that I couldn't stop crying. I grabbed my bag, raced back into the gas station, went into the bathroom, picked the middle stall, and locked the door. Sitting on the toilet, I pulled my knees up, crushing my duffel bag into my chest. The canvas irritated my chin, cutting into my face like razor burn, but I wanted to hurt. I wanted to focus on something other than a choking, horrible fear that Carson would soon burst into the bathroom, kick open the stall, point the revolver directly at my face, and kill me. Images of the glass bottles we had placed on the logs in the woods burst into my vision: the shattering crack as the bullet tore through them, the shards of brown glass in tiny splinters and thick, large chunks spinning in the air and catching the sunlight, the ease with which bullets ripped them apart, and the soft trill of tiny pieces striking the rocks along the creek bed. I held my bag against my chest like a shield, hiding my nose and mouth, and sat there until my legs ached, and then, finally, went numb.

When I eventually stopped crying and set my feet on the floor, the muscles in my back tight and painful, I wondered how much time had passed. Thirty minutes? Was he still waiting outside for me, a smirk on his face and arms crossed across his chest? The lock on the stall clacked loud and echoed when I pushed it aside. No one was in the bathroom. I put the strap of my duffel over my head and shoulders and washed my face, eyeing the door to see if anyone came in. I stepped out of the bathroom cautiously, one hand still on the door, prepared to bolt back inside if I saw him. But he was nowhere in sight. The overhead speakers tuned to a top-forty station announced the time, and I did the math: I had been in the bathroom for almost ninety minutes. On tiptoe, I peeked over the aisles and out the window to the parking lot, and saw that their car was gone.

Back on my heels, feet flat on the ground, I wiped my damp palms on my gym shorts and inhaled the antiseptic soap scent that still clung to my face and neck. My mind emptied. There was a new lightness to my neck and shoulders, and I smiled dumbly at the candy bars in front of me: they had left me behind. Then, as if my stomach could read "Snickers," it grumbled, and I remembered I hadn't eaten lunch. I grabbed two candy bars and a soda from the cooler. There were no customers at the counter, and when the clerk rang up my order I asked him if he could give me some change.

"How much do you need?"

"I don't know. How much is a long-distance phone call?"

Outside, I went to the end of the sidewalk near where Reinhart's Malibu had been parked and sat down in the shadow of the gas station, all the muscles and tendons in my legs groaning and pulling tight as I lowered myself to the ground. I unwrapped a 3 Musketeers bar. I took small bites, eating slowly and methodically, savoring the chocolate, unable to think about anything but the flavor of my food. The entire day seemed impossible and unreal.

I pulled off my duffel bag over my head and set it on the concrete next to me. I balled the candy wrapper in my fist and imagined it was a basketball. I had just survived something big, but even then I had no idea what terrible thing Carson would do just a few hours later, or that it would be several days before anyone, including me, knew about it. Above me, faintly, the speaker system outside the gas station played Springsteen's "Streets of Philadelphia." Even today, that song still makes me cry. I know my sadness has everything to do with the circumstances of hearing the song as I sat staring at the cars pulling up to and then away from the gas pumps, the hot, meaty stench of Carson's breath on my face as he insulted me, his hate still buzzing in my ears, while up above, in a whisper barely audible, Springsteen sang, "I heard the voices of friends, vanished and gone." I imagined that he, too, knew what it meant, deep at his core, to be soul sick and heartbroken, scribbling lyrics furiously while people he knew and loved disappeared.

It's just you and I, my friend.

But I was alone now. The left pocket of my basketball shorts sagged to the concrete from the weight of the roll of quarters the clerk had swapped me for a ten-dollar bill.

When I stood up, the quarters swung forward and batted against my thigh, tugging my waistband crooked. I pulled out the roll, wrapped in material the texture of newspaper but brown, the lettering in chartreuse proclaiming the worth of the coins. I turned my palm up, then curled my fingers around the quarters, my hand now a fist. I held my hand closed like that, clenching the metal tight, the paper roll dampening from my sweat. But I couldn't hold it for long without my hand aching. I loosened my grip, bent down and grabbed my duffel, and walked to the pay phone at the edge of the parking lot.

I picked up the receiver and set my free hand on top of the phone, the dial tone faint as I stared out at the woods. No words came to me. I dialed the number, shoveled in the amount of change the operator demanded, and asked the secretary who answered the phone if I could speak to my mother. When she picked up, my mother said, "Owen?" three times before I could answer.

Finally, I said, "Mom? I need your help."

PART III

XV

It happened just a few hours after I called my mother from Williamsburg, but it was a different world then, back in 1996, and the story didn't reach Cincinnati until Friday morning. When I opened my eyes that day, I was facing the wall, blinking at the scuff marks that must have come from my shoes, though I couldn't imagine why I would ever lie in the wrong direction on my own bed and put my shoes on top of my pillows. I inhaled deeply, and the gentle pressure on my left shoulder turned me over.

My mother sat down heavily on the edge of the bed, her brow furrowed. Even though she must have squeezed hard enough to wake me, the pressure from her hand was light.

"Owen," she said. "Are you awake?"

I turned. Of course I was awake; I never understood why people asked that question. Moreover, it was still spring break—even in my sleepy haze I knew that—and I had taken to sleeping the morning away. My mother showered and dressed in the mornings, left for work, and called around noon to make sure I was awake. Ever since she'd driven me home from Williamsburg, I had effectively grounded myself, not leaving the house at all, spending most of my days on the front porch listening to the radio while reading. I read every article in the daily *Enquirer* with a focused intensity, finding articles about General Electric, the Republican-led Congress's Contract with America, and the daily obituaries of people who had fought in World War II. When I had exhausted the newspaper and heard a top-forty song for the third time in a day, I switched to my history book to try and get ahead when I returned to Rockcastle next week. I read about the Second Industrial Revolution in England, the pollution of the Thames, and the development of epidemiology due to the poisonous water systems of London.

After I had called my mother from the gas station on Monday, I went back inside and bought a *Sports Illustrated* and then returned to my corner spot on the sidewalk to wait. I read the magazine cover to cover before she arrived. When she pulled up to the curb and opened the door, I expected her to fly into a rage, maybe smack me upside the head, demand to know just who I thought I was running off to Florida. As she stepped out of the car, however, the first thing I saw was that she was barefoot. I stood up. Her mouth trembled, her lips split and chapped, and seeing the fear on her face, I started sobbing. She raced over and hugged me and whispered, "It's okay" into my hair. She led me to the passenger side and opened the door, reached in and picked up her dress shoes from the seat and threw them in the back.

She asked me what happened, and I told the story in detail—from playing basketball to walking up the lawn to what I packed. I told her about the two other boys in the car and the songs we rapped along to and wanting Burger King and finding the guns, and how I didn't mean to open the bag but I had to, you know, and I'm glad I did. And I didn't know anything about it, I swear I didn't—Carson just said we were driving to Florida, he didn't say why or what the bag was for, but it was wrong, I just know it, and he's in trouble, and I can't end up like Dad. And Mom, I swear I didn't know, I didn't do anything wrong. Mom responded with silence, her eyes scanning rapidly over the landscape as she drove, her mouth curling up and down into questions she didn't ask, biting her lip, her hands fidgeting around the steering wheel as if it were hot. I had never seen her this scared in my life, not even when my father was arrested. The kind of fury Carson spewed at me would not be coming from her. The headlights of the oncoming and surrounding cars swarmed us, and with each hour fewer and fewer cars were on the road until it was just us and semitrucks. In the slants of light that cut my mother's face into slices, sometimes leaving her eyes in the shadows, sometimes her mouth, she occasionally seemed young and pretty; other times, the lines around her eyes and mouth were deep, creases of age that would become more pronounced each year. Her hands were firm on the steering wheel, the seat pulled upright, her elbows bent ever so slightly, her knuckles unadorned with rings, as if she had tapped a previously deep, unfound resolve. I studied her face for a long time, but I don't remember exactly when it struck me that what I did, leaving without any warning, was such a betrayal to her. I remained awake, tuning the radio as receptions popped in and out along the highway.

When we arrived home, my mother stood in the kitchen, perched on one foot, rubbing the inside of her left calf with her right instep, holding the phone to her ear, and in an urgent but calm tone left a message for Carson's father on their home phone and at his work. After she left both messages, she asked if I was hungry. I said I just wanted to go to bed.

And now, several days later, she was sitting in front of me asking if I was awake.

"Sure," I said. "I'm up. You okay?"

"Carson's been arrested."

I sat up.

"I got a call this morning," she said. "A couple of calls, actually—other parents, and Coach Snyder and Dr. White. It's in the newspaper today and on the news."

"What happened?"

It was the lead story in both the *Enquirer* and the *Post*. Just hours after they drove away from the gas station, Carson and his friends followed a car on Interstate 75 to its home in Cleveland, Tennessee, and attempted to carjack the driver. All three boys had guns stolen from their parents' suburban Cincinnati homes. The driver got out of the car, hands up, cooperating, and gave Carson the keys to the car. But amongst the commotion and their demands for the keys and instructing him to get on his knees and transferring all their bags to his car, they never considered if someone else was home. The boys were startled by the man's wife opening the garage door from the house. One of them fired a single shot from a .32 directly into her face, and then they fled in the stolen car. They were arrested in Panama City Beach, Florida, only because they drove away from a Waffle House without paying their check.

"She's dead?" I asked.

"No, alive. But she's in bad shape, Owen. They don't know if she's going to live or not."

The *Enquirer* was in her lap, her left hand flattening it down as if she could make it vanish.

"Owen?" she said. "They think Carson was the shooter."

• • •

The Kroger on Winton Road was a gleaming new supermarket set back far from the street. At the front of the parking lot sat several large containers: one was for Goodwill, and often garbage bags of clothes and toys, alongside mismatched chairs and small end tables, sat next to the deposit bin. The others were for the community's recycling, one for newspapers and one for plastic bottles and aluminum cans. The parking lot was so large that even when the store was packed, there were rows and rows of empty spots, except after Thanksgiving, when the lot was used for Christmas trees. Once, this Kroger had been a stretch of brick ranch houses, but the owners were bought out, given whatever was deemed fair-market value by a community desperate to keep the largest grocery store in the area happy.

Now, it's just a lot housing a deserted building. In just under ten years, Kroger decided to move back to its old location on Brentwood Plaza, less than a mile south on Winton and closer to Ronald Reagan Cross County Highway, where commuters discovered that stopping for groceries near the on and off ramps of a highway was considerably easier than driving a mile up the road. As for the old "new" Kroger, it was abandoned, resulting in an empty building in a huge parking lot whose night lights are paid for by the municipality. You can still see the remains of the Kroger sign on the brick wall, its texture protected from sun and rain by those large neon letters for years, and now it's a dark reminder, a botched tattoo, of what used to be. There are no plans to put a new business there because the location is poor and no one wants it; nor is there any desire to torpedo the building and build new affordable homes for Finneytown's once vibrant middle-class community. The brick and glass, blacked out as if preparing for a wartime bombing, are the skeletal remains of a community that lost the will to care about its appearance.

But on that Friday night, it was a supermarket so shiny and new that my mother would drive past two IGAs and an Aldi to wander its pristine aisles. We pushed a cart into the store. The produce section stretched the length of the building and displayed a vast section of color—of tomatoes and apples and oranges and bananas. A water system misted the array of broccoli and cauliflower and green beans and celery and parsley—all under bright new tracks of shapely beams of light. Beyond all the colors were loaves of freshly baked breads, muffins, cakes, and donuts, and at the very end was the deli counter that wrapped around the corner, ending at a massive tank of lobsters. The fine mist issuing from the automatic sprinklers was hypnotic.

"Do you want any bananas? Apples?" Mom asked. We had just come from the movies; she had taken off work to keep an eye on me and be around the house, though I spent most of the day trying to process the image of Carson shooting a total stranger. After shooting jumpers by myself all morning, wishing there were a different word than *shooting* for what I was doing, my mother and I had spent the day trying to keep busy with various errands and shopping that involved wandering the mall and buying nothing. We had just come from a showing of *Down Periscope,* a movie that was even worse than its name.

"On the news," I said, "I saw that reporter, Clyde Gray, outside Carson's house."

"He came to our house last year when your father was arrested."

"You didn't tell me that."

"Why would I? You weren't home at the time. I hope those reporters don't follow his sister to her school."

I'd called Caitlin a dozen times since I'd seen the news. She hadn't called me back.

"I'm just thinking," my mother said, "of his father and sister. I know how exhausting it is to be under all that scrutiny."

Of late, Mom seemed to have a new interest in the quality and variety of what we ate, as if these decisions would somehow make me safe from whatever disease of the mind had infected my father. From a great distance, I focused on the deli clerk gliding the meat cutter slowly over a hunk of baked ham.

"It's funny," she continued, "because you think you're the center of the universe, that everybody knows who you are and what you're about. And then the story is over, and the media just moves on. You aren't a person to them. You aren't real. You're just a story. It feels both awful and wonderful to be completely forgotten."

"What? I didn't hear you."

"I know you and Carson are close, but he's clearly a troubled young man, and I'd hate for you to get sucked into his world or be accused of knowing something about what he was planning to do. You've made such strides since switching schools, and I don't want you to feel any obligation to people you don't know just because they've been nice to you these last few months."

"I'm not obligated to anybody." I added a loaf of Wonder Bread to our cart and then steered toward the deli, the cart's wheels squawking loudly. Droplets of condensation ran down the inside of the windows where displays of fried chicken and pizza warmed under the heat lamps.

"I'm sure his father loves them both," she continued, "and has done the best he can. I know how it feels to not have a spouse. But it's different for women. There's just a connection between a mother and her children, something men simply don't have without carrying a child in their bodies for nine months. Not having a mother leaves this horrible void. It's difficult. It's very difficult for any parent to raise children all alone. Especially two of them."

"Can we get turkey and roast beef?" Her face was in profile to me, and we were staring in opposite directions. The hum of the open-air freezers of packaged seafood drilled into my ears.

"Without your father," she said, absently thumbing our grocery list, "I am the only one responsible for you. I know I'm your mother and you have friends to talk to, but all we have is each other, Owen, and there are times when I think about how I could have, should have, done more for you. I should have stood up to your father. I should have asked questions. Demanded answers. I was stupid. I was so stupid. But we're going to manage without him, I promise. We're going to be just fine without him because we've always been without him. You see? Always."

When I didn't respond, she said to the deli clerk, "A pound of both roast beef and oven-roasted turkey, please."

The clerk soaped and washed his hands under a spray of hot water in one of the large stainless steel sinks filled with discarded meat and blood. My nostrils filled with the smell of decay. When he was finished with our order—having slid the meat into a plastic bag, weighing it, hitting the button to print the price sticker, slapping the bag closed, and handing it to me—I acted as if this were some sort of ritual, cradling the meat in my hands and setting it down quietly in the cart like a prayer offering. My mother and I moved forward, the chill of the deli on our backs. She walked to the front of the nearest aisle and stared down its length with an absent intensity.

I said, "You're only talking about Dad because you're worried about me."

"He was shy. People didn't know that about him." She studied my shoes as if deciding whether I had outgrown them. "To tell you the truth, he worked very hard at being friendly and gregarious because he believed that's what people expected of him. But I don't think he liked people very much."

"It never seemed that way to me."

"He was good at parties only because he drank."

"I'm just glad that woman isn't dead."

She raised her enormous brown eyes and contemplated me in such a way that I could not understand her expression. I didn't know why I had said that. I eased the shopping cart forward, hoping she would tell me what aisle to turn down.

We shopped in silence. The only noise I could discern was our cart's loose wheel and the bad music pumped over the speakers, which was frequently interrupted by a recording of what sales were available in what aisle. As if mesmerized by these announcements, we lemminged down every one, even the ones that we knew in advance held nothing we would buy, like the pet food aisle, which for some reason I clearly remember as aisle seventeen. She nudged me down the liquor aisle and took two bottles of Absolut off the shelf, and when I stared at her, she refused to look back at me.

Once we finished our long coil through Kroger, I pushed the cart into one of two open checkout lines; it was late by this time, and most of the clerks looked like they were at the end of a long shift that had been filled with customer complaints and price checks. I didn't pay much attention to my choice, and it took us a moment to realize that in our line, directly in front of us, was Jack Atherton, the anchorman whom I had watched announce my father's conviction.

To see him in front of us was jarring. He wore a dark suit, no tie, and he had the hangdog look of a person suffering from a cold. Which he was: the two items he was purchasing were a triple-pack of tissues and a massive variety of herbal teas. He blinked frequently, as if he couldn't quite bring the cashier into focus.

"You're Jack Atherton," my mother said.

He turned. All the illness drained out of his face, and he smiled, his teeth blindingly white.

"Yes, I am," he said. "I'd offer my hand, but I've been a bit under the weather."

"I can tell."

The cashier shoved the tissues and tea into a plastic bag and set it at the end of the conveyor belt. She gave us a bored blink.

"Do you live in this neighborhood?" my mother asked.

"No, farther north. West Chester. I just stopped in when I realized I was out of Kleenex."

"You weren't on tonight?"

He smiled. "Sure I was. It's almost eleven thirty."

She frowned down at her wristwatch. "My god. Owen, it's eleven thirty."

I looked at her as if she were out of focus. "Mom, I'm on spring break, remember?"

"Where do you go?" Atherton asked me.

"Rockcastle. I'm a sophomore there." I didn't offer my name, and he didn't ask. I didn't want him to connect me to my father. Still, a flicker of something ran across his face. The clerk gave him his total, and he absently handed her a twenty without really taking his eyes off me.

"He's a friend of mine," I said.

Atherton nodded. "I am sorry."

"Can I ask you something?"

"Of course."

"Why didn't you use his name? You're not even saying it now. Everyone knows their names. It was in the *Enquirer.*

But you guys didn't. Neither did Channel 9, and I'm just wondering why not."

The clerk handed Atherton his change, and he held his plastic bag of tissues and tea, one hand resting on his hip as if he were having a friendly, enjoyable conversation at a bar. "You know, I find this really fascinating."

"I just noticed, that's all. I watched it on every station."

"There are two things here," Atherton said, "and I brought up both in our production meeting. Here's the first thing: what does it add to the story? Three teenagers, stolen drugs and guns, a shooting, a police chase, all things that are pretty fascinating on their own. What does knowing their names add?"

A human connection, I thought. But I remained silent.

"The second thing is that they are innocent until proven guilty. I used to be a lawyer, and this is really important to me. I was the only one talking about this in the meeting. They haven't been convicted of anything yet, right? What if they are innocent? I know the idea sounds ridiculous right now, but that's the way our legal system works, and as a news organization, we need to respect and support that system. Even if you're innocent, a serious criminal charge like this stays on a person for a very long time. I know. I've seen it."

"But his name is in the *Post* and on Channel 5 and Channel 12."

"We have no control over that. We needed to make a decision as a news organization. We can't let someone else guide our principles. Your principles only really matter on the hard choices, not the easy ones. This was one of the hard ones. We knew what would be in the papers, and we knew that other news stations would probably use their names."

He shifted his weight with the assuredness of an ex-athlete.

"Technically, one of those boys is a minor. That brings concerns one and two together: minors, innocent until proven guilty, and the potential for long-term damage. We need to think about that. And the other thing—and this shouldn't be that important, but it really is—is that we're new in town. Fox hasn't been here long. How our community views us is a very delicate matter."

I remembered my first week at Rockcastle and the total certainty that everyone viewed me as a person who didn't belong there.

"That's very considerate of Fox," my mother said.

"We try." He smiled, his perfect teeth impossibly white. "Thanks for watching."

And with that, he lifted up his plastic bag of tea and tissues, said it was a pleasure to meet us, and disappeared into the parking lot. The cashier began to ring our items. After my mother paid and I pushed the cart out of earshot of the cashier, I asked my mother if anyone from Channel 19 had come by our house.

"No," she said. "Just Channel 5. Just Clyde Gray."

I nodded. This made me like Jack Atherton even more.

"He makes some very good points," my mother said.

"Carson's not an exam question."

She reached out and cupped her warm hand around my neck.

"You're right," she said. "He's not."

I had never spoken to anyone famous before. I wanted to ask Jack Atherton all sorts of questions about Carson's legal case. I wanted to know how it worked and to be in the presence of a person who was willing to concede that everything might be different than it seemed. Instead, my mother and I stepped into a large parking lot on a March night. The grocery cart squeaked, its wheel shaky and frenetic, as my mother and I walked across the nearly vacant lot. The lot was clean of debris and well-lit, and the feel of the coming spring floated into my skin, the night falling into tune with its own mysterious anthems. Next week I would go back to school, established as my own person: a star basketball player, a studious learner, yet perhaps always an outsider to the club whose rules I was still learning. For a moment I closed my eyes, still pushing the cart, letting my mother guide me to the car.

At home, my mother parked, popped the trunk, and headed up the steps to the house. When the door was open, we heard the phone ringing. She entered the house, and I scooped up two paper bags of groceries and followed. I was inside on the landing, still holding the bags, when my mother appeared at the top of the kitchen steps, holding the phone to her shoulder.

"It's Caitlin," she said.

In the car ride back from Williamsburg, my mother had asked almost no questions: I sputtered out everything about Carson, about the trip, about the guns, about his anger, his absent father, what he meant to me, how confused I was about everything that had happened to me since I set foot in Rockcastle. But I said very little about Caitlin, and when my mother asked, I squirmed the way all teenage boys do when asked about girls. I set the groceries down and reached for the phone, then scurried to my room and closed the door before saying hello.

I closed the door and said, "Are you okay?"

"Yeah, I'm fine. I mean, you know."

"Right. Sure. Are you home?"

"I'm in New York. My uncle is out here and my dad didn't want me home with everything going on. He's down in Florida right now. With Carson."

I sat at my desk and studied the postcards Caitlin had sent me last summer.

"When are you coming back?"

"I don't know, Owen. They're talking about me, like, being near family. My dad and uncle really got into it the other night. I might stay here. Finish school here, you know."

"In New York."

I took the Klimt postcard off my pushboard and set it flat on my desk.

"Are you ever gonna, like, visit Cincinnati, or anything?"

"I don't think so," she said, her voice cracking. "I don't know, Owen. I don't know what's gonna happen to me." She no longer tried to hide her crying, and there was a muffled voice on her end of the line.

"I'm sorry, Owen," she said, clearing her throat. "I gotta go."

She hung up and I sat holding the phone, listening to the silence and then the monotonous hum of an open line, as though it were waiting for me to dial someone, anyone. I beeped the phone off and turned on my desk lamp and looked at all the postcards Caitlin had sent me. I thought about how different my future had looked just a few months ago. I was not one of them: not Carson and not my father. I possessed a boundary that I could never cross with them.

A few months later, Carson Bly would receive a ten-year sentence for attempted second-degree murder, aggravated assault, possession of a firearm, and grand theft auto. Because he was eighteen, Carson was sent to Riverbend Maximum Security Institution in Nashville; Brian Reinhart and Kevin Lordo would begin their shorter sentences at a juvenile facility. For a day or two this was a story, and then it was forgotten by the world. Caitlin sent me a typed letter once, with a return address on the Upper West Side, a letter I still have. Other than that, she, like her brother, vanished from my life as quickly as she appeared. And at Rockcastle, all talk of Carson Bly and his family ceased. Disgraces would not be acknowledged. We simply moved forward as if the past didn't exist.

I know now that anger is its own type of poetry. There was a deep but not yet fully understood pleasure in letting go of certain ambitions, of finding those boundaries in myself, and mapping my life out accordingly. I just didn't know yet what such a map would reveal, what city or town or region, and if I ever got there, when I opened the doors to enter, what would be waiting for me on the other side.

XVI

Once, Queen City Boxing Club was a two-story brick warehouse where all the young Cincinnati fighters trained: Ezzard Charles, Aaron Pryor, Freddie Miller, Carmen Iacobucci, Max Elkus. But as with all things in Cincinnati, the club fell into decay in the eighties. Back before I ever met him, my friend Craig Allen saw the potential of the place as a renovated fitness spot for white-collar professionals who thought boxing was cool, a fun hobby, something to brag about over Heinekens at whatever bistro was trendy at the time. Craig designed the boxing club for an upscale crowd by showcasing a weird combination of nostalgia and luxury: the exposed brick walls and rickety windows remained, but there was new moisture-wicking carpeting in the changing rooms, an abundance of fresh, warm towels, and serenity rocks and fountains placed on the countertops between the touch-free soap and paper towel dispensers.

I arrived an hour early for my fight, and I asked at the front desk if one of the trainers would wrap my hands. I always fought in my corner alone—with no one to give advice, apply ice or close wounds, provide inspiration. The desk attendant said sure, and I entered the locker room, walked past the showers, and dropped my duffel at my feet. I sat down in the training room and studied the lockers. They had a dark cherry varnish and key codes rather than locks, a touch that I found a bit too much. But they were large and roomy, and I thought that feature was worth stealing for my own gym design. After a moment, the "trainer" walked in; he was older than me and started prattling on about how he liked to spar a little bit. I tuned out his voice and watched the lines of tape as they snaked around my hand. First the tape looped my thumb, then went around my wrist several times, back up around the thumb, padding the knuckles in thickening layers, moving back to my wrist, then my thumb again, my pale hands and gnarled fingers blanketed in deep layers of whiteness.

"Test," I said. The trainer, still talking, leaned away, and I flexed my right hand into a fist, the solidness of the wrap strong. I released my fingers and nodded, and the trainer continued, finishing the thumb and wrist, wrapping across the palm and then the knuckles, swinging the tape around my fist several times before circling the wrist once again, my hand now a secure weapon, the tape coming over the top, between the middle and ring finger, then across the knuckles and wrist again, so many times that I had lost count. The trainer cut the tape.

Across the room, out of sight, I could hear laughter. Must be the other boxer. I caught snippets of words like "jab" and "footwork" and "standing count." Both fists wrapped now, a towel around my shoulders, I imagined burying my gloves into this guy's face, his mouth guard snapping loose, his eyes rolling back and closing, and that satisfying thud when a man hits the canvas.

"Need anything else, buddy?"

I shook my head. The trainer left the room, and I stepped in front of the mirror and raised my gloves. I had started fighting in a ring when I went to college. I got what I wanted: Yale. New Haven. About as upper crust and blue blood as I could ever hope for. I stepped into the world that bred all my Rockcastle classmates and sent scores of men from the northeast—from Boston all the way down to D.C.—to become lawyers or doctors, run hedge funds, buy and invest in and build real estate, appear in the pages of magazines. Once I had it, once I made that mysterious and undefined "it," I was surprised at how quickly I came to hate both the place and myself.

Yale is a castle in New Haven; the town itself is working class, filled with the stench of blood and sweat and decay, and late in my first semester, when I took a long walk around the city with my fists jammed deep in my pockets, working through the problems with a research paper for my poli-sci course, I stumbled across the open lights of a boxing gym. Inside and out of the cold for the admission price of ten bucks, I watched my first boxing match. The fight was nothing spectacular—I'm sure no one has heard of Manny "The Grasshopper" Sanchez and Fernando "El Toro" Lopes—but when it was over, I knew that I wanted to train. I wanted to move the way they did, wanted to perfect my footwork and throw all that anger that I had never fully gotten rid of into an organized contest, with real winners and losers and a sense, when it was over, that something greater had been achieved. Because after Sanchez knocked out Lopes in the eighth round, a beating that could have ended five rounds earlier, Sanchez crossed the ring and embraced Lopes. I was too far away to hear them, but he whispered something in his ear, and Lopes nodded and nodded, and when the hug was over and Lopes leaned away, I knew what was running down his swollen, battered cheeks was not sweat, but tears.

I never became a particularly good fighter; I had fought on a couple of circuits, won more than I lost, had my ribs and nose broken. I could take a punch, which was the problem, preventing me from being strategic and smart rather than a brawler. But I loved it all the same—loved the raw adrenaline pounding through my veins before a fight, the primal urge to knock another man down, and then, at the end, win or lose, all was forgiven. Fighters admired each other. They knew what it took to step into a ring and literally risk your life, and they were grateful for the battle. I had felt that way about every boxing match I had ever fought.

In front of the mirror, I bent my knees, stared at my reflection, and threw a jab. A quick snap right at my own chin, and I dipped my head to the side. A fighter can't keep his head in one spot, even when he's punching. Especially when he's punching. I threw another and another and another, quicker combos up on the balls of my feet. I stepped back, rotated my head, and loosened my neck, wiggling my arms like a chimp. A man ducked his head in and asked, "Ready?" and I pounded my gloves together and followed him out.

Queen City had a full-sized basketball court. For boxing matches, the backboards were raised to the ceiling and a thick tarp was stretched across the floor to protect the soft wood from scratches. As my opponent and I entered the gym, the crowd of spectators, almost entirely composed of men in their twenties, clapped and cheered, their voices echoing in the large gym, their white, straight teeth gleaming under the bright lights. Five rows of chairs encircled the ring like trenches. I followed the trainer to the far corner and took the portable plastic steps up to the ring. Opposite me, my opponent was surrounded by several men giving advice, pointing, mimicking fight moves; they wore expensive watches and dress sandals.

I looked down into the front row. Craig Allen sat with his right knee crossed over his left, rhythmically bobbing his foot. He wore a black suit and a chartreuse shirt with the top three buttons undone.

"Hey, Craig, for real?"

Craig cocked his head and gave me an affirmative. I shrugged. He had approached me about going without head gear for this fight. He called it a favor. I told him it was stupid, and he countered by stating the fighter would pay cash. Across the ring, I saw a guy who had taken up this hobby and had no idea what kind of a beating he was about to receive. I saw a blue blood.

In the center of the ring, a balding man in a striped referee shirt and black shorts signaled for us to come together, then he explained the rules in a clear, authoritative voice: six rounds, standing counts, follow his instructions. My opponent looked like a nice guy. Probably a lawyer. He mean-mugged me, and my face glazed over. We touched gloves, his hitting mine too hard, and I stalked back to my corner, positioned my gloves on the ropes, and bounced on my toes.

At the bell, we both bopped toward the center of the ring, fists up around our chins, throwing jabs, feeling out the fight, getting a sense of what we were up against. He was off-balance, leaning a little too hard, but his punches were crisp, better than I expected. We danced for about sixty seconds before I decided to stop fucking around.

My first serious punch hit him right above his eye. His gloves were up, but my glove slid off them and ricocheted against his temple, snapping his head back. He staggered back, and I charged in, slamming a flurry of punches against his raised forearms and gloves. He countered with a low uppercut into my ribs, right under my heart. I stepped back, and he came at me with reckless combinations of jabs and hooks, hammering at my face and arms and shoulders. The bell rang shrill and loud, the first three minutes over.

Across the ring, the guy's buddies—the "corner men"—yelled at him to keep his hands up, stick and move, the kind of generic advice heard in Rocky movies. Someone, I wasn't sure who, had placed a stool in my corner, and I sat down, breathing hard. I stared at the club's logo in the middle of the ring: a pair of gloves crossed like swords and a woman's face (the queen, I suppose?) smiling supremely. *Focus,* I thought. *You're not boxing, you're swinging. Box. Fight. Think*. I chomped down on my mouth guard.

In the second round, I danced around the ring, allowing this guy to jab himself out. Feet spread, knees flexed, gloves raised. He threw a series of jabs, and once he was breathing hard, I slid to his left, feinted, and then stepped in strong and threw a combo to his head. He ducked, countered, and cracked me hard in the side, right at the kidney. I staggered, dropping to one knee. The ref stepped in, his arms spread wide to separate us. I stood and nodded *yes yes yes* to his questions and went to the corner he directed me to; it would hurt tomorrow, but for the moment, I was fine. This guy was a street fighter, and a good one, and I wasn't respecting that. *Don't be stupid.* I stood, nodded at the ref's instructions, and he spread his arms to signal us to continue.

I circled around, stepping away from jabs, and when he threw a wild hook, I ducked it easily, stepped in, focused on his chin, and rapped it with a hard cross. His head snapped back, and I resisted the urge to charge in. I wanted this to last a little longer, so I pedaled away, and when the opening presented itself, I threw an uppercut under his ribs. I heard the whoosh of air, and the guy hit the canvas. The crowd "oohed" with satisfaction, and I walked to the corner the ref pointed me toward. The guy probably wasn't done yet. He got to all fours and shook his head, his corner screaming at him to get up. I hadn't hit him hard enough; I knew he'd get up. He made it in seven, followed instructions, and I let the second round pass without incident. The bell rang.

I ducked and weaved through the third round, punishing this guy with blows to the body. By now, I was in complete control of the fight, but I didn't want to make it so bad the ref would stop it. My opponent was breathing hard, sweat pouring down his cheeks, his right eye beginning to swell, and I worked his ribs into pulp. Each punch shot sweat off his skin, beneath which bones shuddered. Snorts and gasps spouted from his mouth, and I backed off, giving him a chance to breathe. With seconds left in the round, I swung a hard left into his side, and from the noise and the caving of his body, I was certain I cracked one of his ribs.

In the fourth round, I decided to end the fight. He threw out gasping jabs, his left elbow tucked close to protect his ribs. I slipped the jab, snapped out a cross, ducked close, and unleashed a hard, strong uppercut to his jaw. The ref spread out his arms like a plank and yelled "Over!" before the guy even hit the canvas, his body crumbling and going limp on contact.

The crowd leapt to their feet and cheered. I stood in the opposite corner and chewed at the tape around my gloves, trying to unwrap them. Across the way, the fighter had rolled onto his side, blinking rapidly, blood running down the cut above his eye onto the canvas, his friends crouched over him, telling him to take it easy, move slow, breathe.

It had been a few months since I last fought. Years of boxing had left my hands arthritic and battered, had reduced my speed. I had quietly stopped booking fights, declaring myself retired to no one at all. I was twenty-eight years old and considered myself "retired" from something. I liked that: a personal history of which I could be proud.

Across the ring, my opponent was on his feet. My gloves were off, and I crossed the ring and embraced him. He almost collapsed in my arms.

"Great fight," I said. "You hit like a goddamn Mack truck."

"Thanks, man. And thank you for this. This was. Was."

"Yeah, I hear you." I tapped him lightly on the back of his neck; he was acting like a man with a concussion. Which he might have had. "I hear you."

The ref made the official announcement and raised my hand in the air. I wasn't interested in what was coming next; I just wanted to go home and press a can of beer against my closed eyes. The muggy air stuck in my throat. I hustled to the locker room and worked the tape off my gloves.

"Great fight."

I turned. Craig stood in the doorway with his arms crossed over his chest, a big shit-eating grin on his face. He had a tacky quality to his carriage and clothes: shaved head, too much cologne. There was something Cincinnati about him and his loud style of dress. Despite this, I rather liked him.

"What was that?" I asked.

"Guy wanted the real deal, he said. I figured you wouldn't mind earning a few bucks. C'mon, crowd loved it. The next fights are pretty solid. You sure you don't want to stick around?"

"I coulda killed that guy."

"That's really up to you, isn't it, Webb? Plus, you didn't. Payout's in an envelope at the desk. Want me to get it?"

I waved him away. "I know where it is."

"You sure you don't want to stay? Pretty girls here tonight."

Craig had a fondness for women who looked like *Playboy* models: blonde, big tits, wide hips and tiny waists, high heels and low-cut dresses they spilled out of—airbrushing come to life. All of them would be a little bit older than me. Cold beers at home sounded better.

"Another time," I said.

Despite the quick shower and clean clothes, I was still sweating when I sat down on the gym bench, pools of perspiration forming along my lower back. My hands and shoulders ached. I flexed my fingers slow, the pain shooting through my knuckles like I was getting rapped with rocks, and there was a constant popping in my left shoulder. I tugged on a T-shirt and sat barefoot, looking down at the bag between my feet.

"Great fight."

I turned. He leaned in the door frame, his hands in the pockets of his pants, as casually as if he were standing dockside on a cool night and watching the ocean waves lap against the sand.

"You," I said.

Carson, still a sly man, winked. "Me."

It had been twelve years since his hot, angry breath plumed around my face, his teeth bared like a wolf's, a day of cool and reckless freedom darkened in that moment and staying with me for the rest of my life.

Now, he was a stranger to me. He was gaunt, cheeks sunken, and his perfectly coifed hair was long enough to reach his collar. He wore a slim-cut gray suit and black lace-ups. No tie. He beamed, his teeth white and straight, deep crow's feet around his eyes. Still handsome, but he looked ten years older than me. I stood up and crossed the room and appraised him at arm's length.

"You're back?"

"I'm in town. Good enough?"

"Good enough."

He bounced off the door frame and spread his arms wide and majestic. When I hugged him, I swore I could feel his ribs beneath his tailored clothes. He was diminished somehow, almost frail, and I was hyperconscious of how much bigger and stronger I was by comparison. He laughed merrily in my ear and pounded my back as if we were meeting at a high school reunion.

He leaned back, gripping my shoulders. "When did you take up boxing?"

"College."

"You went to Yale to box? You always do things backward, don't you?"

"I guess that's just how I learn." I grinned and stored the fact that he knew where I had matriculated. How long had he been keeping tabs on me? And why?

"Something I picked up," I continued. "It was that or sumo, and I just couldn't eat that much."

"And you're not Japanese. You look great, Webb."

"You too," I lied. "How did you hear about this?"

"However people hear about things. Maybe I saw a flyer between a McCain and an Obama campaign poster."

This didn't make sense, but I let it go. "Let me grab my cash, and then we can head out. I know a place nearby."

"I didn't take you for an Over-the-Rhine guy."

"I just fight here. Besides, the neighborhood has changed since you were last here."

He let that drop, and he followed me through the locker room and into the lobby. Down the hallway came the sounds of the fight. Two or three people in the lobby spoke softly into their cell phones, and the kid at the front desk looked up from a muscle magazine to hand me my manila envelope containing five crisp one-hundred-dollar bills. I counted them, then folded the envelope over once and stuffed it in my inside jacket pocket.

"I've never been to a boxing match," Carson said. "I've seen them on HBO of course, but I've never actually gone to a fight. I knew it was two people hitting each other, and that it doesn't stop until someone goes down. I really did. But the sound. Jesus, the sound that came out of him when you hit him."

"Yeah, man. It's intense."

"You fight a lot?"

"Not anymore."

"So what do you do now?"

"You ever hear of CrossFit?"

He shook his head. "Tell me all about it over a drink. You know a place nearby?"

"There's always a place nearby. Come on."

Outside it was dark, the June air muggy and suffocating. Cicadas softly screeched. It was their time, seventeen years since they had last risen from the ground like the undead, and at night their shrill mating cry softened. At night they are blind creatures, quieter but not silent, drifting toward the few lights they can discover. When they had last emerged, I was in grade school, and boys like me loved to pick up cicadas by their wings and hold them close to our ears, amazed in the way only children can be by the sound of something truly new, the high-decibel buzz of these novel creatures. Boys also liked to pull them from trees and throw them like Frisbees at girls, toss them into their hair, sneak them into school and leave them trapped in desks.

The pavement, hot through my shoes, jarred every bone in my legs as we crossed the parking lot; in the distance, the roar of the cars racing up and down the highway was audible like the first low growls of a dog. I'd forgotten how much fighting took out of me; the ache in my hands was more than I had anticipated, and I wondered, not for the first time, how much damage I had done to my body from all the fights, all the times I had been laid flat on a canvas, staring up at the harsh lights of a warehouse yet unable to recognize which direction was up.

"Where's your car?" he asked.

"You're driving. I don't own a car."

"You're joking."

"I have a bike. When I need a car, I call a cab."

"You're a goddamn hippie. All right, Webb, get in."

He pulled a key fob from his pocket and aimed it at an old two-door BMW. The lights flashed twice to signal the car was unlocked. The wheel wells were flecked with rust, and the bumper had its share of nicks and scratches; it looked like the kind of car a scion hands down to his son, which it very well might have been. There I went, appraising things again. I wrapped the nylon straps of my duffel bag around my right hand. I hadn't been in the habit of cataloging people's worth by their possessions in a long time, and it wasn't a habit I particularly wished to resume. I batted my bag against my thigh, and when I got in the car, I shoved it to my feet.

"So," Carson said, "what's your life been like?"

"My life?"

"I can tell you my last twelve years in about sixty seconds. I bet your story is more interesting. Where am I headed?"

"Mount Adams," I said.

The ignition turned over, and the engine gave a rusty grumble. The speakers, low and quiet, hummed with distortion as a news-radio program kicked in, one of the late-night hacks spewing about how Senator Barack Obama would be the end of America. I glanced at Carson, but he made no effort to hide what he had been listening to by changing the station or turning the stereo—which I noticed had a tape deck and six thick buttons for station settings—to something different. He reached up and used a hand crank to open the sunroof.

"So," he said again. "Your life?"

My life. The drive to Mount Adams and the bar I wanted to go to was five minutes away at most, and even then only if enough stoplights in downtown Cincinnati would slow us down; a few green lights and I'd be out of time—out of time to stretch and expand a story that wasn't all that remarkable. So I talked about basketball and how I had become the focus of the offense (no longer "our" offense) my junior year and led the conference in both scoring and assists. By graduation, I was well-liked at Rockcastle—not the smartest, not the most successful, but well-liked. Dr. White wrote one of my recommendation letters. I went to Yale. I graduated with a degree in economics and worked as a junior lobbyist in D.C. for two years. But the more I boxed, the more I wanted to go home. So I quit, moved back to Cincinnati, and invested in gyms.

"Gyms?" Carson asked.

"I own three. Two for meatheads and a CrossFit. I'm hoping to open another CrossFit soon. I think it's the future."

"The hell is CrossFit?" I noticed he had affected a Southern twang.

"It's a power-lifting workout, but for normal people. Type A people. Group exercise."

"Sounds like Jane Fonda or something."

The climb into Mount Adams followed a steep, winding incline that I had never stopped loving. When I moved back to Cincinnati, I knew this is where and how I wanted to live. Located on the eastern edge of the city, hugged by the Ohio River, bordered on three sides by Eden Park and with a sweeping view of Cincinnati and Kentucky, this secluded neighborhood was removed from the world in a way that I needed. The streets and sidewalks on a treacherous incline made me believe my life on top of the city was continuously earned.

We pulled onto Hatch Street, and I pointed to an open spot directly across the street from the bar I wanted to go to, Yesterday's. It was a dive, dark with shitty neon lighting, but the drafts were cheap and the bartenders knew me. When we entered, we doubled the number of customers; the bartender had been leaning on the counter with a pint of beer, watching the Reds game on the television above the dozens of flavored vodka options along the back wall. When he saw me enter, Matthew smiled broadly and came around the bar to give me a handshake and a hug.

"Did you do your WOD?" I asked him.

"I did. That kettlebell snatch ladder kicked my ass."

"That's why I wrote it that way."

"You're an evil genius, man."

"Matty, this is my old friend Carson. Matty lifts at the gym with me."

"So I gathered." Carson offered his hand. "Pleasure."

They shook, and Matty asked, "Usual?"

"Yeah, we'll take them outside. Anyone back there?"

"Too early. Give it an hour or two."

There was an open door to the back patio, a small courtyard with a privacy fence on one side and a collapsed wall on the other. Matty and the owner had been planning on renovating but hadn't gotten around to it. Cicadas chirped and hummed. Before we could exit to the outside, Carson redirected us to a pair of bar stools. My gums felt dry and filmy. Carson and I stared into the dusty bar mirror between the bottles, and when Carson caught my eye, he raised his hand, slow and steady, pointed his index finger at our reflections, holding his thumb toward the ceiling for just a moment, then dropped his thumb, the clack of the gun, and said so softly that I barely heard him, "Pow."

"How's Caitlin?" I asked.

"I hear she's good." Carson took a long drink from his beer and stared into the empty patio for what felt like a long time. "During the trial, she and my father were there, and she visited me in Riverbend and stuff. But as soon as I was convicted, she stopped seeing me. Had drug problems. Did you know that? You know, on some bullshit about a dead mother and a distant father or some other cliché. Got kicked out of her first boarding school. But she's fine now. She and her husband live in Seattle. I forget what he does. They have two kids that I've never met. They probably don't even know Uncle Carson exists."

"That sucks. I'm sorry."

"I'm not. What do I care about a couple of kids I've never met?"

I squinted at him as if he were out of focus. "Why are you here?"

"After I got locked up, my father relocated the business to Dallas. We still have some interests here and in Nashville, and I'm helping to consolidate and close them off. I drove up this morning and head back tomorrow."

"You're gonna be a Texan?"

"The Bushes moved to Texas, why shouldn't we? What about you? Your mom still here?"

I shook my head. "Arizona. She got remarried when I was in college. Her husband is an electrical engineer. He's a nice guy, he's good to her. I see them at Christmas."

"Where's your dad?"

"I don't know," I said. This was true: I had no idea

when my father left prison, where he went, what he did. Since his release, not once had he reached out to me or my mother. He could be in Ohio. He could be in Florida. He could be anywhere. But the fact of the matter was that I gave no thought to my father. He was gone from my life, cut away like wisdom teeth: painful and surgical, and then forgotten, never affecting how you eat or swallow, the holes healed over, invisible to the world.

"So just you and your lonesome up here. Man is not meant to live alone, Webb."

"You don't strike me as a Bible reader."

He waved his hand. "You get a lot of it in prison, if you run in certain circles. Besides, I know quite a bit about the good book, you know. Benefits of a classical education."

"Which stopped for you at eighteen."

"I'm now educated by the School of Hard Knocks, which isn't a bad thing. Plays well with my father's business partners. I'm both rehabilitated and fairly dangerous." His head swiveled around the room. "Yeah, started working for him as soon as I could. He rented a tiny office in Nashville, couldn't have cost more than $150 a month, and put me to work. It was great, actually, this fourth-floor walkup, nothing but a desk and a computer and whatever files he sent me. Learned the business the hard way. And your business is gyms?"

"That's right. Owner and proprietor." A shiver of pain rippled through my right hand when I picked up my beer. "What was prison like?"

He looked up and watched the Reds game. "Less than great."

I couldn't remember if he liked baseball, so I stayed quiet. He sat on my left, so when I looked up at the game, his face was in my peripheral vision. He was ashen, drawn, almost skeletal, and his coiffed hair contrasted sharply with his worn, exhausted face. I had the feeling that I was sitting with a complete stranger, a different Carson, a poor carbon copy of the boy I once knew. We watched the game for five minutes, then ten. It was the silence of two old men.

Finally, I said, "Rockcastle caught on fire."

Carson put down his drink. "What?"

"Last week. The Upper School. With that building being so old, they first thought it was electrical, but now there's an arson investigation."

"How bad is the damage?"

"The western wing, the administrative offices, main hallway, and the small gym took the worst of it. Fire department arrived in time to save the east wing. Next year all classes are moved to temporary trailers they've set up on the soccer fields."

"The small gym?"

"Gone," I said. "For what it's worth, they were planning on tearing the small gym down next year. It was going to be a new student lounge with leather couches, open work spaces, some sort of combination of a café and a library, minus the books, to show off for alumni and donors."

"Man. That was our spot."

"Why would they keep it?"

"Good point." He shrugged and drank deeply from his beer.

We finished our beers in silence, then ordered another round.

"Whatever happened to Brian and Kevin?" I asked.

"Who?"

"Reinhart and Lordo."

"You never heard this?"

I shook my head.

"Oh, man," Carson smiled, shook his head, then took a long pull on his beer. "Reinhart's parents moved down to Tennessee, not only to get the hell out of Dodge, but also so they could go visit him every week. He became born-again on the inside, and he got out early for good behavior and with some support from the prison chaplain. I think they all still live down there, but honest, I don't really know or care.

"Anyway, Lordo. That fucking guy was a stone-cold moron. The first couple of months after he was transferred from juvie, we were on the same cell block, but we made new friends and drifted apart. And Lordo was just always fucking up. Little things like keeping his cell neat or being late to work, but it was like he didn't even care. He just didn't seem to be all there. Mentally, you know? But then, five years in, he breaks out of jail."

"Are you serious?"

"Yeah. He was on a road crew outside of Nashville, and, apparently, he and two other guys literally just walked off the job. I swear, I heard a thousand stories of how this happened—drunk guards, paid off the guards, a woman, no one really knows. They bring everyone back on the bus to do a count and head back to the prison, and poof, they're gone. Now, one of the guys was a murderer, double homicide in Memphis, and the cops were really worried about him. But there wasn't a peep. None of their old friends or family heard from them. They were just gone. Without a trace and all that."

Carson sipped his beer, then he grinned. "Fast forward to Charleston, South Carolina. There's a report of a break-in at a residence. Few things missing, electronics, jewelry, stuff like that. The big thing missing, though, was a thirty-six-inch television. One of those monsters with the great big heavy tube in the back? Why someone would want a piece of shit like that, no one really knows. So, a roller is going around, checking things out, sees nothing.

The cop stops at a Taco Bell to get a bite to eat, and he gets out of his car and starts heading inside. He looks around. It's eleven thirty, only one other car in the parking lot. And from his vantage point, he sees through the back window of an old Ford Taurus three guys eating in their car. And next to the guy in the back seat is a great big thirty-six-inch television."

"You're kidding."

"Swear to god. These fucking idiots pull a job, and then they get the munchies or something and sit in a Taco Bell parking lot and split a dozen tacos. Cop makes the call, these guys are surrounded, boom, that's it. They didn't even put up a fight. Climbed out of the car with their hands up, fingers covered in sour cream and hot sauce."

"Holy shit."

"I know. They tacked on a few extra years for old Kevin Lordo. He was still inside when I got out." He slapped his palms on the counter and shook his head, his eyes unfocused. A look, dark and distant, ran over his face, and all the muscles in his jaw tensed. I wanted to ask him more about the last twelve years, what prison was like, listen to his stories for the rest of the night, if he ever thought about that woman he shot. Those Ohio woods, the creek bed, the exploding bottles and the roaring sound of a gun: I still heard it, now and then, not in dreams, but throughout my day. At my desk, typing up a new workout for my gym, or at the grocery store reaching for a loaf of bread, or reading late at night in my apartment. As if it were happening in front of me, I would see myself raising a revolver and firing, the slam of the hammer into the bullet's primer, followed by the explosion of glass and metal. Always with remarkable clarity, these images appeared in my mind and would not stop repeating. I bit my lip and struggled to find the words to ask him why. But before I could, he stood and announced he was heading back to his hotel.

"How are you getting home?"

"Walk," I said. "I live around here." He gave me the Rockcastle nod. I left a couple of bills on the counter for Matty and followed Carson out the door and back into the heat.

Out on the sidewalk, he studied his car as if he didn't know how it got there. I listened to the trill of cicadas, and like he was reading my mind, he said, "These cicadas drive me fucking nuts."

"I like it, actually. *Auchenorrhyncha cicadoidea.*"

"What?"

"The Greeks considered them a delicacy."

"We aren't Greek."

We crossed the street, into the dark shade of blackened apartments and homes whose occupants had gone to sleep hours ago. Directly behind his car was a silver four-door Malibu. Carson lowered his chin and glanced into its cabin, stalked around its rear bumper, his eyes narrow and appraising, leaving me at the sidewalk. He crouched down and pursed his lips for several seconds, then he rose up and took two easy steps to the driver's door.

"Come around," he said. When I was next to him, he pointed at the steering wheel with a single, reedy finger.

"At first," he said, "I wasn't really sure what I was doing. But it's easy to do. You see, all you need is a slim jim, a pliable piece of metal, and you slide it down between the glass and the door. Guide it in just over the lock, and once it's down deep enough, you wiggle it a bit until you feel a hitch. It's kinda like going fishing."

I narrowed my eyes at him, but he didn't look up.

"I know what you're thinking,," he continued, "but, you learn a lot in prison about life. How to get by. How to make choices, Webb. Hotwire, carjack. What's the difference? Now, pay attention. There's a little hitch and then a clear metallic pop. You just lift up the door handle and you're in. I believe this model is old enough that the security isn't an issue. New cars, the alarm systems and all that—I mean, it can be done, but it's like hacking a computer. This would be much easier. Watch. Are you watching?"

I said that I was. He held his hands out in front of him, shaping them to match the words spilling out of his mouth.

"First, gain access to the wiring. See this paneling around the steering wheel? It's right below, on the bottom. That's what we want. All we need is a Swiss Army Knife or a small screwdriver, and you glide off the two screws that hold that plastic from the steering wheel shaft. Then it's easy. There are three wires. Now, each of these is just a different key position on the ignition. One to trigger the battery-only position, another for the lights and radio position, and the one we want, in the case of the Malibu, is the red wire. Here's where it gets tricky. I just happen to know with GMs of this particular make, model, and year that this is the correct wire, but you might not know that. You could actually find out in the manual, if you wanted to. But, whatever. Better to have that memorized. You know how easily your brain identifies and catalogs automobiles? America, Webb. America, man. So, now we gotta disconnect it from the cylinder. This isn't hard. Check it out. We strip the rubber from the wire and touch the exposed wires together. Now this burns a little, and you might even see a spark or two fly from your fingertips, but that's nothing compared to the feeling of hearing the engine pop to life. And then it works."

He dropped his hands to his side, and the smile that had begun to creep up his face faded.

"Tell me, Webb: would you get in this time?"

I crossed my arms across my chest and looked at him the way a teacher studies a boisterous student who isn't as smart as he thinks. I easily had twenty pounds on him and years of fighting experience. The last thing I should have been was afraid. But my eyes went to his waistband and my hands fisted at the possibility that he was carrying a gun.

"The hell is wrong with you?" I said softly.

"You think there's this really big line between you and me and the rest of the world, but there isn't." Carson wouldn't look at me. He was in profile, looking out over the car's rooftop into the alley across the way, dark and unlit, the shape of Dumpsters looming along the walls like a threat, the shadows not alive but portending something far worse.

"You left me behind," I said.

"No. You stayed. There's a difference."

He grinned out into the night, his expression contemptuous and self-loathing. He lowered his chin, turned his right shoulder into mine, bumping me hard, and walked to his BMW. He made a great show of using the key fob to unlock his car. He didn't, not once, look back at me. The red lights of the car flashed alive, and he steered out of his spot, drove up the street, and turned left to leave Mount Adams.

I live an unremarkable life. *Unremarkable,* I thought. *Not worthy of being noticed.* I stood in the street, studying the number of cigarette butts in the gutter for no good reason, and braced myself for a barrage of anger, an anger I found an outlet for in sports, first in basketball and then inside the safe confines of a boxing ring. But there was still a great emptiness in my chest. I spit into the street and walked back into Yesterday's.

"Hey, Matty," I said. "Mind if I borrow your truck?"

"Sure, buddy." He fished the keys out of his jeans and tossed them over to me. "You all right?"

"I'm good. I'll be back in an hour or so." I went

outside, walked up to his truck, and turned the ignition, thinking about the wiring hidden from view. I drove west to leave Mount Adams, then north out of the city on 71, two hands on the wheel and using cruise control to stay five miles under the limit. At the end of the Norwood Lateral, I took the exit to Rockcastle, zipping off to the right, then onto the ramp curling up and away from the highway. Across the way, the campus was shrouded in darkness as I cruised to the intersection. With a pair of right turns, I was heading up Red Creek Road, creeping slowly up the street, aware that I hadn't driven past Rockcastle at all since I'd returned home.

The turn into the Upper School was exactly the same: the circular gravel walkway, the structure's long sleepy windows, the stalwart oak trees, and the meticulous surrounding gardens, all of it quiet and still in the night.

But just past the main entrance, where the left side of the Upper School used to be, was nothing. The charred scaffolding was surrounded by temporary orange fencing. I parked the car, popped the glove box, and found a Maglite. Stepping out of the truck, I panned the sharp white light over the perimeter of the damage. On three sides, the orange fencing surrounded the empty rectangle where the left wing had been. My math classes had all been on this side of the building; more than once, I had turned away from the calculus problems on the blackboard to gaze out on the front lawn and picture myself anywhere but in a web of cosine curves. Now there was just scorched topsoil, all the rubble and debris and burned remains of the building excavated away. Over the exposed wall of the Upper School had been nailed cheap plywood covered with plastic. It looked like the kind of place I'd seen in the New Haven ghettos, the sort of building my classmates would laugh at, joking about crack and whores and why the fuck didn't somebody just bulldoze the goddamn thing.

I circled the rubble and spun my light around what did remain, walking the narrow curving driveway that snaked behind the Upper School between the cafeteria and the Fieldhouse, leading to the maintenance barn in the back. The lingering smell of rot and grease drifted from the Dumpsters. My flashlight flickered over the back of the Upper School: black streaks of soot scorched the brick and surrounding windows. The five parking spots for campus vehicles were cordoned off with yellow police tape. Scanning the building slowly with my light, I finally panned over where the small gym should have been.

There was nothing. Instead of the large clapboard building with its second-floor windows and broken gutters, instead of damaged scaffolding and blackened screws and piles of burnt wood and scorched topsoil, instead of orange plastic fencing and ominous yellow tape, there was nothing. My flashlight panned all the way to the other side and cast its light on the small meadow between the Upper and Middle Schools, the row of sycamores lining the walkway unharmed, almost mockingly healthy, I stepped closer. What was once the gym floor was now smooth topsoil, so flat and perfect it was as if the new ground had been laid earlier that day. On one end was a set of double doors to the Upper School; on the other, the doors to the Fieldhouse. Even though I knew that the walls containing these doors once had been interior walls, they looked perfectly normal exposed to the elements. They even had new name plaques screwed into the brick above the handicap button: The Upper School; The Arthur J. Langley Fieldhouse.

Pebbles cracked under my feet. When I swept my flashlight across the sky, arcing it like a jump shot, I could see the trajectory of the ball, its flight from Carson's hands, toward the basket. I turned off the light and stared into that empty space. Would anyone care that it was gone? For years it was just the small gym; the building had never had a name. Rockcastle was a place that could, if it wanted, in a single day of phone calls, raise money for scholarships, new science wings, baseball fields, the pretty Fieldhouse that I so loved. In all the years that Rockcastle had existed, with all the headmasters, teachers, and students who had passed through the campus, not once had anyone bothered to name an old creaky gym. Maybe it had never meant anything to anyone. Maybe Carson and I really were the only two who had ever loved the place.

What would we call this, if he had been standing here with me? I remembered naming his home. I remembered the way we walked through it—boys, just boys—and how giddy I was to be in his presence. Would he still have the wit and vitality to see the rubble of the small gym as a thing he could joke about, a memory he could mock? In some way, Carson had stopped existing for me. My father, too. I had survived them both, just like Rockcastle survived the fire. It would be destroyed and rebuilt. It would go on.

I clicked the flashlight back on and panned it over the empty gravel walkway. My hands ached from the fight, the flashlight suddenly heavy, and I couldn't hear any sounds: no cars, no crickets, no cicadas, nothing. I clicked off the light and continued to look for something there in the dark. I knew I wouldn't find my answers in the remains of this old building.

"I don't believe in ghosts," I whispered.

I don't believe in ghosts.

ACKNOWLEDGMENTS

Thanks to my agent Mark Gottlieb of Trident Media Group for being an early and constant advocate of my work. All writers hope for an agent who reads, understands, believes in, and champions books the way he does. I couldn't have asked for better guidance on this novel.

Thanks to the entire Turner Publishing family: Todd Bottorff, for being a champion of independent publishing; Stephanie Beard, who acquired my novel and has been a stalwart supporter of this book; Jon O'Neal, making the process as easy as it could be and the thousands of behind the scenes decisions a managing editor has to make every day; Kara Furlong and Kelley Blewster, for their sharp and insightful editorial hand; Caroline Herd and Leslie Hinson, for doing all the hard marketing and publicity work of finding this book's readership; and Maddie Cothern, for great design work that gets to the heart of what this novel is all about.

Thanks to my friends who have read so many early and late drafts of this novel: Eve Jones, Keija Parssinen, Gordon Sauer, and Rachel Swearingen. What this book was four years ago and what it is today couldn't have happened without your wisdom, insight, and our long discussions about what my work was trying to explore. I couldn't ask for better, smarter, or fiercer readers. Thank you for endless patience and your invaluable friendship.

Special heartfelt thanks to Jessica Rogen, Danielle Lazarin, Fred Venturini, Adrian Matejka, the entire Missouri Review family, and the unsinkable #CelticsWire crew. The writing life has been chaotic, to say the least, and I wouldn't have gotten through the storm without you. Thanks to my entire family, who have long encouraged this book nerd to spend his time with his nose in a novel and fingers pounding away at a keyboard, trying to write stories that will make people laugh and cry. Hopefully, a little bit of both.

Finally, to my wife, Elizabeth, who has encouraged and enriched my life at each and every step, in more ways, big and small, than I could possibly list on this page. Everything is better with you in my life.

Neglected No More

A novel

By

Richard Jeanty

RJ Publications, LLC

Newark, New Jersey

To Nat,

Happy New Year!

The characters and events in this book are fictitious. Any resemblance to actual persons, living or dead, is purely coincidental.

RJ Publications
rjeantay@yahoo.com
www.rjpublications.com

ISBN 0-9769277-4-8

Printed in Canada

October 2006

11 12 13 14 15 16 17 18 19 20

Acknowledgement

I would like to thank all the usual suspects who have supported me through my writing career and other endeavors.

My family is always number one to me and the addition of my daughter is the most wonderful experience I ever had.

Baby Girl, I will love you unconditionally until my last breath. From now on, daddy will be working diligently for a better future for you and a better society for the rest of the world.

Thanks to my dad for always for showing a lot of enthusiasm about my work. Special thanks go out to all the book clubs and readers who continue to inspire me to get better with each novel. I would like to give a big shout- out to the street vendors and booksellers around the country and all over the world for keeping the world in tune with our literature. Thanks to all the book retailers and distributors who make it possible for our books to reach the people.

A special shout out go to all the New York book vendors and entrepreneurs.

A big shout out go out to my nephews and nieces as well as my brothers and sisters. I would also like to give thanks for being part of the human race.

Last but not least, I would like to thank my fellow writers for making reading fun again for our people.

Introduction

Most of us sometimes dream of being wealthy, as if it would take away all of our problems and stressors. Life is not always about what we carry in our wallets or the number of zeros in our bank accounts. One of the most important aspects of life is being a contributor to society and by that I don't mean that you have to have a great invention or the next billion dollar idea. It's about helping out your fellow man and making sure those around you strive as much as you do.

Being wealthy doesn't take away a terminal illness, it doesn't take away loneliness, it doesn't take away ignorance and it doesn't take away stupidity. However, being a kind hearted and generous person can sometimes lead to a prosperous life even without wealth.

We live in a selfish society where "excess" has been our motto for the last thirty years or so. How many millionaires die and leave their excess life behind abruptly? Many of us seem to have this idea that life ends when we die and that there might even be an after-life. The sooner most of us realize that life never ends the better we will be as a society. Everyone wants to live life to the fullest because we don't want to have any regrets, but what happens to the lives we leave behind? In essence, life never really ends. We really need to reconsider extending the lives of others when we no longer have any more life in us.

Organ donation is one of the most vital necessities in the hood, but we lack donors. We have babies whose lives are cut short everyday because of bone marrow transplant, blood transfusion and kidney failure. My attempt in this novel is to present a situation to the reader where the character's financial wants and needs are fulfilled, but somehow there still remain a void. How can that be if he has wealth? I presented the struggle in Neglected Souls, but what happens after we make it? Do our problems go away?

Never the expert, but I hope I can force my readers to think about some of the issues relevant to the hood and to our growth as a race, community and society. Why is it so hard for some of us to help our fellow man? Shouldn't we want to help make life better for our fellow human beings? Maybe after reading this book some of you will think about it more.

We are not fully to blame because we live in a society where conquest is the key to everything. America has managed to conquer most of the world's resources and position itself as the last standing superpower. And we're brought up to think that our conquest defines our power and strength, but for how long?

Skillful

Back when Jimmy was at U-Mass., he learned a thing or two from the campus skank. There are skanks on every campus across America whose sole purpose is to find the jocks on campus to let it be known that they have a mean head game and they are skillful with the nana. Leslie was that skank, and poor Jimmy was preyed upon during his sophomore year. He and Lisa had decided to take a very brief break from their relationship because it was causing too much stress to her. She worried about the many women who wanted to sleep with Jimmy because he was a star athlete. Jimmy saw their brief break-up as an opportunity to dib and dab in a slew of flavorful available nanas on his campus. Their break-up was only for a semester so she could focus on school, but when Lisa realized that she could lose Jimmy to another prospect, she went back and claimed what was hers to begin with.

Meanwhile, Leslie saw a window of opportunity during a casual conversation with Jimmy when he mentioned that he and his girlfriend decided to take a break from their long-term relationship. The saliva around Leslie's mouth started running like a full open faucet left to run in a kitchen sink, after hearing the news from Jimmy. "What are you doing later tonight?" She asked. "I'll probably study for a couple hours after practice then go to bed around midnight," he answered. Scheming Leslie knew exactly what she was going to do to get a taste of Jimmy's eleven inches that night.

At exactly midnight, she showed up at Jimmy's door wearing a raincoat with a spaghetti thong and spaghetti bra underneath. Leslie was also a breathtaking beauty who was hard to resist. She stood about five feet seven inches tall, weighed one hundred and thirty pounds evenly distributed to the right places with a light complexion. She was considered to be conceited because of her complexion, but her beauty was all real. Her reputation as a head expert preceded her, but don't let her tell it. According to her, only two guys have had the pleasure to get their heads blown by her.

Standing by the door with the coat now open asking, "are you gonna let me in?" Jimmy didn't see any other way, because Leslie was blessed by the creator with curves that are too dangerous to drive on during a snowfall. Her nipples were barely covered by the spaghetti strap holding together what she called a bra, too small for her D cups. And down below, the strap is barely resting on her southern lips and erected clitoris, which forced Jimmy to mum his words like Leon Spinks was his speech pathologist. Leslie had never seen a bulge develop so quickly on a man and she smiled from ear to ear.

Upon stepping into the room, Leslie allowed the rain coat to drop to the floor off her shoulders and without saying a word she got on her knees and went for the gusto. In Jimmy's head, the room started spinning and words like "oh shit, don't stop. Oh God! You're so good," started rolling off his tongue. And Leslie knew that she had that youngen in the palm of her hand. Like most young adults, Jimmy busted a nut less than five minutes after feeling the warmth of Leslie's mouth around his manhood. However, he had more to give and wanted more.

Leslie was directing the whole session and just like an Oscar worthy actor, Jimmy followed his director's orders. She got on his single bed and spread her legs wide open across the bed and pointed to her crotch and ordered him to start eating. Unprofessionally so, Jimmy sat on the floor in front of her and proceeded to suck the hell out of her pussy lips. He almost chewed on them like they were a piece of gum. Leslie had to stop him in his track and slowly showed him how to lick the clit and savor the sweet pinkness spread before him.

Leslie took pleasure in knowing that she was the one shaping this young boy's bedroom skills into a man's. She held back the skin on her clit exposing it to Jimmy and told him to lick it the same way he would lick his favorite ice cream, but slower. Nevertheless, the good student he was, Jimmy had Leslie moaning in no time. She knew that he would lose control early if she straddled him, so she allowed him to enjoy a few strokes from the great view of her round booty because the boy looked like he was in heaven. These sex sessions would go on through the course of a whole semester and by the time Jimmy decided to go back to his girlfriend, Lisa, Leslie was crying and begging because she had become addicted to his long strokes. He was now the lover that she bragged about around campus, not to mention the eleven inch endowment bestowed upon him by the Lord. Jimmy was the man.

However, this night was a different night and it was a different story. Lisa was the beneficiary of Jimmy's polished bedroom skills. He had Leslie to thank for becoming such a great lover. Lisa and Jimmy had just made it home from a fundraising event where Jimmy was honored for his philanthropy efforts in the Boston community. Honestly, Lisa started getting wet from the time the presenter got on stage and mentioned the name of the great honoree whom was her husband. By the time the man was done with his speech about Jimmy, the whole room was in standing ovation for what this great man had achieved. I'm sure if Jimmy read his wife's face correctly he would have noticed the orgasm she reached when he got up to walk towards the podium to receive his award. His speech was classy and brief and everybody applauded him for about one minute, nonstop. He was the type of man that any wife would be proud of and want.

With her wetness still running down her thigh from the night's event, Lisa pulled her husband towards her in the foyer for a long wet kiss when they arrived home. It was the kind of kiss that signaled "my pussy's wet and you better deliver like you never have before." Jimmy had gotten used to it by now and the grin across his face read "fasten your seatbelt and enjoy the ride." Lisa enjoyed that grin and when he picked her up and took her to the family room and laid her down on the bear skin rug, her fire was hotter than a forest fire in L.A in the summer time.

Jimmy threw his jacket to the floor and kicked off his shoes and took off all his clothes as he knelt down to kiss his wife's back. His tongue circled around her shoulders and down to her back as he left light traces of saliva to blow on, causing a little frigid reaction that sent Lisa's nipples to stand at full erected potential, while he unclasped her bra at the same time. He continued down to her ass while palming her breasts in his hands and whispering to her "You know I love you more each day." By the time he came up for air, her underwear was clinched tightly around his mouth and ready to start eating. Not wanting to be selfish, Lisa reached out for his stretched out eleven inch limo of pleasure and started rubbing her fingers on the tip of it.

The sensation of the soothing massage he was receiving at his wife's fingers caused the limo to stretch to its maximum potential and ready to be loaded to capacity. Jimmy extended his elongated body and even more elongated tongue, between his wife's thighs and reached for her clitoris. By now her clitoris was fully exposed like an uncircumcised micro-penis. Jimmy took it in his mouth like he was straighter than straight and Lisa started moaning. Now sitting up to a comfortable position and Jimmy putting in over time between her legs with his tongue, she held on to his head for balance. With each loud moan, he stuck his tongue deeper in her and caressed her clit simultaneously with his mouth. Then came the winding on Jimmy's face and "ooh baby I'm coming. You always make me cum so good with your tongue," Lisa uttered. Not wanting to let her get away from him because of the sensitive nature of her clitoris during climax, Jimmy held her legs tight and forced her to climax multiple times and caused her to shake uncontrollably.

After a taking a moment to regain herself, Lisa saw the big donkey standing before her and all she could think about was riding it. But first, a little oral treatment was in order for the man who had just caused a thunderous vibration to take place between her legs. Palming all eleven inches with both hands, Lisa slowly took the tip of Jimmy's penis in her mouth savoring it like she was partaking in a wine tasting competition. She licked it and took her head back to look at it until she got drunk off of it then stuck the whole thing in her mouth again. Not being able to withstand Lisa's special techniques, Jimmy simply closed his eyes and moaned in pleasure. By the time Lisa straddled him, destination heaven was near. With his hands palming her ass while he lay on his back and she-taking him for the ride of his life, Jimmy's body started a metamorphosis that a grown ass man his size should never succumb to. He was like putty in her hands as she worked her magic on him, causing him to explode and let out a loud roar like a hungry lion that just got fed.

The rhythmic movement of Lisa's ass while he was inside of her continued as Jimmy reached his best orgasm in a long time, but she wanted hers too, again. She grabbed the back of his head and tightened her muscle around the shaft of his penis so he would not lose his erection. A few seconds later the plane was back in the air taking off to Lisa's destination. She tirelessly worked that position until sweat started pouring over her body and his. Recognizing that his wife was working too hard for a nut, Jimmy flipped her over on her back and penetrated her doggy-style because that was her weakness. Before entering, he stuck a couple of fingers in her to check for moisture then took the fingers to his mouth to taste the sweet juices of his wife. After slowly inserting about seven inches inside her, she started begging for more. "Give it all to me, baby," she screamed. She arched her booty up and spread her legs open a little to give him access to her clitoris. While licking his fingers so he could start rubbing her clitoris, he continued to stroke her to the sound of her breath and moans. With each stroke it became more intense and it was a matter of seconds before she reached the promise land.

Sensing that she was about to explode, Jimmy increased his speed to stroke his wife harder and faster so they could climax together. And finally with the gyrating movement of her ass against his sweetest stroke, Lisa and Jimmy both exploded together then fell asleep in each other's arms on the bear skin rug thereafter.

Loving Lisa was always a pleasure for Jimmy, but he couldn't stop thinking about how his mother would react to her if she were still alive. Jimmy would have wanted his mother to love Lisa just as much as he loves her. He even wondered about the rest of the family, if he had a maternal grandmother and grandfather who would spoil the kids that he planned on having with Lisa in the future.

No Future Without A Past

Jimmy and Nina's genetic make-up was a little bleak because their mother, Katrina, had never talked about her family. Katrina held a lot of animosity towards her parents, and she didn't feel that her children needed to know them. After all, her parents had kicked her out of the house when she was just fourteen years old, and they never even tried to look for her. As far as Katrina was concerned, her parents were dead and she no longer considered them family. Of course there were times when she wanted to go back to see her little brother and sister, but the pain that her parents had caused her had forced her to turn her back on her siblings as well.

Since Katrina was hanging on the streets most of her life, she never really had the time to discuss family with her children. The time she spent with Jimmy and Nina was kept to a minimum, and only when she woke them up to get ready for school was she able to talk to them. Nina and Jimmy were so self-sufficient by the age of six; they didn't even need their mother's assistance to get ready for school anymore. Most of the time, Katrina just wanted to stay in bed anyway. Her motherly duties only extended as far as making sure that whatever clothes that her children wore were clean. The last thing she wanted was for the Department of Social Services to be knocking on her door due to the physical neglect of her children.

Although Jimmy and Nina were never told about their grandparents, they both knew that there was a possibility that they existed. They had been told by their teachers at school when they were younger that all children had grandparents. They often wondered what their grandparents looked like, and how grandma and grandpa would have treated them if they were around.

Unfortunately, those thoughts never lasted too long, because they worried about their mother all the time. Jimmy was able to meet his paternal grandparents, however, after he learned that Pastor Jacobs was his biological father. Pastor Jacobs was more than eager to introduce Jimmy to his family as long as his family kept the fact that Jimmy was his son private. The media would have a field day if they ever found out that the Celtics superstar's father was Pastor Jacobs. It would somehow lead to the fact that his mother was a prostitute and a convict. Those investigative reporters knew exactly how to bring about a juicy story that could destroy a black man, especially a well-to-do brother. Jimmy had worked too hard to allow a reporter to destroy his professional basketball career.

Mr. and Mrs. Jacobs had missed the formal years of Jimmy's life and they wanted to make up for it. They fed him like a horse and showed him as much love as possible after they learned of his existence. His grandfather was especially proud because he spent most of his time going to Jimmy's games. The Jacobs also accepted Nina as a granddaughter and spoiled her equally as much. For Jimmy, he had at least found a piece to his family puzzle.

For Nina there were no pieces to the family puzzle. Nina hadn't met a soul from her genealogical tree. As much as she enjoyed being part of Pastor Jacobs' family, she still wanted to meet her own blood relatives. Nina wasn't so much interested in meeting her paternal family members, because she had already accepted Pastor Jacobs as her father figure. She wanted to connect with her mother's family, because she had grown up with her mother. Jimmy was just as curious most of the time, but he didn't let it bother him as much. The fact that they never met any maternal family members was something that Nina and Jimmy had to learn to live with.

A Hunted Past

The only person who ever witnessed the fatal incident between Jimmy and Patrick Ferry in the motel room a few years ago was the comatose prostitute, Jean. Even though Jimmy never intended to kill Mr. Ferry, the crime had been committed, and there was a possibility that he could go to jail if a witness ever came forward. Although the victim's wife, Mrs. Ferry, had decided to call the Boston Police Department to ask them to close the case after she discovered her husband's malicious ways; new evidence could have easily re-opened the case. True, Mr. Ferry's skeletons had been exposed, but Jimmy had no right to play judge or jury and he knew this. Not even the people at the hospital, where Jean was hospitalized, knew that she was connected to the highly publicized murder that took place a couple of years prior.

Jimmy had moved on with his life, and he had been trying his best to repent for his sins by doing more than enough for his community and his family. Deep in his heart, Jimmy knew that what he did for the community was something he would have probably done regardless of the situation. He had let go of the guilt of Patrick Ferry's death, and he filled a void in the community with his services as needed. The secret of what Jimmy had done was between Pastor Jacobs, Jimmy, and Collin.

Since neither Pastor Jacobs nor Jimmy knew that Collin had heard Jimmy's confession to the accidental murder that day; it was believed that the secret only existed between Pastor Jacobs and Jimmy. Collin never hinted that he knew what happened, because he loved his wife too much to jeopardize his relationship with her brother. Besides, Jimmy had become the little brother that Collin always wanted. They spent time together whenever possible, and Collin taught Jimmy a lot during his short life. Collin didn't allow his job as a police officer to interfere with the love for his family.

Jean Murray

Jean Murray, the prostitute witness, had been in a coma for the past two years after she was run down by a drunk driver a block from the police station where she had just been interviewed by Detective Collin Brown. At first, the whole hospital staff thought she would remain comatose indefinitely, but somehow she managed to pull through and regained consciousness a couple of years later. In fact, Jean came out of her coma on the second anniversary of her accident. Everyone at the hospital was shocked that she had finally opened her eyes. She suffered severe head trauma when her body was sent flying fifteen feet into the air when the car hit her.

Jean woke up in the hospital not remembering anything about herself or her life. She could not recall her name, or why she was waking up in a hospital. Amnesia was going to be a new battle that she had to face. Her nurse routinely checked on her to make sure she was still breathing, gave her daily baths, and fed her while Jean was in a coma. Everyone knew that it would have taken a miracle for Jean to wake out the coma, but no one expected for a miracle to really take place. At the time of the accident, Jean suffered a few broken ribs and a broken leg that had healed over the two years. She had no body movement during that time. Jean had to learn to walk all over again.

The hospital staff celebrated Jean's second chance in life by cutting a cake for her. Her doctor was especially happy because he had been very patient with her. The hospital had come close to pulling the plug on Jean, but her doctor had fought to keep her in the hospital because he believed she was strong enough to pull through. The fact that Jean was still breathing when she was brought to the hospital was a miracle in itself. Her doctor truly believed that there was more life left in her.

The recovery road ahead for Jean was not an easy one. She was not originally from Boston, and did not have any family nearby that could help her remember anything about her life. Jean was a run-away teenager who moved to Boston from Delaware when she was just fifteen years old. She got caught up on the streets working as a prostitute in order to survive. When the doctor told Jean that she was brought to the hospital after a near fatal accident, she didn't understand what the hell he was talking about.

The hospital wanted to administer a plan to help Jean regain her memory, but they had no idea where to start. No one had any idea what she was familiar with, and there was absolutely no way for them to find out. Before anything, Jean had to start learning how to walk again. A physical therapist was assigned to her, and she was scheduled to go through physical therapy four times a week in order to expedite her recovery. The state didn't want to pay for Jean's hospital stay any longer, and the hospital wanted to use her bed for other people who needed it.

Jean started making a lot of progress in physical therapy. After a month of therapy, she was starting to take small steps with the help of a walker. She was learning to walk faster, and gaining more strength in her legs while holding onto the rails in therapy. One day while walking the rails, there was a highlight clip of a Celtics basketball game on the television located above her head on the wall in front of her. The game announcer was interviewing the biggest star of the game, and almost instantly Jean remembered hearing a familiar voice. She was startled by the interviewee's voice and fell on her butt. The therapist had to help her back to her feet. The voice brought fear to her and she would have run out of the therapy room if she could.

Jean suddenly recalled the familiar voice telling her "Shut up, bitch!" She couldn't remember when or where the incident occurred, however. The voice scared her to the point where she couldn't listen to it anymore. The therapist took notice of Jean's reaction, and asked if something was wrong. Jean told her that the voice sounded familiar to her, but she couldn't remember where she had heard it.

The hospital took Jean's ability to recognize the athlete's voice as a sign of progress. They wanted to know if she was a Celtics fan or perhaps she had met the Celtics player whose voice she heard. The hospital was quick to point out that the player was quite popular and there was a possibility that Jean could have previously heard his voice on television. For weeks, the hospital tried to help Jean regain her memory, and they got nowhere. Jean, however, was starting to have nightmares and the phrase "Shut up, bitch!" kept echoing in her head. Jean didn't even remember that she used to be a prostitute. She seemed like a lost child and there was no one to identify her.

Jean had completely forgotten about the accident that almost took her life. She keyed in on the incident where someone was killed in a motel room while she was there. She kept thinking about being tied up and helpless while someone was killing the man who had paid to tie her up. After a while, she felt she was losing her mind over something that probably had no significance. She decided to let her memory come back to her slowly instead of trying to force it.

Jimmy's New Life

Jimmy had been playing for the Celtics for a couple of years as a starting forward. He had become the same star-caliber player that he was in college. The community as a whole loved him, and he was involved with many different community groups and organizations. Jimmy and his wife Lisa started a Turkey Give-Away for Thanksgiving during his rookie season, and it became an annual tradition. They also started a Toy for Kids program during the Christmas Season that drew support from many of the local businesses and people from the community.

Life for Jimmy and Lisa was on the upside and they were happy as a couple. They wanted to delay starting a family, because Lisa wanted to spend as much time with her husband as possible before sharing the house with any children. Jimmy was involved enough with the community and the children, that he didn't mind waiting. He also had access to his nephew Collin Jr. better known as CJ to the family, and his niece, Katrina, when he felt like acting like a parent. During the off-season, the kids spent a lot of time at their uncle's house. Jimmy and Lisa spoiled their niece and nephew, and they loved being around them. It also gave Lisa great practice for when she would have her own children in the future. Lisa was great with the children and she didn't mind watching them when Collin and Nina needed to spend quality time together.

Lisa and Jimmy couldn't be happier as a couple, and they shared their happiness with as many people as they could. Jimmy always made time for his fans, and he was never too busy to honor a request for an autograph. He was also fast becoming the leader of his team, and his coach took notice. The following fall when Jimmy returned to camp for the pre-season, he was named co-captain. It was well deserved, because he had demonstrated his leadership qualities on and off the court.

The Celtics' pre-season was off to a great start as they were unbeaten for their first five games. Jimmy took over the lead scoring role that year, averaging twenty-seven points a game along with ten rebounds, two steals, two blocked shots, and seven assists. He had become the all-around player that his coach knew he could be. Jimmy was the focus of every team's defenses around the league. Coaches designed their game plan around Jimmy when they faced the Celtics, and that left his teammates open most of the time for open shot opportunities.

At the end of the pre-season that year, the Celtics lost only one game, and the experts were predicting that they might win the Eastern conference come June. The whole City of Boston was hyped and looking forward to a great season. Most of the Celtics' home games were sold out by early October. Even father Jacobs was having a hard time getting tickets for his kids at the community center. He had to create more stringent requirements for the kids to earn tickets to the games. The kids had to work harder in school, and participate more in their after-school activities in order to be considered for attendance at the games. Good behavior also ranked high on Pastor Jacobs' list for anyone who wanted to attend a Celtics' game with him. The fact that the Celtics had a winning record worked to the advantage of every fan and everyone involved.

The Celtics hadn't been to the Eastern Finals in about ten years, and they were determined to make it that year. The coach relied more on Jimmy who was his star player, but he also placed a lot of responsibilities on the supporting cast as well. The point guard on the team was the second leading scorer, and his favorite target was Jimmy. He had built enough confidence in Jimmy in clutch situations, and that made it easy for him to break down defenses to get open shots for Jimmy.

Jimmy was always the first one to show up at practice, and he was always the last one to leave. Though he was a well-rounded player, Jimmy was never satisfied with his defense. He wanted to improve his defense against the quicker forwards and the guards in the league. He asked his coach to set up special drills for him so he could work on his defense after practice. The more Jimmy dedicated himself to improving his game, the harder the other teams had to work to guard him. He made it almost impossible for any player to score more than fifteen points against him in a game.

Players around the league knew that they were going to have a hard time when they had to face Jimmy. There were a few cocky rookies who did not want to show their respect before going against Jimmy, but after he burned a few of them for forty plus points they started to recognize his prowess on the court. Jimmy was not a vocal leader. He allowed his game and his work ethics to do the talking. He encouraged his teammates to look beyond what was being said in the media, so that they could focus on their game. The media was trying to make a superstar out of Jimmy, but he also knew that they would also delight in his destruction if that should ever happen. Thus, he didn't take the stories written in the papers to heart.

Jimmy didn't care about personal accolades. He knew when he stepped on the basketball court it was his job to perform at the highest level, and he gave one hundred and fifty percent every time. He was admired by the whole Celtics organization, from the owner and the president to the janitors. Jimmy was cordial to everyone, and he would always lend an ear to anyone who needed to talk. It could have been a front that Jimmy decided to change to be a much better person and philanthropist because he evaded jail, but there was something sincere about his way of life. He wasn't doing it just because; it had also become a part of him.

Making a New friend

Jimmy would leave the gym sometimes when nobody but the janitor was around. Every night at the end of practice, he would spend another thirty minutes talking to the janitor about anything and everything. Jimmy and the janitor developed a friendship where they were very honest with each other, and discussed everything in their lives. The janitor was like everyone else who came in contact with Jimmy, he was blown away by Jimmy's kind heart and gentle attitude.

The janitor had become a recluse after a tragedy took place in his family, and he was not comfortable talking to people. Somehow the guy was able to open up to Jimmy and they became pretty good friends. He would tell Jimmy about his upbringing in Hyde Park, how his parents were very religious, how they drove one of his sisters away from home, and another sister had been missing for years and was believed to be dead. The janitor harbored a lot of ill feelings towards his parents, but Jimmy never wanted to butt in. He only listened to the man. Jimmy didn't want to pass judgment or offer any solutions. Most of the time, the janitor was just looking to vent his frustrations. Although the Janitor knew Jimmy's name, Jimmy one day realized that he had never formally introduced himself to the janitor. The janitor felt a little special when Jimmy extended his hand to ask his name at the end of one of their conversations. He told Jimmy that his name was Eddy, and Jimmy introduced himself as if they were meeting for the first time.

Over time, Jimmy learned that Eddy was a bright student who was headed to Northeastern University at one point, but he had decided to forgo school after his sister went missing. He also complained that people saw him as nothing more than a janitor, and he didn't feel like being bothered with people. He lived in a one-bedroom basement apartment in his parents' house, and he had no friends. Jimmy invited Eddy out to dinner one night, just so they could hang out as friends instead of a basketball player and a janitor. They went to a restaurant where Jimmy knew that people wouldn't recognize him as easily, and they had a good time talking through dinner.

The more Jimmy talked to Eddy, the more he realized they had a lot in common. He felt that Eddy was a true friend who didn't like him just because he was Jimmy, the basketball star. Eddy was about eleven years older than Jimmy, but he looked a lot older because of all the stressors in his life. After a period of time, Jimmy started to find talking to Eddy therapeutic, and he started to look forward to their little talks more and more. Jimmy was as normal with Eddy as he had ever been with his own sister and Pastor Jacob. He never really had any friends except for his brother-in-law, Collin. His teammates were more like colleagues than anything. Jimmy cherished his friendship with Eddy. He wanted to reach out to Eddy during his times of need and Eddy was grateful. And that's how they became great friends.

Negotiating the Right Contract

Jimmy had signed a three-year contract with the Celtics when he was first drafted and the Celtics had the option to renegotiate with Jimmy for a long-term deal before his contract expired. The Celtics knew that if Jimmy tested the free agent market they would lose him as a player. Jimmy was already a well-rounded player in only his second year and the whole league knew that he would only get better. Jimmy wanted what was due to him and what was fair to both sides.

Jimmy never wanted anything more than to remain a Celtic his entire career. He was involved in enough organizations in Boston and the rest of the surrounding communities to confirm that he wanted to stay in Boston. As a superstar player, Jimmy could've easily shopped for the maximum salary around the league, and there were plenty of teams willing to pay him top dollars for his services. But it wasn't all about the money with him. It was about establishing something and following through with it. He was already too involved in too many things in Boston to turn his back on the city and the Celtics organization knew that.

At first, the Celtics attempted to insult Jimmy with an offer of ninety million dollars over ten years. The offer was laughable at best. His agent didn't even bother with a counter offer. The Celtics also knew that Jimmy was on his way to an all-star season, and the longer they waited the harder it would be for them to bargain. There were rumors circulating in the media that Jimmy could very well be the highest paid player ever if he went to the right team and those rumors were all over the news. There were teams willing to pay him as much as one hundred and seventy five million dollars for a ten-year contract and

Jimmy knew this. Jimmy knew that he could always maximize his earnings by going to another team, but he wanted to remain a Celtic. Boston was his roots, and he could do a lot more for the city's minority community. The young kids in Boston could identify with him.

Moving to another city to play for a different team was totally out of the question for Jimmy, but he also wasn't going to allow the Celtics to take advantage of him either. Jimmy wanted what was fair to him, and nothing more. He was one of the top ten scorers in the league, top ten in rebound, top ten in assists and steals. Most players with those stats were earning about fifteen million dollars a year or more. The Celtics tried to use all kinds of excuses to try to turn the fans against their star player, but the people had already fallen in love with Jimmy as a person and a player and they wanted him to stay.

Celtics management has always had a problem holding on to great African American players in Boston ever since the departure of Larry Bird, Kevin McHale, Robert Parish and Dennis Johnson. That has also been one of the reasons that they have not made it to the eastern finals in almost ten years. Their last hope of making it to the finals was when the great Reggie Lewis was around and they acquired him for cheap money. Jimmy however, was a different story. Those old ways of maneuvering around a contract were not going to work with Jimmy. His feisty and determined agent made sure of it. The days of finding a new white boy to replace Larry Bird were over. He will always remain the greatest white guy who ever set foot on the parquet floor, but not the greatest player.

In the midst of all the craziness that was going on, Jimmy talked to Pastor Jacobs about what he wanted to do, and Pastor Jacobs advised him to stay focused on his game

and try to improve as much as he could as a well-rounded player. Pastor Jacobs knew that there was really nothing that Jimmy could do except play his best basketball to force the Celtics to cough up the money. He knew that he had to stay focused, but he was worried about going to another team. Jimmy had gotten used to the system in Boston, being the star of the team and he got along with his coach. There was a lot at stake for him, too. Pastor Jacobs explained to him that basketball is not just a sport, it is also a business and
Jimmy had to get used to it.

The deadline to sign Jimmy to a long-term contract was fast approaching, and the Celtics was a playoff-bound team. Jimmy was having a great season, and the Fleet center was sold out for every home game. Celtics Pride was at an all-time high in New England. Jimmy brought back the old Celtics tradition of winning to the city of Boston. The days of sub par records were long gone. People were once again discussing the Celtics by the water cooler on Monday mornings at work. Jimmy made the highlight reel almost every night the Celtics played, and each time was more spectacular then the last. No one was saying that the torch had been passed from Michael Jordan to Jimmy Johnson, but the experts had their hopes up for the future.

The final day to keep Jimmy as a Celtics for the rest of his career was near, and Jimmy's agent didn't want to entertain any offer below one hundred and fifty million dollars over ten years. The Celtics knew that Jimmy was worth every penny, and they also knew that he could get more from another team. The Celtics' first offer was a total insult to Jimmy's game and pride as a player. It was downright humiliating for them to even offer what they did to begin with. Even the experts thought it was a slap in the face for such a great player.

With about five teams with offers topping one hundred and ninety million dollars, the Celtics thought it would be best to lock Jimmy into a contract for one hundred and seventy million dollars over a ten year period. It was announced at a press conference that he would remain a Celtics for the long future. Both sides were happy and Pastor Jacobs reminded Jimmy not to take what the Celtics did personally because it was the nature of the beast.

Jimmy's stock had risen not just in the league, but also in the world of sports period. His number thirty-one jersey was the number one selling jersey in league history during his second year. Nike had signed him to an eighty million dollar long-term contract with his own exclusive line of sneakers. All the other advertisers started pouring in to cash in on Jimmy's celebrity and popularity. Jimmy was hawking close to ten different products and was earning millions of dollars a year. But more importantly, he was one of the best players, persons, and athletes in the world.

Holding His Ground

Everyone close to Jimmy benefited from his newfound wealth, and he was a kind-hearted person who went the extra mile to help the less fortunate. Whenever there was a cause that needed help whether financial or otherwise, Jimmy was called upon because he was always willing to help. Sometimes, he found it difficult to turn anybody down for help. It was getting to the point where Jimmy couldn't spend anytime with his family. Everyone made every event or cause sound more important than the last one. It was starting to take a toll on Jimmy, and his family recognized that some people were trying to take advantage of him.

Pastor Jacobs had a talk with Jimmy, and he thought that perhaps Jimmy should hire a publicist or a manager. Jimmy needed to have a person in his corner who could say no to these people every once in a while. Jimmy didn't know how to go about hiring a publicist or a manager, so he asked Pastor Jacobs to become his manager. After all, Pastor Jacobs was one of the few people who had his best interests at heart. Pastor Jacobs didn't hesitate to accept Jimmy's offer, however, he wanted everything to be done professionally and legally. A contract and salary of one hundred thousand dollars a year was negotiated between them and Pastor Jacobs became the official manager.

Handling Jimmy's entire day-to-day tasks was something that Pastor Jacobs was used to. He had been doing it unofficially for the past couple of years without an official title. Jimmy had always made sure that he was taken care of financially. There was no salary, but Pastor Jacobs received a lump sum amount of money from Jimmy. He was just happy to be a part of his son's life.

Jimmy gave Pastor Jacobs many reasons to be proud, and he was grateful to Jimmy for allowing him to be part of it. The fact that Pastor Jacobs had missed out on the first fourteen years of Jimmy's life was no longer an issue. They had put everything behind them and buried the hatchet.

Jimmy was careful not to mention the fact that Pastor Jacobs was his dad in public. He only shared that information with Nina who he'd sworn to secrecy. He told Nina to not even tell her husband Collin about it. There would be too much scrutiny and scandal if the press ever found out that Pastor Jacobs had fathered Jimmy while sleeping with his prostitute mother. Pastor Jacobs was the only person who could make sure that Jimmy didn't overextend himself to please everybody all the time and he was very tactful with people when dealing with them.

Jealousy and Envy

A couple of weeks after Jimmy signed his big contract with the Boston Celtics, he started getting the cold shoulder from some of his teammates. A couple of the veteran players were especially angry that this young player was able to come in and command such a high salary. Most of them were acting out of anger, jealousy, and envy. If they had taken the time to look at where Jimmy had brought the team, they would've understood why his salary was justified.

All the hard work that Jimmy had put forth to bring his team to playoff caliber status, was being questioned. Some of the players started to refer to him as soft, and Jimmy just allowed their words to roll off his back. The coach sensed the tension almost immediately and he called a team meeting to sort out the disagreements. He noticed that players weren't passing the ball to Jimmy as much and they weren't creating as many opportunities for him anymore. There was one incident where one of the players should have set a pick for Jimmy, but instead he allowed the player to collide into Jimmy which resulted in a concussion. The incident was addressed, and the coach made sure he informed the team about their new franchise player and captain in Jimmy.

Jimmy had become a cash cow, not just because of his plays on the court, but also because he had an infectious personality that people adored. His demeanor on and off the court was always pleasant and he had set very high standards for himself. Jimmy knew that he came from the gutter and he had been given a second chance. He wanted to take that opportunity to help make positive changes in himself, the world, and his community. He didn't take too many things personally, and he tried his best to avoid letting the negative criticism of his game get to him.

The Celtics coach understood that Jimmy was a special player, and he led by example on the court and off the court. Jimmy didn't really allow people to make him reach his breaking point and his teammates tested his will many times. He knew that he was probably the toughest guy on the team, but he didn't have to show it. He would however, occasionally foul some of his teammates harder than he should in practice just to let them know that he wasn't going to let them walk all over him. No blows were ever thrown amongst the players, but the tension was high and the team was starting to lose focus. The Celtics had won quite a few games that season, and their losing streaks never went beyond the two game mark.

The coach noticed that his players sometimes ignored his game plans around Jimmy and the Celtics were on a three game losing streak. He couldn't believe how some of the players were allowing their own selfish anger and jealousy to get the best of them as a team. The coach felt it was necessary for Jimmy to address the team as its captain, and put to rest once and for all the disagreements amongst them.

At the team meeting the coach informed the players that he was meeting with them to sort out the animosity they had towards Jimmy, and he wanted to go back to playing great basketball as a unit. In addition, he told the team that Jimmy would address them toward the end of the meeting. Everyone was to give their full attention to Jimmy and whatever problem they had with him needed to be discussed only at the meeting.

The coach went through the formalities of pointing out what the team had not been doing well on the court, because they hadn't been playing as a team. Through videotape footage of previous games, he pointed out how Jimmy was open on many occasions and he was overlooked by certain teammates. He also pointed out that the defense wasn't helping out when necessary. The coach pointed out all the selfish reasons why the team had a three game losing streak. Some of the players acknowledged their mistakes and vowed to get back to their previous forms and play as a team.

At the end of the meeting, the coach turned the floor to Jimmy so he could address the players as the team captain. Jimmy had a lot to say. "First of all, I would like to address the fact that some of you are angry or jealous of me because of my new contract. I come in here everyday almost an hour before any of you of, and I leave an hour after every one of you. I dedicate a lot of time to perfecting my skills as a player, thus I'm rewarded. If you have a problem with your salary, talk to your agent and don't look at mine. Any player who has problems with me personally should act like a man and come to me to discuss it. I know some of you may take my kindness as softness, but I'm here to tell you that you don't want to test me. We're grown ass men and I shouldn't be hearing about any gripes through the rumor mill. I work twice as hard as everyone on this team to elevate my game to a level that has received recognition throughout the league, so I expect to be rewarded for it. I want to be a motivator that would provoke you into action, not to challenge your abilities."

Jimmy was very sincere and straightforward with the team as he told them that he would give up all the personal accolades and the money just to win a championship with his team. Jimmy was also cautious not to allow his teammates to think that he was soft by pouring out his heart to them. He told every single one of them that if they ever felt that they were tough enough and wanted a chance at him, he would be up to it as long as it stayed in-house. It wasn't a physical challenge, but he told them that he could deal on that level as well.

At the end of Jimmy's soliloquy, some players had their heads down and others took his words as positive reinforcement for the team. The questionable players knew that Jimmy wasn't the type of guy to let down his teammates. Jimmy understood that it was human nature for them to be a little upset over his big contract; however, he also knew that they all had the same opportunities to raise their stocks in the game as he did. Most players are rewarded for their efforts on the court and how well they want to be rewarded is ultimately up to them. The old saying "No pain, no gain" not only applies in sport, but it also applies in life, Jimmy told them.

Nina and Collin

Collin and Nina had stopped seeing their therapist shortly after their second child was born. Collin had been a very loving and supportive husband, and Nina had opened up to him in more ways than one. He was very pleasantly surprised when he came home one day and found his wife wearing a nice negligee with soft music and candlelight throughout the house. Nina had also prepared a nice meal, because she knew that her husband would be hungry when he got home. While Nina's gesture was very nice, Collin wanted a meal of a different kind. He was watching Nina's nice round booty strut to the kitchen in front of him, and he developed a different kind of appetite.

He didn't wait a minute longer to pull his wife towards him as he spun her around to surprise her with a long passionate kiss. As Collin kissed Nina, her body started to shiver as she threw her arms around him to hold on. Collin's hands found their way down to her ass and started gently fondling her until she could stand it no more. Moments later, Nina found herself on the kitchen table with her negligee on the floor instead of at the dining room table where she had planned to have dinner with her husband.

Collin had a way with his tongue, and Nina had never passed up on the opportunity to get a good tongue lashing from her husband. While she was lying on the kitchen table on her back, Collin spread her legs open and started licking her slowly. With every stroke of his tongue she became wetter, and he simultaneously tried to double her pleasure by caressing her breasts with his hands. Collin seemed almost ambidextrous as he caressed his wife's breasts and unleashed the same amount of sensation in both breasts, like Michael Jordan switching hands on his way to the hoop to make a buzzer beater. Only in this moment there was no buzzer to beat, and both he and Nina were going to win no matter what because he made sure it was a win-win situation.

Collin continued to lick the tip of Nina's clit slowly and sensually until he felt her convulsions and her legs tightened around his head and the only words she could utter to her husband were "I love when you eat me, baby. I love you. Don't stop." While his mouth was busy pleasing her, he found just enough time to tell her "I love you too, honey." when he came up for air.

Collin made his way up to her breasts and started suckling on them very gently. He knew that she enjoyed it through the perkiness and the erectness of her nipples. Even after bearing two children, Nina's breasts never lost their form, and Collin was more than grateful. After continually caressing his wife's breasts and rubbing her clit with his right hand, Nina could take it no more and demanded that Collin take her on the table. He dropped his pants to the floor and inserted his ten inch manhood inside of her, and started to stroke her until sweat started pouring all over them.

The sweet moaning sounds of Nina's voice only fueled his passion to please her, and with every stroke he looked into her eyes to see the ecstasy he was unloading on her. After stroking and pleasing Nina while on her back with her legs resting on his shoulders for fifteen minutes, Collin wanted to feel her round booty against his crotch while he penetrated her from behind. He brought her down to the floor and had her lean against the table as he penetrated her from behind. He started stroking her until he exploded inside of her. At the end of their session,

Collin could only say "thank you" to his wife, because she had helped him release the stress from a long day's work. Collin spent the evening in bed with his wife after dinner and they talked most of the night away.

The therapy sessions had really helped Collin and his wife lead a normal life. Their children were their first priority and Collin made sure that he put his family first. Their three year-old son, Collin Jr. looks just like his dad. Their daughter Katrina favors her mother more. Two year-old Katrina has her mother's personality as well as her physical traits. She's a little star in her own right in their household.

Since Nina and Collin's family grew to four, their lifestyle had also changed. Finding time to be with each other intimately had become a task in itself, because the kids were always screaming for attention. Whenever Collin's parents offered to take the children for a night, Nina never thought twice about bringing them over. Collin was transferred to a different precinct after his promotion to lieutenant. However, Nina had not had it so easy with the police department. Although she was promoted to sergeant a few years after becoming an officer, she was also demoted a year later and suspended with pay. The department claimed that Nina was not making enough arrests and did not issue enough tickets. Even though the Boston Police Department was quick to deny that they had a quota system when it came to arrests and tickets in the hood, it was clearly evident that they did when Nina was suspended for lack thereof.

Since Nina's suspension, she had devoted all her time to raising her children. Although Nina enjoyed being home with the kids, she still hired an attorney to file a lawsuit against the Boston Police Department for their unfair treatment of her. Nina was suspended indefinitely until an investigation into her case was finalized. She was hoping that she could get back to work when the kids became old enough to attend school.

Collin's parents tried as much as they could to get involved in the lives of their grandchildren, however, they spent a lot of their time visiting casinos and playing bingo on the weekends. On a few occasions when the young couple needed quality time together on the weekends, Collin or Nina would drop the kids off at his parents' house. The grandparents were always happy to have the children over, but they were spoiling the kids in ways that Nina didn't approve. The children were able to do as they pleased when they were over their grandparents' house and when they came back home to Nina, she always had a hard time enforcing discipline. She felt that every time the kids spent time at Collin's parents' house it was detrimental to their behaviors.

Nina loved the Browns, but she didn't know how to tell her husband that they were spoiling the kids. Collin himself was spoiled by his parents as a kid, and he didn't see anything wrong with the way his parents treated his kids. Nina didn't know how to tell her husband that she didn't approve of the way his parents treated the kids without offending him. Collin always bragged about how great a job his parents did raising him, and telling her husband that she didn't approve of it would be the ultimate blow.

Like most couples, Nina and Collin had their little feuds too. Because Nina wasn't raised by her parents, it was hard for her to grasp some of the things that Collin allowed the kids to get away with. Collin was not as strict a disciplinarian as Nina would have liked. She felt that the kids took advantage of his soft handle on them when he came home from work. Nina would work hard during the day to establish rules such as nap time, play time, reading hour, and snack time with the children, but when their dad came home he would mess up the whole structure. Nina definitely had a problem with that.

Nina kept a tight grip on her kids because of her past experiences. She grew up without much and she had to work hard to get everything she needed or wanted in life. She wanted her kids to understand that sometimes it would take a lot of hard work to get what they wanted. She didn't harbor any resentment towards Collin for having been raised by his parents, but she felt that he took for granted what she didn't have as a child. Collin and Nina tried to keep the lines of communication open between them when it came to their family. When Nina started to explain to Collin the kind of life that she had led, he was impressed with her tenacity, will, and drive. He promised to always support her when it came to disciplining the children in the future.

Collin never realized how lucky he was in life until he met his wife. It was normal for him to have a mother and a father in his household when he was a kid. So, he didn't see anything wrong with spoiling his own children every now and then. Collin was very appreciative of Nina's experience, but he also had to teach her that their job as parents was to make it easier for their children to achieve their goals in life. He didn't want them to go through all the red tape that he went through to get things done. He wanted to help open doors for them.

There was always middle ground with Nina and Collin. It was understood that Nina was the disciplinarian in the house. Collin was especially soft on his daughter. She was his little girl and there was nothing that she could do wrong in his eyes. Nina wanted to make sure that their children knew right from wrong from an early age. She never had anyone tell her what was right or wrong. She figured out most of it on her own by watching her mother do the wrong thing most of the time. Nina understood that just because she now had a middleclass family, it did not shield them from the harsh reality of the streets. She wanted to have a hold on her kids very early on.

Eddy

Eddy was living in his parents' basement at the age of thirty-two and he never wanted to be much of anything. He was satisfied with his job as a janitor at the Fleet Center. Eddy had no motivation in life. He grew up in a very religious setting, but his household was faced with many adversities. Eddy's parents were faithful Christians who truly believed that the Lord had an answer for everything. Sometimes, instead of resolving their own issues, they prayed for an answer from above. It got to the point where Eddy didn't understand why his parents were so devoted to religion and neglecting the real problems they had at home.

His father, Buck Johnson, had tried to raise Eddy and his two sisters to respect other people and to always put God first in their lives. And Eddy was quite religious himself as a youngster. He attended church three times a week with his parents as a youngster and he was involved in the youth ministry. Eddy truly believed that his parents were setting the right path for him and his siblings. However, they didn't always resolve their issues with common sense. Eddy felt that they had placed too much of their responsibilities in the hands of God, which is a common mistake that many Christians make. Buck Johnson never realized that he had to help himself in order for the Lord to help him.

Every problem that Eddy's family faced was dealt with in the church and through prayer. Sometimes, they really needed more than prayer to solve their problems. In one particular case when Eddy's mother, Mrs. Esther Johnson, was diagnosed with a brain tumor, Mr. Johnson was almost adamant that the Lord was the only cure for his wife. He prayed and prayed, but the tumor just got bigger and bigger. His pastor reinforced his beliefs by holding special vigils for his wife each week. It was Eddy who finally stood up against his dad, and suggested that his mother had an operation to remove the tumor. It was just as well because if Esther had waited another day, the doctor said she would have died.

Buck was hard-headed that way, and it was often hard to convince him that doctors sometimes can perform their own miracles in the operating room. The only person closer to the Lord than Buck was his ignorant pastor who had everyone in his church under his spell along with his wife.

As Eddie got older, he became distant from the church and that created a wedge between him and his dad. Eddy was trying his best to open his dad's eyes to the world of modern medicine, but Buck Johnson was stuck on stupid and religion. He never quite understood the balance between religion and medicine. He truly believed that God created certain illnesses for people when he wanted to take them to heaven. Ignorance is bliss and Buck was the poster child for it.

During Eddy's senior year in high school, his younger sister Karen who was just a sophomore in high school thought she was pregnant. She didn't have the courage to tell her parents about her discovery. Karen was smart enough to recognize how ignorant her parents were. Though she did not learn from her older sister Katrina's mistake, she knew that she didn't want to go down the same path as her sister if she was pregnant. Karen wanted to deal with her alleged pregnancy on her own or at least with the support of her brother, Eddy, if need be.

She wrestled with the idea of telling nobody of her possible pregnancy, but after a while she realized that she couldn't go it alone. She told the only person she trusted, which was her older brother, Eddy. He was angry with his sister for allowing herself to get in that situation to begin with, but Eddy eventually came around and was the supportive brother that his sister needed him to be.

Eddy always felt that he contributed to his sister's mishap. Those late night talks they started having about sex, became regular talks. Over time, they both wondered what it'd be like to actually have sex. Curiosity got the best of Karen, and she was persuaded to sleep with Michael, the church's pastor's son. Eddy didn't even know much about sex himself. He was just recycling everything that he had heard from the other boys at his high school. Those guys used to brag about sleeping with women like it was going out of style. It was the same conversation during the bus ride to school every morning, at lunch, during class, and during the ride back home after school. Sex was endless and each story was more intriguing than the last. Although most of it was repetitive, the kids on the bus yearned to hear more of it everyday from different students.

Eddy was always quiet, but he listened and took mental notes of what he heard. This was the closest he ever came to having a conversation about sex. His parents were too hung up on being Christianity to discuss sex with their children. The topic was off limits especially after their oldest daughter, Katrina, became pregnant when she was still in high school. They used Katrina's pregnancy to scare the other two into celibacy. The father did, anyway. How many children really take what their oldest siblings did as a lesson for their own life? The Johnsons did not create an open line of communication with their children.

The old saying "do as I say" was supposed to be the motto in the household, but nothing was being said. The kids found out about everything on the streets. Well, Eddy did and he passed it on to his sister.

Eddy knew what the consequences would be if his sister was pregnant and he did not know whether he wanted her to go through the same ordeal that his sister, Katrina, went through when she got pregnant. He simply left the decision up to Karen to make and he wanted to support her in every way. Eddy and Karen had grown very close since Katrina left home. The two of them did almost everything together. They were only a couple years apart and they both hated the way the parents treated them.

Karen was under a tighter leash because she was a girl. Eddy was given a lot more freedom as a boy. She was under more scrutiny, and her parents made sure she was always under their watchful eyes. Karen couldn't even go to the corner store by herself. Her dad was always suspicious and he threatened to kick her out of the house everyday if she ever got pregnant. Even Eddy was tired of his father's threats against his sister. One day Eddy blew his top and told his father to leave his sister alone. He told his father that he was making them pay for the mistake of Katrina, and that was not fair. His father felt disrespected and told them that as long as they were living under his roof, he was going to tell them what to do and how to do it.

Esther Johnson, the wife of Mr. Johnson and mother of Katrina, Karen, and Eddy never even tried to stand up against her husband. She allowed the verbal abuse of her children to continue on a daily basis. As a mother, she would sometimes try to console her kids after their father lashed-out at them, but she would never let her husband know she was doing that. Eddy didn't like the fact that his mother showed weakness in the presence of his dad. He knew that she was probably a stronger person than his dad, but Mr. Johnson had verbally battered the family so badly that everyone feared him.

The Preacher's Son

Michael was the epitome of perfection in everybody's eyes at the church. He could do no wrong. After all, he was a straight "A" student, the captain of his football team, the star player on the basketball team, the youth ministry director, and he volunteered to help the homeless once a week at a local shelter. Everything about Mike's life was too perfect to be true. All the parents at the church were envious of this young man and they used him as the perfect example of a child when they scolded their own children at home. Most parents at the church used the phrase "Why can't you be more like Mike?!" at one point or another while scolding their children. One would think that he was Michael Jordan or something.

Michael took advantage of the parents' good graces, too. He knew that every parent at the church wanted their daughters to end up with him in a marriage and they wanted their sons to be like him. He was the type of guy who prayed on the weaknesses of others. He used everything to his advantage. Mike had developed an image at his church that was comparable to none. His mother and father praised him every chance they got. They had so many positive stories to tell about their son; sometimes they were just too good to be true.

Mike could do no wrong in the eyes of his parents, Mr. and Mrs. Wallace. They were grooming him to take over the church in the future after his dad retires. His parents assumed that he wanted to follow in his father's footstep as a pastor without ever discussing it with him. But Mike also had a dark side. He was getting tired of being a choirboy. He would go out with his friends after school and commit these petty crimes as a form of adrenaline rush. By the time he reached his senior year in high school, he had become an adrenaline junkie and an avid marijuana smoker. He was able to conceal his dirty deeds from everyone, including his parents.

Mike and his friends would go downtown to Filene's Basement after practice and steal as many clothing items as they could. He would go to the store wearing big baggy clothes so he could stuff stolen items underneath them. He had become so daring that sometimes he would make sure that security was in the store following him before attempting to steal something. Mike believed his choirboy image made him invincible and immune to prosecution. He also wanted to prove to his friends that he wasn't as straight as people made him out to be. Mike relished the fact that some of his close friends thought he was a bad boy outside of the church.

To offset that side of him, Mike created a tutoring program at his church to help other students from his neighborhood that had difficulties in school. Mike seemed like he was almost borderline schizophrenic, sometimes. He had developed so many different personalities that it was getting hard for him to keep up with all of them. He was a young man who was trying to please everyone around him.

Michael also had his eyes on the bad girl of the church. The "bad girl" label had been attached to Karen since she was a little girl. He liked Karen because she was not as conventional as the other girls in the church. She defied convention in every way and Michael loved every aspect of her. He gave her the nickname "Fire Starter", because everything hot that started at the church started with Karen. Though he was a couple of years older than Karen, he found her refreshing and very appealing. They used to flirt with each other a lot in church, but that was the extent of their relationship.

Karen

Karen was never a great student in school. Since she was a child, she always had difficulties learning and her parents never sought help for her. Because her brother and sister were bright, the parents dismissed her as the lazy one in the bunch. They didn't believe that their daughter needed help in order to overcome her difficulties in school. Karen was often disruptive in class and her attention span was very short. She could never sit still for more than five minutes. Her teachers had complained to her parents since she started elementary school, but her parents only knew one way to discipline their daughter. Buck would wear out Karen's behind with his belt after each complaint from a teacher and not even a week would go by Karen would be doing the same thing all over again.

In church, it was the same story. Karen disrupted Sunday school, bible class, service, and whatever else she wanted to disrupt. She would chew and pop gum in church even though it was prohibited. She used to make fun of her teachers and had a very smart mouth. Karen never really cared about the complaints that people brought against her to her parents. Mr. and Mrs. Johnson never really had a hold on their daughter. The beatings and other punishment that she used to receive from her father had become a past time to Karen. She had become immune to the pain of her father's leather belt against her skin. The more beatings she received, the higher her threshold for pain reached. She was becoming devilish, and she didn't care what her father did to her.

Punishment was becoming routine for Karen and she sought attention the only way she knew how. Starting trouble was a way of crying out for help, but Mr. and Mrs.

Johnson believed that Pastor Wallace was the answer to Karen's mischievous ways. By the time she reached age twelve, Karen was smoking in the bathroom at her elementary school with the other girls. It had gotten to the point where she was being suspended monthly for one incident after another.

The fact that Karen might have been suffering from Attention Deficit Disorder was never addressed. Her father continued to try to beat her to a straight and narrow path without realizing that he had already lost handle on his daughter. Only a psychologist could diagnose the correct illness, from which Karen was suffering, but in the Johnson household, God was the psychologist and prayer was the proper medication for all illnesses. Karen could've easily sent her father to jail for physical abuse because that big leather belt used to leave marks the size of a malignant tumor around her buttocks. In her effort to act tough, she kept all the abuse to herself and never said anything to the authorities.

At twelve years old, Karen could have easily been mistaken for a grown woman. Her breasts developed to a size C and the rest of her body was moving right along with her breasts. Karen started messing with the boys at her school downstairs in the basement. She would pinch their butts and feel on their chest as a way of flirting with them. When the school held parties for the special holidays, Karen always had to be separated from the boys. Her dance moves were so seductive and over the top, a special monitor was assigned to her at all times. Karen used to have a field day with her monitor too. She especially loved reggae music because she loved to grind on the boys. And every time the monitor would get between her and the boys, she would walk to the other side of the room with all the boys in tow and the monitor had to keep up.

Without any proof, most the boys at the school started to claim that they had either kissed or felt on Karen at her willing. Most of their claims were unfounded, but because of Karen's attitude in school and around the boys, everybody believed the boys' version. Karen was rather frivolous with her attitude around people, and most of the time misunderstood and misread. She hung around with a rough crowd of friends and she was a little feisty herself. Karen was loud and obnoxious at times, but she had also developed good fighting skills and a temper to match. She was fearless and abrasive.

Despite all the negative characteristics that Karen possessed, she was very respectful towards her brother Eddy. It almost seemed like they spoke a different language around each other. Eddy couldn't understand why people were always making his sister out to be such a bad person. He was the only one who knew the kind of abuse she endured at home, and what it brought out in her. Eddy never allowed anyone to bash his sister. He even started to stand up to his dad to defend his sister.

By the time Eddy reached the age of fifteen years old, he was significantly bigger than his father and his father feared his reactions, sometimes. He was quiet with a deadly streak in his eyes. Eddy felt like he and his sister were placed under a microscope after Katrina was kicked out of the house. He felt like his parents were taking out their frustration on him and his sister for their lack of control on Katrina. He and Karen were also growing tired of the physical abuse that they were suffering at the hands of their father.

One day during an argument with his dad, his father slapped Eddy across the face and it knocked the wind right out of him. Karen was so angry she threatened to poison her father for what he had done. She also told him that if she couldn't poison him, she would kill him in his sleep. The rage in Karen's voice was so real, her father didn't eat any food at the house for a month unless it was prepared in front of him by his wife. He also locked his bedroom door every night when he went to sleep for a long period.

Karen started to put her foot down very early on and her father sensed the change in his daughter's attitude. All the beatings that she had taken from him had mounted to pure hatred for her father. Though her mother was against the way her husband treated the children, she never stood up to her husband or said anything that would go against him. She wanted to be part of a unified front, because it seemed to be the right thing to do at the time.

Karen could only relate and talk to her brother, and she didn't want to see her father abuse him. Even though she was younger than Eddy, she acted like she was his protector most of the time. Karen had also missed her sister since she left. Katrina was her play pal when she was a little girl, and without any notice she woke up and found her sister gone because her father wanted to act like an ass. Karen held a lot of resentment against her dad and even more towards her mother for being submissive to an abusive man.

Doing the Dirty Deed

Mr. and Mrs. Johnson admired Michael so much; they asked his father, Pastor Wallace if he could tutor their daughter, Karen. After discussing it with Michael, they agreed that Karen would go to Michael's tutoring program twice a week after school for help. At first, it seemed like the opportunity that Michael and Karen were looking for. They couldn't wait to start the tutoring sessions at the church.

Under the total guidance and supervision of Michael and Michael alone, the after-school tutoring program was in full fledge at the church in the basement on Mondays and Wednesdays. Mr. and Mrs. Wallace trusted that their son was responsible enough to run his own after-school program, and they also enjoyed the fact that they could always tell their friends how responsible he was. It seemed like there was always a reason behind everything that the Wallaces did when it came to their son.

On Karen's first day at the tutoring session, she did very little homework. She spent most of her time complaining about one thing or another to Mike. As a matter of fact, she was starting to work his nerves. She didn't even bother to bring any homework with her; however, she was cautious enough not to be a total disturbance to the other students who were there. With the assistance of two other tutors from the church, Mike was able to help a few of the students conquer their fears of math and science for the first few days. It was kind of hard for Mike to stay completely focused on the students he was helping because Karen wore some of her most revealing shirts and tightest jeans to the program.

In the past, Mr. Johnson tried his best to keep Katrina from wearing pants and jeans, but the church had changed its old ways. A few of the female parishioners had complained to the pastor about the frigid New England winter weather, and he came to his senses and allowed the women to wear pants like the rest of the modern churches in Boston. It really wouldn't have made much of a difference to Karen, because she was going to wear whatever she wanted to wear, anyway. Karen wouldn't be Karen if she just wore regular pants and jeans. She had to wear the tightest clothes that she could find in order to irk her parents as well as all the other adults at her church.

Despite the fact that the parishioners thought Karen dressed in a threatening and provocative way, Mike enjoyed every minute of it. As a sophomore in high school, Karen looked like a grown woman with a body developed enough to send a grown man to jail for statutory rape. After a while, it became clear to everyone at the tutoring program that Karen was not there to be tutored. She came to the program because her father forced her, but more because she wanted to flirt with Mike until he couldn't resist her anymore. Karen was getting a kick out of seeing Mike sweat over her.

Michael had tried his best to maintain that good image in front of the rest of the students. He was respected and liked by most of the students in the program, because he had helped them improved their grades from the time they started coming to his program. Mike was also smart enough to make the student believe that he would never cross the line with any of them. That is any of them, except Karen. She dominated his every thought and there was no better conquest in his mind.

As much as the Wallaces would have liked for Mike to adhere to their "no sex before marriage" rule, he was laughing behind their backs because as handsome as he was, all the girls at his school were throwing ass at him all the time. Mike was sexually active from the time he was fifteen years old, and his parents had no idea. He went over to the girls' houses after school, and lied to his parents about having extended football and basketball practices. He was banging more girls than Ron Jeremy, the porno star. Mike was an all-around pleaser who wanted to please everyone all the time. He somehow managed to become a pro at it.

As much as Karen flirted with Mike, he didn't know how to react to her advances. He didn't know whether or not she was borderline schizophrenic like him or a complete Sybil. He was going nuts out of his mind for months before he worked up the nerves to say something to Karen. The fact that Karen was very outspoken also instilled a lot of fear in Mike. Since she never held her tongue against anyone at the church, he was afraid that she might not hold her tongue if he said the wrong thing to her. It took him a few months, and one day he finally spoke to her after the tutoring program while the two of them were the last people in the basement. He tried as best as he could to be diplomatic. "Why are you such a pain in the ass in my program?" he asked her. She took his comment as a come-on. "I get nervous around young, handsome athletic boys," she answered. "Is that right?" "Yeah, you make me want to tear your clothes off," she playfully told him.

At that point, Mike thought Karen was a trip and there was no way of figuring her out. He laughed at her comment as he walked passed her to go pick up a few pieces of trash that the other students left on the floor. She extended her hand to cop a feel of his ass and said out loud that his ass felt good. It was then that Mike pulled her towards him and started to French kiss her like she never expected. Her first reaction was receptive, but she turned to her old self again and pushed him off of her. Mike thought that she was playing hard to get because she wanted him to chase her. He pushed her up against the wall and held her firm with his hands as he started kissing her neck and slowly made his way down to her bra. She became agitated and angry and screamed for him to let go of her. He backed off and she asked if he was wimp for giving up so easily.

Karen was one challenge that Mike never anticipated. In the past, he never had to force any woman to sleep with him, and he also never had to fight to convince a woman to sleep with him. Mike was totally confused by Karen's game, so he gathered himself and cleaned up the place as she stood there watching. Finally, after he was about to turn the lights off so he could head out, she grabbed his hand and put it down her crotch and asked if he wanted some of that good stuff. Mike picked her ass up, brought her by the stairs, and sat her down and proceeded to make out with her. He slowly unbuttoned her blouse and buried his face in her chest, sucking on her nipples and her neck. Mike wasn't really as skillful as he thought, but Karen had no one to compare him to. She sat there moaning and groaning and touching Mike all over. And finally he pulled off her pants and she unzipped his pants as they continued to make out. The bulge in Michael's pants could not be denied, and Karen stroking it back and forth only confirmed her desire to sleep with him.

While they could not contain themselves, Mike grabbed his penis and pulled Karen's underwear to the side and inserted it inside Karen's wet vagina. She was wincing in pain, as it was her first time ever with a boy. She couldn't really take all that Mike was giving to her, but she couldn't let go of that tough outer shell and image that she had built for herself. She took the pain and acted like she had slept with someone before. As much as Mike was enjoying the whole thing, Karen was not getting any satisfaction from him, because it was painful for her. She never thought that having sex would be so painful and Mike was especially rough with her, because he wanted to prove to her how much of a bad boy he was. They were both trying to make moot points at this time. They humped and grinded on each other until Mike exploded inside Karen and let out a big roar like a lion. Even though Karen had never slept with a boy, she knew that Mike had come because of the clamoring noise he made while he was coming.

Karen asked Mike if he came inside of her and he said, "No." Not satisfied with Mike's answer, Karen asked him again if he came inside her. In his attempt to sound macho he told her "You think that I'm one of those minute men who would come that quickly?" She then asked, "What was all that noise for?" He didn't know what to say to her and told her that it was just his sex noise and that every guy has a sex noise. He then asked her, "How come you don't make any noise?" She told him she wanted to keep quiet, because they were at a church.

They really needed to read the book called "Sex for Dummies." Karen asked once more, "You sure you didn't come inside of me?" Mike continued to lie to her, and told her he did not come. She knew he was lying also because some of his semen started running down her leg as she stood up to pull her pants back up. They were both lying to each other, but she couldn't lie about the fact that she was bleeding. He told her he noticed blood on his penis, and asked if he was too big for her. She told him, "PPuhlize!! I have had bigger ones than that. It's just that my period is probably coming." Mike's ego was crushed a little bit, so he rushed to shut the lights off while Karen tried to wipe herself clean with some napkins. They left the church without saying another word to each other.

A Weird Moment

A couple of weeks had gone by since Karen had her sexual encounter with Mike. Her menstrual cycle was due on the second Monday of every month, and it usually came like clockwork. She was petrified when she didn't get her period that Monday. All kinds of crazy thoughts went through her mind as she started to think back on the encounter with Michael. She knew that he didn't use a condom and the possibility of pregnancy was very relevant. Karen had also stopped going to Mike's tutoring program, because she felt embarrassed by the whole thing. Mike didn't even try to reach out to her to make sure she was all right.

A week had gone by and no period came. Karen was frantic and she felt the need to call Mike to tell him that she was missing her period. It took a lot of courage for her to even pick up the phone to place that call to him. She knew for sure that if she were pregnant, there was only one possibility who the father might be. As bad of an image as Karen had managed to create for herself, in reality, she was not even close to that image. She had not slept with any boys, and most of the things that she was doing to irritate people were harmless. She merely got a kick out of people making a big deal of her shenanigans. Karen's first sexual experience was with Mike.

The phone rang about three times before Mr. Wallace finally picked it up. It was about six o'clock in the evening and the family was having dinner. He was surprised that Karen was even calling his house to speak to his son. Mr. Wallace had always thought of Karen as a little too hot-to-trot. He had especially cautioned his son not to get caught up with women like Karen. However, his disdain for Karen was only expressed privately to some of the members of his congregation behind closed doors. While he was on the phone with her, he took the opportunity to tell her how fine of a woman she had grown to be, and that God had blessed her with a body that every woman in the church would die for. He also told her that she was one of the most attractive young ladies in the church, and he would especially like to see her come to the church a little more often. Mr. Wallace was a big pervert.

After having somewhat of an awkward conversation with Mr. Wallace for about five minutes, Karen asked if his son was around. He told her sure but they were having dinner at the time and she could call back later. Without hesitation, Karen hung up and told him that she'd call Mike later. Mr. Wallace was trying to whisper a few more words to her, but she didn't give him the chance. He walked back to the dinner table to give his son the message that Karen had called. When his wife asked why he took so long to get back, he told her that he was trying to counsel Karen because she needed Jesus in her life. His wife responded, "That's why I love you so. You always find the time to help those in need." Mr. Wallace just shook his head and said, "That's why the good Lord put me on this earth."

A Restless Night

A couple hours had gone by since Karen's initial phone call to Mike. She waited to hear from him, but he never called. She wasn't sure if Mr. Wallace had given Mike the message that she had called, but she didn't want to sit by the phone to wait for him to call her back. She wanted to call Mike again, but her parents were home and she didn't want them to know her business. There was only a couple of phones in the house, one in the kitchen and the other in Mr. and Mrs. Johnson's bedroom, making it easy for them to listen in on Karen's conversation. She didn't want to take that risk.

The fact that her period hadn't shown rendered Karen restless. She didn't know what to do with herself. She thought about the possibility of having a child, but that thought soon went away when she realized that her father would probably kill her for getting pregnant. Karen also started thinking about her other options as well. Since she wasn't too much into Mike, she didn't even think about being married to him. She knew that if she told her parents and his parents that she was pregnant they would force her to marry him, but she knew that she couldn't be tamed at the tender age of sixteen. Karen didn't want to be tied down with a baby and a husband at such a young age.

She soon realized that she might really be faced with the same decision that Katrina had to make when she got pregnant. Karen was tough, but she wasn't tough enough to be on her own. And this was one kind of news that she couldn't take to her parents, because the pastor at her church had been stressing to the kids the dangers of premarital sex. She even thought about having an abortion, but that thought soon went away as well because she would need her parents' consent as a minor. Karen was running out of options. The only thing she could do was pray to God that her period was only late, because of all the stress she had endured after having sex with Mike.

Karen knew that she shouldn't have had unprotected sex with Mike, but she made a stupid decision that put her in a situation that was not at all favorable to her. To make matters worse, even after Katrina was kicked out of the house, Mr. and Mrs. Johnson never even took the time to talk to Karen and Eddy about sex. They figured that the pastor touched upon the subject enough on Sundays to get through to the kids. Never once did they think about a personable parental approach about the subject with their children. Karen really felt that if they had taken the time to talk some sense into her, she might not have slept with Mike.

That night, Karen didn't watch any of her favorite shows on television. She was too busy worrying about her next move if she were pregnant. By eleven o'clock, she had fallen asleep hoping for a miracle to happen the next day when she woke up. It was an unusual night for Karen too, because her brother Eddy religiously went to her room every night to chat with her before they went to sleep. She didn't even have Eddy to listen to her sorrow that night. For some reason, he just did not go to her room that night. She fell asleep clutching her pillow in a fetal position.

Karen tossed and turned that whole night and it was hard for her to get any real sleep. It would be an even longer day the next day when she woke up, because she had to wait until she got out of school to seek Mike to talk to him. When Karen woke up the next morning and noticed that her period still hadn't come, she was losing her mind. She even started to contemplate suicide. She thought about swallowing enough aspirins to put her to sleep indefinitely while she was in the bathroom getting ready for school. At the sound of her brother's knocking on the door to use the bathroom; she woke out of her nightmarish thoughts. Eddy needed to get in the bathroom to get ready for school himself, and he told his sister if she didn't come out he was going to break down the door. Karen and Eddy fought over the bathroom every morning before school.

Karen finally made her way out of the bathroom and said nothing to her brother. Eddy knew that his sister was bothered by something when she didn't say anything to him, so he asked her "what's wrong?" as she walked by him. She told him that nothing was wrong. She went to her room to get dressed and walked down to her bus stop to head to school. That day at school, the teachers noticed a change in Karen's behavior also. She wasn't being her usual disruptive self, but she wasn't participating in class either. Her body was in school but her mind and spirit were somewhere else. She didn't even want to be bothered with the people that she normally hung out with at school. The possibility of being pregnant dominated Karen's thoughts and she wouldn't have peace of mind until she spoke with Mike.

The Confrontation

When school finally let out, Karen made her way to the First Baptist Church in Dorchester to meet with Mike. She was agitated, frustrated, confused and most of all, scared. She needed someone in her corner for support and comfort, and she was hoping that Mike would show his support for what she was about to tell him. As usual, when she entered the tutoring hall in the basement, Mike and the other tutors were helping a group of students with a science project. Karen pulled out her notebook and started writing what she wanted to say to Mike down on a piece of paper. She did not know what kind of reaction to expect from him, but she was hoping for the best. After writing some of her key points down, she became bored and started drawing pictures of a baby on her note pad.

Karen sat through the tutoring program for two hours while Mike helped the other students without saying a word to him. He didn't even bother to greet her, and that set a red flag in her mind. She knew that they hadn't spoken in a couple of weeks, but he was acting like he didn't know her, all of a sudden. She paid him no mind, because she didn't want any of the other students in her business. She had something to discuss with Mike privately.

Meanwhile, Mike looked a little suspicious and was even sweating a little by the presence of Karen in the room. He kept his head down the whole time while he was helping the other students and avoided eye contact with Karen. It was almost like he felt guilty for doing something to Karen that he shouldn't have done. Mike knew damn well that he had ejaculated inside Karen that day when they had sex, and he knew that there was a chance of her becoming pregnant. Not that Karen added to the pressure that he was under, but she would smile every time he tried to sneak a peek at her from the corner of his eyes. She kept her eyes fixated on him after a while, because his curiosity kept forcing him to take a peek at her.

It seemed like Mike was trying to glance at Karen in some sort of weird way in an attempt to try to decipher her body language. He knew he was in for something, but he didn't know what. The last thing he wanted was for Karen to get loud with him in front of the other students. He wanted to make sure that the wild streak in Karen was tamed until tutoring session was over. As much of a fool he thought Karen was, he was even a bigger fool to think that she would divulge her personal business in front of other people. She was able to somewhat manage her personality when she wanted to, and that day she definitely showed her behavioral management skills and self-control.

The moment of truth finally came after the last student threw her backpack over her shoulder and headed out the door. Karen slowly approached Mike and asked him why he didn't return her call. He didn't really know what to say to her, so he came up with an excuse. He told her that he had a lot of homework, and by the time he was done with his homework it was too late to call her house. It seemed well enough and she bought it. She told him that she needed to talk to him and it was better if he sat down. By this time, Mike was sweating bullets and would probably wet his pants at the sound of a mouse. He knew it was going to be the inevitable and he was not ready. Karen sensed his discomfort, so she tried to reach out and grab his hand for security. He pulled his hands away from her and told her to say whatever it was that she had to say.

The meaner side of Karen resurfaced as she told him, "Suit yourself! I'm here to tell you that I might be pregnant and the baby is yours, 'cause I ain't been with nobody else. There, I said it!" Mike's mouth almost hit the floor when the word "pregnant" came out of Karen's lips. The jig was up and Mike had to either claim responsibility or deny that it was his. Unfortunately, he did what most scared teenager and most men would do and said to Karen, "There's no way that you're pregnant by me, because I didn't come inside of you. As much as you have slept around, you better go somewhere else with that shit."

Karen couldn't believe her ears. She jumped across the table and smacked Mike dead in his face as hard as she could. He fell to the floor and told her if she touched him again he would beat the crap out of her. The forceful edge in Mike's voice conveyed to Karen that he was very serious and she had better not trip again. She wanted to try the diplomatic approach and told Mike that she had never slept with anybody other than him, and that if he didn't want to help her perhaps his parents would be happy to hear about their little fling. That was as diplomatic as Karen could get. Mike saw it as nothing but blackmail and was outraged.

Mike went into a futile diatribe saying, "You think a little ho like you can go to my parents and tell them that I slept with you and they would believe you? Everybody in the church already knows your reputation as a ho, and there's no way that people would take your words over mine. You've caused nothing but problems in the church since you were twelve, and now your skank ass want to tell me that you're pregnant with my baby? Bitch, please!"

The forceful edge that he had in his voice earlier had lost its effects after he called Karen a bitch. She jumped on him and started punching him all over his face and body.

He had to run away from her and stand across the table to keep her from getting to him. Karen was pissed that Mike had only thought of her as ho and she didn't want to talk to him about the pregnancy anymore.

She simply told him "God don't like ugly. You're gonna get what's coming to you. It may not be today, it may not be tomorrow, but you're gonna get yours. I shouldn't have never allowed myself to sleep with your sorry ass and if I'm pregnant, I'm gonna keep it just to show your dumb ass parents how perfect their little son is. A blood test will not lie and the only way you can say you're not the father is through a blood test. You just opened a whole new can of worm for your ass, chump!"

Karen walked out the door leaving Mike bewildered without saying another word. He couldn't even fathom what Karen's next move was going to be, but he knew that he had made a big mistake by calling her names. As confident as Mike sounded about his image with the people at the church and his parents he also knew that if subjected to a blood test that paternity could easily be established, and he could be determined as the father of Karen's baby. Mike was in a catch twenty-two situation.

A Bloody Mess

When Karen left the tutoring program the previous day, she had hoped to never see or speak to Mike again because he was a jerk. She was convinced she was pregnant and she was trying to figure out a way to deal with it. She knew that her brother would support whatever decision she wanted to make, but the fact of the matter was that she still needed her parents to sign for her to have an abortion if she decided to have one. Karen started to get a little depressed that day in class, but when all the students started pointing at her and laughing as she walked down the hall to her next class; Karen wondered what the hell was so funny. She didn't know why people were pointing at her, and she became very confrontational with one girl. She went up to the girl and grabbed her by her hair and asked her if she wanted to get her ass beat for laughing at her. The other student was so scared; she took off running and left behind a big chunk of her hair in Karen's hand.

Karen was going down the hall confronting all the students and they were all too scared to tell her why they were laughing at her. As she got near her class, one of her friends pulled her to the side and told her that her pants were bloody red from the crotch down. Karen ran to the bathroom to take a look and she noticed that there was blood running down her legs. Any other time Karen would have been upset, but that day, she was happy and relieved that an embarrassing situation brought ease to her state of mind. She stood in front of the mirror and smiled a sigh of relief. She bowed her head for a few minutes and gave thanks to God for giving her a second chance. Karen was happy that she was not pregnant and felt like a load had been lifted off her shoulders.

Karen had come to the conclusion that she was pregnant, because her period was almost a week late. She did not even bother to bring a pad or a tampon with her to school. In the past, she was always careful; she either wore a tampon or brought one with her at school when her period was expected. This time she endured the embarrassment at school and was particularly angry with the students who were laughing at her, but she was relieved that she was not pregnant. None of the students knew what Karen was going through in her life because of her tough outer shell which she always used as a defense mechanism. No one got close enough to know her.

Karen was able to go to the nurse's office to get a tampon to keep the blood from running. The embarrassing smell of the blood was something she didn't want to take with her on the bus on the way home. She asked the nurse to use her phone to call her father to pick her up from school. Her father was at work at the time, so she decided to call her mom instead to explain what had happened and her mom was very sympathetic. Her mom called her dad to explain thc situation, but it was a different situation when Mr. Johnson got on the phone to speak with his wife. He thought Karen was negligent, and that he shouldn't have to leave work to go pick her up at school just because she had created an embarrassing situation for herself. Mr. Johnson acted like a jerk and told his wife that Karen would have to find her own way home, because he wasn't leaving his job early to go pick her up.

Karen broke down in the nurse's office after her mother told her that her dad wouldn't pick her up. Knowing how distressing the situation was for Karen, the nurse offered to take her home. Karen was grateful, and asked the nurse if she could stay in her office until the end of the school day. The nurse didn't really have much of a choice. She knew that if she had sent Karen back to class it would have resulted in a fight, because everyone at the school was aware of Karen's temper. The nurse tried as much as she could to help Karen clean some of the blood off her pants with alcohol. She also found out that day that Karen was not as bad as she portrayed herself to be at school. They spent a few hours talking, and the nurse learned that Karen was a frightened little girl who didn't want to end up like her older sister. She even told the nurse about her pregnancy scare.

Karen, for the first time, was able to discuss sex and the precautionary measures that she needed to take to avoid getting pregnant if she was to continue to be sexually active. The nurse was really delicate and overly nice with Karen. She highlighted the fact that Karen didn't need to sleep with boys to validate herself to anybody. The nurse explained to Karen that any woman with self esteem would wait for the right man to come along before she decided to have sex, and that her body was her temple and she needed to take care of it. Karen learned a lot about her body, sex, boys, and nurse Baker. In a way, she was glad that her day happened the way it did, because it taught her a lesson and she discovered new things that she wouldn't other otherwise have known.

Peace of Mind at Last

After nurse Baker dropped Karen off at home, she ran directly to Eddy's room to let him know the good news. Everything seemed to work out perfectly that day because Eddy had switched his scheduled day off with another worker at his part-time job to help alleviate his sister's worries. When he left for school that morning, he knew that his sister didn't seem right to him, and he wanted to make sure that he was home to talk to her after school.

Karen didn't even bother to knock on Eddy's door before she entered. He was a little startled when she barged in, but he held his arms open to give her a hug after seeing her standing there. He didn't know what state of mind she was in, but he wanted to console her. Though Karen was happy about not being pregnant, tears of joy started running down her face when she saw her brother standing there waiting to hug her. She knew that he would've been there for her, but the gesture he made towards her confirmed the closeness of the relationship that they already shared. Karen had always felt misunderstood by everyone except her brother, and he had shown that he would be there for her even in her darkest hour.

She tried as much as she could to fight back the tears. They came rolling down her cheeks and Eddy just held her tight against his body as he told her that everything would be all right. Karen nodded her head in agreement, and told Eddy that she knew for sure that everything would be fine because her period had finally come. They both started jumping and dancing around in Eddy's room. Eddie offered to take her down to Brigham's, a neighborhood ice cream parlor in Mattapan Square to celebrate. First, he wanted to talk to his sister about not repeating the same mistakes ever again. Eddy was very frank with his sister about keeping her legs closed and not giving in to the temptation of these young boys on the street. He also told her that they didn't really have a concrete plan if she had indeed become pregnant, and she was just lucky.

After Karen explained how the whole thing initially happened with Mike, Eddy was a little irate because his parents were always quick to throw Mike's name in their faces like he was a saint. Eddy felt like Saint Mike was manipulating everyone at his church, including his parents. He wanted to get back at Mike for treating his sister so disrespectfully, so he came up with a plan to make him sweat for the next few months. Karen was more than eager to make Mike pay for the way he treated her, so she jumped right on board with Eddy's plan.

Sweating It Out

For the next few months Eddy and Karen would have their way with Mike. Eddy had his sister showing up at Mike's school wearing a small pillow under her shirt that made her look like she was carrying a baby. Each time Karen showed up at the school, she antagonized Mike as much as she could with threats of naming him as the father at the hospital, and forcing him to take a blood test to establish paternity. She told Mike that he wasn't going to go away to college to become this big football star that he had planned on becoming, because he was gonna be playing daddy at home. The more she talked, the more it was driving him crazy.

Karen really got to Mike one afternoon when she threatened to take the pregnancy to his parents and the church if he didn't start owning up to his responsibilities. Mike didn't know what to do with her after a while. The more scared of the situation he became, the more she pushed him. Eddy even got in on the fun when he started to call Mike at home to tell him that he hoped he'd be a good brother-in-law and a good father to his nephew or niece. Mike feared that Karen might have told her parents about the pregnancy if she told Eddy. Karen's parents had not gotten in touch with Mike's parents yet; however, he knew he had to keep his cool in order for her not to let the cat out the bag.

One day Karen called Mike and told him that she had a doctor's appointment and asked if he was gonna take her. He told her to get the hell out of his face, that he had his tutoring program to run, and he didn't want anything to do with the baby. As scared as Mike was, he was still trying to stand his ground as a conniving liar. Karen threatened to come to his tutoring program with her stomach showing. He knew that if she came to the program looking pregnant the other students would tell the whole church how pregnant she was, and it would be a matter of time before she revealed he was the father. He agreed to go to the hospital with her. He asked the other tutors to cover for him while he made plans to meet Karen at the hospital the next day.

Meanwhile, Karen wanted to milk her little game for all she could. She found reasons to stop attending church on Sundays with her parents so Mike couldn't see that she wasn't really pregnant. She told Mike that she would meet him at Massachusetts General Hospital at 3:30 pm the next day and to wait for her because she might run a little late. As planned, Mike went to the hospital and waited for two hours for Karen to show and she never did. He went to the front desk to enquire about an appointment for a Karen Johnson, but the nurse told him that no such person existed in her appointment book. Mike was furious and angry that he had gone all the way down to the hospital and Karen didn't show up.

Mike was so pissed when he got home, he didn't even bother calling Karen for an explanation. She, however, called him to tell him how sorry she was for telling him to go to Massachusetts General Hospital to meet her when her appointment was actually at Boston City Hospital. Mike could sense she had a smirk on her face as she told him that, so he hung up the phone in her face and vowed that he'd get her back for humiliating him.

A Game Gone Wrong

Karen and Eddy had exhausted every opportunity to make Mike angry, and Mike had had enough. Mike had conjured up his own plan to get even with Karen. She had called Mike about another appointment at Boston City Hospital, but this time he offered to pick her up from school in his dad's car. Karen thought she was going to play another one of her jokes on Mike, but it turned out that she would be the one getting a dose of a serious medicine.

Mike showed up at Karen's school right when the last bell rang at the end of last period. He had parked his father's car around the corner and walked over to meet Karen at the front. He wore a black baseball cap to hide his face with a black a pair of jeans and sweatshirt. Since Karen knew that he was going to pick her up, she ran to the bathroom to put on the pillow to carry her fake stomach as planned so she could have her little fun with Mike. He still had no idea that she wasn't really pregnant, but he was tired of her game.

Karen got in Mike's car, and told him to head towards Boston City hospital. Her plan was to get him there, and after they got there she would tell him that she mixed up the days for her appointment and he would have to come back the following day to take her back to the hospital again. She thought she had her plans laid out. Mike however, decided to take Karen for a little ride a little farther north than she had intended. He drove up to New Hampshire with her instead, and when he got to a wooded area he told her to get out of his car. Karen fought him and told him she wasn't getting out and he couldn't force her out because she was pregnant. After telling Karen to get out for about ten minutes while she refused, Mike got out and went to the passenger side of the car to pull her out. They struggled at first, but he finally pulled her out and locked the door. He went back to the driver's side and got in the car and drove off.

Mike only wanted to teach Karen a lesson for messing with him. He drove to the other side of the wooded area to watch Karen cry her little heart out, because she thought she was left stranded. After a half hour of watching her being hysterical, he went back over to pick her up and demanded that she apologize for all the headaches she had caused him. She refused to apologize and an argument ensued. Karen attacked Mike and in an effort to try to defend himself against her, he hit her across the temple with the back of his hand and she fell unconscious to the ground. Mike was so stupid he didn't even check for a pulse or find out if she was breathing. He attempted to revive Karen through CPR but his efforts were futile. He didn't even know what CPR was. He was only trying it on her because he had seen it on television. After about fifteen minutes of calling himself "trying to bring Karen back to life," he realized that he might have had a dead corpse in his hands.

Mike panicked and he immediately picked up Karen's body and threw it over his shoulder to put her in the trunk of the car. As he threw Karen over his shoulder, he felt a cushion against his shoulder and when he pulled up her shirt, he realized she wasn't pregnant at all, and that she had been wearing a cushioned pillow to play a game with him all along. He became angrier because she had played him and now he believed it led to her death. He drove to a U-Haul equipment rental center not too far from where they were and bought a big cardboard box. He then proceeded to go back to the wooded area in New Hampshire. He put the box together and placed what he thought was Karen's lifeless body inside the box under a tree.

What may have started out as a prank ended up being a homicide, he thought. Mike never set out to kill Karen that day, but it seemed misfortune was upon him. His bright future was somewhat distant from his mind as he drove down Interstate 95 South towards Boston after leaving Karen's body in a box to rot. All Mike could think about was life behind bars, and the disappointment that his parents would see in him. He knew that it was a matter of time before someone discovered Karen's body, and all the fingers would be pointed his way because Eddy was in on the game that they were playing. He knew Eddy would tell the police to go after him. Mike thought about ways to get rid of Eddy too when he got back home, but that thought quickly faded because he wasn't really a killer.

Startled

Mike was too shaken to drive straight home. He pulled over on the side of the expressway to think about the consequences of what he had done. He started banging his head against the steering wheel as tears welled up in his eyes. He blamed himself for sleeping with Karen in the first place and he blamed his parents for forcing him to live up to an image that he couldn't really live up to. He was really remorseful about what he did, but he was too scared to think about going to the authorities.

As Mike sat in the car on the side of the road pondering his next move, a Massachusetts State Trooper pulled up behind him to see if everything was okay. Mike was startled when the officer knocked on his window to ask if everything was all right with him. The first thing that came to mind when he saw the officer was that Karen's body had already been discovered. The officer noticed the dry streaks of tears on Mike's face, and he asked if he was okay. He told the officer half-heartedly that everything was fine and that he was sad because he had lost his girlfriend. The officer told him that it was nothing to cry about, because there were a lot more women in the world and he was only a young man and that all men have gotten their hearts broken at one time or another.

Mike wasn't really paying attention to all the gibberish sentiment that the officer was dishing out to him. He was just happy that he hadn't been caught. The officer told him that he couldn't stay on the side of the road, and that he needed to head home to deal with his issues. Mike didn't even wait to hear another word from the officer as he put the car in drive and drove straight home. When Mike got home, every little sound of a police siren increased his paranoia. In an attempt to make sure that he was eliminated as a suspect in her disappearance, he placed a phone call to Karen's house. When Eddy picked up the phone, he asked if he could speak to her. Eddy told him that Karen hadn't gotten home yet, and he told Eddy to let her know that he called. He was surprisingly cordial for a guy who had been tormented by Eddy and Karen for the last few months. Eddy wondered what was up with him, but did not say anything.

They hung up the phone and Mike was a little relieved that Eddy wasn't at all suspicious of him. Although Mike felt guilty about "the accidental death of Karen," he wasn't ready to spend the rest of his life in jail. After all, he had been fooling everybody into thinking how great a young man he was for the sake of his parents. Being normal again however, was going to be a challenged that Mike hadn't yet faced.

Saving Karen Johnson

Dinnertime had come and gone and Mr. and Mrs. Johnson had not seen Karen. They wondered why she did not make it home on time for dinner, but she had done that in the past as well. Karen had missed so many dinners with her family in the past, her father simply told her mother and brother to ignore her after a while and start eating. The Johnson family had to learn to adjust to Karen's behavior, and sometimes they felt like they were walking on eggshells with her because of what happened with Katrina. Mr. Johnson didn't really give a damn about the past, though. He wanted things done his way and it didn't matter what the outcome was.

Also, in the past when Karen didn't make it home for dinner, it was because she wanted to piss off her father for something that he might've done to her. It was normal for Mrs. Johnson to ask her husband if he had done anything to Karen before she went off to school earlier in the day. Mr. Johnson told his wife, "as a matter of fact, I spoke with her earlier while I was at work because the school had called me about her disrespecting a teacher. I told her she was gonna get a beating when she got home and that's probably why she ain't here."

Mr. Johnson went on to explain to his wife and Eddy his plan to send Karen to military school in order to save her life. He felt like he was losing control of his daughter, and she no longer feared him or reacted to his threats. As much as Mr. Johnson hated the fact that he had pushed one of his little girls out of his life, he didn't want to lose a second one and he was willing to do whatever necessary to make things right for Karen. Mrs. Johnson had a lot to do with his new way of thinking. She began to slowly to assert herself when it came to the decisions regarding the family by empowering her husband. She would make suggestions to him and fooled him into thinking he was the person that came up with the plan. She took away the threatening feeling that her husband had for many years.

Mr. and Mrs. Johnson were very excited about their new plans for their daughter. Even though Eddy didn't agree with them totally, he knew that his sister needed more structure than his parents could provide. He thought that military school might do her some good. Eddy loved his sister and wanted the best for her as well. Of course, he did not want her to leave him alone in the house with his parents. Although severely misunderstood, he also knew that she wasn't a completely responsible person. If anything, he wanted the military experience to scare her straight, because he knew that she wouldn't stay there for too long. Eddy was the only person who understood that Karen didn't like restraints, and if she felt that people were trying to hold her down she would find a way to get away from them.

It was decided at the dinner table that night, Karen would be transferred to a military school in upstate New York as soon as her parents could make the arrangements. Eddy was told to keep quiet about the plans, and Mr. and Mrs. Johnson were going to ease up on her so she wouldn't suspect anything. It was painstakingly hard, especially for Mrs. Johnson, to discuss sending her child to some military school to straighten her out. She felt like she had failed her daughter as a mother, but she couldn't stand by and allow her to drift away to nothing. She wanted started to want more out of life for herself now, but she also wanted a lot more for her children.

The Agony of a Missing Child

The clock on the kitchen wall read nine o'clock in the evening, and there was still no sign of Karen. Everyone knew that she had never stayed out that late before during a school night, but they hadn't started to worry yet. Karen was always unpredictable to her family, and they were used to her erratic behavior. They were ready to deal with one more of her surprises. Mrs. Johnson didn't want to appear worried, but her facial expression and body language said otherwise. By midnight when her husband shut the television off to go the bed, she asked him if he was going to sleep knowing that her baby girl still hadn't come home.

He responded, "There's nothing I can do at this time. I'll deal with it in the morning because the police department won't take a missing report unless she's been gone for twenty four hours." Mrs. Johnson had to beg her husband to call the police to demand that they do something about her missing daughter.

That day, the Johnson family learned that reporting a missing child is easier said than done, especially a missing black teenager. When Mr. Johnson dialed the police station to ask to speak to someone about his missing daughter, he was immediately asked how long she had been gone. When he told them that she was missing since the end of the school day; they told him exactly what he hadn't expected to hear, that it hadn't been long enough to file a missing report on his daughter.

Furthermore, they started grilling Mr. Johnson about his relationship with his daughter. And the fact that he and Karen had a disagreement earlier in the day also played a big factor in the police stagnancy with the report. Mr.

Johnson was told that he had to wait a full twenty-four hours from the time that his daughter got out of school to report her missing, because it was the last time she was seen by someone. The Police Department also assumed that it could have been an act of defiance from a daughter toward her father.

Meanwhile, Mrs. Johnson spent the whole night tossing and turning in her bed. Eddy also could not sleep, and he did not understand why his sister would want to take a threat from his father this far. Karen never feared a beating from her father and Eddy knew that. He figured it had to have been something a lot more serious for Karen to stay away from home. He kept tossing and turning, trying to figure why his sister hadn't come home. Karen also failed to tell Eddy that she was going to run a prank on Mike on that day. She didn't get a chance to call Eddy to tell him about it, because Mike picked her up from school.

The fact that Karen was missing did not seem to interfere much with Mr. Johnson's sleep. From down the hall, he could be heard snoring in his room. Eddy was worried about his sister, but he worried more about his mother. He knew that she couldn't handle losing another child. After Katrina left, Mrs. Johnson was never the same. She anticipated a knock on the door from her daughter every single day for the first five years, and every knock on the door only intensified her anticipation of Katrina's return. It almost drove her insane, and Eddy didn't want to have to relive that episode all over again. He tried his best to reassure his mother that Karen was fine and that she would eventually come back home.

The whole evening came and went and there was still no sign of Karen. Her parents drove to her school to see if she showed up, but she didn't go there either. Mr. and Mrs. Johnson drove straight to the police station after leaving the school to file a missing report on their daughter. They used the recent picture that Karen took at Sears that Mrs. Johnson kept in her wallet to help the police identify Karen when and if she is found. Mrs. Johnson was sobbing uncontrollably, and she couldn't maintain her composure. The police officer who was taking the report sympathized with her, but it would take a veteran like Officer John O'Malley to help make the process easier on Mrs. Johnson. He understood exactly what she was going through, because during his five years on the force he had encountered many similar cases and the outcomes weren't always positive.

His assignment to the "special missing children unit" propelled Officer O'Malley's desire to become a detective. After completing the missing report, Officer O'Malley advised Mrs. Johnson to put up posters of her daughter around the neighborhood in case someone had seen her.

The Ends Justify the Means

Karen had been missing for over a week and the police hadn't gotten a clue yet. Detective O'Malley asked his superior officer if he could be assigned to the case. It was the first case that was assigned to him in a long time, and it would bring him closer to the family than he ever wished. Detective O'Malley worked relentlessly to find clues and a link to Karen's disappearance. He talked to everyone who knew Karen and from the stories he heard, she didn't have too many friends. Most people could only recall a negative encounter with Karen, which placed O'Malley at a disadvantage. However, the one person that would bring him closer to a suspect was Eddy.

Eddy explained to Officer O'Malley about the little game that he and his sister conjured up against Mike because he had disrespected her after they slept together. As many people Detective O'Malley spoke to about Karen, it was her brother that he found to be the most helpful. He explained to the officer how his sister had lost her virginity to Mike, and he had turned his back on her when she thought she was pregnant. Though Officer O'Malley felt it was a cruel joke that Eddy and Karen played on Mike, he still felt that it didn't warrant her disappearance.

Armed with the information that he received from Eddy, O'Malley went to the Wallace home to speak to Mike. When he arrived at the Wallace home, Mike hadn't gotten home yet. He spoke with Mike's parents and told them that he needed to talk to Mike, because he was known as a friend to Karen. The whole church knew of Karen's disappearance, and the Wallaces were more than cooperative with the police. They assured Officer O'Malley that they would give their son the message and they would also make him available for questioning.

When Mike got home that evening he was shocked to learn that a police officer had come to his house to question him about the disappearance of Karen. The pressure was on, and he didn't know what to do. He felt like he had no one to speak with about his situation, and even worse he felt ashamed for what he had done. The fake image that Mike was trying to uphold had caught up to him and he was not ready to face the music.

Mike sat in his room and started thinking about all the bad things that he had been doing and all the witnesses who could jeopardize his freedom. He thought about the times he and his friends went down to Orchard Park Projects to get high everyday. He thought about the time he went to Filene's and Macy's to steal clothes just for the thrill of it. He thought about the many women he had used and abused to get his way. Mike thought about all the times he had cheated on the field by shooting steroid to get bigger and stronger than his opponents on the football field. He had done so many wrongs, and yet his parents and people at the church thought he was the perfect gentleman. How would he explain all the bad things that he had done when it was all found out? He thought. It was something that Mike didn't have the solution to.

Mike did the only cowardly thing that he could muster the courage to do. He pulled out a pad of paper and a pen, and wrote down his confession before he swallowed a whole bottle of ibuprofen. By the time his parents discovered his body in his bedroom, Mike's heart had given up and there was nothing the paramedics could do to revive him. In Mike's confession however, he didn't leave any clues as to where the police could find Karen's body. He only confessed to what he thought was murder.

A Woman on a Mission

When Mrs. Wallace discovered her son's body in his room, she was hysterical as she ran to her husband to let him know that their only son had taken his life. His body was lying on his bedroom floor with no life left. Mrs. Wallace cradled her son's body until the paramedics arrived. She talked to her son and told him how much she loved him and that he could have come and talk to her before taking his life. Mrs. Wallace was also clutching in her hand, the suicide note that Mike left behind describing the details of the dark side of his life.

Mr. Wallace fought back tears as he stared at his son on the floor. He wanted to be strong for his wife, but he was too angry with her. He started blaming her for forging an image that Mike had to live up to. Mrs. Wallace always wanted to be part of high society, and as a result everyone in her family had to live up to the hype that she created about her upscale family. It was Mrs. Wallace who talked her father into allowing her husband to take over the ministry at the church after his retirement. Mr. Wallace was never interested in becoming a pastor, but his wife pushed him to take on the role and he accepted it as a way to please her. He felt like he was always trying to please his wife and he didn't want to do it any longer. Mr. Wallace missed out on a lot in his son's life, because his wife kept the boy busy doing things in the community for her own benefit.

Mr. Wallace never got to spend time with the boy, since his mother had mapped out his life from the time he was born. The only thing that Mike ever enjoyed doing was playing football with his friends, but his mother didn't see any reason why he should play football with his friends just for the fun of it. She forced him to join the football team in high school, and she pressured him to compete with everyone and everything in his life.

Mrs. Wallace gained her competitive spirit when a man who married her best friend dumped her. The man was a physician, and she became caught up with his profession and his high profile image in the community. He thought she was too stuffy for him, and she wanted to run his life. Her best friend however, was easygoing and attentive and they got along very well. The man decided to pursue a relationship with her best friend and they married a year later and had a son. Mrs. Wallace married her husband who was an accountant and a member of her church a year later as well. She tried to talk her husband into getting his MBA, and when he refused she forced him to become a preacher because it would bring prestige and adulation to her family. Mrs. Wallace wanted to be with a prominent man to show her ex that she was worthy.

Mrs. Wallace also gave birth to Mike who was about the same age as her ex-best friend's son. Her friend's son was a natural born athlete and leader who always made the high school sports headlines in Boston. In order to continue her competition with her ex-best friend, Mrs. Wallace forced her son to become an athlete and a leader. Mike never understood the motivation behind his mother' aggressive push for him to be great at everything, but her husband knew very well where her intention came from. Her break-up with her ex was the talk of the church for a long time, and Mr. Wallace ended up paying the price because his wife was a woman scorned.

Concealing the truth

Mr. Wallace finally asked his wife if Mike revealed any reason why he took his life in that letter. At first, she ignored his question because she knew what he was saying sounded too familiar. Mike had written on the note that he was tired of living up to an image that his parents had created. Now that he was gone, Mrs. Wallace didn't even want to face the reality of the situation. Her husband asked to see the letter, and she refused to give it to him. He demanded to see his son's last words, and before she handed it to him she asked him to promise that he wouldn't go to the police with it. Mr. Wallace didn't understand why he would have to conceal a suicide note from the police, and he told his wife that he would make no such promise.

Mrs. Wallace was up to her old tricks again. Even as a grieving mother, she still wanted to uphold her image. She didn't want people to find out that her son had committed murder before he took his life. The little perfect image she had helped to create was going to stay intact as far as she was concerned. Mr. Wallace didn't want to be part of any conspiracy to hide evidence from the police. He snatched the letter from his wife, and as he read it tears ran down his face. He shook his head in disgust at his wife. She had pushed the kid to the brink of disaster, he thought. He felt bad for never standing up against his wife and for not being a voice for his son.

From the letter, the phrase "You guys have forced me to live up to an image that I couldn't uphold" kept echoing in Mr. Wallace's head. He knew exactly what Mike meant by this. Mike was never given the opportunity to be a normal teenager, and as a result he had led a double life and he kept secrets from his parents. Mr. Wallace was sickened by the whole situation. He told his wife that if she wanted him to continue to be a part of her life, she would have to stop acting so selfishly and stop living for other people. Mr. Wallace lost his only son, and he accepted part of the responsibility for his son's death. The worst part of the letter was when Mike admitted to delivering the fatal blow to Karen's temple. Mr. Wallace knew that his son was no murderer, and it had to have been an accident that he killed Karen.

Mr. Wallace wanted to do the honorable thing by calling the police, and tell them about the letter. The whole congregation had been made aware of Karen disappearance, and they were praying for the best. Mr. and Mrs. Wallace would have to tell them that Karen was killed at the hand of their son, and that was something that Mrs. Wallace was totally against. It would all lead back to her selfish nature. This time however, Mr. Wallace took his position as a man in this relationship and his position as a man of God and called the police to report the suicide and the letter found.

There was rage inside Mrs. Wallace as her husband picked up the phone to call the authorities. Before he could finish his first sentence on the phone, she attacked him and told him that he didn't care about the reputation of his family. She kept swinging at him while he was on the phone, and he kept dodging as he told the cops to get to his house quickly. He finally hung up the phone, and she picked it up and threw it at him in full attack mode. Mrs. Wallace was like a woman possessed, and her husband had no idea that he had made a deal with the devil. He tried to subdue her, but she kept kicking and screaming that she was going to destroy him and that without her he would be nothing.

Mrs. Wallace was saying things to her husband that were unforgivable, and she didn't seem to care. Mr. Wallace, meanwhile, had made up his mind that he was going to leave his wife and the ministry because his wife had crossed the line. He knew that she was on the Board of Directors at the church, and he did not want to have to plead for his job and wanted to wash his hands off with "the crazy psycho wife of his." Mr. Wallace was very tactful in the way that he had planned to leave his wife. He didn't want to end his marriage in turmoil and he wanted to be there for his wife through her bereavement period.

The Moment of Truth

The moment of truth had finally arrived for Mr. and Mrs. Johnson. They were about to receive the worse possible news that any parent could have received about their missing child. It was also one of the worse predicaments that Officer O'Malley had been in since he became a police officer. He had to deliver the bad news about Karen, but even worse he had to tell them that their pastor's son was responsible for her disappearance and he had committed suicide without leaving any clues about the body. Officer O'Malley wrestled with his approach as he had never done this in the past. There was no gentle way to deliver the message to a parent that their child had been murdered. O'Malley had developed a close relationship with Mrs. Johnson through the course of his investigation, and he knew that she had anticipated finding her daughter alive.

The fact that Mrs. Johnson had divulge to Officer O'Malley that her oldest daughter, Katrina had left home pregnant when she was fourteen years old weighed heavily on her heart. He didn't know how much more her heart could take, but he had a job to do. Every conversation Mrs. Johnson started with Officer O'Malley began with Katrina's name, and she had hoped that he would find out information about her whereabouts as well. O'Malley never discovered any information on Katrina, because she had been using the alias Star Bright whenever she was arrested. Easing the pain for Mrs. Wallace was a chore in itself, and O'Malley was just the right person to do that. Though he wasn't always philosophical, O'Malley found a way to make delivering the news to Mrs. Johnson easier.

He knocked on Mrs. Johnson's door early that afternoon, and found her sitting in front of her television watching the news. She was wishing and hoping to find out any little information about her daughter from the mid-day news. But nothing was reported about Karen. It seemed like the media had no interest in the disappearance of a little black girl. There were more important issues to cover like which neighbors' cat had to be rescued from a tree by the fire department or which animals had to be saved from an unkempt shelter. There always seemed to be something more important in the news than the lives of black people.

The only kind of news that the media yearned for was the "shoot 'em up bang bang" that took place among the black people. A good black-on-black, shoot out, murder-rampage would make the headlines any day. The depiction of savages in the hood killing themselves is what the media hungered for. Why would the life of a missing little black girl make the local news? It was common for the local news to report little white girls being kidnapped in states as far as Montana, however. Their lives are more important and national alerts needed to be issued for these white kids.

America's media is so biased that it can be sickening at times, Mrs. Johnson thought.

The police department wanted to inform the Johnson family that someone had confessed to killing their daughter before they went to the media using O'Malley as the messenger. O'Malley tried his best to ease the situation for Mrs. Johnson by holding her hands and showing a lot of sympathy. He told her that someone had confessed to killing Karen, but he had not mentioned where he left the body. Mrs. Johnson almost fell to the floor after he delivered the words. They seemed to cut through her heart like a knife. What O'Malley feared most was her reaction when she found out that it was Mike Wallace who had confessed to the murder.

When Officer O'Malley finally told Mrs. Johnson that it was Mike who had confessed to the murder, she seemed aloof at first. She then acted in anger and told Officer O'Malley with as many expletives as she could that she never trusted the bastard. Mrs. Johnson was totally devastated, but she knew that her daughter was a fighter and a part of her refused to believe that she was actually dead. She wanted to find the body in order for her to believe that her daughter was really gone. She was angry that Mike had given closure to his parents, but left her bewildered.

Mrs. Johnson never really bought into that perfect image of Mike that everyone had spoken of at the church. She had seen him smoking weed with a group of boys once while coming home from the supermarket. She never said anything because her husband had always tried to use Mike's good image to motivate his own kids, and she didn't know how to tell him that Mike wasn't at all what he appeared to be. Mrs. Johnson also felt guilty, because if she had said something to somebody about Mike maybe her daughter would still be alive.

The Media Nightmare

After the Johnson family was notified of the possible death of their daughter, the police department released a statement to the media about Mike's confession. Immediately the media felt it was a situation that was newsworthy, because a young man whom people believed to have been on the straight and narrow path had committed a heinous crime. Every television station in Boston focused on Mike's suicide and confession. They referred to him as a coward who didn't want to face his fate in the justice system. They had totally forgotten about the young girl who lost her life. When they finally talked about her, they tried as much as they could to find information about her young troubled past.

The Johnson and Wallace families were furious at the portrayal of these two young people in their moments of sorrow. The media even alluded to their love affair as the reason why Mike was pushed over the edge. Everyone was trying to draw their own conclusions. The media succeeded once again in creating the image of the young man as a cruel, calculated murderer while Karen was portrayed as a young female victim who was too hot-to-trot. The media's distorted version of what actually happened had everyone at the church turning their heads at Pastor Wallace and his wife.

Mr. Wallace had decided to tell his congregation that he was stepping down as pastor because he and his wife were getting a divorce the Sunday after his son's burial. The media camped outside the Wallaces' home waiting for a statement, and when that didn't work they went to the church and waited for them there. A few people at the church took the opportunity to let the world know that Mike and Karen were great kids, but those statements never made it to the television screen on the news. Mike's ex-cohorts managed to capitalize on his misfortune by accepting money to talk about some of the bad things that they did together when he was alive. The media had managed to turn Mike's so-called friends against him with a fist full of dollars.

Pastor Wallace's departure from the church was something that he wanted to deal with privately within the church, however, the media got news of his resignation and they drew their own conclusion about that as well. It was not favorable toward Pastor Wallace at all to say the very least. The church didn't really know what to make of everything that came to light that week. It seemed as if the pastor didn't even have a hold on his own family while preaching the good word of the Lord to his congregation.

Mrs. Wallace, meanwhile, fell into a deep depression because everything that she had worked so hard to build was destroyed publicly, and she couldn't face the embarrassment. Mr. Wallace tried his best to be supportive and sought help to get her out of her depression, but she continued to verbally abuse him until he could take it no longer. He walked out on her while she was at the hospital, and left her parents to deal with their lunatic daughter.

Dealing with a New Tragedy

After Mike's confession was discovered and made public, the Johnson Family no longer wanted anything to do with the church. They had discovered that they were around a bunch of fair-weather Christians who ran to the media like parrots with their opinions about the tragedy. Mrs. Johnson didn't want to be around the people at the church anymore because of their judgmental attitudes. When Katrina left a few years earlier they started spreading rumors about her being a little tramp that had to be sent to upstate New York to be tamed. Since it was just a rumor, the Johnsons didn't really know who started it, and they didn't really want to deal with it because she had truly left the house because of her pregnancy.

This time around, things weren't going to be as easy for Mrs. Johnson. With Katrina, she was still hoping that one day that she would walk back into her life, because she had no confirmed report that Katrina was dead. She prayed everyday that Katrina would have a change of heart and would want to reconnect with her family. Mrs. Johnson was very hopeful. She wanted to have the same positive attitude with Karen even though Mike had confessed to killing her. It had to be a mother's hunch.

A few years passed and Karen's body was never discovered. Everyone in the house had grown depressed over her disappearance. Mrs. Johnson stopped all physical relations with her husband and Eddy became a recluse. The Johnson household was not the same without Karen, and everything changed for the worse. Eddy isolated himself in the basement of his parents' house. After he graduated from high school, instead of going to Northeastern University as planned, he took a job as a

Janitor with the Fleet Center and invested all his earned money in turning his parents' basement to an apartment.

Eddy didn't interact much with his father, because he felt that he had contributed to the destruction of the family. His mother also blamed herself for not standing up for her kids when her husband was beating them. A part of her truly abhorred her husband, but as a Christian woman, she couldn't harbor ill feelings towards him. She continued with her wifely duty in the household except when it came to sexual relations. She made sure that Eddy had a plate of food to eat everyday, but it was easy to see that they were a dysfunctional family.

Mr. & Mrs. Johnson

Since kicking Katrina out of the house, Mr. Johnson was trying his hardest to keep Karen under lock and key. Mr. Johnson didn't want Karen, the only daughter he had left, to end up pregnant at a young age like Katrina. The only place he allowed Karen to go to alone was the tutoring program at the church. The fact that he had turned his back on Katrina really bothered his conscience, but he didn't want to show this to his family. His wife, Mrs. Johnson, became very resentful toward her husband... Her eldest child had been gone for a long time and she wondered everyday what became of her. The family never really expected for Katrina to be gone from their lives forever. The stubborn Mr. Johnson allowed his pride to get in the way of finding his daughter.

Mrs. Johnson used to cry herself to sleep at night thinking about Katrina and how she just disappeared from her life. She was so dependent on her husband that she never even learned how to drive a car. From the time she married her husband, Mr. Johnson informed her that he was the man of the house and whatever decisions he made regarding the family, she was to support him. She was a wonderfully subservient wife for most of their marriage; that is, until Katrina was kicked out of the house. Mrs. Johnson missed her daughter so much that she started talking back to her husband. She no longer wanted to listen to his idiotic rants about how a family should be.

Mr. Johnson's idea of a functional family was so out of line with the times that he could easily be mistaken as a man from the Stone Age. He didn't want to accept the fact that his daughter, Katrina, was a good person and that he drove her away. He was constantly suspicious of Katrina for no reason. Katrina had never failed any classes in school and didn't really do many bad things at home for him to think that she was a bad child. Because his wife sat back and said nothing about his parenting, Mr. Johnson thought everything he was doing was correct. He drove Katrina out of the house. This same behavior was now causing his daughter, Karen, to do bad things.

Mr. and Mrs. Johnson never discussed Katrina's disappearance from their lives. Their silence about the whole situation was eating away at Mrs. Johnson's heart. Her husband would be driving her in the car, and she would suddenly see someone and think it was her daughter. One day Mrs. Johnson chased a woman down just because she walked a little bit like Katrina. She saw the lady from behind and was overcome with joy. Mrs. Johnson ran after the lady hoping to give her a big hug. Upon reaching the woman and tapping her on her shoulder, however, she realized it wasn't Katrina because the woman turned around and appeared significantly older. Mrs. Johnson was once again disappointed and had started to become a little delusional even from these random Katrina sightings. She wanted to see her daughter at any and all cost.

While her husband was away at work, Mrs. Johnson would search the phone directory looking for Katrina's name. One day she got on the phone and called about two hundred people whose first name started with the first initial K and the last name Johnson. As a mother, she knew that she had not done right by her daughter. Mr. Johnson had never revealed to the church that he had kicked his daughter out of his home and family because she was pregnant. Instead, he told the congregation that Katrina was sent/to upstate New York to live with his mother. He felt that Katrina had brought shame to his family by getting pregnant and he didn't want the church to find out.

As much as it would have seemed like the First Baptist church was a receptive place that would accept everyone with open arms and without prejudice, it was also a place where people gossiped about each other. The congregation could and would have the private business of a family spread from Boston to Tallahassee in a matter of minutes. Rumors and gossip played a big role in the church. The women who held each other's hands and prayed together every Sunday were the same women who dogged each other's families behind their backs. It was understood by the Johnson Family that the church was not always as welcoming as they would have people believe. So, Mr. and Mrs. Johnson made sure that they got their story straight with their children, Karen and Eddy, as far as what they needed to tell the church about Katrina.

The pastor at the church found it odd that Katrina suddenly stopped coming to church with her family. When he asked her father where she was, Mr. Johnson had to lie to maintain his good standing and reputation within the church. The commandment "Thou shall not lie" had been totally ignored by the Johnson Family. In fact, Mr. Johnson was the biggest hypocrite in the church. He had kicked his daughter out of his family's life for lying, and he turned around and asked them to lie to the church about Katrina's absence.

Mrs. Johnson may have been passive and subservient, but she was not naive. She was the one who pointed out to Mr. Johnson how much of a hypocrite he was. She was getting tired of living for people whose opinions had absolutely no significance to her. Mrs. Johnson told her husband that he had allowed his faith in ignorance to destroy their family and she was tired of it. She also reminded him that she was the one who introduced him to the life of Christ, and now he wanted to show her how much more of a Christian he was than her. Mrs. Johnson was furious when she realized that she had lost her daughter for good. The agony and the pain that she suffered over the years was all because her husband did not want to let go of his stubbornness.

As bright and honest as Mr. Johnson wanted to appear to his family, they had lost all respect for him because of his ignorance. His remaining children stopped talking to him after a while, and his wife vacated their bedroom altogether. Mrs. Johnson moved into Katrina's bedroom years after she was kicked out. She had forbidden her other children, Eddy and Karen to ever go into Katrina's room in hopes that her daughter would one day come back home to the family. For years, she went in that room every Saturday and cleaned it spotlessly. She never changed anything in the room, as she needed every little reminder when she thought about Katrina.

Moving into Katrina's room after fifteen years of marriage was the final step to Mrs. Johnson's declaration of independence in the household. She had grown tired of listening to her husband, her pastor, and the congregation at her church with regard to the way she was supposed to live her life. It was because of them that she never set out to find her daughter to begin with. Mrs. Johnson had become bitter towards her husband and her church, but by the time she had decided to do something about it, it was a little too late. Katrina was long gone and she had missed out on the opportunity to see her daughter and grandchildren grow up. Mrs. Johnson prayed and wished everyday that her daughter was okay out there in the world.

Despite all the animosity Mrs. Johnson felt towards her husband and her church, she continued to prepare her husband's favorite meals at home and attend the church with her family every Sunday. Though she and her husband hardly spoke any words to each other, they had created a new way of communicating silently. They were both two miserable souls who were unable to connect to the modern world. Mrs. Johnson couldn't see herself leaving her husband, her children, or her home. The fact that Mrs. Johnson was financially dependent on her husband also weighed heavily on her mind.

In her late forties, Mrs. Johnson was encouraged by Karen and Eddy to do more with her life. First, she had to find a way to earn her GED. With the help of an adult education program and a little extra tutoring, Mrs. Johnson earned her GED by the time her son entered high school. She wanted to be a role model for her children, and she also wanted to show them that it was never too late to accomplish certain goals in life. Mr. Johnson, however, felt threatened by the fact that his wife was able to earn a GED. He had always made it seem like he was the most intelligent person in his household even with a sixth grade education. It was his way of elevating himself while downgrading his wife. Mrs. Johnson started to learn more and more through her readings and writings. She discovered how a lack of education kept her husband in total darkness.

She began to realize why her husband had been acting so ignorantly during the course of their marriage. She wanted to teach him about her discovery and love for reading, but he fought her every time. He even tried to belittle her achievements on a few occasions by telling her that she would never be more than a wife and a homemaker to him no matter how much she had learned through her readings. Though Mr. Johnson quit school in the sixth grade, his reading skills were at a third grade level and he had never tried to improve them. When he went to church with his wife, he pretended he was reading from the bible, but he had actually memorized the scriptures after his wife had read them aloud to him at home. Mr. Johnson had proven that most illiterate people are usually pretty smart at concealing their deficiencies to the rest of the world.

Mr. Johnson concealed much of his life and he wasn't open to any new changes, unless directed by his pastor. In the process, he created a barrier of communication between himself and his wife. It was so important for Mr. Johnson to be the head of his household; he chose to stay ignorant so that he could lead by force instead of common sense and intelligence. It was no fault of his own that Mr. Johnson never finished school, but he was too proud to allow people to know that he was deficient in any way.

Mrs. Johnson decided that she wanted to become a counselor to help other families with various social adjustments and issues and also to be an inspiration to her children. At the urging of her daughter and son, Mrs. Johnson enrolled at UMASS in Boston as a non-traditional student to major in Social Work. In just three years, she completed a Bachelor's Degree, and after graduation she accepted a position at a local center to help families on welfare.

A Forgiven Heart

Eddy felt he had lost both of his sisters because of his parents and their overly religious nature, he did not want to ever set foot in another church again. One night he was having one of his regular talks with Jimmy after a practice session, he mentioned that he had never gotten a chance to grow up with his sisters because his parents had pushed them out of his life. Jimmy could see the hurt in Eddy's face as he expressed this pain. Before he could say anything more about his parents' religion Jimmy asked him "When was the last time that you've been to church?" Eddy was embarrassed to tell Jimmy that he had not been to church for over fifteen years since the disappearance of his sister Karen. Although Jimmy didn't hear the whole ordeal about Karen and Katrina's disappearance from Eddy, he knew that he sympathized with him, because Jimmy himself had questioned his own faith in the past when his mother disappeared out of his life.

Jimmy invited Eddy to his church where the vibrant Pastor Jacobs was able to touch somebody's soul every Sunday. He knew if Eddy came to his church he would see the difference, and he would not hold everyone to the standard of his old pastor. Eddy was apprehensive about the invitation at first. However, after much convincing and a promise from Jimmy that he would never ask Eddy to come back if he didn't like it, Eddy accepted Jimmy's invitation.

Jimmy had talked to Pastor Jacobs the Wednesday before Sunday's service about his good friend, Eddy, and how Eddy was depressed about the loss of his sisters. Jimmy also recalled his own feelings when he learned of his mother's death and how he was able to deal with it through the help of Pastor Jacobs and his sister. The good pastor assured Jimmy that he would have a special service on Sunday about loss and the loss of a family member, sibling, or a close friend. Pastor Jacobs referred to his good book, the almighty Bible, to prepare himself for service on Sunday.

As expected, Eddy showed up at church for the 9:00 am service. Jimmy was very happy to meet and greet him at the door. Jimmy introduced Eddy to his wife, Lisa, his sister, Nina, and Nina's husband and their two children. They all welcomed Eddy like he was family. That Sunday Pastor Jacobs was able to hit a note with Eddy when he talked about letting go and forgiving the sins of others in order to liberate the mind from bondage. Eddy paid close attention to Pastor Jacobs' words and when Pastor Jacobs explained that people sometimes placed too much of their responsibilities in God's hands and religion, he understood exactly where the pastor was coming from. Pastor Jacobs explained that in order for God to help a person, that person must also help himself or herself. As a preacher he is only human and no one should look to him to help solve all of their problems.

Eddy started recalling how his parents relied on prayer for years to solve every little problem without taking the appropriate actions. He also thought about Pastor Wallace, who enforced those beliefs for years, and now he was finding out something different from another pastor who had admitted that he had a dark past himself. Pastor Jacobs had always proudly taken the opportunity to tell the church about his dark past, and how without his past he would not have been a pastor. The perfect image that Pastor Wallace had tried to build was something that Eddy had always had a problem with. He was happy to hear a pastor admitting to human mistakes, and he embraced the words and the wisdom of Pastor Jacobs.

Eddy had a newfound faith in the church. He knew that he had to let go of all the hatred that he harbored over the years toward his father because his dad didn't know better.

Toward the end of service, Pastor Jacobs asked everyone who needed prayer to come to the front of the church, and Eddy was one of the first one to get out of his seat to walk toward the podium. Jimmy also got up to hold his hand for support. Pastor Jacobs asked the Lord to cleanse the souls of the people who harbored ill feelings toward others, and to show them the way to forgiveness. Through the pastor's prayer, Eddy could feel his words going through his spirit. By the end of service, Eddy felt rejuvenated like he had been to a place where the Lord had heard his cries and took away all of his pain.

After church, Jimmy introduced Eddy to Pastor Jacobs and he invited him to have brunch with his family. Eddy was gracious in accepting the invitation to brunch. Everyone drove to The Cheesecake Factory, which was one of Jimmy and Nina's favorite spot for brunch on Sundays. Pastor Jacobs couldn't make it, because he had another service at 11:00 am that Sunday but he promised to continue to pray for Eddy.

Discovering an Illness

As Jimmy and Eddy's friendship grew stronger, they started spending more and more time with each other. Eddy still kept his family life discussion to a minimum because he was still trying to deal with the pain of losing his two sisters. Pastor Jacobs' Sunday service had helped, but it didn't erase Eddy's pain completely. Eddy still needed time to heal. He talked as much as he could with Jimmy about the Bible, and his effort to forgive his mother and father. He also told Jimmy about how he wanted his mother and father back together for happier times. Jimmy encouraged his efforts, and even offered to come by his house to see if his parents would give Pastor Jacobs' church a try.

Everything seemed to be normal in Jimmy's life, and he was very happy that he was able to help Eddy. Even Lisa had taken a liking to Eddy, and she invited him over her house for dinner with Jimmy on many occasions. When Jimmy started feeling restless, had difficulty sleeping, and was tired all the time during the off-season, Eddy was the first person that he told. It seemed as if all of Jimmy's energy was gone, and he didn't know what was going on with him. Jimmy didn't want to tell his wife and sister, because he didn't want them to worry. It was at the urging of Eddy that Jimmy finally went to the doctor to see what was wrong with him.

Unfortunately, Jimmy received the worse news that he could've gotten from his doctor at the Beth Israel Deaconess Medical Center that day. Jimmy was told that there was a possibility that he was suffering from kidney failure during a routine check-up. Jimmy explained to the doctor that he was fatigued all the time, his skin was dry and itchy, he was nauseated and vomiting, there was an abundance of fluid retention, he couldn't fall asleep, his thoughts were confusing, and he had a metallic taste in his mouth all the time. Dr. Morris ordered him to undergo a complete physical the following day. It was then that the doctor discovered that Jimmy's kidneys were failing him. He told Jimmy about the few options that he had as a patient, and one of the recommended options was dialysis. Dr. Morris told Jimmy that he could undergo Hemodialysis treatment for a few weeks. If there was no progress made he would need a transplant if he wanted to continue to live, much less play basketball.

Jimmy was not left with too many choices. After receiving the news, Jimmy called Pastor Jacobs, his sister, and his wife in a meeting to inform them about his health. Everyone was more than willing to sacrifice a kidney for Jimmy. Everyone believed the person with the strongest possible match was Pastor Jacobs because he was Jimmy's father. Without hesitation, Pastor Jacobs scheduled an appointment with Jimmy's doctor to see if he was a possible match. Meanwhile, the Hemodialysis treatment was not working for Jimmy.

When Pastor Jacobs went to the hospital, Dr. Morris explained the pros and cons of a living donor to him, but no negative impact could persuade Pastor Jacobs to think twice about saving his only son's life. Pastor Jacobs was also informed that he could lead a normal active life after recovering from surgery without any special restrictions. "The body can function perfectly with one kidney as long as the donor has two healthy kidneys before the operation," Dr. Morris explained. Dr. Morris also told Jimmy the advantages of a living donor. "A patient who receives a live donor transplant has a better immediate outcome and long-term kidney transplant survival than a patient who receives a deceased donor transplant," he said.

Things looked very optimistic. As required by the hospital, the resident Nephrologist subjected Pastor Jacobs to undergo a thorough evaluation to determine his general health and kidney condition. Pastor Jacobs went through a complete medical history and physical examination. He was tested for diabetes, cancer, high blood pressure, kidney stones, and poor kidney function. An X-ray was taken to evaluate his lungs, an EKG was taken for the heart, a blood and urine test (including HIV testing) was given, a spiral Computed Tomography (CT) scan was administered to determine any abnormalities in the kidneys or the blood vessels that lead to them, and a final cross match to check for antibodies within one week of transplant were all completed. Pastor Jacobs also met with the nurse and social worker at the hospital for an evaluation.

Though the hospital Nephrologist administered many tests, it was determined that Pastor Jacobs was not a match for Jimmy. The process of elimination had begun. Lisa was the next person to see the doctor in an attempt to save her husband's life, but she was not a match either. Nina went through the same process, and unfortunately she also was not a match. Jimmy was starting to get scared, but Nina's husband Collin instilled hope in Jimmy when he offered to go see the doctor to check if he was a possible match. The other people who had offered to donate a kidney to Jimmy were almost automatic, because they were his father, wife, and his sister. Collin didn't have to offer to do it, and Jimmy thought it was very big of Collin to offer him a kidney. Even though he had long considered Collin a brother, it was a gesture that he didn't expect.

Unfortunately, Collin would not be a match either. Meanwhile, Jimmy continued to deal with his illness. He had not been spending time with Eddy. He didn't even tell Eddy about his diagnosis. It was when Jimmy and the Celtics decided to hold a press conference to tell the public about Jimmy's illness that Eddy found out about it. At first, Eddy didn't understand why Jimmy didn't call to tell him about it, but he understood that Jimmy was going through a lot and he had to deal with his family first. Eddy wanted to give Jimmy time to deal with his situation before calling him. He also knew it was unlike Jimmy to go a couple of weeks without calling him.

One More Offer

Eddy finally received a call from Jimmy after a few weeks of dealing with his search for a kidney. When Eddy picked up the phone he could tell that Jimmy wasn't his normal upbeat self and he knew why. Jimmy started explaining to Eddy how things were not looking so optimistic for him, because he had a rare blood type and everyone who had offered to give him a kidney thus far was not a match. Eddy was not overly educated about kidney failure, so he started asking Jimmy all kinds of questions. It almost seemed as if he was prying, but because he and Jimmy had developed such a comfortable relationship Jimmy didn't mind sharing the information with him.

After learning from Jimmy that he could live a long, healthy life with one kidney, Eddy did the most selfless thing he could think of. He offered to give Jimmy one of his kidneys. Jimmy was taken back by Eddy's gesture, but he was not surprised. Jimmy always knew that Eddy had a kind heart, and he didn't want to force Eddy into doing anything out of pity. Jimmy explained to Eddy if death was to be his fate because he couldn't find a kidney, he was alright with that. He didn't want to force anyone to make any sacrifices for him. Jimmy truly believed that he had been blessed during his short life and if the Lord wanted to take him away he was willing to go.

Eddy took a long deep breath on the phone, and he started to address Jimmy in a very emotional tone, "You are the first person in a long time that has taken the time to talk to me and tried to get to know me since I've been working at the Fleet Center. You've never made me feel out of place or less than you. I feel connected to you somehow. If that connection was going to come through by sharing my kidneys with you, then so be it. Donating my kidney to you is not at all a sacrifice, but a situation that God had created to bring together two souls from two different spectrum of the world. The only thing that I would need from you is for you to pay my hospital bill."

Just when Jimmy thought his luck had run out, and there was no way out because the transplant waiting list for a kidney was so long, God sent an angel his way named Eddy. The optimism in Jimmy resurfaced as he asked Eddy jokingly if he could at least take him out to eat so he could have a full stomach when they visited the doctor the next day. Eddy laughed at Jimmy's comment as they made plans to meet for dinner later.

A Meeting by Chance

The next day Jimmy drove himself to Eddy's house in Hyde Park to pick him up for the doctor's appointment. When Eddy rang the doorbell, Mr. Johnson answered the door and he immediately recognized Jimmy as a Boston Celtics player. In fact, Jimmy was his favorite player on the team. Mr. Johnson was a little puzzled, at first, because he didn't know why a basketball superstar would show up at his door. Jimmy quickly explained to him that he and Eddy were friends and he was there to pick him up. Mr. Johnson called for Eddy to come upstairs as Jimmy waited in the living room.

Mr. Johnson and his wife were admiring Jimmy, because they had never seen a basketball star up close and personal before. If Jimmy had examined Mr. And Mrs. Johnson's faces closely, he would have recognized the obvious resemblance, but he was timid and did not want to be treated like a star. He kept his eyes glued to the family portrait hanging on the wall in the living room. In the portrait was a picture of Katrina, Karen, Eddy, and Mr. And Mrs. Johnson. While staring at the picture, it was as if Jimmy almost recognized his mother even when she was a little ten year-old girl. He chose not to say anything to Mr. and Mrs. Johnson because Jimmy was not the type to believe in coincidences. As far as he knew, he didn't have any maternal family.

Eddy finally came upstairs after about ten minutes. Before he and Jimmy could leave, Mr. Johnson asked Jimmy for his autograph after he went to his room to get a basketball jersey with his favorite player's name on the back, J. Johnson. Eddy pleaded with his father to leave Jimmy alone, but Jimmy didn't mind signing the jersey for the old man. Mr. Johnson also joked that they could be family because they shared the same last name. Mrs. Johnson offered him a home cooked meal, but he declined and told her that he had just eaten. Jimmy left the Johnson household that day without realizing that he had just come into contact with his maternal kinfolks.

Dos Amigos

On the way to the doctor's office, Jimmy and Eddy talked more about their lives and how they grew up. He felt like Eddy's parents were the perfect couple and thought about what he would've done to grow up in a family setting like that. Jimmy was a little emotional when he was talking about his childhood. Without mentioning his mother's name, he told Eddy that she was a drug abuser and a prostitute who didn't spend much time with him when he was growing up. Although he held her dear to his heart, a part of him was angry sometimes because she wasn't around to be part of his success. He told Eddy that his mother and his neighborhood were his motivation, while his sister Nina was the enforcer. He said that whenever he saw his mother, the only thing he could think about was a way out of his neighborhood, and a life away from drugs, prostitution, and the streets all together.

Jimmy went on to tell Eddy that as much as his sister tried to shield him from his mother's business on the streets, he always knew what was up and he just never said anything. Jimmy mentioned how his mother came up to him one day to solicit a blowjob for crack, and he gave her his last ten dollars without her ever realizing that she was talking to her own son. There were things that happened with his mother that he never even told his sister, because he knew she wanted to protect him. He told Eddy how close he and Nina were, and that he would not be where he was in life without her support and strength. Eddy just listened as Jimmy talked about his childhood and upbringing. Jimmy also never failed to make Pastor Jacobs the highlight of his stellar basketball career. He didn't refer to Pastor Jacobs as his Dad, but Eddy quickly made the connection between the two.

After realizing that he had been the only one talking during the drive to the doctor's office, Jimmy stopped and apologized to Eddy for unloading all his problems on him. Eddy told him, "That's what friends are for. If I can't sit here and listen to you vent or talk about issues that bother you, then what's the point of being friends?" Eddy's statement to Jimmy was reassurance that Jimmy indeed had a true friend in Eddy. As much as Jimmy wanted to have the perfect upbringing like he thought that Eddy had, Eddy wanted to set him straight about the misconception he saw back at his house. After Jimmy made a comment about Eddy being brought up in a loving family, Eddy said to him "What's on the surface is not always what it seems." Jimmy didn't understand the comment, and he asked Eddy to elaborate. Eddy started to divulge to Jimmy how his father had allowed religion to control his life, and in the process his family had lost two of its members. Eddy could only recall waking up and not seeing his older sister in the house anymore. His father told him that his sister was sent to Upstate New York to live with relatives. He never questioned what he was told, and still believed that his sister was still alive. Before Eddy could get too far in the story they reached the doctor's office.

It's a Match!

Jimmy never got to hear Eddy's whole story, and he was nervous when he walked into the doctor's office. Whenever he came to see his doctor, the medical assistant always took time out to flirt with Jimmy. Even when Jimmy was accompanied with Lisa, she would try to flirt with him. "Some people will take their chances on lust regardless of whom they disrespect." Lisa always said. Jimmy was too worried about his future to pay any attention to the Medical Assistant's advances. He was focused on finding a kidney so he could extend his life a few more years.

Dr. Morris had become quite familiar with Jimmy over the years and he sympathized with him because he was one of the doctor's favorite patients. Jimmy had inherited his father's infectious personality, and there was a silent campaign to help find him a kidney. The doctor was very excited to tell Jimmy that he had about five potential donors who wanted to help him any way possible. Dr. Morris had grown fond of Jimmy because he didn't act like a spoiled millionaire like most of the other athletes he had come in contact with. Jimmy always took the time to play videogame with the Doctor's son when his son was in the office. Sometimes, it seemed like Jimmy never even had a childhood because he enjoyed the videogames just as much as the doctor's son. It was that part of his personality that everyone fell in love with.

While Jimmy was in the office talking to Dr. Morris, Eddy nervously waited in the waiting area. He had no idea what he was up against, but he sincerely wanted to help out his friend. After flipping through the pages of the numerous magazines, Eddy was relieved to find Jimmy and Dr. Morris standing in front of him moments later when he raised his head. Dr. Morris sensed that Eddy was nervous, so he tried easing his mind with straightforward honesty. He reassured him that it was going to be a rigorous process, but at the end of the procedure he would walk away fine.

Just like a scared little kid who was going to see the doctor for the first time, Eddy followed Dr. Morris to his office almost shitting bricks. The Doctor administered a few tests before deciding to draw a sample of Eddy's blood. Eddy was then taken to the transplant Nephrologist so he could administer the rest of the tests.

It would be a week before Dr. Morris received the results from the tests, and Jimmy and Eddy were impatiently waiting. Eddy did not even understand the significance of what he was about to do for Jimmy. Since Jimmy was deemed suitable for transplant he was not worried about himself, but he was hoping and praying that Eddy would be a match for him. Dr. Morris called Jimmy a few days later to explain to him a new discovery in kidney transplants, and how it would increase his chances for a donor. According to Dr. Morris, "To increase the possibilities for organ donation, the Center used new clinical protocols that made it possible to transplant kidneys across different blood types." Jimmy was very happy to hear that his chances for a transplant would increase. He went on about his life and he prayed to God everyday for an answer. Pastor Jacobs held special prayers at the church for Jimmy and deep down in his heart, he knew that the Lord was gonna find a way to keep his boy alive.

A week passed and Dr. Morris called Jimmy with the good news that Eddy was a perfect match. Jimmy was speechless on the phone for almost five minutes. Dr. Morris thought he had passed out for a moment, but when Jimmy screamed aloud, “Praise the Lord!” through the phone, Dr. Morris was assured that he was still alive and well. Everyone was happy for Jimmy, but he had to call his savior, Eddy, to tell him that he was a perfect match. Eddy was overjoyed with the news and he wanted to get the operation out of the way as soon as possible.

The Surgery

Since Eddy was determined a good match, Dr. Morris scheduled surgery immediately. Jimmy's family stayed at the hospital the whole time he was in surgery. His wife, Lisa, was restless as she silently prayed for her husband to make it out of the operating room alive. Even though Dr. Morris had tried his best to ease Lisa's worries, she couldn't contain herself. The surgery took almost five hours. A board-certified surgeon performed the operation successfully. After the operation, Eddy and Jimmy were taken to the Post Anesthesia Care Unit where they received state-of-the-art monitoring and individualized care from specially trained nursing professionals and well-trained doctors.

Eddy never even told his parents about the good deed that he was doing for Jimmy. Eddy knew that his father's selfish ways and attitude might have interfered with a decision that was all his own. Eddy didn't want his dad to talk him out of doing what he wanted to do for Jimmy, so he waited until after it was done to call and tell them that he was in the hospital. Mrs. Johnson rushed to see him and brought him a home cooked meal. She also commended her son for having a great heart, and she told him she was proud of his gesture.

Both, Jimmy and Eddy remained at the hospital for six days, and the doctors tried their best to show Jimmy and Lisa how to care for his new kidney. Nina was also very involved in the after-care of her brother. She stopped by the hospital everyday to make sure he was okay. Jimmy had requested to share a room with Eddy at the hospital, and over the course of six days the two families became acquainted. They mostly discussed Eddy and his big heart. Pastor Jacobs also came to the hospital everyday to see Jimmy and Eddy. Mrs. Johnson was drawn to Pastor Jacobs almost instantly at the hospital, and she promised to visit his church the upcoming Sunday.

Mrs. Johnson, Nina, Lisa, and Pastor Jacobs were all trained by the nurses at the hospital on how to care for Eddy and Jimmy. The guys were treated like babies during their stay in the hospital. Mr. Johnson never even bothered to come by the hospital to see Eddy, because he thought what Eddy did was foolish. He told Eddy that there was no guarantee that one of his kidneys wouldn't go bad and questioned why he would give one of them up. Eddy expected his dad to have a negative attitude about what he did, but he never thought that his dad would be a total ass about it.

Jimmy decided to leave the hospital early, because he didn't want the press to start hounding him daily. Eddy didn't want the media to find out who he was, because of his good deed. The media had nothing but praise for him even though they had never seen him. Jimmy showed his gratitude when he offered to buy Eddy a home of his choice anywhere in Massachusetts. Although no amount of money could have saved Jimmy's life, he felt the need to compensate Eddy for helping him. Eddy; however, graciously declined Jimmy's offer. He knew that the media would quickly conclude that his intention was to be an organ seller instead of a donor.

Staying Healthy

Before Jimmy and Eddy were discharged from the hospital, Dr. Morris stressed the fact that Jimmy had to commit to a healthy lifestyle in order for him to prosper with his new kidney. Jimmy was to follow up with the hospital regularly to ensure proper care, and to lower the risks of side effects from prescribed medication and kidney rejection. The doctors wanted to make sure that the risk of infection was minimized so that Jimmy's body could withstand the new kidney.

It was also explained to Jimmy that he ran a greater risk of high blood pressure, diabetes, high cholesterol, and a certain form of cancer after his transplant. It was made clear to him that he had to adapt to his new lifestyle because a transplant is not a cure, but a treatment for kidney failure. Treatment for Jimmy's kidney would be a lifelong process in order to deal with the different elements of the treatment plan.

As an athlete, Jimmy was already committed to a life of exercise, but he needed to develop a healthier diet than he was used to prior to his transplant. Eddy also joked that Jimmy had better not abused his body or he would take back his kidney. Maintaining good health was not an issue for Jimmy, because he was not a smoker and he didn't indulge in alcohol. Jimmy would no longer be able to sit in the sun by his pool, however, because overexposure in the sun could negatively affect his health.

The complications were less risky for Eddy as a donor. He wouldn't have much physical adjustment, but he had to watch his diet and exercise regularly as well. He and Jimmy made a pact to develop an exercise regimen that they could both enjoy. During the recovery period, Jimmy and Eddy developed a bond like brothers. They kept their doctor appointments together, and they managed to keep an exercise schedule that was suitable for both of them.

The surgery forced Jimmy to sit out the upcoming season and Eddy took a six-month leave of absence from his job. The doctors at the hospital didn't want to scare Jimmy, but they had to inform him that the national statistical average survival rate for kidney transplants from a live-donor was twenty one to twenty two years. Jimmy had a higher rate of survival, because Eddy was an exact genetic match.

Nina was so concerned about her brother's health. She absorbed as much information about kidney transplants as she could from the website www.ustransplant.org. Nina knew that education was the key to keeping her brother healthy. She also brought home as much information as she could from the library for Lisa to make sure that she was aware of everything as well. Jimmy's recovery went pretty smooth, and he was given the green light to return back to basketball a year after his transplant.

Becoming An Organ Donor

While going through their ordeal, Jimmy, Nina, and Lisa found out through research how uninvolved African Americans were regarding organ donations. Yet, African Americans suffered the most from kidney failure. After Jimmy's recovery, the whole family decided to sign up as organ donors. They saw the need and they took action. Had Eddy not sacrificed his own organ to help Jimmy, no one knew how long he would have survived on a failing kidney. Jimmy was more than happy to sign-up, because he knew that extending someone else's life in need would be the only thing he could do to show true gratitude.

Pastor Jacobs and the rest of the clan signed up as well when they learned the statistics for African-Americans and the chances of survival through organ donation. They felt very ignorant about their lack of knowledge about organ donation. If Jimmy had never gone into the hospital for his surgery, they would have never known about the need for bone marrow transplants, kidney transplants, blood transfusions, and many other illnesses that African Americans suffer that they could collectively help their community fight.

The family was also very weary of the myth: "If one of them was involved in a serious a car accident, the hospital would most likely allow them to die in order to use an organ from them to save someone else." That myth keeps many people from becoming organ donors, not just in African-American communities, but in all communities.

Reconnecting With Family

As Jimmy and Eddy grew closer as friends, certain subjects could not be ignored. Eddy never really got the chance to finish his conversation about his two missing sisters with Jimmy prior to the transplant. It was something that bothered Eddy since Karen went missing. He never before had a buddy like Jimmy, and he could not talk to his parents because he felt they were responsible for the loss of his sisters. One day while they were working out, Eddy asked Jimmy about his mother. In the past Jimmy had kept his mother a secret, because he didn't want anybody running to the press with his mother's story. Since he and Eddy were practically connected at the kidney, he told Eddy that his mother had committed suicide when he was a little boy and he didn't know much about her because she was on drugs most of the time when she was alive.

Eddy saw the pain in Jimmy's eyes, and he could feel the pain in Jimmy's heart as he revealed the story. Eddy asked what his mother's name was and Jimmy told him Katrina. After Jimmy told him his mother's name, Eddy thought about it for a few seconds. He shook his head as if to say it would be an impossible coincidence. Jimmy wanted to know why he shook his head the way he did. Eddy told him that his oldest sister's name was Katrina, and that she had left home when she was fourteen years old. They never heard from her after she left. The description that Jimmy gave of Katrina was not the same description that Eddy remembered. Eddy was only seven years old when Katrina left and because the family hadn't taken many pictures; he could only remember Katrina the way she was in her last picture with the family when she was twelve years old.

It felt a little strange to both of them that they were both connected to someone named Katrina Johnson. Jimmy's inquiring mind wanted to know more. He asked Eddy if he wouldn't mind coming over to Nina's house to talk more about his sister. Eddy said, "It would be my pleasure." Jimmy picked up his cell phone and called his sister to tell her that he wanted to come by with Eddy to talk about something very important. She told him "No problem. By the time you get to the house I will have dinner ready." Collin had not yet gotten home when Jimmy spoke with Nina. He would show up at the house with his friend and best man, John O'Malley, later.

O'Malley loved to go over to Collin's house because he enjoyed Nina's cooking. He knew that since Nina was suspended from the force she was home everyday and she cooked almost all the time. Jimmy and Eddy arrived at the house first and Collin and O'Malley showed up a half an hour later. Before anything was ever discussed Nina had the table set with food because she knew her husband was on his way home and she wanted everyone to eat together. She wasn't expecting John, but she was not surprised that he showed up. Collin had called his wife earlier to make sure she was cooking and whenever he did that, Nina knew John would show up at the house with him.

That day Nina went all out with the meal, because she was expecting a new face to come eat at her house. It was also her way of thanking Eddy for saving her brother's life. Nina's children were sitting next to their mother at the table so she could monitor them. Nina was some kind of woman. She had slaved over the stove all day while watching her children. She had to make sure that they were entertained. She read to them, bathed them, fed and monitored them while she was cooking. Sometimes, her husband wondered where she got the strength or even the talent to do all these things simultaneously. He showed appreciation by doing the little things for her that most kind hearted women would appreciate. It was not unusual for Collin to come home to rub her feet, give her a bath, or just take her to a spa for the day to pamper her. She received flowers regularly from her husband, and he never went to bed without telling her how much he loved her.

While everyone was sitting at the table eating, John O'Malley who had not formally met the adult Eddy yet noticed something familiar about him. Collin pointed out the fact that Eddy was the man who donated the kidney to Jimmy. John was staring at Eddy for a different reason, however. He had seen Eddy before, a long time ago in Hyde Park, when his sister Karen was reported missing by his parents. John had the case when it was first opened, but it was transferred to another officer and still remained open with the Boston Police Department. John asked Eddy if he had a sister named Karen who went missing a few years ago. Eddy answered "Karen has never been found." John had gotten pretty close to Eddy's family, and he remembered his mother saying that she had not seen her oldest daughter, Katrina, in years as well. John also asked, "Did your other sister ever go back home?" Eddy answered "No."

The topic was now open for discussion. That is when Jimmy told Nina that Eddy had a sister named Katrina who left home at a very young age and he was wondering whether there was a possible link to his mother and Eddy's sister, Katrina. Other than the obvious first and last names, there was no other connection between Katrina that they knew of. It was fine to have this coincidence with Katrina, but it was rare that Jimmy and Eddy shared the same blood type as stated by the doctors at the hospital. Jimmy and Nina were getting excited about the possibility of discovering their family. The more they spoke to Eddy about Katrina, the more they were convinced it wasn't a coincidence.

As police officers, even John and Collin knew that there were too many pieces connected to that puzzle. The fact that Eddy told them that his sister left home at fourteen years old almost confirmed that they were, indeed, related. Eddy could not tell Jimmy and Nina that his sister was pregnant when she left home, because his parents had kept that a secret from him. They were starting to connect the dots. The only thing left to do was to set up a meeting with Eddy's parents to find out if their mother was pregnant when she left home. Eddy was also sad to hear that his possible sister had committed suicide, and that he never really got a chance to know her. At least, he knew then that his sister was resting in heaven and that was a form of closure for him. Eddy was almost certain that his sister Katrina was the same woman who gave birth to Nina and Jimmy.

Everyone was excited about the prospect of Nina and Jimmy discovering their long lost family. Even John got involved in the "tear shedding" at the table. Collin was very happy that his wife was finally going to discover her roots, because it had long been bothering her. She wanted so much to accept her husband, Pastor Jacobs, and Jimmy as her only family, but she wasn't totally satisfied without her complete family. Collin could see the joy in his wife's face after she learned the possibility of discovering her kinfolks.

Eddy was excited as well. He couldn't believe that he had been interacting with his own nephew this whole time without knowing it. He picked up the phone and called his mother to arrange a dinner at her house with Jimmy, Nina, and her family. Mrs. Johnson had seen Nina and Jimmy at the hospital when she visited her son, but they didn't really get too chatty with one another. Eddy didn't even tell his mother what the dinner was about. He simply told his mother that he wanted to celebrate life with his friends and family, and asked if she could cook his favorite meals. His mother and father hadn't done anything remotely enjoyable since Karen was gone, and Eddy wanted to foster change in their lives.

A Family Connection

A dinner was scheduled for 6:00 pm on Sunday evening. Mrs. Johnson was very excited about hosting a dinner party at her house for a celebrity athlete. Unbeknownst to her was the fact that this athlete was possibly her grandson. Everyone showed up on time, but Mrs. Johnson had anticipated for some of the guests to be late. Dinner wasn't quite ready when Jimmy, Lisa, Nina, Collin, their two children, and Pastor Jacobs showed up at the house. Everyone got reacquainted with each other and Mr. Johnson introduced himself for the first time to the clan. Eddie and Mr. Johnson played host until Mrs. Johnson got dinner ready. Mr. Johnson was enthralled by the presence of a star athlete in his home and that was the only reason he took part in the dinner.

While everyone waited in the living room, Jimmy and Nina looked through the family's photo album, and in it they saw plenty of pictures of their mother. Nina recognized her mother almost instantly as she flipped through the pages of the photo album, her eyes were getting teary. She started reminiscing about all the times her mother was struggling to keep her head above water. A part of Nina resented being at the Johnson's house, because she knew that even though her mother didn't tell her much about her grandparents that they were somewhat responsible for her downfall. A feeling of uneasiness came over her. Her husband Collin noticed the change in his wife's composure. He went over to her and placed his arms around her for comfort. She whispered to him that she didn't think she could go through with telling these people that she was their granddaughter.

Although Collin wanted to support his wife's decision, he also felt that it was necessary for her to learn about her family heritage. He called Jimmy over so they could talk to Nina and show support. Mr. Johnson had no idea what was going on between Nina and Jimmy. Eddie was busy playing with Nina's two children while Mr. Johnson talked Lisa's ear off. Every little wrinkle on Mr. Johnson's face that day said something to Nina and none of it was pleasant. She could see a callous man who had not a clue about anything, but thought he was in charge of everything. It seemed like he was forcing his antisocial behind to take part in this dinner, and they could all sense it. Mrs. Johnson, however, was very pleasant and kept checking on everybody while the food was being prepared.

Mrs. Johnson reminded Nina of her mother, and she took the opportunity to offer her help in the kitchen so she could get to know her grandmother better. When Nina went back to the kitchen, she didn't expect Mrs. Johnson to drop a load on her. Mrs. Johnson was teary eyed as she told Nina her wish of having a happy family that consisted of her children and grandchildren. She went on to tell Nina some of the hidden family secrets about her two missing daughters. Mrs. Johnson felt comfortable enough with Nina to open up to her right away. After listening to Mrs. Johnson divulged some of her family's deepest secrets, Nina knew there was no turning back. She was talking to a woman who had longed to see her missing daughters, and was very resentful of her stubborn husband whom she almost allowed to destroy her family completely.

Mrs. Johnson didn't have to tell Nina that her husband was stubborn and sometimes ignorant. She was able to read right through the man from the little time that she had spent with him in the living room. Nina knew that Mrs. Johnson was probably not responsible for the hard life that her mother had led on the streets. She felt that Mrs. Johnson could have been the voice of reason and at least tried to reach out to her daughter, however. Though sympathetic, Nina wasn't completely forgiving. She stood there in the kitchen playing the scene in her head where she would reveal to Mrs. Johnson that she was her granddaughter. She imagined laughter and happiness on Mrs. Johnson's part, but she couldn't see Mr. Johnson as a welcoming grandfather. The man seemed too miserable to be happy about anything.

The food was almost ready. Mrs. Johnson asked Nina to return to the living room while she set the dining room table and put everything together to serve her guests. First, she gave Nina a hug and thanked her for listening to her pain. Nina told her it was a pleasure and not to worry about it. Nina walked back to the living room and found Jimmy and her husband fully engaged in a conversation with Eddy and Mr. Johnson about the Patriots while watching a football game on television. Mr. Johnson was talking about the obvious racism that clouded the city of Boston when it came to their African American athletes. Mr. Johnson emphasized the fact that the sports organizations in New England are always looking for a white superstar represent their teams. He also discussed the fact that a great quarterback like Donovan McNabb or Michael Vick would have never been given the opportunity to start for the Patriots regardless of their talent.

Jimmy saw something in his grandfather that he also possessed. Mr. Johnson had a fire and determination in him to succeed at all costs, despite the odds. He wanted to prove to people, or specifically to white people, that he was just as good as they were. Perhaps, it was that determination and fire that drove him to push his daughter out of his life because he was ashamed of her for some reason. Jimmy was determined and fiery, but he was not living for anybody other than himself. He didn't care much about what white people thought of him, he simply wanted to take care of his family and help those less fortunate in his community. Collin also took part in the conversation and brought up the fact that the Boston Police Department had suspended his wife, because she wasn't making enough arrests and didn't write enough tickets. "Sure, they said there was no quota for arrests and tickets written in stone anywhere, but it was understood that the police officers had to make a certain amount of arrests once they were walking the beat on the street, especially in the hood," Collin stated.

Nina was a little idealistic in her views of community policing. She did not see the need to antagonize young black males just so she could take them to jail, creating a barrier against their future. She was getting tired of watching the white officers go into the black community, and harass the young black males. When these young men reacted to the maltreatment or harassment, they usually found themselves in the back of a police cruiser being taken to the police station to be processed on trumped-up charges that were fabricated by the police officers. Nina knew what it was like in her neighborhood and she wanted to educate people first before arresting them. Half the young black males in the hood didn't know or understand the significance of a police arrest record. They heard stories of people glorifying the fact that they had been to jail, but they didn't see the doors being shut down on them as adults looking for work because of a criminal record.

Nina was aware of the fact that most of the times, these felons couldn't even get a break to get started in life. When the time came for them to start a family of their own, they would sometimes become desperate and have to resort to selling drugs or committing other criminal acts in order to provide for their families. As a police officer on the side of the law, Collin highlighted those points as well to make sure that Eddy and Jimmy understood their stance in society with the police. He also stressed that ninety percent of the time that the judges went with the police officers' accounts of events because they're both on the side of the law. No amount of money or star status could keep a black man from being arrested for no reason at all. He gave a great example of this when Dee Brown, the former Boston Celtics player, was arrested in Wellesley while waiting in his car for his wife. He was guilty of a crime until proven innocent and the crime he committed was driving around in a BMW in Black skin in a white neighborhood.

While Nina stood in the doorway listening to her husband defending her honor, Mrs. Johnson came to the living room to announce that dinner was served. Nina gleefully smiled at her husband as she made her way to the dining room behind Mrs. Johnson. Everyone followed to the dining room promptly after. Mr. Johnson was seated at the head of the table while Mrs. Johnson sat on the other end. Eddy was all smiles, because he was about to reveal the happiest news to his family.

Everyone found some of the best tasting southern fried chicken, collard greens, black-eyed peas, macaroni and cheese, white rice, corn bread, and Kool-aid prepared by Mrs. Johnson in the dining room that day. The mood was quite festive. Mrs. Johnson wanted to treasure every moment in the presence of her new friends. She knew that once they left, she would revert back to her old ways with her husband and she would be sad all over again. However, this time she would find out news that she never expected.

Before anybody could dig into the serving bowls to fill up their plates, Pastor Jacobs asked them to bow their heads in prayer. The food smelled so good it ended up being the shortest prayer known to mankind. Everyone loved Mrs. Johnson's cooking and Nina's children kept comparing Mrs. Johnson's food to their mother's. Every time they made a comment about their mother being just as good a cook as Mrs. Johnson, Collin shook his head, because he knew that Nina was not as great a cook as her grandmother, however, she was good. Mrs. Johnson encouraged everyone to eat as much as they could because she didn't cook like that very often. Mrs. Johnson fed Nina's children like they were her own grandchildren and they kept asking her if she was their Grandma. Little did Mrs. Johnson know, she was about to find out that she was a Grandma and Great-Grandma that day.

Finally, after everyone finished their food, Nina asked to have everyone's attention because she had something important to say to the family. As everyone quieted down to allow the food to digest, Nina commenced speaking "I never thought that this day would ever come. My brother and I always dreamt about this special day and through the grace of God and the kindness of someone we thought at first, was a complete stranger to us, made being here today possible. Jimmy and I went through a lot as children because our mother neglected us and most of the time we didn't know where our next meal was going to come from."

Nina continued as she pointed to Pastor Jacobs, "God didn't just bless my brother and I once; he blessed us many times over. One of those times was when he brought Pastor Jacobs into our lives. I know that we have never formally thanked him for all that he has done for us, but we want him to know today that we love him from the bottom of our hearts, and he's the only father that we have known. But, today is another blessed day for us. We have finally found our maternal family with the help of Eddy who's not only my brother's lifesaver and angel, but also a great friend and newly found uncle to him. When I was looking through the photo album in the living room, I fought back tears as I reminisced about the good times that my mother shared with us. After spending time in the kitchen with Mrs. Johnson, I realized that my mother inherited her affectionate ways from her. So without further ado and more rambling from me, I just want to tell Mr. and Mrs. Johnson that we are your grandchildren and your daughter Katrina was our mother."

The room fell silent for a brief moment after Nina revealed that she was part of the Johnson family. Mrs. Johnson had long thought that she would never again in her life reconnect with her daughter, Katrina. She had given up hope and wondered what became of her daughter. Of course, the next question out of Mrs. Johnson's mouth was "Where's Katrina?" with great anticipation. The room was about to become silent once again and the joyous emotion that lived there momentarily was about to be replaced with anger, pain, hatred, and feelings of loss. Since Nina had delivered the good news, Jimmy took it upon himself to tell Mr. and Mrs. Johnson that Katrina passed long ago when they were teenagers. She was in Heaven somewhere watching over her family.

Throughout the whole announcement, Mr. Johnson didn't show any emotion at all. It was as if this man was emotionless and didn't care if people saw his inhumane side. But Mrs. Johnson ran towards her grandchildren and tried to spread her arms around them as much as she could to hug them as she broke down in tears at the news that her daughter was dead. Eddy tried to comfort his mother, but his father remained stoic in his seat without saying a word. It was almost like the old man had forgotten that he ever had a daughter named Katrina. Nina's children were trying to hug their mother, asking her if she was all right. Collin took them away to give Nina and Jimmy time to embrace their Grandmother and Eddy.

The lack of emotion from Mr. Johnson angered Lisa and Collin, and they both wanted to say something on behalf of their spouses. Before Lisa could open her mouth to say something to Mr. Johnson Collin reminded her that she was in his house and disrespecting him would only be stooping to his level. While Jimmy, Nina, Eddy, and Mrs. Johnson mourned Katrina's death all over again in the dining room, Mr. Johnson got up from his chair and went to his bedroom. He didn't say anything to anybody and nobody paid him any mind. Perhaps that was his way of mourning.

The family realized that day how hard it was to bring someone out of darkness who chose to remain there. Mr. Johnson's action only reassured his wife that his ignorance was almost beyond repair. She was happy to meet her grandchildren, but she was angry that she had to remain in that house to continue to live with her husband. The sight of him was making her and Eddy sick to their stomachs. Nina and Jimmy didn't particularly care for him either. They were satisfied for having found their uncle and grandmother. Mrs. Johnson also informed them about their aunt, Karen, whom had been missing for years. She noted that they couldn't find her, because they lacked the financial resources to offer a reward for information leading to her whereabouts.

Jimmy wished he had met his family a long time ago, because he would have put up a reward for Karen from the moment she disappeared. He promised his grandmother that he would do all that he could to help locate Karen's body so she could have closure. Nina shook her head in agreement as she told her grandmother that she would ask her husband to put the word out on the streets again about Karen. Mrs. Johnson ended up having one of the most joyous days since she last saw her daughter, Katrina.

Getting to Know the Family

It had been a few months since Jimmy and Nina found their maternal grandparents, and everything was going well with the family. Nina and Jimmy tried as much as they could to catch up, and make-up for the time they'd missed with their grandmother. Nina's two children, Katrina and Collin Jr., enjoyed being spoiled by their great-grandmother. Mrs. Johnson especially spoiled Katrina, because she was named after her daughter. Little Katrina shared a few similar traits with her grandmother, Katrina as well.

Jimmy had asked his uncle, Eddy, to resign from his position as a custodian with the Boston Celtics and to begin working for him as an Assistant Director to Pastor Jacobs with his nonprofit after-school program for disadvantaged youths. Eddy had always been an intelligent man, but because he didn't know how to deal with the loss of his two sisters he never maximized his potential. He was a quick learner under the tutelage of Pastor Jacobs. Eddy learned the functions of his new job in no time, and he became one of the favorite staff members to the kids. Jimmy also helped Eddy with the purchase of his first home. Jimmy's story had lost interest in the media, and he was glad because he wanted to spend the time to get to know his family.

Since Eddy bought his home, Mrs. Johnson spent very little time in the house with her husband, because she was miserable there. Nina and Collin had finished the basement in their home and they turned it into an in-law apartment for Mrs. Johnson and she spent a lot of time there getting to know Nina, Collin, and their children. She didn't want to spend too much time around a grumpy, miserable, old man. Mr. and Mrs. Johnson were too old to even bother filing for divorce, even though they couldn't stand each other. Things became very tense in the house, especially after they both retired. Even though there were hardly any words spoken, the tension in the house was at an all time high. Mrs. Johnson started to resent doing everything for a man who didn't want to treat her with respect and didn't show her any appreciation.

Nina and Collin could sense how unhappy Mrs. Johnson was in the house every time they visited with her. When they offered to remodel their basement so she could spend more time at their house with them and the children, Mrs. Johnson jumped at the opportunity to get away from her husband. Meanwhile, Nina and the Boston Police Department had reached a lucrative settlement for her unjust termination, and she decided to resign altogether from her job to become a homemaker. During that time she was also trying to get pregnant with her third child, and having her Grandmother in the house with her eased the burden a little with the other two children.

Mr. Johnson was as grumpy as ever, but this time there was no one in the house for him to take out his frustrations. He would sit in front of the television all day to watch sports, and would only step out on his porch to grab his newspaper and mail. For the sake of Jimmy and Nina, Pastor Jacobs would occasionally stop by Mr. Johnson's house to see how he was doing. He also tried to get him to open up about some of the issues that were bothering him. Pastor Jacobs would visit the old man for hours and he wouldn't exchange but a few sentences with Pastor Jacobs during the visits. Those few sentences were the usual greetings such as "how are you?" or "What brings you to my neck of the woods today?" Pastor Jacobs knew whatever it was that kept Mr. Johnson from expressing his feelings to his family had to be dealt with, and only a professional psychologist could get him to talk about his feelings.

One day during a visit at Mr. Johnson's house, Pastor Jacobs asked Mr. Johnson how he would feel about seeing a specialist about the loss of his two daughters. Surprisingly, Mr. Johnson was open to the idea. Even though it was little progress, Pastor Jacobs was happy to report to Jimmy and Nina that their grandfather had agreed to see a psychologist about his issues. Of course, Jimmy offered to pay for the sessions. Pastor Jacobs scheduled the first appointment as soon as he could before the old man changed his mind. Jimmy also agreed to pick up his grandfather to bring him back and forth to the doctor's office for his appointments. It was his way of trying to connect with the old man.

Breaking Down the Wall of Silence

As much as Jimmy wanted to ignore his grandfather for being ignorant and stubborn, it was bothering him deep down in his heart that his grandfather was not as loving and receptive as his grandmother. He wanted to break through the old man to show him that he didn't have to be so mean and emotionless all the time. It almost seemed like the days of working in the cotton fields never ended for Mr. Johnson. The man did not know how to be happy and he did not want to embrace happiness. Jimmy would have none of it. Jimmy was planning to have children with his wife, and he wanted them to know their Great-Grandfather, because he had experienced what it was like to live without knowing his whole family.

Jimmy was very sympathetic towards his grandfather and he wanted to see a better side of him. While the rest of the family was all but eager to abandon the old man, Jimmy wanted to try a little harder. He felt that the old man gave everyone the cold shoulder because he felt like he had failed Katrina. He thought, with enough cffort and encouragement, everyone would find the good in the old man. Even Mrs. Johnson had never gotten the better side of the old man during their entire marriage. Jimmy wanted to see his family together and happy, and the only person standing in the way of complete happiness was Mr. Johnson. He had to be dealt with.

When Jimmy picked up Mr. Johnson for the first time for his appointment with the doctor, the old man almost changed his mind. He thought that the doctor would label him a lunatic just like the family had thought of him. He told Jimmy "I know that I agreed to see this shrimp, but I'm not gonna let nobody tell me that I'm crazy, because I ain't." Jimmy had to correct his grandfather and told him that the proper term was "shrink". His grandfather responded "Shrimp or shrink, they're all the same to me. They all like to tell people how crazy they are." That was the most words Mr. Johnson had spoken since Jimmy met him and Jimmy knew that there was another side to this man. He just sat back in the car and smiled at his grandfather's confusion of the word.

When they finally made it upstairs to the Psychologist's office, Jimmy asked his grandfather if he wanted him to come in with him for support. Mr. Johnson told him "I ain't afraid of nobody. I can take on this shrimp by myself. He just better not tell me I'm crazy." The doctor came out to greet Jimmy and his grandfather, but before he brought him into his office Jimmy asked if he could have a word with him. Jimmy explained to the doctor the circumstances in his grandfather's life such as the loss of his daughters and the discovery of his new family. The doctor shook Jimmy's hand and assured him that he would take great care of his grandfather.

The doctor asked Mr. Johnson to walk inside his office in front of him. Mr. Johnson answered, "Why I gotta walk in front of you? Are you planning to stick a knife on my back or something? It's your office, you should go in first." He turned to Jimmy and said "Don't never let nobody walk behind you because you don't know who's gonna stab you in the back." As Jimmy made his way out to the lobby, the doctor turned to Mr. Johnson and told him "Nobody's going to stab you Mr. Johnson. I'm here to help you." Mr. Johnson responded "I know you ain't gonna stab me, because you want me to stab you, so you can say I'm crazy. But I ain't gonna stab you either. I just want to get to know my grandchildren and my great grandchildren. Can you tell me how to go about doing that, doc?" The doctor suddenly keyed in on the fact that Mr. Johnson was interested in getting to know his family better. It was an opening that the doctor was praying for and Mr. Johnson brought it right to him. The doctor locked the door behind him as Mr. Johnson took a seat on the couch in his office.

Mr. Johnson came out of the psychologist's office a couple hours later, acting like a new man. He was so talkative during the ride home Jimmy wanted to drown out his voice with the radio. Mr. Johnson wouldn't let him. The old man was talking about things that Jimmy had no idea about. He started telling Jimmy about the time when he met his wife and how they fell in love, how he always wanted the best for his family, and the great joy that Katrina brought him and his wife when she was born. The old man went on and on in the car. As annoying as he might've been, Jimmy knew that it was a huge breakthrough for the family. The doctor had scheduled two more appointments to see the old man during the week. He would subsequently see the old man twice a week for the next three months until the old man learned how to express his feelings of loss and guilt to his family. Mr. Johnson pulled out a treatment plan and a schedule from his back pocket, and handed it to Jimmy. Jimmy was surprised at the progress that his grand-daddy had made after just one visit.

He was excited about seeing the doctor, but most importantly he was excited about the possibility of winning his wife and family over again. Mr. Johnson was learning to grieve the best way he could, and the doctor encouraged his rambling during their session. That was the type of therapy that worked for him. The doctor would speak to Jimmy every time he brought his grandfather to the hospital and update him on his progress. The old man was slowly coming around. He was starting to do more things outside of the house, and he even suggested that he and Jimmy see a movie together. Jimmy was most pleased at the suggestion. As mean spirited as Mr. Johnson was in the beginning, Jimmy learned that he was also resilient. It was perhaps from him, he and his sister had inherited that trait.

Over the next few months, Jimmy and his grandfather became very close. Mr. Johnson expressed his pain to his grandson about the way he had treated his family in the past. Most of his maltreatment stemmed from the lack of nurturing from his own father when he was growing up. Mr. Johnson had been ridden with guilt since Katrina left home, but because he wanted to stand by his decision to kick her out of the house he never went to look for her. Mr. Johnson had never before shed any tears and after learning about his harsh upbringing, Jimmy was surprised when Mr. Johnson got teary-eyed when he talked about his family. He had missed out on the formal years of his grandchildren's lives, and he didn't want to hold on to that bitterness anymore.

Meanwhile, Jimmy took every opportunity to tell his grandmother about the new changes in his grandfather. Even Nina and Lisa agreed that the old man had started to see a better way in life. Mrs. Johnson was not so easily convinced. She had been with that man for over thirty years, and she knew that no psychologist could help change him that significantly in such a short amount of time. She still wanted nothing to do with him. It would take Jimmy, Nina, Lisa, and Collin to try to persuade Mrs.

Johnson that her husband had made great strides in counseling and that he deserved a second chance.

Jimmy was starting to feel connected to his grandfather and he wanted to help him win over his wife. As much progress as the old man made, he wasn't ready to learn how to be romantic. For Mr. Johnson, love was understood not expressed. He had never learned to express love to anyone. As long as he provided for his family and protected them that was enough love from him. Jimmy would show his grandfather another way. The old man was apprehensive at first. Every time he thought about the lonely nights he spent at his house without his wife, he agreed little by little to follow Jimmy's suggestions to get his wife back.

Since Nina knew how romantic her husband was, she suggested that Jimmy talk with Collin about ways that Mr. Johnson could woo his wife back into his arms. Collin was more than willing to help. First, Mr. Johnson had to establish a way to communicate with his wife. They had not spoken in so long and there was so much to be said. Mr. Johnson thought a simple apology would have his wife running back to him. When Collin explained to him how much damage control that needed to be done; he started to realize how badly he had hurt his family.

Teaching an Old Dog New Tricks

Before any plan could be established for Mr. Johnson, he first had to learn to express himself through writing. Mr. Johnson had done a great job concealing his literacy deficiency most of his life, but Jimmy was able to pick up on it when his grandfather was adamant about him reading articles in the newspaper to him all the time. He found many excuses for not being able to read the article himself and Jimmy knew it was more than meets the eye. However, approaching such a sensitive subject with Mr. Johnson would prove more difficult than Jimmy initially thought.

The fact that Mrs. Johnson was able to obtain a college degree weighed heavily on Mr. Johnson's ego. For years he had managed to manipulate the woman into thinking that she was nothing more than a subservient wife, but she would go on to prove to him that she was more than what he thought. Jimmy could've easily used his grandmother's achievements to motivate the old man, but he knew that would only add fuel to the fire. Mr. Johnson didn't understand the value of an education because he hadn't gotten one and was able to function well in life, according to him. Never once did he realize that his ignorance had cost him his family.

Tact was the most important weapon to use to get through to the old man and Jimmy was very tactful when he brought up the fact that Black people have achieved a lot considering the fact that they were prohibited from earning an education for over four hundred years in America. "Grandpa, we probably would've been much farther in life as a people if we were allowed to learn how to read the same time as other folks," he said. "Despite the setback in our timing, we have produced quite a few notable figures in society. That's also one of the reasons why I went back to school to obtain my degree in accounting. Basketball is not gonna be with me forever, but I can always use my accounting skills," he continued.

A light smile came across the old man's face, he was proud that his grandson was so intelligent, and Jimmy felt he had found his angle. "Striving to improve your skills in life is a nonstop task and you shouldn't limit your intelligence because you were deprived once upon a time. Your grand kids are looking forward to you reading to them and I think it will be great to hear a story told through the voice of their grandfather," Jimmy said. "Well Jimmy, my son, I think you make a good point. I've been stubborn my whole life because I had to hide from the world what I didn't want them to know, but now I'm a grown ass man and I can do whatever the hell I want and I'm gonna learn how to read and write to get my wife and my family back," Mr. Johnson said.

Jimmy cracked open the door that had been shut for many years and the old man didn't feel threaten at all by his approach. Jimmy came by the house with books he picked up from the library, and everyday he dedicated a couple of hours of his time while in recovery to teach his grandpa how to read and write. Mr. Johnson would go on to earn his GED and was motivated by his wife to earn a Bachelor's degree in education by the time he turned seventy. It took a little longer to earn his degree because he wanted to take his time to do it right. Mr. Johnson didn't just do it for himself, he also did it for his grandchildren and for those people who never believed that they could walk away from darkness in their lifetime.

Getting Back in the Groove

Jimmy and Collin came up with a plan for Mr. Johnson to win back his wife's love and affection. They made him agree to write her a letter everyday for a month explaining to her why he had been so callous and mean, and how he planned on showing her that he was a changed man and a new person all together. There was a theme for each day and each letter had to end with the words "I Love You." Mr. Johnson never realized how hard it was to be romantic.

In the first letter, the theme was "Asking for a moment of your time". At the top of each letter, Mr. Johnson wrote his theme and handed the letter to Jimmy to give to his wife. In his first letter, he wrote to his wife to simply ask her for a few minutes of her time. He wanted nothing more than to show her how wrong he had been most of their lives, and how right he wanted to be this time around. He went on and on about situations in the house with the kids, as well as his wife, and how he didn't act like a gentleman when he should have. He rambled on paper the same way he rambled at the Doctor's office. Mrs. Johnson instantly noticed the change in her husband from all the rambling that he had done in his letters. Mr. Johnson used to be a man of few words, but all that changed. Even though he wasn't totally literate when the letters were written, his wife was able to understand his writing and noticed the improvement.

By the time Mr. Johnson wrote his twenty-fifth letter, he was doing some serious begging for forgiveness. He had also been required to send roses to his wife everyday starting with the first day he wrote his first letter. Each bouquet was equal the amount of letters he had written.

For the first time, Mrs. Johnson felt like a teenager in love. She wondered what came over her husband. The last letter she received from Mr. Johnson, he was requesting a date with her. Jimmy had arranged for a limousine to pick up his grandfather at his house. The chauffeur was instructed to go to Nina's house to pick up his grandmother. Collin made sure that Mr. Johnson was aware of the fact that he had to get out of the limousine to hold the door open for his wife, and to have two dozen roses in his hand waiting for Mrs. Johnson.

A date was set at a nice restaurant in Boston. Mr. and Mrs. Johnson ate their favorite meals, and then they were off to an annual ball for Seniors held at the VFW hall in West Roxbury. The couple had fun dancing the whole night. Mr. Johnson held his wife like a teenager in love, and she was finally happy to have fun with her husband after over thirty years of marriage. She wished he had been so sweet, kind, and romantic when they were younger, but she was indulging in the moment. At the end of the night, Mr. Johnson wanted his wife to come back home with him, because he had Viagra on ice at the house. She declined, because she still wanted to take things one day at a time. She told her husband that she appreciated all the effort that he put forth in trying to win her over, but she wasn't going to give in so easily to him. As much as Mrs. Johnson wanted to go home and be with her husband, she stuck to her guns and stayed at Nina's house.

Mr. Johnson accepted his wife's decision and he would go on to write her love notes everyday that he woke up. The letters didn't stop coming even after Mrs. Johnson moved back into the house with her husband. They both were avid watchers of Home and Garden television. Mr.

Johnson got the idea to create a secret garden of roses especially for his wife after watching a program on Home and Garden television. She woke up everyday to find a rose on the kitchen table along with a love note from her husband.

Mr. Johnson might have missed out on the lives of Jimmy and Nina, but he more than made up for it with his great-grandchildren. Collin Jr. and his sister, Katrina were always going somewhere with their great-grandparents and that gave Nina a lot of time to spend with her husband. Collin took great care of his wife when she finally became pregnant with their third child. Collin, however, also told Nina that he wanted his children to start spending time with his parents as well. Since the Johnsons came into their lives Collin Jr. and little Katrina hadn't spent much time with their paternal grandparents. Nina had complained that they were undermining the way she disciplined her children by spoiling them every time they went over there. Collin was quick to point out that Mr. and Mrs. Johnson were doing the exact same thing and Nina made no big deal of it.

Nina was a big enough person to admit her bias and Collin was able to show her that the grandparents were doing nothing wrong by showing love to the children. It was hard for Nina to swallow this, at first, because she was never spoiled as a child. When her grandparents came around she knew that she had missed out on a lot, and that made it okay for her children to be spoiled by them. The children would split their time between the two sides of the family when Collin and Nina needed to spend time together.

After reconnecting with Jimmy and Nina, Mr. and Mrs. Johnson were interested in saying their goodbyes to their daughter Katrina. The guilt of Katrina's death hadn't disappeared from their mind and they knew that they needed closure in order to move on with their lives.

Katrina's Grave revisited

The Johnsons had never gotten a chance to say goodbye to Katrina. Even Eddy wanted to speak to his sister even though she was dead. The family made plans to go to the Longwood Cemetery to visit Katrina's grave on Memorial Day. Mr. and Mrs. Johnson, Eddy, Nina, Collin, and their two children all met at Jimmy and Lisa's house for the short drive to the cemetery. Jimmy and Nina had been visiting their mother every year on Memorial Day, and leaving fresh flowers on her grave every other week. It was an emotional scene for Mrs. Johnson, her husband, and Eddy. Mrs. Johnson was especially emotional, because she felt that she didn't do a good enough job fighting for her daughter.

Mr. Johnson was able to contain himself for only a short period as he burst out in tears, and knelt down in front of his daughter's grave to ask for forgiveness. Although he had never told his daughter how much he loved her when she was alive, he couldn't stop telling her how much he missed her and how he was an imbecile who didn't know any better. He would carry the pain of her loss with him forever. Eddy was satisfied with saying his goodbyes and thanking Katrina for bringing two beautiful children into the world that he loved dearly.

Mrs. Johnson asked for a special moment with her daughter away from everyone else. She talked to her daughter about some of the activities that they never got a chance to do together. She told her daughter that she wished she had taken the time to act like a mother instead of an obedient wife to her husband. She told her daughter that she had never forgotten about her, and that her spirit continued to live within her from the time she left home.

Most of all, she told her daughter she loved her and she was always proud of her.

The whole family left the cemetery that day teary-eyed. Lisa comforted her husband, and Collin held on to his wife the way she needed to be held. Eddy simply put his arms around his Mom and Dad as they walked away from Katrina's grave. The family went out to celebrate Katrina's life at Jimmy and Nina's favorite Chinese restaurant in Saugus, Massachussetts.

Finding Karen

Jimmy and Nina had brought closure to the Johnsons when they reconnected with their grandparents, but there was still a missing piece to the Johnson family. They also had a daughter named Karen who had been missing for years. When Karen went missing she was presumed dead, because her body had never been found and the confessed killer left a note without revealing where the body was. That situation created a whole different kind of limbo in the Johnson's household. Jimmy and Nina had never met their aunt, but they could feel both their grandparent's and Eddy's pain whenever they talked about Karen. It seemed like they had given up hope, and Karen was starting to become a painful memory like Katrina was.

Jimmy and Nina could sense that the family wasn't completely happy, despite the fact that they found each other. Mrs. Johnson remained hopeful and sad at the same time. She wasn't too optimistic after she learned that Katrina had passed. Even worse was the fact that someone had admitted to killing Karen. She resonated with the fact that Karen was dead, but the family wanted to give her a proper burial.

Jimmy hired a private investigator to help find Karen. About a week later, the investigator found out that it was never reported that a State Trooper had checked on Mike on the side of the expressway. The investigator backtracked as much as he could to figure out what Mike may have done with Karen's body. There was never any report of any bodies of a black woman turning up on any rivers in the surrounding area, and the investigator hit a brick wall with the case. He urged Jimmy to start a national campaign nationwide for Karen.

A picture of Karen when she went missing at the age of sixteen was plastered on every milk carton at every supermarket in the country for a month. At first, it was a hard sell to feature Karen as missing, because her family had been told that she was killed. Jimmy was able to convince the people from the milk company that it was worth a shot to feature his Aunt as part of the campaign even if it was just for one week. When the folks from the milk corporation agreed to feature Karen for a month on their milk cartons it was a blessing from above. The whole family kept their fingers crossed, but was ready for the worse.

Karen had been gone for so long, she would have been in her thirties and looking a lot different than she did as a teenager. An expert forensic artist tried his best to make a composite of what Karen would look like in her thirties at normal weight. Jimmy tried as much as he could to get the case exposed nationally in the media. It was unusual for a missing black woman to receive any kind of national attention on television. Jimmy used his celebrity status as he embarked on a crusade to help find his aunt's body.

Jimmy was featured on many talk shows while going through his treatment for a kidney transplant, and he took every interview opportunity to talk about his missing aunt while he was on the air. He was relentless. He continued to feed the press with his hope of returning to basketball the following year while he plugged his missing aunt to the world. Jimmy also became the spokesperson for the Kidney Foundation. He wanted to educate people about kidney failure, but most importantly he wanted to urge all people in the African American Community throughout the country to sign up as organ donors. His other crusade was to find his aunt and bring closure to his grandparents.

Blackmailed

While Jimmy was traveling around the country to raise awareness for kidney failure, he was being closely watched by an old foe. Jean, the prostitute who recognized Jimmy's voice when he unintentionally caused the death of Mr. Ferry in that hotel room a few years back, had made herself very familiar with Jimmy's scheduled television appearances. One day during a taping of a talk show in New York, Jean traveled there to be part of the live studio audience, just so she could see Jimmy. She lied to the producers and told them that Jimmy was her biggest source of inspiration when she came out of her coma from a car accident in Boston. The producers found her story moving, so they arranged a private luncheon for her to meet with Jimmy. Since Jimmy was the type of person who always tried to reach out to people, he agreed to meet with Jean for a private lunch after the show.

Lunch was set up at a nice restaurant downtown Manhattan. Jean was brought to the restaurant early to wait for Jimmy. He arrived about fifteen minutes later in a limousine. The press was barred from the lunch meeting. After about ten minutes into their meal, Jean burst out "Look, I'm not here because I'm a fan of yours. I can care less about your little kidney failure campaign and your struggles to get back to basketball." Jimmy was surprised by Jean's comment. "Who are you?" he asked. "It don't matter who I am, but I know the real person behind the mask that you're wearing," she told him. "All that fake good-guy image that you're trying to portray on television is about to be exposed unless you write me a high six figure check to make your problem go away." Jimmy didn't know what hit him. He definitely knew that he had hidden skeletons, but he never thought that they would one day catch up to him.

He tried acting ignorantly by asking her what she was talking about. Jean was very sarcastic in her tone and demeanor. "Do you suddenly have amnesia?" she asked "What are you talking about?" Jimmy answered. Jean turned to him and said, "Look, I'm the one who was lying up in that hospital for almost three years in a coma, all right? I'm the one who was suffering from amnesia, but thank God my memory came back. I know that you don't want me to blurt out to everyone in the restaurant that you were the man who stabbed Ferry that night in the motel room when I was tied up to the bed?" Jimmy didn't know how to respond to Jean. He simply asked, "How much do you want?" The possibility of going to jail ran through Jimmy's mind and he was scared. He didn't know how serious Jean was, and he didn't want to take any chances. She requested three quarters of a million dollars in the form of a certified check. Jimmy asked, "How exactly do you plan on explaining to the IRS the reason why you'd be receiving such a large amount of money from me?"

She knew that he had a point and she needed to come up with another plan. "Well then, I guess you're gonna have to give me the money in cash," she said. "Just how am I supposed to get my hand on seven hundred and fifty thousand dollars in cash?" he asked.

"You'll find a way. I'm sure you have a safe hidden somewhere with some cash for emergencies," she said. Jimmy was starting to believe that the car hit Jean a little too hard on the head, because she sounded delusional. Even though Jean posed a threat to his career and livelihood, Jimmy sensed that she wasn't bright enough to follow through with her demands.

It had taken Jean a few months to regain her memory. The only thing she was familiar with was Jimmy's voice, and the incident that took place in the hotel room the night she was with the murder victim and nothing else. She had no friends or family to report this to, and she did not even remember whom she talked to about the case. Jean almost did not believe that incident really happened. She could not remember the details of the case and the doctors at the hospital told her that she would never fully regain her memory. Jean did not know where to begin if she really wanted to report Jimmy to the authorities. The case had been closed for two years and all the records were sealed at the widow's request. But Jean tried to threaten Jimmy, anyway. She told Jimmy if he didn't give her the amount of money she asked for, she would go to the police.

Jimmy wanted some time to think about his next move, so he agreed to a payment plan with Jean. He told her that because of government regulations, he could only give her nine thousand, nine hundred, and ninety nine dollars a week so that the IRS would not question the source of the money. It sounded like a good start to Jean, but it would be a great stall for Jimmy. Jean thought she had Jimmy cornered, and she couldn't wait to start spending his money lavishly. She had planned to leave the shelter where she was staying, and move into a suite at the Westin Hotel downtown Boston. Over nine thousand dollars a week for almost seventy-six weeks could go a long way. Jean was betting on that money to start living the good life. She handed Jimmy a piece of paper with a phone number where she could be reached, and Jimmy left the restaurant after shaking Jean's hand to confirm their deal. It was almost like a hand-scripted publicity stunt the way Jimmy shook Jean's hand and gave her a hug in front of everyone. Even Hollywood couldn't have written a better script.

Cornered

Jimmy left the restaurant feeling bewildered about the whole situation. He thought about going to the police to turn himself in. That thought quickly faded when he came to the realization of spending the rest of his life in jail for defending himself and his family against a scumbag who was going around molesting and raping young children. "As many children as Patrick Ferry molested when he was alive, my life and freedom should not be on the line," he whispered to himself. There had to be a different way to deal with his problems. Giving the money to Jean wasn't an issue, but Jimmy knew that the money wasn't going to keep her away. Greed has a way of rearing its ugly head when it's least expected, and he knew that Jean would come back and ask for more money. He would always have the incident clouding over his head.

The only person Jimmy had ever confessed the incident to was Pastor Jacobs, and he needed to speak with him immediately. Jimmy left New York and rushed to get on a plane to go home to Boston. He asked his publicist to cancel all his future television appearances and interviews until further notice. While on the short plane ride to Boston, Jimmy thought about his options. He had never actually thought about murdering anybody with his bare hands, but that is exactly how he felt when he was at the restaurant with Jean. He wanted to wring her neck until there was no life left in her. As much as he was trying to be a good citizen and beat the odds of where he came from, there was always something in his way that seemed to want to pull him to the life of crime.

Jimmy had created his own destiny, and he wasn't ready to let somebody else change that for him. He knew there had to be a way to get rid of Jean, and he couldn't wait to get home to talk to the man who always helped him find a solution to his problems. That man was none other than his father, Pastor Jacobs. Jimmy relied heavily on Pastor Jacobs' guidance to get through the tough times in his life, and he never had to face anything tougher.

When Jimmy arrived at the airport, Nina was there to pick him up. He would normally leave his car parked at the airport when he went away on short trips, but he had planned a five city tour. He didn't feel comfortable leaving his car parked at the airport for too long a period. When Jimmy got in the car, he was not his normal cheery self, and Nina noticed almost immediately. Nina knew her brother and she knew that something was bothering him. He simply thanked her for picking him up, because his wife, Lisa, was attending a charity event in Boston and couldn't pick him up. Jimmy didn't say much the whole ride to his house. He was somewhere that he hadn't been in a long time and getting out was going to be harder to do this time.

Jimmy couldn't even talk to Nina about his problem because he had kept the incident a secret from her as well. She wondered why her brother was so silent, but he didn't offer an explanation. "Did something happen on your trip?" She asked. "I don't really want to talk about it Nina," he told her. Nina knew very well when to leave her brother alone. She didn't say much to him in the car during the ride. She simply left him to wallow in his mess.

After Nina dropped Jimmy off at his house, he took his luggage into the house. He then hopped in his car and drove straight to Pastor Jacobs' house. He needed guidance and this matter was more serious than any matter he has ever had to face in his life. Jimmy was going out of his mind while driving to Pastor Jacobs' house. He was hoping that Pastor Jacobs would have the solution to make his problem go away. He had come too far to let some bimbo hooker ruin his life, but he also knew that the bimbo hooker now held his future in her hands. Jimmy arrived at Pastor Jacobs' house in no time.

He rang the doorbell. When Pastor Jacobs opened the door he knew that something was wrong, because Jimmy's face was flushed. As they made their way into the living room, he asked his wife to bring Jimmy some water to calm down his nerves. Pastor Jacobs asked Jimmy to take long deep breaths to recollect his thoughts before saying anything. Pastor Jacobs was trying his best to make him feel comfortable and secure, but he had no idea about what Jimmy was about to unload on him.

After about fifteen minutes of long soothing, deep breaths and a few sips of Poland Spring Water, Jimmy was calm enough to start telling Pastor Jacobs about the re-emergence of Jean from her coma and her plan of blackmail. Pastor Jacobs sat there and listened to Jimmy. He knew that Jimmy's blood pressure was rising as he told him of Jean's demands. The first words out of Pastor Jacobs' mouth "can you find a way to stall her until I can come up with a plan?" "I might be able to stall for a little while because I told her that I will be given her about ninety nine hundred and ninety nine dollars a week," Jimmy told him. "That was good thinking on your part. I should be able to come with a plan very soon. Meanwhile, you might have to make a payment to her until my plan comes to fruition," Pastor Jacobs told Jimmy.

This was one situation where Pastor Jacobs didn't readily have the answers as easily and quickly as usual. Blackmail was new to him, and he didn't want to offer any quick solutions. Jimmy's livelihood was dependent upon his plan. He asked Jimmy if he had a way of contacting Jean, and Jimmy handed him a phone number. He took the number in his hand and looked at it for a few seconds. He shook his head and wondered why this chick had to come and mess up something that was going so well. Pastor Jacobs told Jimmy to go home and not to say anything to anybody. Being a pastor took a backseat to his son, it was time for him to revert to his old street ways to get Jimmy out of trouble.

The Plan

After Jimmy left Pastor Jacobs' house, Pastor Jacobs told his wife that he would be in his office and not to bother him for a while. He pulled out the piece of paper with Jean's number from his pocket and dialed the number. A female voice answered on the other end and said, "Kind Street Inn, may I help you?" Pastor Jacobs quickly told her he had the wrong number. Pastor Jacobs knew that he recognized the number when he saw it, but he wanted to make sure. He had done some volunteer work at the Kind Street Inn Shelter and had a few contacts there in that shelter. Pastor Jacobs' plan to help his son out of the situation was suddenly getting clearer and easier.

He figured that Jean did not really have a leg to stand on as far as her story against Jimmy, so he had to find a way to expose her before she exposed Jimmy. The lure of prostitution was the only way that Jean knew how to make a living. The shelter did not allow prostitutes to take their well-deserved beds. If Jean thought she could blackmail Jimmy, Pastor Jacobs wanted to show her that two could play that game.

He did some background work and found out that Jean had only been at the shelter for a week. She was used to a certain lifestyle and with all the restrictions at the shelter; he knew that she wouldn't be able to stay there much longer due to all of the restrictions. It was a matter of time before Jean would find her way back to the streets to begin prostituting herself again. Pastor Jacobs was patiently waiting. He had come too far with his son to allow someone to destroy all his life's work. Pastor Jacobs had only one son, and he was not ready to lose him to the penal system. Anybody who got in his way was going to be dealt with whether he was a man of the cloth or not.

A Teenage Girl and a Dream

While Jimmy was going through his ordeal in Boston, far across the country there was a beautiful woman who had lost her memory due to a blow to the head. She had received this blow at the hands of an angry young man when she was just sixteen years old. A wealthy widow who always dreamed of having a child found this young woman. While taking a leisurely walk through the woods of New Hampshire, this lady came upon the hidden young woman's unconscious body breathing heavily in a card box. When the lady heard the young female voice groaning, she was startled at first because she didn't expect anybody to be in that part of the woods. At first, she tried to help the young lady by asking where she was from and if there was anything she could do to help. The young lady had no idea who and where she was. She didn't even know her name. She was suffering from a serious case of amnesia, and the lump on her temple was evidence that a blunt object may have hit her.

Since this young woman's disappearance only made the local news in Boston, nobody in New Hampshire had even heard of her. Unfortunately that day, she would find herself being cared for by a wealthy woman who wanted to be her mother and nothing else. Her new name would be Sonya Watson. The rich lady called herself Regina. There was no ill-will on Regina's part, but she knew that the young lady had a family somewhere. Her selfish needs prevented her from ever attempting to find the young girl's family. She decided that they were going to be a family, and she moved far across the country to California to prevent the authorities from ever finding out about her new daughter.

Regina took great care of Sonya, and gave her all the things that a little, poor, ghetto girl could ever have dreamed of. Regina had a big house on the hill and she was able to convince Sonya that she was her mother. She realized that the girl didn't know who she was. Sonya was somewhat suspicious of Regina, at first, because Regina was asking questions about her family. After realizing that the girl could not remember anything about her family, Regina claimed she was only playing with her and that she was her mother. Sonya, however, couldn't recall ever having Regina as a mother. When Sonya asked about her father, she was shown a picture of a man in a wedding picture with Regina. That man had died and left them all his fortune. Sonya would go on for the next fifteen years believing that Regina was her biological mother.

It was just Regina and Sonya for a while. The story was forged out of desperation, and for over fifteen years Sonya had been questioning that story. There was nothing around to remind her of her past, so she simply accepted the kind-hearted woman as her mom. Regina treated Sonya like a princess and offered her the world.

There were no family pictures when Sonya was young, and she wondered why. When she asked Regina why there were no pictures of her as a baby or a little girl, Regina told her that their house had burned down and all the pictures burned along with it. Sonya was also blamed for the fire, because Regina wanted to keep her from asking so many questions. She told Sonya that she was the reason why they lost all the pictures and other family heirlooms as a way to keep Sonya in-check with guilt. Regina genuinely loved Sonya and it was a perfect situation for her when she found Sonya. Regina never liked little or young kids, she wanted to have a daughter who was about fourteen years old because she didn't have the patience for younger kids. She was even a foster parent at one point in her life. Her door was always open when the Department of Social Services needed a placement for their foster teenagers. It was good for a while, but none of the girls Regina took in wanted to be adopted. She started to lose her patience with them. She stopped being a foster parent all together.

Sonya, for the most part, fulfilled a life long dream for Regina. In her own delusional and twisted ways, Regina believed that she was a great parent and that she had done a great job raising Sonya. She also made Sonya believe that her childhood was filled with happy thoughts and wonderful experiences. After all, Sonya graduated top of her class at the University of California in Los Angeles. She became a top-notch attorney and Regina was the driving force behind her success. Sonya was grateful, but she was never comfortable calling Regina mother. Regina, however, insisted on it.

Unbreakable Bonds

It was during Jimmy's tour as a spokesman for Kidney Foundation that Sonya saw him on her television screen. He was always pleading for anyone who had information regarding his aunt Karen to come forward. Jimmy also used a sketch artist to draw a picture of what Karen would look like in her thirties that he always carried in his pocket. At the end of each talk show, he would always show the picture of the young Karen and old Karen in hopes to help find her.

When Sonya saw the picture of this woman who looked so much like her, she became curious. She never knew Jimmy, so she couldn't identify with anything that he was saying. She wrote down the phone number to contact the family. Sonya's suspicions grew even more, and she wanted to confront Regina about it. She picked up the phone to call Regina and when Regina picked up she could hear the television program in the background. Regina quickly shut off the television. It was the same program that Sonya was watching, and there was something suspicious about the whole situation. Sonya demanded an explanation from Regina, but Regina wanted nothing to do with it. She told Sonya that it was figment of her imagination to even think that she was the actual woman that Jimmy had mentioned on television. Regina stepped up the guilt trip again by telling Sonya that she had been imagining things in her mind ever since the fire.

Although, Regina had provided a great life for Sonya, she always felt that she was being manipulated. Regina never wanted her to discuss anything about her family life with strangers and she was not allowed to have friends. Sonya was always leery of the woman who claimed to be her mother. Sonya had been home schooled by Regina. When she wanted to live on campus in college, Regina threw a fit and told her that she didn't want to stay in the house by herself. She bribed and convinced Sonya to stay home and commute to school by purchasing a convertible BMW for her. All those things only added to Sonya's suspicion of the woman who had possibly kidnapped her when she was a teenager. Now, she had a possible connection to her real family and Regina wanted make sure that she destroyed it.

After badgering Sonya for about ten minutes on the phone for thinking that Regina was not her mother, Sonya couldn't take it anymore because she had heard enough. She wanted to hang up on Regina. Regina became enraged and started calling Sonya an ingrate. The guilt-laden tongue-lashing she received from Regina only reinforced her belief that Regina was not her biological mother. She knew that a real mother would never consider her own daughter an ingrate. She hung up the phone before Regina could say anything more to her. After Regina heard the phone slammed down in her ear, she started cursing Sonya. She began talking to herself, "I lost a daughter already and I'm not about to lose another one," she said.

Regina had a biological daughter named Sonya who was about the same age as the Karen, whom she found in the woods. She couldn't deal with the fact that her daughter had drowned in the lake where she had discovered the girl's body, so she decided to replace her real daughter, Sonya, with the girl she found. Since Karen had forgotten who she was it was a perfect scenario for Regina. She even shaved two years off Karen's age to make her believe she was her real daughter. Regina had a birth certificate from her real daughter and she used it as proof to convince Karen that she was her daughter.

Sonya's curiosity got the best of her after she hung up the phone on Regina. She called the hotline for the number listed on the television show by Jimmy and a lady answered. "I just saw the basketball player named Jimmy on this show and I believe that I can be the missing person that his family has been looking for," she told the lady. The lady took down her name and number and promised to have Jimmy call her as soon as he could. Everything seemed surreal to Sonya at that point. She was trying to remember if people ever referred to her as Karen, but she drew a blank. Something deep inside Sonya made her feel that Regina was not biologically related to her. They looked nothing alike, and the man Regina claimed was her husband and Sonya's father also looked nothing like her.

What to do?

Sonya wrestled with the idea that she possibly grew up with a total stranger and imposter who might have taken advantage of her memory loss and kept her away from her real family. Then, she thought about the luxurious and fabulous upbringing that she had with Regina, and she decided that she didn't want to harm Regina in any way, shape or form. Regina had been nothing but loving and kind to her. Occasionally, they had their disagreements and she acted less than a mother, but for the most part, it was a loving upbringing and she was well educated and successful.

Sonya really wanted Regina to be her biological mother because of her kind heart, but the fact that she could be somebody else's child was taking over her spirit and mind. She started to feel pity for Regina, because she knew that Regina was afraid of being alone and that could have been the reason why she kept her away from her family. Sonya had no idea that Regina had actually lost a daughter. Everything in Sonya's life seemed like a fairytale. She had a caring mother, she lived in a mansion, she had a mother who stayed home to take care of her, they went on vacation around the world every summer, and she had a father who was wealthy enough to leave his family financially well-off for the next five generations. Who wouldn't want such woman to be their mother?

Sonya didn't understand her situation at all and she still had not spoken to Jimmy or the Johnson Family. She felt like she was getting ahead of herself and racking her brain to deal with a situation that she wasn't even certain about. It started taking a toll on her mentally. She decided to stop thinking about the whole situation, and just waited for the Johnson family representative to call her.

The Rescue

Although the Johnson family never gave up hope, however, they never anticipated finding Karen alive. It had been so many years and so much had happened during that time, there was no way that Karen could've possibly lived away from her family for so long, they thought. The family decided that Mrs. Johnson should place the call to Sonya. Everyone gathered in the Johnson's living room on that fateful day to find out if they had finally found Karen. Mrs. Johnson's hands were trembling as she picked up the phone to dial the number. She didn't know what kind of reaction to expect from the woman on the other end.

The phone rang three times before Sonya finally picked it up and almost instantly she recognized the voice on the other end. Sonya knew that she had heard that voice before, and it was a voice that brought joy to her when she was a little girl. Mrs. Johnson also recognized Karen's voice on the phone when she answered, "Sonya speaking." Mrs. Johnson was shocked to hear that familiar voice referring to herself as Sonya. Mrs. Johnson told her, "You sound like my baby, Karen, and there's no way that your name is Sonya." Sonya told her that her voice sounded familiar too, but she couldn't fully recall who Mrs. Johnson was. Mrs. Johnson started telling Sonya about the family she left behind in Boston, and that everyone had been agonizing over her disappearance for over a decade. She wanted to go back to the time Karen went missing, but none of it sounded familiar to Sonya.

Regina was not a stupid woman. After she found Karen, she took her to a hypnosis specialist who was able to hypnotize Karen. He made her believe that her life began at sixteen years old when she was found, and that Regina was the only family that she had. At the time, Regina told Sonya she wanted to help her remember her Dad, but under hypnosis she had other plans. Though the specialist was able to get Karen to believe that Regina was her mother, he was not able to erase her memory about her real family. He had no pictures or names to use as reference. Regina had paid the hypnotist handsomely and told him that Sonya was really her daughter.

Sonya found it strange that Mrs. Johnson had been grieving over her for so long, so she made arrangements with them to fly to Boston to meet the family the following week. Meanwhile, she continued to go by Regina's house as usual to see her and pretended that the mother-daughter relationship they had was still intact. Sonya never gave Regina any indication that she was seeking the truth about her family. When she was leaving to go to Boston, she told Regina that she was going on a short vacation to Cancun. Regina insisted on coming along, but Sonya brushed her off and told her that she needed some time alone.

Sonya arrived at the airport in Boston a week later. The whole family greeted her. Jimmy and his wife, Nina and her children, Eddy, and Mr. and Mrs. Johnson all waited at the terminal entrance for her. They didn't have to hold up any signs with Sonya's name, because Karen always shared a very close family resemblance with her mother. Eddy recognized his sister right away as he ran towards to give her a hug. She could see that he was almost a clone of her as she reluctantly hugged him back. He held her in his arms and told her how much he's been missing her and how growing up without her was unbearable. For the first time in her life, Karen recognized the family resemblance. He took her luggage and headed towards the rest of the family. Sonya was shocked to see the two people who looked most like her were standing in front of her. Mr. and Mrs. Johnson didn't want to let go of their daughter. They held her tight in a bear hug almost suffocating the young woman. She was introduced to the whole family and one by one each member of the family hugged her and told her how much she was missed.

Eddy was so overcome with joy, because he had missed his sister more than anybody. Karen and Eddy were very close when she went missing, and for the first year while she was gone, he cried himself to sleep thinking about her. His face also brought joy to her, because she could only recall good things about him. Karen kept smiling at her brother all the way home.

Karen was directed to the stretched limousine waiting outside. Once everyone was in the limo, they started pointing to her face, and the fact that her looks hadn't changed much since she was a teenager. She was still Sonya as far as she was concerned, but everyone in the car kept referring to her as Karen. Her mother and father pulled out pictures of her with the family from the time she was a baby to the time she went missing. With every picture, her memory was starting to come back to her. They showed pictures of her, Eddy, and Katrina together. It brought out different emotions from her. She recognized young Katrina and remembered that it was not a pleasant experience for her. As they were talking in the car, Mrs. Johnson told Karen that she kept her room the same way she left it before she went missing. She also stated that it would be nice to have her back in her room again. To their dismay, however, Karen told them that she was planning to stay at the Sheraton Hotel.

Before Karen left for Boston, she wasn't sure if these people were actually going to be her long lost family. So, as a precautionary measure, she booked a room at a hotel. On the way to the house, Karen told the family about Regina, the life she had led, how she was an attorney, and that Regina was a very good mother to her. But every time she referred to Regina as her mother, Mrs. Johnson got offended. Karen explained to them that she had no memory of what happened to her, but she was always suspicious of Regina. She also told them that Regina was a good person, and she didn't want to get her in trouble with the law. When the limo pulled up in front of the Johnson home, Karen started to remember running up and down the stairs in front of her house when she was younger. Mrs. Johnson didn't even have to lead her to her room, because she remembered exactly where it was. Karen was starting to regain her memory and the first thing that came back to her was how mean her dad was. She was almost frightened by him all of a sudden, and Mr. Johnson could sense it.

The Johnsons knew they had found their daughter, but Karen had also started a new life back in California. Her job, home, and everything she had known for the last fifteen years or so was in California. She would have to get to know her biological family all over again, and she wanted to know why Mr. Johnson frightened her. The whole family had to explain to her that her daddy was a changed man, and that he had come a long way to be a better father to Eddy and a husband to his wife. Karen was happy with the news, and she made plans to spend a week in Boston with her family. She was able to cancel her reservation at the Sheraton, and stayed in her old room at the Johnson house.

That week Karen discovered herself all over again. The family explained the tragedy with Mike, and how all this mess came about. Karen herself started to recall the events that led up to her disappearance. She also told her parents that she was lucky to have been found by Regina because she provided her with the best care and the best that life had to offer. She wanted her family to meet Regina. She told them that if they didn't mind, she would like to keep the name Sonya Watson. It would be too much trouble to change her name back to Karen because all of her professional achievements were attained in that name, and everyone in her professional life knew her as Sonya Watson. She still wanted her family to keep calling her Karen.

Even though it took a lot of work for Karen to finally find her family, the reality was that if Jimmy was not a star athlete with unlimited means, it would have been impossible. Unlike the Natalee Holloways of the world, Karen was a little black girl who went missing and the country didn't give a damn. Natalee Holloway went missing in Aruba and the whole world knew about it a few hours later, all because she had no melanin on her skin. Even in Aruba, a heavily populated black country, the black man was the first person to be under suspicion when she disappeared. Jimmy knew that young white boys all over the world know that they can always pull a fast one on the authorities everywhere by blaming the black man for violent acts. Society continues to perpetuate those sentiments by acting hastily to get these black men locked up.

It was easy for the Johnson family and Karen to keep their discovery from the media. The case had been closed and nobody except the family had been relentless enough in their search to find her. "So many young black girls have gone missing, and the police and the media hardly pay any attention to it. It seems almost as if these people's lives do not matter as much. The Jon Benet Ramseys, the Natalee Holloways and the Staci Petersons are the only types of women that the world seem to care about. Even when witnesses come forward with information about missing, little, black girls they are ignored. The young black girl who was found decapitated in Florida could've been saved if the police acted on the information from a witness. The struggle goes on for equality in a different way. Most people in the hood have no idea that there is still a struggle going on and a fight to be fought," Jimmy told the family.

Though Karen was happy to be reunited with her family, she had decided to go back to Los Angeles to stay because it had become her home and she did not want to leave the place that she had grown to love. Karen knew that a part of her truly loved Regina for all that she had done for her, and she didn't want to abandon her. She promised to keep in touch with her family and visit them as often as possible. Karen was happy to finally rediscover her true roots, but she was grateful for the life that she led under the care of Regina. Saying goodbye to her family on the last day of her visit wasn't easy. It was especially hard when her brother, Eddy, got teary eyed from the joy of finally seeing his sister again. Eddie was also happy that she was staying in California, because he now had someone and a new place to visit.

The Set-up

Despite the fact that Jimmy had helped reunite Karen with the family, his problem still hadn't gone away. Pastor Jacobs had devised a plan to deal with Jean, and his plan required him to spend endless amounts of time following Jean around. He knew that old habits were hard to break. Jean could not really give up prostitution and all the other bad habits like being a shoplifter and booster as well as a heroin addict. Pastor Jacobs started following Jean around with a hidden camera and it was easy for him to do, because she had no idea who he was. Jimmy had pointed Jean out to Pastor Jacobs one day while Pastor Jacobs purposely drove by the shelter.

Instead of getting up and go out to look for work everyday as required by the shelter, Jean had other plans. But Pastor Jacobs also had plans of his own. He invested almost a thousand dollars in a small camera that he was able to attach to his cap. Watching all those undercover stories on Dateline and other investigative shows on television taught Pastor Jacobs a thing or two about surveillance. He followed Jean around for most of the day and captured every criminal act she committed on camera. He saved the footage for the day when he would use it to get rid of her permanently.

Unaware that she was being watched, Jean was committing grand theft, shooting drugs, prostitution, and all kinds of other petty crime on the streets. The footage that Pastor Jacobs captured would have been great for an undercover story about Jean's life of crime. There were also other victims captured in this footage, and most of them happened to be very well known fathers and husbands getting blowjobs from Jean in the back of different cars. It was the type of footage that Jean and her clients did not want to end up in the hands of the media or the police. Pastor Jacobs had every intention on getting the footage to the police and media. Being from the streets had its advantages, and Pastor Jacobs was a force to be reckoned with. His son was the most important person in his life, and he was willing to go to great lengths to protect him.

After gathering enough evidence for about a week to ensure Jean's permanent departure from Boston, Pastor Jacobs called Jimmy to set up a meeting with Jean for the initial payment. The meeting was to take place at a motel in Boston, and Jimmy was supposed to bring close to ten thousand dollars to keep Jean from going to the police with her story. Jean was very excited when she received the call from Jimmy, and was glad that her plan to blackmail him was finally coming to fruition. After the meeting was scheduled, they both hung up. Pastor Jacobs told Jimmy that he had everything under control and the matter would be taken care of. There was a sigh of relief from Jimmy as he crossed his fingers.

While Pastor Jacobs and Jimmy were planning their moves, Jean was making plans of her own. Jean was not as stupid as Jimmy and Pastor Jacobs thought. She wanted to protect herself in case things didn't go accordingly. She was also from the streets, and she had learned a thing or two while she was on the streets as well. The meeting with Jimmy was taking place a week later, and Jean wanted to make sure that she captured everything from that meeting on camera. She rented a room at the far end of the motel, and she invested in a few equipments of her own. Jean had set up hidden cameras all over the room.

She made sure that Jimmy's face would show in every position when they would discuss their arrangements.

Reaching Out to a Friend

While the Johnson family was going through their ordeal in Boston, the missing piece to their family puzzle was desperately trying to reconnect with her children. After Candy moved to Phoenix and left Katrina back in Boston in the jungle to fend for herself, she had learned through the grapevine that Tony, her pimp, was killed on the streets. She wondered how Katrina was surviving on her own. Candy had made a special trip to Boston to seek out Katrina. Unfortunately, she had learned that Katrina was incarcerated at Framingham State Prison.

Since Candy left the streets and moved to Phoenix, she had changed her life completely. She opened a center for runaway teens. With her past experience, she wanted to help keep kids off the streets. She was able to hire a grant writer to write a proposal for her, and she got the local as well as the federal government to fund her program. Candy's proposal was passionate and the lady she hired to write the grant believed in her cause. She wanted to help young teens transform their lives, and the only way she could do that was if she started her own program. The city of Phoenix also welcomed her efforts to help keep runaway teens off the streets. Her program has been a success since its inception.

Candy, however, could never get a young girl named Katrina that she left behind in Boston out of her mind. She was now in a position where she could help Katrina. She decided to take a trip to Framingham to visit with Katrina at the prison. After visiting with Katrina during her visit in Boston, they decided to continue to communicate with each other through letters and the occasional collect calls that Katrina would charge to

Candy's home phone. It was a relationship that Katrina really needed because the staff at the prison was worried that she was becoming suicidal. Candy's letters gave her strength and Katrina started coming out of her depressed funk.

Candy sent money to the prison for Katrina's commissary, and she also sent books that helped keep up her spirit while she was in jail. Candy knew that Katrina's children were a sensitive subject to her, so she avoided talking about her children. It would only have demoralized Katrina's progress. The two of them were like sisters. In no time, Candy was coming to the prison to visit Katrina on a monthly basis. She told Katrina about the Teen Center she opened back in Phoenix, and that she had a job waiting for her when she got out of prison. Candy also felt that Katrina's experience in jail would be a great asset for her program because the participants would hear of her experiences firsthand. Katrina had gone through things that many of these young women could never imagine, and Candy wanted to be proactive with her participants by having a staff that lived through it all talk to them.

Candy's friendship kept Katrina sane while she was in jail, and Katrina's spirit gave Candy hope for her program. She knew that Katrina's pains were going to make a great difference in these kids' lives, and she wanted to encourage Katrina positively while she was in Jail. Candy gave her hope and strength, and Katrina taught her determination.

Establishing Her Position

When Katrina first got to the prison she had to establish her position there. She could either be a weak link or a leader. She chose to be a leader. Many of the women were trying to test her fighting skills, and Katrina was not shy about whipping an ass or two. In no time, she was known as one of the most feared women in that jail and nobody wanted to mess with her. Katrina had gotten into scuffles with some of the toughest women in that jail, and she came out victorious most of the time. After a while, people started going to Katrina for favors or they would ask her permission before they acted on anything. Katrina surrounded herself with a group of young women that were tough enough that they didn't need actions. Their words were loud enough. They taught each other how to box and they lifted weights to get strong and their clique was formidable.

There was one girl in particular that Katrina took under her wing when she first came to the prison, and she soon became known as young Star at the prison. No one at the prison knew Katrina's real name, so everybody referred to her as Star. This being the name she used whenever she was arrested. After a few of years of mentoring young Star in the prison, it was time to pass the baton to her as the next leader in the prison. Katrina was confident that young Star was strong enough to hold her grounds when she decided that she wanted to transfer to Arizona to be closer to Candy. Katrina asked the prison officials if she could finish the terms of her sentence in Arizona where Candy lived. Young Star was transferred to Katrina's cell and she took over Katrina's leadership role as Katrina was granted a transfer.

Young Star, however, was not as strong as Katrina thought. She was not ready to assume the leadership position that Katrina had created for her. Soon after Katrina left, it was a total disaster at the prison. Young Star didn't know how to keep the girls in Katrina's old crew in check and everybody started to turn against her. She woke up everyday fighting someone to prove herself. After a while, she got tired of fighting. As feisty as young Star was, she didn't want to go on fighting everyday of her life for the remainder of her forty-year sentence for double murder. She wasn't as strong as initially perceived, and her weakness was starting to show. Young Star decided that she didn't want to deal with all the hassles that were going on with the women at the prison anymore. She got tired of fighting for her life and a role she didn't know how to handle.

Young Star decided to end it all by tying the body of her uniform shirt around the bars on her cell. She then wrapped the arms of the shirt around her neck and hung herself. It was a shirt that Katrina had left for young Star with her prison number on it. It was also a gift that young Star treasured from her mentor. Her lifeless body was discovered the next day by one of the prison guards. On the record, she was buried as Star Bright, because the prison officials failed to document that Star Bright AKA Katrina had been transferred to a prison in Arizona to finish out her sentence.

A Second Chance

In Arizona, Katrina thrived at the prison. She decided to take a different approach to prison life when she arrived in Arizona. Her reputation as a tough woman and a fighter back in Framingham followed her to Arizona. The inmates there knew better than to mess with her. Katrina also used her reputation to foster change in the prison system in Arizona. Of course, she had to make an example of the baddest and toughest woman at the prison when she first arrived to confirm her reputation, but after that it was smooth sailing. She had proven herself to her fellow inmates. The only thing she realized she could do with the fear that she instilled in them was to make them see things in a positive light.

Katrina became a model prisoner in no time and whenever there was trouble with the inmates, the guards sought her help to bring about peace. Katrina was on a first name basis with the warden, and she did more to assist them than any prisoner who had been at that prison in previous years. She also received a lot of privileges that other inmates didn't have. Candy visited with Katrina twice a week. Katrina was even able to convince the warden to allow Candy to bring a group of girls from the program to see what it was really like behind bars.

Katrina also ran a substance abuse group while in prison. She helped the younger inmates deal with their addiction while discussing her own past and addiction on the streets. Katrina never let anyone in on her private life, though. Nobody at the prison knew that she had children, and she made sure she didn't mention her family even during emotional moments in group with the other women. Katrina was a role model for many of the inmates at the prison. She inspired many of them to change their lives while in prison, and to stay positive after they were released back to society.

After serving almost half of the remaining sentence, Katrina was up for parole. She went before the parole board. With the help of the staff at the prison, she was granted parole and released from prison after serving thirteen years. The day before Katrina was released the guards and the inmates threw her a going-away party. Everyone was teary- eyed, because they knew that no one at that jail deserved their freedom more than Katrina. They also knew that they were losing a friend and a great person. Katrina left the prison with tears of joy as well as tears of loss, because she knew that she was going to miss her friends very soon. But freedom was a lot better.

Free At Last

When Katrina walked outside those prison gates, she also left behind the name Star Bright. She decided to go back to using her real name Katrina Johnson. After making her way outside the prison gates, she found Candy waiting in her BMW, X5 SUV. The first item on the menu was to get Katrina home into some better clothes and then take her shopping for a new wardrobe. Katrina could not believe that she was out of prison, and was about to face the world all over again. Candy had mentioned to her that Jimmy had become a professional basketball player and a good humanitarian and that her daughter Nina was a police officer. While visiting Boston, Candy went back to the old neighborhood to make sure that Katrina's children were okay. Katrina's mind was at ease knowing that her children had made it in this cruel world, but she wasn't ready to face them just yet. She felt that she had so much to prove to them for letting them down, but she didn't know where to begin.

Katrina had been denied a bath for the last thirteen years, and one of the things she was most looking forward to was a simple soothing bubble bath. Candy was so happy to see her friend out of prison, she didn't even argue Katrina's request. She drove straight to her four-bedroom home in suburban Phoenix to allow Katrina the luxury of a bath. Katrina's mouth almost hit the floor as Candy drove through her exclusive neighborhood with posh homes and well manicured lawns lining the streets. She couldn't believe that her friend had come so far. Candy had taken her fifty thousand dollars and invested it wisely.

When she first got to Phoenix, she enrolled in an adult education degree program offered at University of

Phoenix. She pursued a Bachelor's Degree in Counseling while she worked as a receptionist at a counseling center during the day. Candy completed her degree in two and a half years and then went on to pursue her PhD in Psychology. She kept all her personal achievements from Katrina when she was in jail because she did not want Katrina to think that she expected her to live up to those expectations.

Candy didn't waste too much time after she left Tony. She wanted to change her life and she knew that the only way she could do that was to go back to school and earn a degree. Someone with her background would have had too much of a hard time making it in the world. Candy had also regained custody of her daughter who was now an adult working as the Executive Assistant Director at her mother's center. Katrina was in awe of Candy and she knew that she couldn't ask for a better friend. Candy was the kind of friend who only used positive reinforcements with Katrina, and she never once made Katrina feel like she was above her because she was a doctor.

Candy pressed the automatic garage door opener in her two car garage as she pulled in the driveway, and Katrina noticed the brand new CLK 320, Mercedes in the garage. Candy handed a set of keys to Katrina for the Benz as well as keys to the house so she could come and go as she pleased. Katrina didn't know what to say to Candy, but she was even more shocked after she entered the house. The door from the garage led them right to the sit-in style kitchen where Katrina saw the most beautiful hardwood floors, stainless steel kitchen appliances, and furniture that money could buy.

Katrina was even more shocked when she raised her head to the twelve-foot vaulted ceilings from the kitchen to the formal dining room. The chandelier hanging from the ceiling in the dining room looked like something a person would find in the home of a movie star. Candy had come a long way, and she didn't spare any luxury in that house.

All the bedrooms in the house were fully furnished with top-notch furniture from some of the hottest, high-end designers in the business. In the back yard, there was an Olympic size swimming pool, as well as a Jacuzzi that was big enough to accommodate a whole football team. Candy led Katrina to the guest bedroom, located on the first floor of the house. There was a full bathroom and plenty of room to help her adjust from a ten-by-ten jail cell to a life of luxury. Life as Katrina knew it was about to change and change for the better. The first thing she did when she entered the room was to fall back on the plush bed covered with satin sheets. She took off all her clothes and headed to the bathroom. Katrina took one of the longest baths that day as she savored every minute of her newfound freedom.

Later that night, Candy cooked Katrina the best meal that she had ever had. Candy had learned to become a great cook after she regained custody of her daughter. As a mother, she couldn't rely on McDonald's and other restaurants to keep her daughter healthy. She might have been a career woman, but she was also a mother and a mother who cared deeply for her daughter. Having been neglected by her own parents, Candy made sure that she gave her daughter the attention that she needed. As a result, her daughter also became a doctor. Candy's new task, however, was to help ease Katrina's assimilation back into society.

Adjusting to Her New life

Candy knew that life behind bars was rough on Katrina and she wanted to help make the transition as smooth as possible. As a psychologist, she wanted to counsel Katrina, but there was a conflict of interest because Katrina was her friend. She knew that every little banging noise would send Katrina in a state of paranoia because of the slamming sound of the prison doors, so she kept her noise to a minimum during the first few months of Katrina's release. She also gave Katrina time to recuperate and decide which direction she wanted to take her life.

Of course, Candy had a job waiting for Katrina at the center, but she left it up to her to decide when she would be ready to work. Katrina's experience as a drug counselor was invaluable to Candy's program because many of the children who came to the center were victims of drug abuse as well. It took Katrina a few weeks to get acclimated, but she was ready to tackle the challenge. Katrina had an infectious personality, and when she started working at the center the girls gravitated towards her almost immediately. She was running her own groups in no time, and the young girls could not wait to hear about her hard life in jail and on the streets. As entertaining as Katrina's life sounded to them, she warned them to take her stories seriously because she didn't want any of them to fall victim to the circumstances she did. Katrina tried as blatantly as she could to tell the young girls in the program about her harsh life behind bars and on the streets. Unlike most people from the ghetto who served time, Katrina didn't want to glorify prison life and made it a point to tell these young girls about the barriers that a prison record could create.

Everyone at the center loved Katrina, and Candy could depend on her to make sure things were running smoothly when she had to go away on conferences. Candy's daughter had become a younger sister to Katrina, and they even hung out sometimes. Katrina stayed away from all the bad elements that sent her to jail, and Candy made sure that she received counseling from one of her colleagues twice a week. Everything in Katrina's life was finally coming together, and she had Candy to thank for her successful transition.

After living with Candy for close to a year, Katrina was ready to be on her own. She knew that Candy had made adjustments in her own life to accommodate her while living with her. She didn't want to be a burden any longer. When she told Candy that she was ready to get her own place, Candy only asked where she wanted to live. They went apartment hunting together, and with the help of Candy and her daughter, Katrina secured a nice apartment in a middle-class neighborhood on the outskirts of Phoenix. She continued to work for Candy and she earned a healthy salary. Katrina, Candy, and her daughter would sometimes hang out together. They would have a ball laughing at the men who tried to pick them up when they were out. The ladies were all appealing and attractive in their own right and they flaunted what they had every chance they got. Katrina managed to regain her beauty after sobering up. She was able to get her teeth replaced because Candy knew a great dentist who did magical work with veneers.

Family's Never Lost

Despite all the positive changes in Katrina's life and all the progress that she had made, one thing remained constant; the inability to face her children. The psychologist worked with Katrina on the issues relevant to her children, but she was always too ashamed to muster the courage to face them. She had written letters to them while she was in prison, but she never got a response from them. Actually, the letters never made it to Jimmy and Nina, because they had moved from the house by the time she started writing to them.

Candy didn't want to pressure Katrina about her kids every time they hung out, but she urged her to try to reconcile with them. It was at least worth a try. She even offered to fly to Boston with Katrina to face her children. Katrina did not know where to begin, and she did not know where to find her kids. Candy put those worries to rest very quickly when she got on her computer and did a search on Nina and found out that she lived in Hyde Park with her husband. Katrina had no idea that her children had reconnected with her parents, so Candy also looked up her parents on the Internet. She found out that they still lived in the same house where Katrina grew up. Candy told her it was still worth a try to reach out to her parents, and burying old hatchets was very important to new beginnings. Candy also suggested that Katrina go back to her old neighborhood to see what people had to say about Jimmy and Nina, so she could have a better idea on how to approach them. "People in the hood are always honest about certain things. They always seem to know what is going on in people's lives even after they are long gone from the neighborhood." Candy told Katrina.

The decision to face her children was something that Katrina really struggled with, and the feeling of failure continued to linger within. Katrina had seen Jimmy grow up to be a very handsome man only on television, but she never had a chance to see Nina. She wondered if her little girl had grown up to be a lady. There was so much on Katrina's mind, she decided the best thing to do was to face the situation. She booked a flight to Boston to go see her children alone.

A Jungle No More

Katrina landed in Boston a changed woman. She rented a car at the airport and headed straight to her old neighborhood. Katrina didn't even bother to go to her hotel downtown to check in. She was eager to see all the old familiar faces in her neighborhood. Unfortunately, there were no more familiar faces left. The neighborhood had changed drastically and all the bad memories had been erased. The derelict tenements had been refurbished to look brand new again. The street was newly paved and lined up with trees. The front yards of the homes were filled with beautiful gardens and well-manicured lawns. Even the old house where Katrina rented her first apartment looked different. Since Nina bought it, she added new vinyl siding, windows, and a new front porch to compliment the totally renovated interior.

Katrina was back to square one. There was no one that she could reconnect with or ask questions. All her old friends had been swept off that street to make room for the re-gentrified group of yuppies and buppies who found their way back to the city due to the convenient commute to the center of town. She didn't even know that her daughter had bought the house where she once lived. Katrina felt like she was in a strange place. Her only hope now was the address that she had for Nina in Hyde Park. There was no one on Kentworth Street to help her prepare for the meeting with her daughter. It was then or never; Katrina had come too far to turn back. She was about to do the hardest thing ever in her life as a mother, which was facing the children that she had neglected years ago.

The Jungle that Katrina left behind had been transformed to a beautiful garden. It was a matter of time before

Katrina got word that a new jungle had been created about thirty miles south of Boston in Brockton. Most of the crack heads that were forced out of the hood found their way to an old factory city that had lost its luster when the factories were shut down. The great white hope Rocky Marciano had made Brockton famous when he became the only undefeated boxer to retire with his heavyweight belt featuring a record of 49-0. Katrina knew that Larry Holmes broke that record when he fought Leon Spinks, but the white world was not ready to give up Marciano's record to a black man. Not to mention the countless times that Rocky Marciano himself lost to other great black boxers who were cheated because the white judges were not fair to them. Katrina knew this because she was a boxing fan and she used to watch the fights with her dad as a little girl. It was the only thing that they ever did together.

Katrina also knew that White people have never been fair to black folks since they visited the African continent. They were not fair to her and her children. They were not fair to the people on Kentworth Street. They were not fair to the people in Africa whose resources they have stolen since the beginning of time. They were not fair to the Indians whose land they stole while annihilating most of the population. They were not fair to the Mexicans whose land they stole in the West and now try to ridicule them by tagging them with the label "illegal immigrants." They are not fair to the Haitian people who helped them fight off the French for the great state of Louisiana and the great battle in Savannah, Georgia. They are not fair for supplying the hood with crack and illegal guns. They are not fair for allowing the devastating disease known as AIDS to massacre almost half of Africa, India, and Asia. They are not fair for trying to become dictators to the rest of the world and Katrina knew this now because she spent a lot of her time reading in jail reading history books as well.

Katrina was now better equipped to understand that White people pretty much want to control the world and to some extent they do. They originated from Europe, but somehow they managed to own the majority of land and wealth in some of the richest parts of the world. They managed to own all the gold and diamond mines in Africa, they control parts of Asia, they took America from the Indians and the Mexicans, and now they are trying to conquer the only part of the world where they have never been able to stake claim, the Middle East. So Katrina knew that the hood was only a dot on the map and it was at their disposal for the taken whenever they chose. She also noticed how quickly the ghetto can be cleaned up when White folks want to make it their home again. In the grand scheme of things, these people had also contributed indirectly to her harsh life on the street.

"What happens locally in our neighborhoods has taken place globally since the beginning of time. Whatever is convenient for rich white people can easily become an inconvenience not just black people but poor people all over the world," Katrina thought to herself. Katrina's old neighborhood was part of the new convenience and the old crack heads were made to be inconvenient somewhere else. Thus, Katrina had lost all her connections to her old neighborhood.

Facing the Music

True to form, Katrina was a survivor and not a quitter. She hopped back in her car and drove straight to Nina's house in Hyde Park. On the way to the house, Katrina's emotions of guilt overcame her, and she started to break down and cry in the car. As a mother, she had failed her kids, and it was the one thing that she couldn't go back and change. Moving forward was one thing, but looking your little girl in the eyes and trying to explain to her that drugs and prostitution were more important than being a mother was another thing all together. The survival argument would not work because Nina had to survive herself and she didn't turn to prostitution. Katrina wanted to face the music, but she didn't know what tune to expect.

She couldn't make up her mind about what she wanted to say, and she drew a blank every time she was trying to rehearse something from memory. Everything was failing Katrina, but she didn't want to fail her children again. She had no idea about the agony the children went through when they thought she was dead. Katrina only believed that her children turned their backs on her while she was locked up, but the children were living with the pain of her death for years. Katrina figured that only two things could happen as she pulled up in front of the house; Nina could reject or accept her. She knew that forgiveness would take time, but acceptance would open the door for her to earn Nina's forgiveness.

Katrina was all smiles as she pulled up in front of the big Victorian house. She double-checked the numbers of the address on the piece of paper in her purse to make sure it was correct. From the look of the house alone, Katrina knew that her daughter had made it out the slums of Boston. She looked in the mirror to make sure that her hair and make-up were right before stepping out of the rental car. Walking up the ten steps to Nina's front door seemed like eternity. Katrina was nervous and happy at the same time. Before ringing the door bell, she took notice of the Mercedes Benz parked in the driveway near the garage, and she was all smiles. "Her daughter had indeed made it out of the slums," she thought. She fixed her clothes once more as she rang the doorbell. It took a little while for Nina to come to the door because she was trying to feed her youngest child. Meanwhile Katrina contemplated leaving, because it was taking too long for someone to answer the door.

She began to think she was making a mistake and as she turned to walk back down towards her car, a voice called out, "Can I help you?" Katrina took a deep breath before she turned around to face her daughter. As Katrina turned around and said, "I'm looking for Nina?!" Nina ran towards her and exclaimed, "Mom!" She was elated to see her mother as she reached her and gave her an eternal embrace. The butterflies in Katrina's stomach, before she saw her daughter, were replaced by joy and happiness. The two women hugged until tears started flowing like rainfall dropping out of the sky during hurricane season in Florida.

Nina couldn't believe her eyes. "How is it possible that you're still alive?" she asked her mother. "It's a long story and I will tell you all about it as soon as I'm able to stop rejoicing in this moment," Katrina answered. She invited Katrina inside as she made her way back to her daughter in the kitchen. She introduced Katrina to her children. She started telling her about her husband, children, and grandparents like two friends who hadn't seen each other in years and needed to catch up in life. Nina made Katrina feel so welcomed that the guilt that Katrina initially felt started to resurface. She realized that her kids had no idea that she was alive and again she had failed to reach out to them to make sure that they knew where she was. Nina hadn't even brought up the fact that the prison officials had categorized her as "dead." The joy in Nina's face completely took away Katrina's pain and suffering for all the time she didn't see her children. She went over and hugged Nina once more before the tears started flowing again. She sat there and watched how beautiful and gorgeous her daughter had turned out to be. She also took notice of Nina's growing stomach with her third grandchild.

After feeding her daughter, little Katrina, Nina told her mother that she had named her daughter after her. After she learned from the prison officials that her mother had committed suicide, she wanted to keep her name alive. Nina explained to her mother that the prison officials had listed her as dead. Katrina had gotten news that young Star had committed suicide after she left the prison in Massachusetts, but she didn't know that the prison officials had mistakenly listed her as the person who died. She explained to Nina that it was mistake that the prison officials had made, but she made her own mistake by assuming that her children had turned their backs on her. They even started laughing at the fact that everyone cried for her at young Star's funeral.

Katrina was anxious to learn about Jimmy. She knew that he was a basketball star from watching him on television all the time, but she wanted to know how he dealt with the fact that he thought his mother was dead. Nina tried her best to explain to her mother that it was harder for Jimmy to cope with the loss at first, but he had forgiven her and was able to move on with his life. She also told Katrina that her presence was going to be the biggest surprise in Jimmy's life. "If there was one thing he could use right now that was some good news because he hadn't been in a good mood lately." Nina told her mother. She started telling Katrina about Jimmy's battle with kidney failure. Katrina told her she missed the whole thing, as it unfolded on television, because she couldn't bear to watch her child suffer.

There was so much that Katrina wanted to say to her daughter, but she simply sat back and relished in the moment as she watched her daughter and her grandchildren. There was really no word to describe the feeling that overcame Katrina on the day she saw her daughter. The word that would come closest to it would be "rapture." Katrina was caught up in the rapture and she didn't want the moment to end. She kissed and hugged her grandchildren many times over.

While Katrina may have been elated to see Nina, Nina couldn't wait to get on the phone to invite Jimmy over for a special visit. After dialing Jimmy's number, it took forever for him to pick up his cell phone. When he finally did, he was not in the best mood and Nina sensed it almost instantly. Jimmy was still trying to figure out a way to deal with his problems with Jean, and Pastor Jacobs hadn't come up with anything solid to make her go away completely yet. Nina told Jimmy that he needed to drop whatever he was doing and head to her house immediately. He asked, "Is it an emergency?" She told him "Yes!" He asked, "Are the kids all right?" She told him "Yes!" He then asked, "What's the emergency?" She informed him that she couldn't tell him on the phone, but he needed to bring his butt to her house right away. He told her that he would be right over then hung up the phone.

A Great Surprise

Jimmy hopped in his car instantly to go find out what was up with his sister. While driving over to her house he wondered what was so important that she wanted him to come over right away. He hoped that it was not something serious that needed his attention. Jimmy had his hand full with Jean, and he was looking for relief not more headaches. He was relying on Pastor Jacobs to make his problem go away, but Pastor Jacobs was not coming up with a solution that was quick enough for him. Jimmy did not want his life ruined in the media and he damn sure did not want someone to take advantage of something that he had worked hard for all his life. There was no point of beating himself up for something that he felt he had no control over. He crossed his fingers hoping that the situation would be resolved with the help of Pastor Jacobs.

Jimmy pulled up in front of Nina's house and noticed the burgundy, Ford Crown Victoria parked outside. The first thing that ran through his mind after seeing the car parked in front of the house was that Jean had called the police to scare him into paying her. It was a well-known fact in Boston that all the undercover cops drove the big Ford, Crown Victoria. Jimmy hesitated, at first, because he thought he was about to get caught and the police were using his family to get to him. He thought about running, then he realized that there was nowhere in the world he could go without being recognized. A well-known basketball player, there was no place to hide.

Jimmy sat in the car and sweat for a little while before deciding to face his fate. As much as he anticipated a big hoopla with the Boston Police Department, he was about to dance to a whole different beat; a beat that would bring a bittersweet feeling. After ringing the doorbell a couple of times, Jimmy braced himself for the handcuffs that he expected the cops to slap around his wrists. He stood there sweating for about thirty seconds before Nina came to the door. Jimmy realized that there was nothing wrong from the big smile his sister was wearing on her face. He was relieved to see that she was happy, but he still wondered why.

As the two of them stepped back into the living room, Nina told Jimmy that she had a pleasant surprise for him, and it was something that he would have never expected. When Jimmy stepped into the living room, he recognized his mother right away. He ran towards her and gave her a bear hug, lifting her up from the floor leaving her feet suspended. She was begging for Jimmy to put her down. Katrina had never expected her boy to develop into such a huge man, and she also didn't expect the reception she got from both of her children. Jimmy was elated that she was still alive, and for a moment he'd forgotten about all his problems.

Jimmy and Nina sat in the living room as Katrina tried to bring them up to date to what she had been doing since her release from jail. She told them about her best friend, Candy, who helped her get her life together while she was in jail as well as the poor decision she made to stay away from them. She told them that she had been sober for years, and that prostitution and drugs were in her past and she intended to keep it that way. Jimmy had the same questions as Nina about her supposed death, and she explained to him it was all a mistake by the prison the department. Also, she appreciated all his effort in making sure that Young Star received a proper burial, because she was also a great person who deserved the same treatment. Jimmy was so happy to see his mother he didn't know what to do with himself. He kept holding her in his arms and didn't want to let go.

She told them about her new life in Phoenix, and that she really enjoyed being out there making a difference in the lives of the young girls in her program. Katrina was grateful that her kids had forgiven her, and was looking forward to getting to know them and catching up with their lives. Nina and Jimmy felt that the best part was yet to come as they told their mother that they were able to reconnect with their grandparents and Pastor Jacobs. Katrina's reaction to the news was not at all positive. She blamed her parents for a long time for the way her life turned out, and she was not ready to forgive them for turning their backs on her.

It was hard for the kids to read Katrina's facial expression, but they were hoping that she would be happy with the news. Katrina had never mentioned her parents to her children in the past because she harbored ill feelings towards them. She never anticipated that a family reunion would take place between her children and her parents. She didn't even bother to ask them how her parents were doing. She did, however, ask who Pastor Jacobs was. When Jimmy told her that Leon, the hustler, had become a Pastor, the first words out of her mouth were "I guess he found a new hustle!"

The kids didn't want to condone the negative vibes they were getting from their mother about Pastor Jacobs and their grandparents. They had come a long way to bring the family back together, and they didn't want their mother to come in and destroy all the hard work that they had done. Katrina was just as guilty as her parents when she turned her back on them, and they made sure that they let her know it. She was the pot calling the kettle black, and the kids didn't want to hear anything negative from her about the people in their lives.

If Katrina wanted to be part of their lives, she would have to learn to forgive just like they did. There was no other way. As happy as Nina and Jimmy were to see that their mother was still alive, they were not willing to create a division in the family because of her. Forgiveness was something new to Katrina, and she had to learn from her children how to forgive and forget. The kids made no qualms about the fact that they were happy to see her and wanted her to be part of the family again, but they were not willing to take her side against their grandparents and Pastor Jacobs.

Nina and Jimmy tried as much as they could to explain to their mother how sorry their grandparents were for turning their backs on her. Even Pastor Jacobs was a new man who wished that he had never turned his back on her. While behind bars, Katrina thought about writing her parents to ask them to help care for her children, but she never followed through with it. She knew that she had no right to hold grudges because she would be just as bad as the people she was holding the grudge against. Katrina made a pact with her children that she would forgive her parents and Pastor Jacobs, because the most important thing to her was their happiness. She had failed them once; she didn't want to ruin it again the second time around.

Jimmy and Nina asked how long she was in Boston for and Katrina told them she was not sure, because she did not know how they were going to receive her. Extending her stay in Boston was only a matter of a phone call to Candy. She told them that she only brought clothes for a couple of days, however, Jimmy and Nina told her not to worry about clothes because they could always take her shopping. They asked her to stay for a couple of weeks, splitting her time between Jimmy and Nina's house. Katrina took out her cell phone to tell Candy the good news, and Candy had no problem with her extending her stay in Boston. She was more than happy to grant Katrina a two-week vacation.

After finalizing her plans with Nina and Jimmy, Katrina called the hotel to cancel her reservation. A dinner was planned at Jimmy's house in two days at six o'clock in the evening so that they could bring the whole family back together. Everybody was expected to be there to welcome Katrina back to her family. Nina told her kids not to say anything to their father about their grandmother coming to the house, and if they kept her secret she would take them to get their favorite ice cream the upcoming Sunday.

Getting Acquainted

Nina and Jimmy kept Katrina's presence a secret from their grandparents, Pastor Jacobs, Eddy, Karen, and Collin. Everyone was called and invited to Jimmy's house for a special dinner in a couple of days, and the time was rescheduled for eight o'clock in the evening in order to accommodate everyone's schedule. Jimmy even placed a call to his aunt Karen in California to ask her to come to Boston promptly due to an emergency. Karen did not even question Jimmy's motives as she called the airline to make reservations to come to Boston the following day.

The only person who knew about Katrina other than Jimmy and Nina was Lisa, and that was only because Jimmy brought her over to his house to stay with him for the first week. When Katrina first arrived at Jimmy's house, she couldn't believe her eyes. She thought she had seen the nicest house that she would ever see back in Phoenix when Candy took her home. Jimmy's house was ten times bigger and twenty times more beautiful. Candy was doing well, but she didn't have millionaire money like Jimmy did.

Getting accustomed to seeing high priced homes and luxuries that Katrina never before knew existed was going to be a huge adjustment for her. It was a big one hundred eighty degree change for her. Jimmy's house was lavish and everything in the home was grand. His money was well spent by Lisa when she decided to decorate the place herself. The spiral staircase overlooking the foyer at the entrance of the house is reminiscent of a castle from an old kingdom. The twelve-foot ceilings added to the Victorian flair and the grandiose stature of the house.

Katrina requested a tour of the house and Jimmy obliged. Jimmy had the house completely renovated, and added a gym fully equipped with every kind of exercise equipment that he could find. He had free weights as well as universal weights and a regulation size indoor basketball court. He wanted to start with the gym because that was where he spent most of his time. By the time he made his way back to the family room, he asked Lisa to take over the tour while he lounged on the couch. Katrina's mouth remained open throughout the tour, and she couldn't believe how far her son had come. She was just as impressed with Lisa. She noticed that Lisa was well mannered, easy going, caring, and sincere. They instantly bonded. Lisa had grown up to be a beautiful woman and her assets had grown in all the right places. The little shy girl that Jimmy met in high school was no longer. She had blossomed to a gorgeous woman with a great sense of style.

As they were going around the house, Katrina and Lisa engaged in a conversation that involved Jimmy. She wanted to know if her son was happy and if they were planning on having children any time soon. Lisa and Jimmy had been trying to get pregnant, but since the re-emergence of Jean, Jimmy's mind had been elsewhere. Lisa knew her husband, and she figured in due time he would come around and they would start having great sex once again. Katrina acted more like a best friend with Lisa, and she loved it. When they were done with the tour, Katrina was impressed and hungry. Lisa offered to cook dinner as her husband was hungry, too.

Katrina went back to the living room to catch up with her son while Lisa went into the kitchen to whip up something to eat. Katrina was sitting in the family room staring at Jimmy as if she could not believe her eyes. He was actually sitting in front of her with all his wealth and success! He had grown to a mature and handsome man, but she could tell that something was on his mind. Even though she had been away from him for a long time, she still had motherly instincts. Her motherly instincts told her that something was bothering her son.

She asked 'do you have something on your mind that you want to talk about, son? I may have been away from you for a long time, but I can still sense when something is bothering you, you know?" He told her that it was nothing that he couldn't handle on his own. She wanted to know what it was, and she told him that he never knew what solution she could come up with as a mother unless he told her his problem. Katrina was walking a thin line with Jimmy, because Jimmy got involved in this mess to begin with because of her. If he had not confronted his mother's john, he wouldn't have been implicated in a murder. The more she tried to get Jimmy to talk, the more enraged he became. After pestering him for a while, he blurted out to her, "it's your fault that my life may be ruined by this woman." Katrina had no idea what Jimmy was talking about. The television was loud enough to drown out the sound of their conversation away from Lisa.

Jimmy decided to tell his mother about Jean and the murder of Patrick Ferry, and how it was now coming back to haunt him. After hearing Jimmy's story, Katrina felt that if she ever wanted to get in her son's good graces again, she had better come up with a solution to help him get rid of Jean. Jimmy told his mother that he never involved his wife in the situation, because he didn't want to worry her. He had intended to keep it that way.

Mom to the Rescue

Being an ex-con and a former street prostitute was no deterrent for Katrina after she heard Jimmy's story. She simply asked him for Jean's name and address. After eating the best spaghetti and meat sauce dish ever cooked by Lisa, Katrina grabbed her car keys and headed straight to the Kind Street Inn where Jean was staying. She told Jimmy she was going to visit an old friend and she would be back later that night. Her experience in jail had toughened Katrina up to the point where she was fearless, and physical confrontation was the least of her worries.

Armed with a gray wig, bifocal glasses, and a cane that she purchased from a joke store before her visit with Jean, Katrina was determined to help Jimmy out of his situation. She tried as much as she could to disguise herself by wrapping a silk scarf around her head on top of the wig, and she changed her voice to that of an old, frail woman. Katrina went to the front desk and asked for Jean Murray. She was told that Jean had not reported back to the shelter, but she was due back in less than a half hour in order to beat the shelter's curfew. Katrina decided to wait for Jean down the block in her car for forty-five minutes.

Katrina moved her car a few blocks down the street and she started losing her patience. After noticing this woman walking into the shelter, she went back to the front desk and once again asked if Jean came back. This time the lady at the front desk pointed Jean out to her as Jean was making her way through the lobby. The lady called for Jean to come back to meet with Katrina. When Jean turned around, Katrina told the receptionist "Never mind! That's not her." Katrina was able to take a good look at

Jean, and made sure she remembered her face. Katrina was also from the old school, she knew from Jean's attire that she hadn't fully given up prostitution. She would find a way to sneak out of the shelter later that evening to go work the streets. After all, Jimmy's big checks hadn't started rolling in yet.

She went outside and waited patiently in her car for Jean to reappear. As expected, Jean snuck out through the back door, and Katrina met her in the back alley. She approached Jean and asked her, "Do you know Jimmy?" Jean responded, "What business is it of yours?" Katrina rebutted, "If you know what's good for you, you'd leave him alone and not ever try to get in touch with him again." Jean sarcastically answered, "What you gonna do, beat my ass, grandma?" Katrina told, "Leave Jimmy alone and everything will be all right. If you come within a hundred feet of Jimmy or his home, you will have me to deal with!" Jean could only laugh after she heard Katrina's statement, and then told Katrina that if Jimmy didn't pay up she'd make sure that his life was ruined.

At this point, Jean was starting to wear out Katrina's patience. The tough ex-con was about to emerge once more. Katrina tried to grab Jean's arm in an intimidating way to show her that she was serious. Before she could grab a hold of Jean's hands, Jean pulled out a knife that she usually carried for protection. She extended the blade and cut Katrina across the hand as she was reaching out to grab her. Katrina backed up to watch the blood spill out of her hand, and before Jean could flinch she hit Jean over the head with the cane in her right hand. Jean fell to the ground. The cane slipped out of Katrina's hand as she hit Jean again. Jean charged at Katrina flinging the knife at her, trying to stab her with it.

She had pushed Katrina all the way back against the wall away from the cane, and there was nowhere for Katrina to go. With one last attempt to stab Katrina in the heart, Jean swung the knife as hard as she could, but Katrina ducked and was stabbed on the shoulder instead.

Jean tried jumping on her to finish her off, but Katrina was able to push Jean off of her. She noticed a piece of lead pipe lying on the ground. She dove to the ground and picked up the pipe, as Jean got back on top of her attempting to stab her again. Katrina was able to get her hand on the lead pipe, but not before Jean stabbed her twice on her right leg. She was able to kick Jean off of her with her left leg, and used the lead pipe as support to get up from the ground. They were now facing each other: Jean with a knife in hand and Katrina with a twenty-inch piece of lead pipe and a few stab wounds. Jean took a couple of swing at Katrina with the knife and missed. Reverting to her fighting skills back in prison, Katrina was able to set Jean up with a left hook, and as Jean got closer to her she hit her across the head with the pipe. Jean was knocked out.

Katrina became angry as she got on top of Jean, and continued to beat the crap out of her using the lead pipe. By the time she was able to regain her composure, Jean's lifeless body lay on the ground. Katrina picked up the lead pipe, her cane, and the knife from Jean's hand and hobbled off to her car. Unfortunately, there was an eyewitness who watched the whole thing unfold from her window in the back alley. When Katrina got to her car around the corner, she took off the gray wig and placed it in a bag along with the knife and lead pipe. She then locked the bag in her trunk with the cane. She was profusely bleeding from her wounds, but the hospital was the last place she wanted to go.

The meeting between Jean and Jimmy in the motel room would never take place, and she would never get the money that she anticipated would change her life forever. Jean's demise was Jimmy's fortune, just like his demise would have been hers. As a mother, Katrina seemed to have been able to reconnect with her family just in the nick of time. But now, she needed to make sure that the sound of steel bars and gates would not be her fate once again.

United Once More

Katrina called Jimmy at his home to ask for Pastor Jacobs' number. Jimmy had mentioned to her that Pastor Jacobs was the only other person who knew about Jean and he was the only one helping him. Jimmy wanted to know why Katrina needed Pastor Jacob's number, and she told him she just wanted to call and thank him for watching after him and Nina. After Katrina got off the phone with Jimmy, she immediately placed a call to Pastor Jacobs. Mrs. Jacobs picked up the phone and Katrina asked to speak with her husband. Pastor Jacobs had a surprised reaction to a female calling his home so late at night.

When he got on the phone, Katrina told him that she had an emergency and she needed his help because it had to do with Jimmy. Pastor Jacobs didn't believe that the caller was Katrina because as far he was concerned, she was dead. She told him that she couldn't go into details on the telephone, but he needed to meet her in the parking lot of Roxbury Community College as soon as possible if he didn't want to see Jimmy end up in jail. Katrina was familiar with the Roxbury Community College area because she had driven by it on her way to Nina's house earlier in the day. She noticed the changes right away, and she was pleased with the new buildings at the school and the total renovation of the area.

It was one thing for Pastor Jacobs to be suspicious of the caller, but it was an entirely different thing when it involved the livelihood of his only son. Katrina said things to him on the phone about their old time together, and he realized that only, she, would know such things as the place they used to have sex and which motel. Pastor

Jacobs jumped out of bed and told his wife that he had an emergency that he needed to tend to. He got up and threw on a sweat suit, and headed to Roxbury Community College to meet Katrina. On her way to Roxbury Community College, Katrina could see the barrage of police headlights and siren headed to the South End where she knew that she had just killed Jean. She was trying her best not to look suspicious as she carefully drove through traffic towards the college.

At one point on her way to the college parking lot, a police cruiser pulled up behind her with flashing lights and siren. She thought that they had caught up to her as she pulled over to the side of the road. But relief soon followed, as the police cruiser continued to head up the street pass Katrina. The police officer driving the cruiser was only trying to clear his path on his way to a dispatched call for another crime. All Katrina could think about at that moment was the fact that she had come back to Boston to get locked up again, and this time she knew it would be for good. This would be her second stint in jail for defending her children and there wasn't going to be any leniency on the part of the court.

After Katrina finally made it to the parking lot of the school, she impatiently waited for Pastor Jacobs to show up. She was bleeding profusely, and if he didn't get there soon she was going to pass out. She tried her best to apply pressure to her wounds, but there were too many wounds. After about ten minutes of fighting to stay awake, Pastor Jacobs pulled up in the parking lot in his Mercedes Benz. He noticed Katrina's rental car in the lot, and immediately ran towards it. He found her slouched in the front seat covered with blood. Pastor Jacobs never forgot her face, and he recognized Katrina instantly. He was asking her how she got stabbed, but she didn't have enough strength to answer. When he suggested taking her to the hospital, she shook her head saying, "No!"

Due to the nature of his work with children, Pastor Jacobs always kept a First-Aid Kit in the trunk of his car for emergencies. He was able to patch up Katrina's wounds and gave her a couple of aspirin to take away the pain. After Katrina regained her strength and consciousness, she tried to explain to Pastor Jacobs how she was attacked by Jean when she went to talk to her about Jimmy. After getting the full story from Katrina, Pastor Jacobs knew that taking her to the hospital was out of the question. She could not go on with just patches on her wounds. She needed to get stitches. While Katrina was in jail, she had to learn many things and stitching a wound happened to be one of them. Pastor Jacobs went to Walgreen's and bought Katrina a pack of dental floss and some needles. They went to his church and she sat in the basement stitching her wounds without so much as a scream from the pain inflicted by the needle. She had truly come a long way from the weaker Katrina that Pastor Jacobs met many years ago.

Pastor Jacobs wanted to know how Katrina was even still alive, but she was getting tired of telling the story over and over. She told him that he would have to wait until the family dinner at Jimmy's house in a couple of days to hear the story along with everybody else. "My presence was supposed to be a surprised but now you know!" she said.

She needed a plan to avoid going to jail and Pastor Jacobs was just the man to help keep her out of jail. Katrina also did not want Jimmy and Nina to know what she had done because she did not know how they would react. First, her car had to be cleaned of all the blood she had spilled. Pastor Jacobs took Katrina back to the parking lot to pick up the rental car. He had her follow him to his house so she could park the car in his garage. After securing the car in the garage, Pastor Jacobs took Katrina back to Jimmy's house. She tried her best to look presentable. Jimmy was too tired to notice how badly she really looked when he came to open the door. She was also wearing an overcoat that Pastor Jacobs took out of his wife's closet. She used it to hide her wounds from Jimmy. Before leaving, Katrina asked Pastor Jacobs not to say anything to her children about the incident. In fact, she wanted him to act like they had not seen each other yet at the dinner.

Katrina went to the guest bathroom and washed up before she went to sleep. She changed the gauze on her wounds and wore a long t-shirt to bed. She also took a couple of aspirins to ease her pain. It was an adventurous night for Katrina on her first day back to Boston. While she was lying in bed, she knew that Boston was not a place that she wanted to be because she constantly had a chain of bad luck following her. She knew that it was a matter of time before she perished for good in Boston. She vowed to stay in the house until the end of her visit in order to stay out of trouble.

Everyone's got something to hide

Katrina woke up the next morning to the smell of bacon, eggs, toasts, and freshly squeezed orange juice. She ran to the bathroom to brush her teeth. When she came out, she threw on a robe that Lisa left for her on the hook of her bedroom door. Jimmy and Lisa allowed her to get a good night sleep. Lisa decided to run to the kitchen to make breakfast before Katrina was fully awake. She wanted to make a good impression on her. Katrina could not go back to sleep when the aroma of lean bacon hit her nostrils. She just had to give in to the good smelling breakfast. When Katrina entered the kitchen, she found Jimmy and Nina wearing their robes waiting for her. Jimmy was reading the newspaper as he usually did every morning, and Lisa was drinking a glass of orange juice.

Katrina was trying her best to keep from limping due to the stab wound she received at the hands of Jean the night before. Jimmy was also surprised to learn in the paper that a prostitute listed by the name of Jean Murray was found dead in the back alley of a homeless shelter. According to the paper, an investigation was under way to find the murderer. The police mentioned the fact that there appeared to have been a struggle between Jean and her killer and that the killer could possibly be walking around with some wounds. Jimmy raised his head to look across at his mother while reading the paper, and she smiled at him. He was a little suspicious of her, but he shook it off when she got up to walk to the fridge to get some butter without showing any signs of pain.

They all sat at the table and ate breakfast, but Jimmy said very little to his mother. Katrina, however, was a little too talkative that morning. She was running her mouth a mile a minute, and most of what she was saying had nothing to do with anything. Her conversation went from how long Jimmy had known Lisa to how long Lisa had known Jimmy, information that she had heard from them the day before when she first came to the house. Jimmy's suspicions resurfaced and he knew that his mother might have had something to do with Jean's death. Getting it out of her would be a different story. It was easy for Jimmy to believe that his mother had murdered Jean, because he knew she was more than capable. She had killed before and right away she was under suspicion again.

Jimmy also acknowledged the fact that both times that Katrina had committed a crime; it was to protect her children from people who were trying to exploit them. It may have been a stupid move on Katrina's part, but Jimmy knew that he no longer had to worry about Jean exposing him. A tape of Jean committing sexual acts with johns in the back of cars and shooting drugs up her arms had also surfaced at the police station in Boston. It had a post office box listed in New Hampshire that would throw off the police department's investigation. An open case of a serial killer reigning terror on the prostitutes in the streets of Nashua, New Hampshire threw the cops in Boston for a loop. They wondered if the serial killer had finally made his way down to Boston wreaking havoc on the city.

The police did not know where to begin because all the clues that they had tied Jean's death to a serial killer who liked to videotape his prostitute victims in action prior to killing them. There was no trace of fingerprints. The police department in New Hampshire had received many tapes from the serial killer taunting them, showing the prostitutes and their johns before they're killed. The tape with Jean on it was all too similar and the police somehow connected Jean's murder to the serial killer in New Hampshire.

The serial killer's ammo was to expose the johns while he disposed of the women who committed petty crimes and sold themselves for money on the streets, because they could never satisfy their hunger for the green paper. He was like a vigilante who took it upon himself to clean up the streets in the Northeast. It now appeared as though he was making his way down to Boston from New Hampshire. After reading that part of the story, Jimmy was thrown off course, and the thought of his mother killing Jean was completely gone from his mind. He was somewhat relieved of the thought that he had a repeat murderer under his roof, even though she was his mother. He wanted to believe that Jean was killed by somebody else.

Karen had also arrived from California for the big dinner, and Eddy went to pick her up. After he picked up Karen, he called Jimmy to see if he could swing by to see his favorite nephew to update him on his progress at his new job with the foundation. Realizing quickly that his mother was sitting across the table from him, Jimmy told Eddy that he was going to be busy, and that they could catch up on things the following day at the dinner. Jimmy did not want Eddy to know that Katrina was back until the dinner. He wanted to have his family in a dinner setting, so whatever animosity or grudge they had towards each other would be forgiven once and for all. Lisa was sworn into secrecy about the fact that Katrina was in Boston, as well.

Pastor Jacobs also called Jimmy early that morning to make sure that there was no suspicion about what took place the previous night with Katrina and Jean. He acted like he was checking on Jimmy and Lisa, and he made no mention of having seen Katrina. He asked Jimmy if he should bring anything for the dinner, and Jimmy told him that everything was all set to just bring his good heart. He meant that literally, because he didn't want Pastor Jacobs to have a heart attack when he saw Katrina. Pastor Jacobs also had to lie to his wife about leaving home in the middle of the night to go meet with Katrina. He told her that he had to go help one of the girls from the community center who was considering running away from home. He did not even bother mentioning the fact that he took one of her overcoats from the closet. She had so many of them, she did not even notice the one missing.

Feeling relieved that his problem had gone away; Jimmy was trying his best to keep Katrina's return to Boston a big secret for the dinner party. He wanted to pleasantly surprise his entire family with Katrina's presence. His family was finally going to be back together and Jimmy wanted to savor the moment. Meanwhile, Katrina tried her best to tend to her wounds without letting Jimmy know that she was responsible for Jean's death.

Before Dinner

The day of the planned dinner finally arrived and the scheduled time of six o'clock in the evening was fast approaching. Katrina and Lisa spent the whole day in the kitchen cooking together. Katrina's culinary skills had improved tremendously since she last saw her children. While in jail, her duties were shifted around a lot based on need. Katrina was an opportunist who looked for ways to improve her stay while in prison. During the third year of her sentence, Katrina realized that the inmates would go to great lengths to perform special favors for the cafeteria staff so they could have extra food. Katrina managed to have her duties shift from the laundry room to the cafeteria, and it was there that she learned how to make a few dishes.

While performing her duties in the kitchen, Katrina became the best student under the guidance of the head cook. She learned how make lasagna, potatoes au gratin, steak tips, and a few other dishes. For the dinner, Katrina wanted to make her favorite potatoes au gratin and lasagna. Lisa decided to make shrimp scampi, clam chowder, garlic bread, and her favorite dessert, chocolate soufflé. There was enough food on the table to feed a family of thirty. The ladies knew that they had done a great job with the food, and they could not wait to see the people's faces when they start eating.

After a long day in the kitchen, Lisa and Katrina spent a few moments relaxing in the game room located in the basement of the house. Katrina almost poured her heart out to her daughter-in-law. She told Lisa how she felt about neglecting her children, and that she had had a hard time dealing with the fact that she had allowed her weakness for drugs to control her life. Turning her back on Jimmy was especially hard, because he was her youngest child. Lisa told Katrina that Jimmy was more than happy to learn that she was alive, and in due time she knew that her husband would forgive his mother completely.

After relaxing in the game room for about an hour, the ladies returned to the living room to continue their little girl-on-girl talk. Katrina realized that Lisa was not just physically beautiful, but she was also a beautiful person inside and out. Lisa also realized how harsh a life that Katrina had led, and she was surprised that Katrina was even able to maintain her integrity to live on. The time that Lisa and Katrina spent together was very essential because all the bias that Lisa carried with her for Katrina was almost completely erased. She knew that her husband was lucky to have been born to a mother like Katrina.

Meanwhile, Jimmy was in the family room watching ESPN. He was listening to all the doubters who still believed that it was going to be too hard for him to ever come back and play, much less dominate on the basketball court like he once did. Since his mind was now free of worry, he wanted to concentrate on returning to basketball to prove his doubters, once again, how wrong they were about him. Jimmy's body responded well to the kidney, and he wanted to start playing pick-up games as soon as he could.

A Family Reunion

Everyone was dressed by 5:45 pm and Jimmy wanted his mother to stay in the guest room until after everyone arrived. Katrina was lying down in her bra and underwear on the bed anticipating seeing her parents again for the first time in over twenty-five years. She had forgotten what her younger brother Eddy and her younger sister Karen looked like. What she worried about most was the mean streak in her father that caused her departure from home when she was only fourteen years old. She wondered if he had changed at all or if he had gotten meaner over the years. She also felt bad for her mother who stayed because she didn't want to desert her family. Katrina was also overcome with joy, because she had made her way back into the lives of her children and now she also had grandchildren.

As Katrina lay on her back thinking about her long journey from the time she was fourteen to the present, tears started flowing down her cheeks. She knew that it was a long journey, and the only reason that she made it at all was because the Lord wanted to keep her around, so he performed a miracle. She got off the bed and knelt down on her knees and started praying and thanking the Lord for all that he had done for her. Katrina had never lost faith, and it was her faith that carried her through the years.

She could hear the doorbell ring as the people started to arrive one by one. Pastor Jacobs and his wife were the first people to arrive. Then it was Collin, Nina and their children. Katrina started getting dressed after Nina and her family arrived. Nina excused herself and signaled to Lisa that she wanted to go up to the bedroom to see

Katrina. She told her husband to watch the kids while she went upstairs to see Katrina.

Before she could reach the first step her son, Collin Jr., asked, "Is grandma gonna eat with us today?" Nina turned around and played it off, "Sure. Nana is on her way now." She said this as if she was she was talking about Katrina's mother, Mrs. Johnson. Collin Jr. then replied "Not Nana, our new Grandma!" Nina ran back towards Collin Jr. and whispered in his ear, "If you still want Mommy to get you ice scream, you need to stop telling people about grandma, ok?" He said, "Yes, Mommy!" Nina ran back towards the stairs to go find her mother.

Nina found Katrina standing in front of the mirror on the dresser looking at herself and smiling. She was wearing a light blue strapless dress and a light blue cardigan sweater. She asked Nina if her choice of dress was right. The big smile on Nina's face and the big nod she gave her mother took away all the doubts about the dress. This was actually the first time that Nina ever shared the experience of watching and helping her mother get dressed. The two women acted like two sisters who had never been apart. Katrina looked extremely good for her age, even though years on the street as a drug user had taken away some of her youth. The beautiful veneer implants she got in Phoenix brought back the beautiful smile she once had.

Nina could not believe how amazing her mother looked, and she knew that Pastor Jacobs' wife had better watched out because Katrina was about to have a whole new affect on her husband. After Nina helped with applying Katrina's make–up, she was ready to go downstairs and stun everyone. First, Nina had to talk to Jimmy about how they wanted to introduce their mother to the family. While

Jimmy and Nina were in the kitchen talking, the doorbell rang and it was Mr. and Mrs. Johnson, Karen, and Eddy. The last of the group had arrived and everyone was ushered into the formal dining where Lisa had set the table for thirteen people. Everyone took a seat at the dining room table, but there was still an empty seat left. Mr. and Mrs. Johnson asked why there was an extra seat at the table, and that is when Jimmy asked to have everyone's attention. He had a big announcement to make.

"First, I would like to thank everyone for being here today. Nina, Lisa, and I wanted to take this opportunity to invite everyone over to share in our joy of reconnecting with someone we all thought was taken from the family forever. It's not often that people are given a second chance in life, but as a family we have been given more than our share." At this point, everyone turned to look at Karen. It seemed as if Jimmy was referring to Karen in his speech, and everyone was ready to applaud. Before they could put their hands together, he told them that he was not done yet.

Jimmy continued, "I know that we agonized over the fact that aunty Karen was missing for years, and by the grace of God she was returned to us intact and we are grateful for that and want to celebrate her presence as well. But this time, God used his power in ways unimaginable to all of us. He has brought to us the final missing piece that links our family, a mother, a daughter, a sister, a grandmother, and an all-around wonderful woman. Ladies and gentlemen, please put your hands together and welcome my mother, Ms. Katrina Johnson, back to our family." Jimmy was eloquent in his introduction.

There was silence in the room across the table where Mr. and Mrs. Johnson, Collin, Karen, and Eddy were all sitting for about thirty seconds, because none of them could believe that Katrina was still alive Pastor Jacobs, Lisa, Jimmy, and Nina were clapping like they had just won the state lottery. Everything seemed like a miracle as Katrina appeared wearing her light blue dress with light blue stilettos; a nice pair of dangling platinum earrings, and a nice platinum charm bracelet courtesy of Jimmy. Mr. and Mrs. Johnson's jaws almost hit the table. Eddy could not contain himself as he ran towards Katrina, and lifted her off the ground in a bear hug. Karen joined her brother in hugging her sister, but Mrs. Johnson was too emotional and dumbfounded to move from her seat. She sat there idle with tears running down her face and smiling at the same time. Mr. Johnson was too embarrassed to say anything to his daughter. After Mrs. Johnson nudged him on his side, he got up and walked over to his daughter and told her how he had missed her and how sorry he was for acting so cruel when she was younger.

Katrina was taken back a little by her father's sudden change of heart. She didn't realize that Mr. Johnson had changed over time, and that her kids were able to bring life into an otherwise scorned man. Pastor Jacobs took notice of Katrina's beauty almost instantly as he walked over to hug her as if he had just seen her for the first time in over twenty something years. Katrina had transformed herself into the beautiful woman that she once was, and everyone was happy that shc was still alive.

After hugging, kissing, and holding Katrina for close to thirty minutes it was time for Pastor Jacobs to say grace and bless the food. In between bites, Katrina would tell everyone the tales of her old life and her newfound one in Phoenix. She had a new zeal to live life and be the mother and grandmother that she had always wanted to be for her children and grandchildren. Mr. and Mrs. Johnson couldn't believe the inconceivable ways in which Katrina had to fight to survive while she was on the streets and in jail. Jimmy and Nina confirmed some of her detailed accounts about her battle with drugs and the neglect of her family. Katrina made sure that everyone knew that she was a better person, in a better place, and that the street life and drugs were a lesson that she had to learn in order for her to become the strong woman that she was.

There was so much that Katrina and her parents needed to catch up on. She had to call Candy in Phoenix to ask her for yet another week extension on her vacation. Candy was more than happy to honor her request. Everyone in the family was happy that Katrina was going to be spending an extra two weeks with them in Boston, and her time would be split among her children, grandchildren, her brother and sister, and her parents. Katrina was also happy to finally meet Collin, whom she thought was adorably handsome and extremely well-mannered.

Tying Up the Loose Ends

While the festivities were going on and everyone was celebrating the return of Katrina to her family, Katrina asked to speak with Pastor Jacobs in private. Mrs. Jacobs gave her husband an okay nod to go speak with Katrina in private. She was self-assured that her husband would never cross the line with another woman; even a woman who looked as fine as Katrina and who had given birth to his son.

Katrina wanted to speak to Pastor Jacobs for two reasons. The first reason being to thank him for looking after her children while she was absent from their lives. Jimmy and Nina had made it clear to Katrina that without the help and guidance of Pastor Jacobs they probably wouldn't have made it this far in life. For that, Katrina was grateful. She wanted to make sure that she expressed her gratitude to Pastor Jacobs for being a father to both of them. The second reason she wanted to talk to Pastor Jacobs was to ask him about what she should do with regard to Jean's murder. Katrina was very sorry for killing Jean, but she was in a situation where she was either going to kill or be killed. Katrina started to explain to Pastor Jacobs Jean and her aggression toward her during the confrontation, but Pastor Jacobs told her that he was already aware of the situation. She wanted to make sure he knew that she only went to talk to her to ask her to back off her son. While she was very remorseful about the murder, she didn't really want to go to the police. Pastor Jacobs reassured Katrina and told her not to worry because he had taken care of everything.

During the past few months he serial killer who had been killing prostitutes on the streets of Nashua, New

Hampshire had dominated the news headlines from Lowell to Boston and every town in between around the New England area. The total count of his victims had amounted to nine. As a cautionary measure, the police department and the media alerted the public. Pastor Jacobs was an avid newspaper reader and a well-informed person. He read the Boston Herald, Boston Globe and the New York Times daily. He had been following the murder spree in the paper and he figured out the ammo that the killer had been using. Initially, he wanted to use the footage of Jean on camera to try to negotiate with her and if she refused his deal, he was going to send the tape to the police station. However, his plans to use the footage changed when Katrina became entangled in the murder.

Pastor Jacobs told Katrina that he decided instead to use the captured footage of Jean on camera to help derail the police in their investigation, so that she's not found out. Pastor Jacobs was well aware of the steps that Katrina had taken to change her life and he knew that she was far more valuable to the teenagers in her program in Phoenix than she would have been behind bars. Armed with the knowledge of the pattern of the killer, he knew that the police would blame this new murder on the existing killer and Katrina would be able to walk away without getting caught. There was nothing left at the scene to tie Katrina to Jean's death and Pastor Jacobs got rid of the evidence that he found in Katrina's car.

After he detailed the car himself, he drove it to the parking lot of the church where Katrina could pick it up. She hadn't told him about the excuse she used to explain to Jimmy why she didn't drive herself back home on the night of the murder, so he asked her to repeat everything to him so he could be informed. She told him that she told

Jimmy that she was too tired to drive herself home that night and that she left the car over her friend's house and that she would pick up the car when she was ready. Pastor Jacobs thought it was a good enough excuse as he made plans to pick her up the next day to go pick up the rental car.

Katrina was still a little nervous about the witness who told the cops that she saw an old woman running from the scene. But Pastor Jacobs assured her that the police would think that the killer used a disguise to throw them off and their search would be for a male serial killer. Pastor Jacobs told Katrina that prayer would do her a lot of good and only God could forgive her for taking someone else's life. The two of them had been in the room for close to fifteen minutes and Pastor Jacobs knew it was a matter of time before his wife came looking for him. He wanted to wrap things up and made sure that Katrina knew what time he was going to pick her up the next day to get the rental car.

Know When To Let It Slide

As Pastor Jacobs and Katrina made their way out of the room, they could hear the toilet being flushed in the bathroom. It was Collin, he had gotten up to use the bathroom and while he was in the bathroom he couldn't keep from eavesdropping on Pastor Jacob and Katrina's conversation. He heard their whole conversation and was in a position as a police lieutenant to make an arrest and solve a murder that he would be highly recognized for. Collin found himself once again in the midst of a confession to a killing by a member of his wife's family. But this time, he had to fight his conscience for but a few seconds to decide that he wasn't going to do anything about it.

Collin thought about the way the Boston Police department treated his wife and the way they forced her out of a job and he came to the conclusion that the crime was committed out of his area and therefore out of his hands. Arresting a woman who was defending herself against an attacker wasn't going to do anything, but add to the stereotype that black people are savages who kill at will no matter what the situation. Collin also realized that the life of a white prostitute was probably going to be downplayed in the media as someone who was struggling to make it in society instead of the criminal that she really was.

At the end of the day, it was going to be one more strike against the black race and Collin didn't want to add to the daily grief of black folks in the ghetto. He walked back to the living room without saying anything to Katrina or Pastor Jacobs. However, Katrina and Pastor Jacobs had good enough sense to know that Katrina should go back to Phoenix the following day until the Boston Police Department came to a conclusion for Jean's murder.

A Sudden Change of Heart

Pastor Jacobs drove to Jimmy's house the next day to pick up Katrina so she could pick up the rental car from the church parking lot. Luckily Katrina had parked the car away from the alley, because the witness didn't where she fled to. Jimmy and Lisa had gone out to run a few errands, so they weren't there to see her leave. When Pastor Jacobs pulled up in front of the house, he found Katrina waiting with her bags packed and ready to leave town. It was hard for Katrina to depart so suddenly, but it was something that had to be done. Pastor Jacobs popped open his trunk and got out of his car to help Katrina with her luggage. Katrina was very sad as Pastor Jacobs peeled out of Jimmy's driveway to head to his church.

She cried silently in the car and wondered why everything always went so wrong whenever she was around her children. Pastor Jacobs simply told her "there's a reason for everything that happens in life and sometimes people have to let go of the big expectations in order to savor the small moments in life." Katrina wanted so much to stay in Boston for an extra couple of weeks to get to know her family, but at the risk of being arrested for Jean's murder, she made the wise decision to leave.

Pastor Jacobs told her how great it was to see her again as he loaded her baggage in the trunk of her car after he arrived at the church parking lot. He gave her a long hug and a kiss on the cheek as he wiped the tears from her yes. He assured Katrina that the whole family would come to Phoenix as soon as they could to spend time with her and they would be looking forward to meeting Candy, the woman, who helped her get her life together.

Katrina drove straight to the airport to catch her flight to Phoenix, Arizona. After boarding the plane, while Katrina was sitting in her seat waiting for the plane to take off, she called Jimmy's house and left him a message. She started "I know that I'm looking like a bad mother to you again, but situations beyond my control have forced me do leave you so suddenly. I wish that I could explain to you in more detail why I had to go, but I can't. Just know that I love you and your sister very much and your spouses and that I will be looking forward to seeing you guys in Phoenix very soon."

Never Say Goodbye

Just as Jimmy started to play the message that Katrina left for him, he turned on the television and the police chief was talking about Jean's death and the possibility that there could've been a copycat killer. Jimmy knew then what his mother had done and it was a sacrifice that he was more than grateful for. He knew that if his mother had extended her stay in Boston, there was a possibility that she could've been tied to the murder and he would have to go without her for another twenty-five years of his life. Knowing that she was just an airplane flight away from him was satisfying enough. He never wanted to say goodbye to her because he knew that he would see her again very soon.

Although Nina didn't get a message from Katrina, Jimmy was able to convince her and his grandparents that Katrina was needed in Phoenix and she had to leave abruptly due to an emergency. Nina was a little sad that she didn't spend much time with her mother, but Katrina left a good enough impression on her heart that would last until the next time they saw each other.

Katrina went to Boston and discovered a new family that was very different from the one she left behind when she went to jail. Her father had changed, her mother was happy, her brother and sister were responsible adults and her children were successful beyond her dreams. She realized that she had asked God for a lot in her life, but she never thought that he would deliver so much. Katrina was happy that she didn't say goodbye to her family because she knew that they would be with her in Phoenix and took with her the memories of a wonderfully happy family.

She was even happier when the whole family showed up in Phoenix six weeks later for a surprised visit. Everyone stayed at her house and some people slept on the floor reminiscent of when she was a child. Back then, she had to give up her bed and sleep on the floor with her siblings when her grandparents, aunts and uncles came to visit in Boston. She didn't mind doing it this time for her children, grandchildren, brother, sister and her parents. It was the beginning of the Johnson family becoming a tight knit family for the first time.

Stay tuned for the very first part of this trilogy.

Ignorant Souls

(The Prequel)

Malcolm is a wealthy virgin who decides to conceal his wealth From the world until he meets the right woman. His wealthy best friend, Dexter, hides his wealth from no one. Malcolm struggles to find love in an environment where vanity and materialism are rampant, while Dexter is getting more than enough of his share of women. Malcolm needs develop self-esteem and confidence to meet the right woman and Dexter's confidence is borderline arrogance.

Will bad boys like Dexter continue to take women for a ride?

Or Will nice guys like Malcolm continue to finish last?

Tina develops an insatiable sexual appetite very early in life. She only loves her boyfriend, Darren, but he's too far away in college to satisfy her sexual needs.

Tina decides to get buck wild away in college
Will her sexual trysts jeopardize the lives of the men in her life?

Faith Jones, a woman in her mid-thirties, has given up on ever finding love again until she met her son's best friend, Darius. Faith Jones is walking a thin line of betrayal against her son for the love of Darius. Will Faith allow her emotions to outweigh her common sense?

Richard Jeanty

Motherhood and the trials of loving too hard and not enough frame this story...The realism of these characters will bring tears to your spirit as you discover the hero in the villain you never saw coming... Neglected Souls is a gritty, honest and heart stirring story of hope and personal triumph set in the ghettos of Boston.

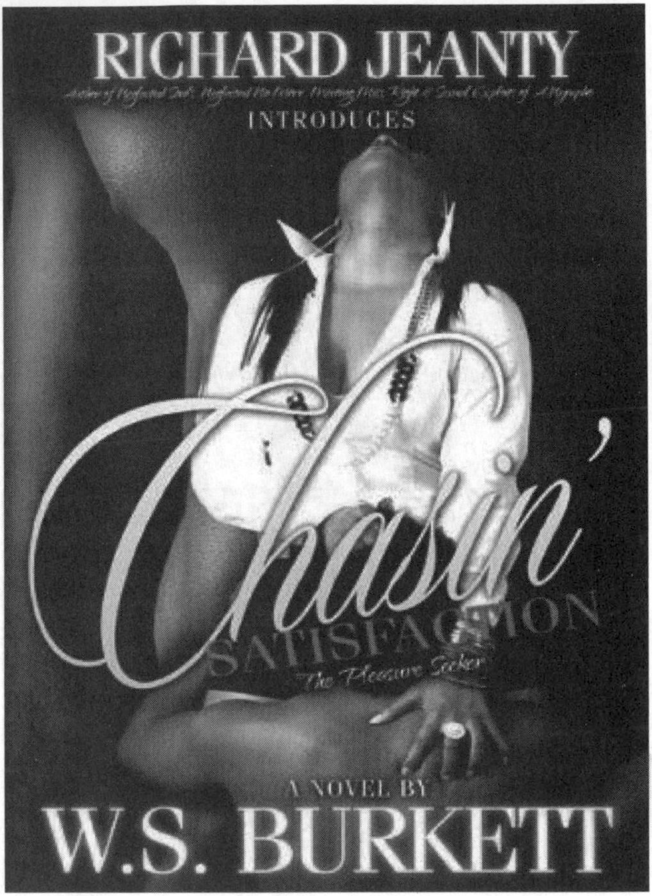

Betrayal, lust, lies, murder, deception, sex and tainted love frame this story... Julian Stevens lacks the ambition and freak ability that Miko looks for in a man, but she married him despite his flaws to spite an ex-boyfriend. When Miko least expects it, the old boyfriend shows up and ready to sweep her off her feet again. Suddenly the grass grows greener on the other side, but Miko is not an easily satisfied woman. She wants her cake and eat it too. While Miko's doing her own thing, Julian is determined to become everything Miko ever wanted in a man and more, but will he go to extreme lengths to prove he's worthy of Miko's love? Julian Stevens soon finds out that he's capable of being more than he could ever imagine as he embarks on a journey that will change his life forever.